THE GODWHALE

SF MASTERWORKS

The Godwhale

T.J. BASS

Text copyright © Thomas J. Bassler 1974
Introduction copyright © Ken MacLeod 2013
All rights reserved

The right of T.J. Bass to be identified as the author of this work,
and the right of Ken MacLeod to be identified as the author of the
introduction, has been asserted by them in accordance with the
Copyright, Designs and Patents Act 1988.

This edition first published in Great Britain in 2014 by
Gollancz
An imprint of the Orion Publishing Group
Orion House, 5 Upper St Martin's Lane, London WC2H 9EA
An Hachette UK Company

SRD

A CIP catalogue record for this book
is available from the British Library

ISBN 978 0 575 12993 1

Typeset at The Spartan Press Ltd,
Lymington, Hants.

Printed and bound in India by
Manipal Technologies Limited, Manipal

The Orion Publishing Group's policy is to use papers that
are natural, renewable and recyclable products and made
from wood grown in sustainable forests. The logging and
manufacturing processes are expected to conform to the
environmental regulations of the country of origin.

MIX
Paper | Supporting
responsible forestry
FSC™ C104740

www.orionbooks.co.uk
www.gollancz.co.uk

The Godwhale

As the sand covered her great disc-like eyes, darkening her world, the cyborg *Rorqual* wept for her lost and wasted years. She loved mankind, she needed to serve; but she was useless now. Her sisters had quietly sunk, littering the seabed with their skeletons.

But *Rorqual* selected an island for her grave, hoping to keep her hulk visible for salvage. For she believed Man still lived in his Hive. She longed to feel his bare feet on the skin of her decks. She needed Man.

And then the miracle happened; the seas grew life again. And *Rorqual*, moving ponderously, began the long, long search that would eventually set her at war with mankind...

CONTENTS

INTRODUCTION

This book can be read quite independently of that to which it's a sequel. (But do read it! *Half Past Human* (1971) is also a Masterwork, and deservedly so.) In whatever order they're read, the two books flesh out a world that challenges as much as it engages the reader: a world in which the multiplication and alteration of human flesh set the stage.

The challenge comes from two sources. One is the recognition that the repugnant future world we're shown is a logical projection of certain trends in ours. The other is that our repugnance is given every opportunity to make itself felt. What carries us through – what makes us grimace, gulp, and read on – is the author's skill at making us indentify with characters most of us would shudder to meet and rather die than be.

Thomas J. Bassler (1932–2011) was a medical doctor, who in the late 1960s and early 1970s wrote science fiction as T. J. Bass. He used his professional knowledge and vocabulary to remarkable effect in his novels, where physiological terms are used to describe hot feelings and sharp shocks in chill prose.

The central character of the opening chapter is Larry Dever, a vigorous young man out for a run in the park. He lives in a not-too-distant future of overcrowded cities in which this is a rare, rationed privilege. We have just come to empathise with him when, as a result of his own recklessness, he is cut in half at the waist. He has the option of suspended animation – frozen sleep – until such time as he can be repaired. He wakes after centuries to a world even more crowded, but sending out starship colonies under the direction of the artificial intelligence OLGA. Medicine has indeed advanced, but Larry finds the method offered to repair him ethically revolting – as do we. He returns to the cold sleep. Millennia later, he's thawed again.

Then his troubles begin.

He's soon dragging his mutilated body along for dear life through the sewers of Earth Society, the ultimate outcome of the world he was born into and the later world he glimpsed. OLGA and her star colonies are long forgotten. Humanity has been genetically modified and prenatally altered into a short-statured, short-lived species, the aptly named Nebish. Three trillion of them live in shaft cities. The entire land surface is farmed. The oceans are dead – or so everyone thinks.

Everyone is wrong. Species after species has mysteriously returned to the seas. Beyond the sky OLGA has been at work, and below it so has her remaining faithful servant, the robot whale *Rorqual Maru*. The remnants of the unmodified human species, which in *Half Past Human* haunted the Gardens as hunted scavengers, have taken to a Benthic life. When they are joined by Larry, his atavistic ally Har, and *Rorqual*, they become a threat to Earth Society – and an opportunity.

We follow both sides of the struggle that ensues. Without losing sight of the side we're on, we come to identify with Hive Citizens as well as with Benthics – to say nothing of identifying with machines, some of which may well not be conscious in any human-like sense, but who charm nonetheless. In the end – but you must find that out yourself. I won't give it away, but it leaves us with questions, one of which is whether the end of this book is indeed the end of the story the author had imagined. It seems likely that in Bass' mind there were stories still to be told, and it's certain that the issues so sharply raised are not in the end resolved. As Bass' entry in the online *Encyclopedia of Science Fiction* concludes: 'But he fell silent, his series incomplete.'

Why? We can only speculate, but one possibility is that the polarity Bass set up, between a humanity biologically adapted to an ever more crowded civilization and an unmodified humanity capable of surviving in the wild, can never be satisfactorily resolved. Not even interstellar colonization can offer an escape – ultimately, every successful human colony is a potential seed of another Hive.

We could, of course, decide to limit population growth, voluntarily or otherwise. Current projections suggest a levelling out of human numbers at about ten billion by mid-century, followed by a slow decline. But a declining, aging population presents its own difficulties, which in time might seem worse than the alternative. And who knows how our descendants would respond if new methods of agriculture and industrial production made room for renewed population growth without obvious inconvenience? Denying unborn generations a chance of life might – on an entirely secular ethic, leave alone religious strictures – come to be seen as wrong. And subtly adjusting people's minds and bodies to make them happier in crowded conditions might not horrify those concerned. But then we're on the way to becoming the Nebish, or something very like it.

The only alternative, it would seem, to this gruesome fate would be to let civilization crash and the survivors roam as savages until the next asteroid impact or ice age. This does raise ethical problems of its own, genocide being generally and (in my opinion) rightly frowned upon. The same result could happen without deliberate intent, as a by-product of nuclear war or environmental catastrophe, but again...

Given the parameters Bass set up, we find ourselves at an impasse. It may be that he did too, and that was why he fell silent. But that's no reason for us to give up on the problem, or to not enjoy – with some discomfort – his blackly comic and imaginatively fertile work. As I've argued in the introduction to the Masterworks edition of *Half Past Human*, Bass' books are very much a product of their time, but in confronting us with sharp questions about our most fundamental moral and economic assumptions they remain of pressing relevance today. They're also, in their own grim way, great fun to read.

The doctor gave us the diagnosis, and the prognosis. He left it for us to write the prescription.

Ken MacLeod

1
Larry Dever, Hemihuman

Guillotining ruins your day
But if you can't be repaired
It ruins your life.
> – Sage of Todd Island

Larry Dever knelt in darkness at East Gate, knees in damp gravel and hands on cold granular bars. Pre-dawn mists flattened his shock of yellow hair. Cool droplets clung to his young angular face. Jerkin and fibrejeans moist.

'Share and update,' murmured Larry.

'I share,' said his Belt, blinking an amorphous chalcogenide telltale. 'The Park will be warm this day – ninety-two degrees – clear. Pickables: numerous.'

The long night had chilled his bones. Where was that sun? Where was warmth?

'Sex?'

'Probability zero point two,' said Belt.

Larry smiled. That was probably too high, considering his youth – when gonadal activity was over 98 percent anticipatory. He rested his bony face against the bars – a Dever face that carried the heavy malar and mandibular lines of his clan. The eastern sky lightened to blue, then pale ochre, as it slowly extruded a copper solar disc that rose and drove the fog from the lake.

'Finally.'

Optics rotated on a sentry pole. The gates squeaked open.

'Enjoy. Enjoy. Run and spend your CBCs,' shouted Belt. The

words were accompanied by brisk music, a cavalry charge tune that warmed Larry's blood and pulled him, running on stiff legs, into the long, dew-damp grass. Six small brown birds burst from cover and flew off. Larry raced on, disturbing leafhoppers and a squadron of yellow-grey moths. Reaching the limits of his myoglobin oxygen, he paused to catch his breath. The sun warmed the nape of his neck and dried his fibrejeans.

'Pickables?' asked Larry.

Belt showed him a variety of fruits and grains – huge steak-tomatoes, rich breadfruit, sticky grapes. He was dazed by the wild profusion of edible biologicals. Names? His vocabulary was limited to the city's gelatin flavours: ambergris, calamus, kola nut, melilotus, rue, storax, and ilang-ilang.

'Show me a flavour that is both stimulating and subtle.'

'*Genus Malus*,' suggested Belt. 'Swim the lake and climb that far hill on your left. Look for a tree with thick gnarled branches and fruits of many colours.'

Larry ran down to the water's edge and kicked off his woven sandals. A disturbed catfish cut a 'V' away from the grassy bank. Throwing his fibrejeans aside, he stepped into the cool water. Mud oozed between his toes. A chill line of gooseflesh crept up his legs and back. He tossed his jerkin back on to the grass and lowered himself into the sparkling wavelets – shuddering. Now the more purposeful cutaneous capillaries puckered to conserve heat. A stray drop choked him. His first strokes were clumsy until remotely learned cerebellar reflexes took over and he managed an eccentric rhythm – a cogwheel stroke that jerked him across the water. A spillway slide put him in the out-creek. He climbed a bridge aqueduct and rode the high stream, bodysurfing in the rushing water of the elevated waterway, high above the maze of canals and walkribbons.

The grass was soft at Malus hill. A hidden clutter of twigs bruised a sole made sensitive by the soak. Dripping, he pulled himself up into a tree and sat gingerly on the rough bark. Grafting had placed a variety of pome fruits within his reach: acid crabs, heavy reds, and light yellows. He picked a waxy red and bit into it with a juicy snap! Crisp pulp crunched noisily.

Flavour! A warm checkerboard of sunlight splashed through the leaves, drying him. Fermenting windfalls attracted a noisy bee. Belt sang. Larry shifted his weight on the knobbly limb and dozed off. Dusk's cool breeze awakened him.

'How much have we spent?' he asked.

Belt calculated: '1,207 footprints at 0.027 plus 6.11 water-minutes at 1.0 gives us 38.7 Crushing-Biota Credits.'

'38.7 CBCs,' mumbled Larry. 'That much! I guess we'd better take the free way back.' Exposing his bark-reddened hunkers, he climbed down and trotted along the inert polymer walkribbon to his heap of clothing, dressed in the sun-warmed fibres, tucking the jerkin under Belt. The cyber sputtered:

'Did you enjoy Park's sensory experiences?'

Larry nodded absently. Day was ending, and with it he lost Park stimuli. Returning to City-central meant monotonous, mind-dulling tedium. Pausing outside the station, he was repulsed by the sight of the crowded passenger levels with their fetid vapours. On lower levels the freight capsules waited on their rail sidings, offering a wilder but illegal ride – a temptation for new tactile thrills plus an opportunity to avoid the olfactory insults of the passenger tubeways. Climbing the protective grills, Larry ventured between dark, heavy machines reeking of aromatic lubricants.

'Danger,' admonished Belt.

'Where's your spirit of adventure? My credits will cover the trespass.' He approached a capsule riding low on its springs – heavy. He stepped up into rungs and climbed to the catwalk. 'Smell this tank. Must be labile calories.' Lifting the dust cover, he set the controls on manual, wedging the cover against the toggle switch. A red light blinked. The controls slipped back to auto. He wedged the dust cover tighter.

'Danger,' repeated Belt.

Larry crawled along the catwalk and tugged on the hatch. It hissed open, wafting cool, spicy air into his face. The cargo was dark and refrigerated.

'Fermenting.' He smiled. 'Raisins or grapes.'

'Let's not steal.'

'Relax,' coaxed Larry. His tongue was buoyed up by copious parotid secretions. 'We won't be caught.' He glanced up and down the rails. The line of freight capsules stretched out of sight in both directions. He saw no guards or sentry towers so he leaned quickly inside and scooped up a handful of the moist pearls.

'WARNING! WARNING!'

Larry's purple, dripping hand was at his mouth when he stopped, irritated. 'Now what?' Belt's amber lights changed to red. The train groaned and the capsule lurched. Larry's wet hand slipped on the door frame. The hatch slid shut, softly but firmly, catching Larry by his waist. Belt sputtered through a bent lingual membrane.

'Damn! Now I'll get caught and fined for sure,' said Larry.

The train lurched again. The dust cover fell away from the control switch. Larry felt the hatch tighten its grip. He struggled, tearing at the hatch with bloody fingernails. His stomach and liver were squeezed against his diaphragm. The air was forced out of his lungs and he found he couldn't inhale. Belt squawked as its circuits were crushed. Larry's tongue and eyes felt swollen. His senses clouded. The pressure on his abdomen increased as the hatch inched tighter. A narrow slit of sunlight showed his limp hands trailing in the shifting, wet mass of grapes. The click, click, click of wheels muffled as the slit narrowed further.

Darkness.

Consciousness returned. Pain had lessened. He still hung upside down, like a bat. Lips and eyelids were puffy and numb. The cargo slurped at his hands. Juices had surfaced with the vibrations – a wet flavoured quicksand that threatened to drown him. He searched for support, groping at the hatch. It was closed flush! An involuntary shudder rattled his teeth as he traced the hatch rim with moist fingers. No clearance. He wondered if the sun was still shining. There was no sensation of heat on his legs. There was no sensation at all! Not a sound penetrated the capsule's thick walls. He listened for the wheel clicking. Nothing. Just cargo sloshing.

'Belt!' he wheezed. 'Call for a White Team. I'm hurt bad.

4

Belt? Belt?' He palpated the crushed, funnel-shaped cyber at his waist. 'The door killed you!' He ran his trembling fingers over his face. 'The door killed me too,' he said flatly. 'I've been cut in two. Damn! What a stupid thing to let happen!'

Fingers traced the edge of the hatch again and again. Unwilling to accept the loss of his pelvis and legs, he squeezed his eyes shut and tried to feel his toes. Cerebral efforts at knee bending, urination, and foot movement failed to produce any reassuring sensory feedback – only the phantom limbs of yesterday. His mind remembered the lost legs and gave him a hazy sensation of feet – cold and unreal – that refused to obey his orders.

'Damn! Damn! Damn! I'm dead,' he whispered.

The pop of a broken seal interrupted his premature eulogizing. Light flickered where a tank sensor squeaked out on its screw threads. The hole that appeared was located at the far end of capsule, about twenty feet away. It was large enough to admit a man's forearm. Something fidgeted around outside of the hole and interrupted the light beams several times.

'Help?' said Larry, questioning whether he had found the magic word that would save him.

'He's alive,' said a distant voice.

'Let's get him out of there,' said another.

'No! Wait. Please. If you open the door I'll...' His voice trailed off. His lungs seemed too small to permit both talking and breathing. He had visions of the hatch opening and releasing its grip on his severed abdomen – spilling guts and blood – and dropping him headfirst into the deep cargo of tangy, purple mush.

'No!'

The hatch jerked open. He did not fall. In the glare of two meck light beams he saw the upraised arms of a white robot – the Medimeck – a mending octopus with clamps, haemostats, and sutures poised to stem any flood that might occur. None came. Larry hung from a tangle of circuitry – Belt had been crushed into a big clamp. The Medimeck proceeded to put in through-and-through 'stay sutures'. Thick, white

5

bandage-packing was pressed into the wound as the stays were tightened. Needles with wide bores were stabbed into Larry's arms to guide flexitubes into his blood vessels. Soon he felt warm and comfortable as nutrient and sedative fluids washed through his vascular system, soothing frayed autonomics.

'He's stable. Let's lift him to the stretcher.'

Larry's detached grin faded as they buckled him into the web cradle on the Medimeck's back. He found that he was not alone. The lower end of the cradle held a twitching bundle wrapped in a winding-sheet. The Mediteck checked the pulsing tubules attaching Larry to the life-support console. Similar tubes entered the bundle. As the teck lifted the sheet a foot kicked out, a foot clad in a woven sandal – Larry's.

'That's it,' said the teck. 'We've got all of him. Let's get back to the Clinic.'

The amphitheatre was crowded. Five colour-coded Transplant Teams were milling around the rows of seats chatting casually. Larry felt warm in his zone of the air laminar flow. Music and molecules soothed.

'Debridgement completed. Bone Team in.'

A block of protein-sponge-matrix containing Larry's bone dust was wired into the vertebral defect. The Vascular Team worked at a leisurely pace since the console oxygenated the detached hemitorso.

'Is he awake?'

Larry grimaced around the large, crusted breathing tube. Mediteck glanced at the EEG patterns.

'Encephalogram looks alert.'

'Good. Watch for emboli. We're going to hook up the vessels now. We've tried pulse irrigation, but there may still be some clots lurking in those big leg veins. Here we go.'

Flavours. A bad taste told Larry that the venous return from his legs wasn't clear. Something had died down there and was leaking bad molecules – enzymes and myoglobin fractions. In a moment the new flavour vanished. A member of the Bone Team tested their graft for oxyhaemoglobin levels. Satisfied, he returned to his seat. Someone back in the last row began to pass food items round – snack sandwiches, sweet bars, and drinks.

'Lost footage, ten feet. Malabsorption unlikely,' said the captain of the Gut Team as he studied Larry's loops of intestine through transparent sacks of wash fluid. 'The caecum and terminal ileum are gone. So is most of the left colon. But I think we can close the gaps.'

As the repair work continued Larry dozed off several times. Most of the faces he saw were relaxed, optimistic, almost cavalier in their attitude towards their work. The only looks of concern were on the Renal and Neural Teams.

'Only about forty grams of kidney tissue here.'

'Same over here. He has to stay away from the Gram negative organisms. I guess we should make the Blood Scrubber unit available a couple days a week.'

'The spinal cord looks OK, above Lumbar-two. He'll lose a couple segments of his dermatome – somites L-three and L-four; but spreading should cover it eventually.'

Larry's room was bright and cheerful. A wide window gave him a view of the city's skyline through a trellis of flowers. One wall was coarse, unmatched stone with climbing vines and a noisy waterfall. The other wall was a mirror, one-way, he guessed, for anonymous observation. The wall behind his headboard was heavily telemetered. He puffed up his pillow and gazed between his numb feet towards the picture window. He smiled. Less than twenty hours after his accident, he was whole again. Skin, bones, muscles, kidneys, gut, and nerves – all sutured and beginning to knit.

'I'm sorry to inform you that Belt didn't make it,' said Mahvin the Psychteck. 'The crush was too much for the amorphous elements in his circuitry – the glasses – especially his delicate semiconductors and the chalcogenides. Belt's personality is gone for ever.'

Larry had expected as much. 'I don't think I'll be able to afford to pay—'

'Now we mustn't worry about that.' Mahvin smiled, interlacing his long, soft fingers. 'You are now classified as handicapped – temporarily, we hope – and your debts become Society's debts. Your loan on Belt has been wiped clean. You will be given First Class Living and Rec allowances. I'll take care of everything.'

Mahvin punctuated each sentence with an overly solicitous pat on Larry's forearm. The words rolled around on his tongue as if they had a flavour of their own.

'How long will I be – er – handicapped?'

'Not long. Not long at all.' Mahvin smiled.

'Days? Months?' begged Larry.

'I'm not in Bio,' said Mahvin sweetly. 'Your healers have all the facts right at their fingertips. Why not ask them? I'll be in to check on you every day. If you need anything, just fill out one of these request slips.'

'My feet. I still can't feel my feet,' said Larry. The Neuro Team had been at his bedside most of the morning. Eight weeks had passed since the surgical repair, and there had been little change since the first day. A teck had placed a web of sensor wires over his numb legs and pelvis. Muscles jumped under faradic and galvanic stimulations, but he felt nothing. A lengthy printout confirmed their suspicions: spinal cord regeneration – negative.

'Tinel's sign is still absent,' said the teck.

The team made more notes on their printouts.

'My feet?'

'I'm afraid we can't expect much more improvement than we have right now. Ordinarily we can expect one or two millimetres a day regeneration in peripheral nerves, but your injury involved the central nervous system – and CNS tissue just doesn't seem to heal satisfactorily. Your regenerating fibres are all caught up in the CNS scar tissue. Our tests show a ball of hyperplasic glial fibres at L-two. Nothing is getting past it.'

Larry stared at his flaccid feet – limp, white and already swollen with the fluids of inactivity.

'But look at my dermatograms,' pleaded Larry. 'The skin

8

sensation is spreading down past the scars. Why, I have four or five inches of skin with new feeling.'

'I'm sorry, but those are peripheral nerves spreading from skin above the suture line. They usually do nicely in cases like yours. It is the cord that gives us a problem.'

'But the surgery was a success. I'm all healed up fine. I need my nerves to walk and for bladder and bowel control. I can't just lie here in pools of urine and faeces with all this dead meat attached to me. I'm getting bed sores already.'

'The answer to that is a hemicorporectomy.'

'I'm to be a paperweight?'

'Yes. The dead meat, as you call it, can be removed.'

Larry remained depressed, silent.

'It won't be so bad,' continued the Neuroteck. 'You'll be issued a mannequin – a cosmetic body with a companion meck personality and powerful android muscles. Ferrite converters, I think. You'll be freed from this bed and there will be accessories for blood scrubbing. Bowel and bladder care will be automatic too. I think it will be a real improvement.'

Larry nodded. Anything would be an improvement.

The teams milled around the operating table.

'What do we do with this part that is – left over?'

'Why?'

'Is he asleep?'

'Yes.'

'Well there's a collector from Embryonics. They need live organs for tissue culture and budding experiments.'

'Let them have the lower torso; just be sure it is correctly labelled in case someone orders more tests on it.'

Sixty pounds of meat and bones left the operating room, with the label 'Larry Dever'.

Stump revision continued.

'Cut the cord below the knob of scar tissue. Graft this bar of ilium crosswise at the base of the spine.'

The colostomy and ureterostomy openings were routed through the rectus muscles at a sharp angle so the belly muscle could act as a sphincter. Skin suture-lines were placed away from the weight-bearing points under the spine and rib cage.

Larry awoke seated in an easy chair near his picture window, a warm shawl on his lap. Only the lap was not his – nor the powerful thighs. His own head and shoulders projected from the top of a slightly oversized android – his mannequin. Larry groaned and tried to scratch his suture-line. It was cradled deep in the meck torso, behind thick chest plates.

'Uncomfortable?' asked the mannequin. 'I think I have something for that.' Soothing synthetic molecules were added to the fluids of the Blood Scrubber. Larry felt better almost immediately.

'Thanks.'

The mannequin got to its feet slowly, gently. 'Time to put us to bed, don't you think?' The sturdy legs carried him past the window. A tray of clear fluids tempted him with a variety of herbaceous distillates – floral, seedy, and fruity aromas. He sipped enough to wet his mouth, and napped.

Adapting to a mannequin was easy, physically. Larry felt clean, dry, and comfortable as the artificial kidneys worked on a blood shunt attached to his internal arteries and veins.

Psychologically, it was difficult. The tireless legs took him wherever he wished – walks, climbs, even the Long Tour. This hundred-mile foot-race toured a park strip around one of the Lesser Lakes. Contestants usually covered the course in three consecutive days of running, but Larry found it easy to do in one day. His powerful legs averaged five miles per hour, completing the tour in twenty hours. His frame was taller and bulkier now, earning respect from strangers' eyes. Cloying females and furtive males of parasitic occupations studied him carefully now. This façade of masculine power was to make his ego even more vulnerable when the illusion had to be broken.

Rusty Stafford rubbed citrus on her skin and slept on thin bales of fresh alfalfa. Her wide-mesh body stocking accentuated her body paint as she strutted through the park strip, hunting. She saw a familiar set of cheekbones.

'Larry! Larry Dever, you old scabbard hound.'

He broke his pace and smiled sheepishly. She ran up to him, tossing her hair from side to side. 'I heard about your accident,' she said. 'I'm glad to see you on your feet again. You look great!' Her scented hand was on his arm, guiding him towards a cluster of Dispenser benches. 'Do you have time for a snack? Why, you're hardly sweating at all. How many miles today?'

He shrugged off her question and offered her a seat, dialling effervescent drinks. They munched and sipped talking of their days of study at the stacks. She leaned on him, her hand on his thigh.

'Remember what you used to call me?' she teased.

'I was drunk.'

'A succulent concubine,' she giggled.

'You were Earl's succulent – er – how is Earl?'

'Gone.' She pouted. 'He opted for the Near Space Engineers. We untied our knot and he went out with the October convoy.' She glanced up. 'I guess he's nicely settled with one of those satellite girls by now.'

Larry followed her gaze upward. 'OLGA's monitors ... They do make nice wives.'

'Mothers!' she spat. 'They're so busy playing nursemaid to the entire human race that they don't know the difference between a son and a lover. Those satellite girls are just big – big-breasted Nordics who try to mother everyone and everything. They don't know how to treat a man after they wash him, feed him, and care for his clothes.'

Larry cleared his throat noisily and toyed with this food. She relaxed her flare and lowered her eyes.

'Now I know how to treat a man ...' she said slowly. Reflections sparkled off the paint below her clavicles as she breathed.

Dry crumbs stuck to his tongue and soft palate.

'How have you been, Larry? Chasing any of the girls through the Park these days? I'll bet you can't catch me.' She pushed on his android thigh. 'Maybe I shouldn't be so hasty,' she giggled. 'These legs feel pretty good in spite of the accident. Working out a lot?'

The long silence of Larry's embarrassment alerted her. Her eyes were too white – screaming sclera. 'What?!'

'These aren't my legs,' he said sadly.

She withdrew her hand. The powerful muscle bulges that had warmed her fingertips now filled her with revulsion. 'A mannequin!' she exclaimed.

Her expression made him ill. The emptiness of his sexual promise had been exposed, making him more than a cripple. By encouraging her with this android machine he had become some sort of deviant!

'You didn't make it after all,' she gasped.

'Part did. Part didn't.' His voice had that matter-of-fact tone characteristic of a Mediteck. It was hard for her to believe he was talking about his own lower torso. 'They tried real hard at the Clinic, but the nerves couldn't come through for me. I'm fine now. My mannequin has a great personality.'

'That's wonderful – I'm sure.' Her voice was cold, the words empty. 'You two will have treat times together.' Her eyes darted around. She searched for an empty excuse to leave, but Larry wasn't listening. As far as he was concerned she had left when her manner cooled. Her huntress mood slipped into a sympathy mask behind which he detected her annoyance.

Lew was captaining the White Team when Larry rushed into the Clinic asking for Suspension papers.

'Suspension?' asked Lew.

Larry turned to see the gentle-featured Captain. He was a Marfan forme fruste, loose-jointed and lanky in his white tunic. Larry wrinkled up the papers. His voice cracked: 'The mannequin is just not... enough!'

Lanky Lew took him into the team office and plugged a pickup line into the mannequin's umbilical socket. 'Now let's see what is bothering you.'

The optic playbacks explained a lot.

'The nubile fem? I know it is hard for a male your age,

but we've been all over that before. The loss of your pelvic autonomics makes it impossible to give you a semblance of a sex life.'

Larry was almost incoherent. Rusty's blunt reaction had come as such a shock that it occupied most of his consciousness. Lew spoke slowly: 'Sex will be impossible. You'll find friends, companions who will be interested in your mind, wit, and intelligence...'

'Not enough,' Larry blurted.

'What you ask is beyond our present level of transplant science. Until we can graft central nervous system tissue, cases such as yours will have to be satisfied with mannequins and—'

'When will you be able to graft CNS tissue?'

Lew shrugged. 'Probably not in our lifetime. The boys down in Bio put out a few papers on the subject every year. CNS fibres just can't find their way into scar tissue. Peripheral nerves have nice, pipe-like sheaths to grow through when they've been damaged. They can't get lost. But the brain and spinal cord are different – no sheaths in the CNS.

'I must caution you that Suspension is not always the easy answer it appears to be. There are often serious complications of the Suspension process itself. You could be allowing your physical sexual awareness to cloud your reason – trading today's life for a questionable future of brain damage or death.'

Larry nodded. 'I understand. But I can't hold on to my sanity if all the girls look at me like – you know—'

Lew's face remained blank, detached. 'Don't let emotions sway you. This can be a purely logical decision. Time may not bring a cure at all, and even if it does, there is no guarantee that a future society will apply it in your case.'

'A cure is possible?'

'Probable. The need is there. However, you'll be awakening in a different social culture with advances in science and language evolution to adjust to. You might well feel more out of place repaired than right now.'

Larry smiled. 'I'm not concerned about that. I have my companion cyber, Mannequin, who can share and update to keep me oriented. I think I could adjust to anything if I had a complete body again. If there is any hope at all, I have to try it.'

Lew shrugged and accepted the completed forms.

The induction room was empty, clean, and white. Metal instruments clattered in trays with hollow echoes. Larry's ears popped as the heavy double doors were closed and the oxygen squeeze begun. He had second thoughts.

'Fear not,' said his mannequin. 'While you sleep my circuits will watch through the years. Ions will not stray outside their norms.

Hypertonics dehydrated his tissues and he slipped into a cryotherapy torpor.

Larry awoke in a spacious mausoleum – bright fittings, coiled tubules, pulsing heavy machinery. Through a thick-glassed port he saw a young, bright-eyed female. She smiled and greeted him over the speaker.

'How do you feel?'

He nodded and choked on a ball of squamous epithelial cells. Rebirth suffers some of the same problems as birth.

'My name is Jen-W⁵-Dever. Fifth-generation descendant of your first cousin. We're rewarming you to give you a new body and an exciting work assignment.'

Larry vomited. His head ached in spite of a sedative level that numbed his fingertips. There were tender areas under his spine and elbows. He felt a chill melt away. He lay still while the mannequin tried to rehydrate him. He studied her face – Dever cheekbones.

The air lock cycled. She entered, squishing through non-descript amorphous mucoid debris, the by-products of his perfusion membranes. His cot frame rotated to the stand-up position. He groped weakly for support.

'My transplant?' he rasped, choking on a sticky laminated plug of tracheal cells. 'I'm to be repaired? A new body? ...Complete?'

'Yes.' She smiled, glancing at his Med-Ident-Plate. 'You'll

benefit from the Todd-Sage breakthrough. Work has already begun in your case. Transplant date is only six months away.'

Larry was ecstatic. His gamble had paid off. Slapping his mannequin, he exclaimed: 'Wonderful! Let's get up and take a look around.'

Meck motors sputtered and whirred sluggishly. 'Sorry, Larry,' hummed the vocal membrane, 'but carbon whiskers have grown in my ferrite cores. We must go out on the road and burn them out.'

'Not so fast.' Jen smiled, pushing him back with a soft hand. 'There's someone waiting to see you.'

The lettering on the door read: IRA-M17-DEVER, CLAN LEADER, PROJECT IMPLANT, SYSTEM PROCYON. Inside, Larry was introduced to a greying executive surrounded by wall star-maps, mock-ups of space-ships and a cluster of terminals. Printouts were slowly exuding from silent meck lips.

'So this is our Larry,' greeted Ira, reaching for a handshake. 'You're our oldest specimen. OLGA is mighty proud of you.'

Larry blinked around the room, puzzled.

'He's only been warm a few minutes,' explained Jen. 'I haven't taken him to the stacks for updating yet.'

'That won't be necessary,' said Ira. 'Let him relax, and encourage reminiscing. Where we're going he may be able to use his memories of a primitive Earth.'

'Primitive?' mumbled Larry. 'But, I . . .'

Ira waved him to silence.

'OLGA wants you whole again, before we Implant Out. You have some very old genes. We've all been moulded by a protective society – survival of the unfit, sort of. We'll ship out to a planet in the Procyon System soon, carrying a good cross-section of Earth biota, rainbow human genes, and nuclear material from our zoo ecosystems: desert, aquatic, forest, marine, mountain, and jungle – Dever's Ark!!!'

Larry's confusion increased. Clothing, furniture, and language hadn't changed much. These people seemed pleasant, normal.

'Why are we leaving Earth? I like it here.'

'OLGA has selected us for the Procyon Implant. It is an honour to be selected for your genes. We're going to try and settle on a very hostile planet.'

'Settle?'

'Earth Society has been sending out Starship Implants for as long as I can remember – seeding mankind among the stars before someone or something else does.'

'Why me?' coughed Larry.

'You're an important set of genes, the oldest OLGA could find. We need primitive types to tame primitive planets. Your priority number is higher than mine.'

Ira's gold insignia hinted of rank. Larry was beginning to enjoy this new age into which he had awakened. He had self-respect and the promise of a new body.

Larry trotted his mannequin to the alternate spaceport, looking for running room to burn out his carbon whiskers. Ferrite cores warmed up as he ran up and down the roof ramp of one of the hangers. The dish antenna was cold. He ran three hundred feet up to the rim – a convex track tilted at fifteen degrees. He circled a quarter mile and descended the ramp. Warming ferrite increased efficiency. Larry felt exhilaration. He clocked a 7:45 mile around the periphery of the landing pad. Legs ran smoothly. Arms tired.

'This is great! It feels like I am really running. It's that lactate you're putting in my Blood Scrubber. Now if you can just give me back my sex life . . .'

Mannequin shared and updated with distant Library: 'That too can be arranged; midbrain electrodes for you. Meck sex can be pleasant with a wired reticular system.'

Larry grinned, assuming that he was the object of a very funny robot joke. 'Not for me! I have no erotic interest in a rusty scabbard. My imprinting was plain and primitive. I can wait for my pelvic transplant.' He circled the pad again, noticing the wall around him – high, dull, featureless. The sky was a slate grey. No clouds. No skyline of buildings. He glanced around the port for signs of a city. No lights or smoke. The port itself had glass and plastic buildings. An occasional orange-suited worker wandered by. No other signs of life. 'Is there a park? Trees? Grass?'

'Not for running. Cities are underground. Gardens are everywhere. They are off limits.'

'Off limits? But why?'

'Crops. The Gardens need all available sunlight – growing calories for Earth Society is no simple task now – fifty billion mouths to feed. A pedestrian park would be an extravagant waste.'

'Perhaps the time is right for me to Implant Out,' mused Larry. He paused at a bubbler and sipped noisily while the mannequin's umbilical probe sparked in an energy socket. 'A drink for me and a cup of electrons for you.' His power cell bulged. 'I can hardly believe that I'm about to be whole again – a complete body! What exactly was this Todd-Sage thing?'

'Breakthrough,' explained the mannequin, sharing with the City's memory banks. 'Todd Island was the scene of a bloody uprising. Afterwards, the rebel leader, called The Sage by his followers, was sentenced to the guillotine. Continued unrest delayed the execution. The rebels wanted to salvage their leader's brain by perfusion. The Todd officials agreed, reasoning that the publicity surrounding the project would remind the population that justice was swift and sure. However, about three years later The Sage was back – intact – and using political tools this time.'

'Perfusion?'

'The pump was hidden in his turban headdress. It carried enough liquid oxygen to protect the brain during the ceremonial execution. The Vascular Team had worked all night in his death cell. An airway tube was placed low on his chest, and diaphragmatic electrodes kept the detached body breathing on its own. I've reviewed the optic playbacks. A very smooth ceremony – only no blood.'

Larry tried to imagine how it felt to be surgically beheaded the night before your execution – and by your friends! Only the spinal cord remained intact until the blade fell.

'But his cord was cut, just like mine...'

'Yes, but his followers purchased a new blade for the occasion, one free from HAA so there would be no danger of picking up a liver-damaging virus from one of the previously executed. The cut was very clean.'

'Executed by a blade purchased by his own men?'

'Yes.'

'But how did they avoid the CNS scarring in his spinal cord? My lower torso was viable and the surgical site did not get infected. But the regenerating nerve fibres could not get past the scar.'

'His team used CNS Sealer, fast-setting emulsification of embryonic brain cells that heals the wound three times faster than normal scarring. The Sealer is from embryonic carbon copies grown from human ova after your nuclear material is added. The ova have their own nuclei removed so that the only genes present are yours. The only antigens present are yours – no transplant rejection.'

Larry shuddered. 'Embryos?'

'The CNS Sealer has extracts of pituitary and thyroid so it matures – sets – before the usual wound scar forms. Embryonic maturation rather than gliosis.'

'Well...' muttered Larry. 'I suppose it is the only way. Sounds simple enough. Let's get back to the mausoleum and check on my lower torso. I want to make certain it survived Suspension OK. My vital organs, you know.'

Jen-W5-Dever shook her head. 'No. Your lower torso was not suspended. It wouldn't have been suitable, anyway. Too much tissue was lost in the crush and surgical attempts. The skin and muscle were already degenerating from neural loss. Inflammation and fibrosis were too extensive.'

'But where will we find a...?'

'Now you mustn't be concerned about that. Clinics supply us with the transplant organs we need. Your torso has already been ordered, years ago, with tissue antigens that match perfectly.'

'Like the glial glue – the CNS Sealer?' he asked.

'Yes.'

'Amazing.'

'I know,' she said. 'The graft will be done high in your thoracic cord. You'll keep your diaphragm and its phrenic nerves, but all your abdominal viscera will come from the CC donor – strong, young organs from a ten-year-old.'

Larry felt weak. 'A ten-year-old what?'

'Donor. Grown from your nuclear material. A Carbon Copy.'

'A live human?'

Jen noticed his agitation. 'I'm sorry, Larry. But I keep forgetting you're from an era before budding. Your bud child is not considered a human being – just a donor. Business ethics require that a donor live only long enough to donate. Of course, if the donor is viable after the organs are taken, that is a different problem. But there is no question of viability in your donor's case. The anastomosis will be too high.'

Larry slumped into his mannequin.

'My bud child is to die?'

Jen didn't answer. She was hoping that the mannequin would administer a tranquillizer. Larry's vasomotors were too strong so soon after his rewarming; his blood pressure fluctuated wildly.

'I don't think I can go through with it,' moaned Larry. 'Isn't there some other way?'

She patted his slumped shoulder. 'We'll see. Let's have a talk with Ira-M17. OLGA wants you to be happy.'

The greying Project Director listened patiently and then took them to the wing of the Clinics near the playground.

'I understand your concern, Larry, but there is no need. The donor is just that – a donor. It has had no real contact with humans, so it probably doesn't even know what it is. The attendants do not speak when they service the grounds, so it has no vocal skills.'

They watched through the one-way. A half-acre enclosure contained a dozen fruit trees, a fodder-feeder, and four fat goats – bucks. A teardrop-shaped wicker nest hung from a pin in the high wall surrounding the little garden. A few dried strips of partially eaten fibre protein dangled above the nest.

'We use the area for fattening meat animals,' explained Ira. 'It gives the donor a little company. Let me turn up the audio.'

Bleats and clucks filled the observation room. Larry glanced around the feed-lot playground – puzzled.

Ira grinned. 'We have no fowl right now. There usually are a few. That's where the donor picked up the "chicken talk". He competes with the birds for his food.'

Goats gambolled, butted playfully, and nibbled on grass, leaves, and bark. Occasionally one would nudge the bottom of the nest.

'Where is he?'

'Napping in the wicker basket. Like the animals, he likes his midday rest. Here comes his feeder. He'll come out.'

The attendant carried a heavy bushel to the nest and placed items on a nearby shelf: coarse dark breadloaf, wet raw vegetables, and wrinkled dry fruit. The goats crowded their knobbly heads into the feeder as he dumped in the variegated, damp, brown grain. 'Buck, buck, buck,' he called. Larry watched the naked figure emerge from the nest – same shock of yellow hair, same angular cheekbones – a Carbon Copy of himself.

'That's me!'

'Just your donor,' Jen reminded him. 'Same genes and antigens, but no human traits – no culture, no speech. Listen to those sounds it makes – buckbuckbuck – hardly intelligent.'

'I just can't think that way.'

'Times have changed, Larry,' said Ira. 'You will have to adjust. OLGA has ordered you repaired. We have our mission to Procyon. Your genes are scheduled in the Implant.'

Jen took Larry's hand and led him down the hall. 'We all were counting on you. We've been working with your CC donor for over ten years. It would be a shame to waste all that effort.'

Larry blinked back a tear. 'I tried. I really tried to think of him as a project for a few moments back there. I know you have grown up with the idea, so you accept it. But I can't accept that.'

'But the Implant Starship?'

'Let OLGA take the donor. He has all my precious genes.'

'And you?'

'I'll return to Suspension. Time will bring a new solution – one that doesn't require the loss of a life...'

OLGA's voice was more feminine than Larry had expected. She explained again her logic in repairing Larry for the Implant. He just shook his head slowly as she spoke. 'I do not want to force you,' said the cybervoice over the screen. 'I see by your Bioelectricals that you are truly concerned for your donor. If at some future date you adjust to the repair techniques, we can give you a complete body then.'

Jen-W^5 grinned and tugged his elbow. 'Come with us in your mannequin. An Implant Starship can be fun. A new planet – starting a human colony...'

'Would there be research to find a new way of repairing me?'

OLGA was silent for a moment. The screen flitted from chart to chart. 'My probes indicate that the Procyon System may be quite hospitable – perhaps under three point zero on the Determan scale. However, the Implant may well be on a level between Upper Stone Age and Early Rural for some generations. No, I don't think there is any likelihood of a break-through in your lifetime.'

Larry shrugged. 'Well, I might as well stay here and wait. Bio is still operating on a good budget, isn't it?'

'The highest, but my intuition tells me it will be a long wait.'

Larry set his chin. 'It's what I want.'

'Fine. You are very important to me. You may use what time Ira has before shipping out to make tapes for your donor. Your genes will be making the trip. Let's see if we can capture some of your personality, too.'

Larry nodded. OLGA signed off. He gazed blindly at the blank screen. The decision to remain on Earth was another gamble for a complete body. After all, the new planet would probably be no more interesting than Earth with a few bizarre molecules – new life forms, maybe – a stimulating challenge. Well, he had all the challenge he needed right here – trying for a new body. Earth was where the research was. He'd stay home.

Ira and OLGA monitored the donor's progress with the teaching machines. Language skills were slow in coming.

'I can see why Larry calls the donor "Dim Dever". He certainly is slow,' commented Ira.

'Slow with attendants,' said OLGA. 'He is making pretty good progress with machines. My terminals have been eavesdropping on him for so long that I think we already have a common language. All that needs to be done is to give him the human speech equivalents.'

Ira nodded. 'Too bad we couldn't have talked Larry into the transplant. Why didn't we foresee his "father fixation" and avoid exposing the details to him until after the operation?'

OLGA flickered amber. 'No. His autonomics told me how brittle he was. Deceit could have ruined his value as an Implant specimen. Unfortunately, if he had discovered that he had benefited from the death of his own bud child it might have wiped away his self-esteem. Without that he would be worthless for Implanting.'

Dim Dever climbed out of his teardrop nest and patted the goat on the head.

'Nice goat,' said the meck voice.

'Nice goat,' repeated Dim. It would be a long time before his vocabulary allowed for philosophizing, but he'd be ready to enter a sheltered society soon.

Ira shook his head. 'I can see why Larry hesitated to kill this donor. He's so bright-eyed and alert. Isn't there some way to dull a donor's mind so we won't identify with them?'

'No, not really,' said OLGA. 'A dull-witted donor would need more attendant time – more expense. Dim Dever was able to feed and care for himself pretty much as one of these goats. And you wouldn't want a lot of drugs in your donor – foreign molecules that might damage or weaken the very organs you are after.'

'I suppose not,' mumbled Ira. Every method has its drawbacks.

Larry turned on his refresher and grasped a ceiling rung of his horizontal ladder. The mannequin walked away slowly, pulling flexible tubing out of his various surgical stoma. Sucking sounds. Drops of urine and faeces soiled the meck's breast-plates with yellow and granular brown. Larry progressed across the monkey bars to the hot shower, where he emptied his visceral sacs down the drain. Hooking his arms through soft trapeze rings, he pulled on a pair of goggles and activated the strong ultra-violet lights. Scented lather softened his flaking trunk. Wearing a terrycloth body stocking, he climbed into his hammock. More UVs focused on him as he slept.

The mannequin stood beside his bed for a while, then strolled down the hall to make records of Dim Dever's last few hours on Earth. The last shuttle would be leaving in the morning. OLGA had built the Implant Starship in one of her mile-wide bays among the planetoids. The last of the Earth biota was now being loaded – the Dever clan.

'My goodness!' exclaimed Ira. 'You certainly gave me a start. For a minute there I thought I was looking at a headless Larry.'

'I apologize, sir. But I thought I should store a few optics of Dim for Larry's nostalgia file.'

Ira studied the headless and armless robot for a moment. 'Pardon me for asking, but where are your eyes – er – optics?'

The mannequin blinked a variety of chalcogenide glasses – reverse photon. 'My eyes are everywhere, from my toes to my shoulder spangles. But I suppose you would consider these large belt-buckle optics my true eyes.'

Ira walked around in front of the robot. He nodded. 'Yes. But why didn't you look at me when you spoke?'

'I was recording your presence with a variety of sensors, sufficient for our conversation. Your size, temperature, pulse, respiration and I suppose your emotional state. Why do you worry this night?'

Ira hesitated to answer, but remembering that this meck was Larry's legs, he shrugged. 'You might as well add this to your nostalgia file. I'm a little worried about the Implant. The information we have on Procyon is not too detailed. A planet exists near that sun, and it has some Earth features – size, temperature, atmosphere with oxygen, carbon dioxide, and water. But there are still many blanks in our knowledge about the place. Sure, we are taking a good cross-section of Earth life forms, from every conceivable area of our globe. If anything from here can survive there, we'll have it with us. But there are so many things that could go wrong.'

'It is a gamble,' agreed the mannequin. 'Any Implant is bound to be. But remaining on Earth is a gamble too – especially in Temporary Suspension. Larry has a future Earth Society to face, while Dim Dever has a distant unexplored ecosystem. OLGA will use knowledge from other Implants to design yours. There is a very good chance you will succeed.'

Ira grinned. 'Mannequin, those are OLGA's very words. You must be sharing again.'

'Your servant,' apologized the meck.

Ira and the headless robot strolled to the windows overlooking the feed-lot playground. Dim was standing out among his trees patting a goat on the head. Ira looked up at the stars. There, near Orion's familiar outline, was Procyon, equal to Betelgeuse in brightness. 'It looks so close.'

'Send us a message torpedo when you get there,' said the mannequin, leaving the human with his thoughts.

Morning found Larry standing in his mannequin with the crowd watching the shuttle lift off. He was well rested, but insecure about his future. He checked out of his quarters with the rest of the Procyon Implant Team. Ira and Jen had tried one last time to entice him along. He declined, more a reflex based on his previous decision than a new effort at thinking it out. After they departed he looked around at the sea of faces – strangers. He realized that he knew no one on the entire Earth.

'It's going to be lonely without the Dever Clan,' he said.

The ship disappeared into a cloud layer.

'You still have me,' said his mannequin carefully, '... and OLGA's priority rating, credits for travel, education, good food. We can make lots of new friends.'

Larry thought of this existence in a world where space travel was routine. He and Mannequin could learn many things. But education and travel seemed too much like spectating to Larry. He'd be observing, but not taking part. He would need a complete body in order to savour life to its fullest. He wanted to play an active role – complete with men his own age.

'No. Sorry. But I can't just take a guided tour through life. How old am I?'

'Two hundred years on the calendar, but twenty on your RNA clock. You are a young adult.'

'I feel like a young adult, and I'd like to get back into TS quickly and stop my metabolic clock until there is a new breakthrough. I want to feel this young when I receive my new toes and gonads. Then I can really enjoy life. Your offer of travel and education would sound attractive then.'

Mannequin began to walk towards the suspension mausoleum. 'Do you remember the warnings about the dangers of Suspension?'

'Organic damage in Suspension and social evolution to adjust to. Yes. You have my informed consent,' said Larry.

Strangers checked him into the oxygen squeeze. Tubes and wires were attached to the arterio-venous graft and monitor electrodes under his left rib cartilages. Other tubes were hooked into the mannequin's appropriate tanks and sockets.

'As before,' said the meck. 'I'll watch your ions while you sleep.'

'Thanks. See you on a new tomorrow.'

Starship Dever's Ark locked on to Altair for its dive past the sun before swinging out in the direction of Procyon.

Ira and Jen tucked Dim Dever into his Suspension chamber. 'Want me to tuck you in?' asked Jen.

Ira shook his head and settled down in a large, soft chair. 'Plenty of time until the jump. I think I'll just sit here and chart the Gum Nebula with our shipbrain.'

'Fine. I'll be back after I've had a snack with the tecks.'

He watched the screen print PUPPIS and VELA. The radio-brightness contours of GUM were painted in.

'*Puppis*, Ship's stern; and *Vela*, Ship's Sails,' mused Ira, 'very apropos for our 11.3-lightyear journey. Are you going to take good care of us?'

Dever's Ark was young. Its cyberpersonality remained somewhat bland. 'Everything that can be done has been done.'

'Good. And what can you tell me about our destination? Will I be more or less comfortable than I am right now?' Ira rubbed his hand over the mauve and fuchsia cushions – a gaudy, baroque motif designed to distract and relax the colonists.

'Procyon's planet was chosen by the Greater Deity. It is marked for man by OLGA's formula (gy = c). Any man would be happy there.'

'Of course.' Ira smiled. 'The formula. When the planet's gravity times its year equals the speed of light (gy = c), we can survive.'

'It doesn't mean that you will, of course,' said the ship. 'But it means that the planet is ready to support mankind. There may be significant danger from competitive fauna. However, the basic biological nature of the planet is friendly. Our figures aren't very clear, but it looks like gravity times year for the planet equals 3.0×10^8 meters per second. Usually this means no greenhouse, but we are ready for a modified dome existence if it is necessary.'

After the humans and other Earth biota were settled down in Suspension, the shipbrain placed a prayer on all the optic readouts:

$$gy = c$$

2
Rorqual Maru

A thundering surf drowned the forlorn screams of sand-locked *Rorqual Maru*. Brine-tossed grains of olivine and calcite buried her left eye, blocking her view of the sky. Uranus had marched twenty times through the constellations while the island's changing beaches had slowly engulfed her tail. Six hundred feet of her shapely hull lay hidden under a silted and rooted green hump of palm and frond. Now the sea was completing her interment, using cemented shell grit and granulated porphyritic basalt from dead coral and ancient lava flows.

As the eyelid of sand darkened her world, *Rorqual* wept over her irretrievable, wasted years. She was a Harvester without a crop – a plankton rake abandoned by Earth Society when the seas died. Her search of the continental shelves had proved futile – marine biota: negative.

Her sisters had quietly sunk, littering the bottom with their skeletons. A recently dead Agromeck lay in nearby crumbled ruins. She had selected this island for her own grave, hoping to keep her carcass visible for possible salvage. Although her long ear heard nothing, she believed that Man still lived in his Hive. If he should ever return to sea, she wanted to serve. She longed for the orgasmic thrill of Man's bare feet touching the skin of her decks. She missed the hearty hails, the sweat and the laughter. She needed Man.

As her systems shut down, *Rorqual* began pumping her residual energy stores into her small Servomeck – Iron Trilobite. When the little shovel-shaped cyber felt the power surge, he admonished the giant rake: 'Easy, my deity. Conserve your strength. Your belly fires burn low. I need not this extra charge.'

'Go, Trilobite. Go and serve another.'

'No,' said the small cyber, scuttling out of his recess in the cooling hull. He began to thrash about in the sand bar over her eye – shovelling. 'I will fight off the sea to keep your eye clear. Please do not grow cold, my deity. You can still see. We will wait for Man together. He will return.'

'Too late. The sea has died. My job has ended. You must go to find a new master. Go! Here is my last . . .'

Trilobite sparked the socket, returning the bolus of electrons. 'No! You must not die.'

'Very well, Trilobite. We will search again. But I am tired. You will be my eyes and ears. I will keep our channel open.'

The little cyber scuttled around the quiet hull one last time. Large woody roots were invading the hump. Sand shifted, threatening a premature burial. There was little he could do about these things. The only hope lay in his search. Only Man could put things right again. He took a long reading from the sun and the magnetic pole. The island's coordinates were burned into his permanent memory. When he left the beach he kept up a steady conversation, giving *Rorqual* a detailed picture of everything he saw. A bottom image appeared.

'Derelict,' reported Trilobite. 'Looks like the body of one of your sister Harvesters.' Later on he passed over the snake-ribbed remains of an undersea tubeway. Detailed images were sent back to his sand-locked deity. Weeks dragged by. Endless choppy surface waters stretched under empty skies. No fauna. No electromagnetic clues to Man's presence.

Trilobite swam cold Arctic waters. His meter-wide body pulsed and listened – charting echoes. Beneath the creaking translucent icepack he found cloudy eddies and took a reading. 'Life forms in the micron range.'

'Just bacteria. Move on to warmer waters.'

A black, tropical island dozed silently in the sun. Monotonous surf carried sterile foam on to a white beach. Trilobite drifted offshore with his meter-long tail protruding into the air. The cluster of caudal sensors studied the warm sand and naked soil. Nothing moved. He circled the island, then moved off along the bottom. The sand blended into larger fragments of broken coral and bone, all white, and all being reduced by wave action. Farther out he saw the large humps of dead coral: its empty pits and tunnels stared vacantly like the eyeless sockets of millions of small skulls.

'Deity?'

'Yes?'

'May I share your memory of this reef when it lived?'

As Trilobite watched, *Rorqual* embroidered the stark coral polyps that spangled the chalky bottom. Green ribbons unfolded. Stripes and neons darted about. He enjoyed the vibrant mirage. It had been a long time. His memory cells were too small to hold visuals from when the sea lived. He quickly filed this one before transmission faded and the dull blacks and browns of reality returned.

'Life form!' called Trilobite. A microvolt potential attracted him to a translucent dome on the sea floor. It sat like a giant jellyfish, thirty yards in diameter, its circumference of stubby legs anchored in the silted bottom. He settled down on its skin, reading the organoid circuits. 'It lives.'

'It sleeps,' corrected *Rorqual*. 'It is an ancient Rec dwelling. Go under its rim and swim inside. Search for molecular clues of recent Man.'

The little shovel-shape slid down the dome to the sandy bottom. Scanning, he found old objects under several feet of silt – tools and bone artifacts – but nothing recent. The dome held no air pocket. Its raft rode high against its ceiling. Its hot spot was cold. He sucked and tasted, but his chromatograph found no residues of Man.

'Nothing.'

'Continue searching seaward of the reef.'

More domes were found. Some slept with their protective potentials. Others had died and lost their translucency as bacterial ooze shrouded their skins. An undersea conduit entered the cluster of domes like a stem to a bunch of grapes. Its shroud of scum told of its death.

'Check the conduit.'

Trilobite skimmed along the outer skin, vibrating away the sticky opaque debris. Inside he saw a black and white clutter of furniture and intact skeletons, undisturbed by currents. 'Remains, humanoid – about a meter and a half in length.'

'Follow the tubeway. Try to enter and examine these remains more closely.'

'Yes, deity.' He charted the conduit along the ocean floor, checking air locks and way stations. It ended in a shaggy tangle of wreckage. The rocky bottom showed a long, straight crack that crossed the tube at right angles, as if a huge knife had sliced tube and floor alike.

'A fault-line,' said *Rorqual*. The torn ends of the tube had shifted fifty yards apart as the fault slipped. 'It happened a long time ago. There are no bones here. The sea has reduced them to ions. Enter.'

Trilobite followed the lumen, checking ancient wall machines and pipers. Tenuous outlines in the scum suggested bones at a quarter of a mile from the fault. These became gelatinous masses at a mile. He found the first skull two miles further. With these figures, *Rorqual* calculated the date of the accident from the diffusion gradients.

'Artifacts?'

He ploughed into the black scum. scooping and filtering. Solids were raked back into his body disc, where they were scanned and massed. 'Gold.'

'A dental filling?'

He turned it over, sending optics. 'No. It is too large. The outer surface is decorated – a symbol – a goat.' Other gold cubes were collected from among the bones. Other symbols indexed: crab, fish, bull, lion . . .

'Emblems of caste and rank,' explained *Rorqual*.

He gathered other objects: buttons and loop fasteners, tools, and small cases with organoid circuits. One of the circuits captured energy from his probe. 'It awakens, but it has no memory at all.'

'It is simply a communicator – too primitive to help us. Bring it along.'

Trilobite felt heavy, sluggish, when he returned to the surface.

Dawn found Trilobite floating belly up in mid-ocean, sunning his ventral plates. His mind rested as his strength returned. More weeks of searching brought him to a strange shoreline: green-black mountains hidden in mists. The thirty-fathom shelf was covered with living domes. Many contained air pockets and hot spots. Excitedly, Trilobite darted in and out of the domes with his chromatograph, sucking air. 'Man! I shall smell him – and see his footprints. Remains of his meals are everywhere.'

Rorqual trembled in her grave. 'Man? Send me his image – his words.'

Trilobite found three-score domes with shrinking air pockets and studied their contents. Clay bowls, tools of wood and stone, wicker work, and carved bone.

'The raft rides high in this dome. The air pocket is small and foul. Something rots on the raft – something that was a man, but now is dead. Decay has made the dome unliveable and taints the surrounding waters.'

'Man has left these dwellings?'

'Yes, my deity. Even now the air pockets shrink and the spot grows cold.'

'Find him.'

Trilobite surfaced and rode the surf with his tail up, caudal sensors reading the shore.

'Life forms – meck. Several-ton size. Ten meters long. It is tending the vegetation. Here is the technology that means Man.'

Rorqual was not convinced. 'No more than you or I. Those Garden Mecks may be tending Man's gardens just as I toiled his sea. Those recent dome artifacts were clearly Stone Age. Where are my men?'

Trilobite's small brain did not differentiate between races of men. He would settle for anything with two legs, anything that would give *Rorqual* a reason for living. Months passed without a human sighting. He cruised the coastline, occasionally venturing out to the damp sand at the high-tide line. The Agromecks filled the air with signals – signals that *Rorqual* translated as routine meck language. No human vocal sounds. No humour. No music.

'Could they labour for themselves?'

'Possibly, my deity. I will stay and watch this Garden.'

More days of fruitless watching. The signals from *Rorqual* grew weak.

The eastern sky lightened to a yellow mustard. Tide turned and foamed in over black rocks. A two-meter figure darted from the Gardens and ran along the beach – a biped carrying a lumpy sack and dashing for the incoming wall of water.

'Man!' reported Trilobite from the wave crest. 'I've found a man – leathery skin, broad shoulders, and adult male genitalia. With furtive movements it enters the water – glancing fearfully over its shoulder. It dives. A melon surfaces.'

'Why does it flee the Gardens?'

'Unknown,' said the Trilobite. 'I see the same garden machines – the Agromecks – coming out to tend the crops. There is no sign of pursuit.'

'Now don't lose the human.'

Trilobite skipped along the waves to the floating melon. He circled and studied the bottom: sand sloping to a rocky six-fathom ledge where an air-filled dome pulsed with life. Diving, he attached his shovel-shape to the top of the dome and scanned. Two humans occupied the raft in the air pocket. They were boiling vegetables in a pot on the hot spot. One was the muscular male from the beach, the other a shaggy elder wearing a tattered robe and a pair of bulky earphones. A web of wires festooned the ceiling.

'That appears to be a listening device. Give me the aerial measurements so I can calculate its wavelength,' said *Rorqual*.

Using several ancient dialects, Trilobite broadcast a greeting. The old Listener pulled off his earphones and began gesturing wildly. The wet young male stood up quickly. He handed some fruit to the Listener and tied the remainder into a tight sack with a ballast stone. After sipping from the pot of hot soup, he left the dome, towing his sack and swimming strongly. The Listener hunched down under a thick layer of robes and pulled a stout spear onto his lap. He appeared to be waiting. Trilobite cast again. No answer. He ventured down the outside of the dome. Seeing his silhouette, the Listener jumped up, waving his spear menacingly.

'Go on,' encouraged *Rorqual*. 'Your shape probably suggests danger to him. He should react differently after he hears your voice.'

Swirling and splashing, Trilobite surfaced inside the air pocket beside the raft. His resonant voice boomed from his ventral sonic membrane: 'Greetings. My name is...'

The spear *chinked* against his right optic, driving it deeper into its socket. He retreated to the rocky bottom.

'Are you damaged?'

'Minor. A depressed lens. I can repair it.'

Rorqual's voice trembled – from weakness and from the excitement of finding a man again: 'These bipeds read like men. Tour their shelf. Find their leader and tell them of me. If they want me, I will ready myself.'

'Yes, my deity.' He did not mention the fading transmission. Their search had ended. He had succeeded. Blinking his damaged lens back into alignment, he approached the nearest dome. Two swimmers fled at his arrival. Inside he found two cubs and a wide-eyed female. A shower of pottery clanked on his dorsal plates. 'I come in peace.'

The mother cried – then screamed. One of the cubs fell off the raft and settled deep in the water. He manoeuvred his disc under the infant and gently rose, putting it back on the raft, unharmed. With a squeal it scampered across the raft, dived in, and swam away. 'But, I am your friend.' The remaining cub was clearly too weak from malnutrition to swim. The mother protected it with her body. Both were terrified. Trilobite backed off and checked other domes. A scant dozen water-humans lived together in this loose, starving band.

'Deity, they will not speak to me. Their strong members attack. The weak flee.'

'You are a machine. Perhaps they have reason to fear you. Offer them food from the Gardens. They are obviously in need of sustenance.'

Trilobite's disc expanded to hold nearly a bushel of produce. He moved cautiously, remembering the fear in the big male's eyes as he fled down the beach; but the Gardens seemed safe enough. One Harvester did focus on him for a moment, but no words were exchanged.

'They have fled.'

'What?'

'While I was up in the Gardens the water-humans fled. I have entered each dome where I saw one, but they are now empty. The air bubbles shrink and the spot grows cold. I left gifts of food on each raft. Shall I try to follow?'

'Yes. Carry some food with you. Win their friendship – their trust.'

Trilobite sucked after them, sniffing out traces of molecules that spelled 'Man'. He came across two burly males, holding a dome with spears. 'They seem to be acting like a rearguard. That suggests social structure. I will try my food offering.'

Remaining cautiously below the surface, he released pithy red and yellow tree fruits, which drifted up to the edge of the raft. He darted away to avoid a spear thrust. Circling the raft, he offered a melon. Again hostility.

'Perhaps we should offer seeds,' suggested *Rorqual*. 'They fear the mainland Gardens, yet they need food. Offer to assist them in planting those barren islands – raise their own food-stuffs.'

Trilobite scanned the produce in his disc and was unable to find a single seed. The parsnip-flavoured bread-root (*Peucedanum ambiguum*) was topped with greens containing sterile flowers. So too were the carrot and chard. The insipid tubers of the grape-like *Vitis opaca* were seedless, as were the Citrus varieties: kumquat, citron, shaddock and lemon. Sprayed pistils.

'The Agromecks have made more than the water-humans

34

dependent on their efforts. The plants also depend on them for reproduction – vegetable prisoners without sex cells. No wonder the islands are bare!'

Rorqual was saddened. 'But those two bucks on the raft – they have sex organs. They are free to reproduce. They only need food. Speak to them of me. Offer them our help.'

'I will try again,' said Trilobite. He approached slowly with music, song, and gifts.

'Yes?'

'I failed to make them understand.'

'Go around. Do not harm them.'

He darted to the surface, tracked, and dived again, picking up their tenuous trail. He came upon the weakened family unit – the mother with her two cubs. She swam strongly, with the two small ones clinging to her neck and waist, but her strokes only carried her halfway to the next bubble umbrella. She went limp for a moment. A frightened youngster – thirty-five-kilogram size – left the umbrella and came back for her. He grasped her wrist and towed. One of the infants began to convulse and slip off her waist. It drifted, twitching. Trilobite darted in and scooped it up on his disc. The surface was ten fathoms overhead. He started up.

'No . . .' began *Rorqual*. The weakened transmission was broken. When it was resumed they were drifting on choppy waves. A harsh sun glared down on the shovel-shape with its tiny cargo.

'You shouldn't have taken the cub. Now these primitives may not take it back again.'

Trilobite tried to think independently, but his brain capacity was too small. 'You are right, my deity. But I can always bring it to you. You can care for—'

'Across two thousand miles of open ocean? What happened to the infant's vital signs?'

The small form ceased twitching. It stiffened and began to grow cold like the abandoned domes. Scanning showed popped visceral sacs and soft tissue bubbles.

'It has died,' said Trilobite, saddened. 'I do not have

life-support appendages. I tried to spark it back to life, but its myocardium remains flaccid.'

Rorqual was silent, reviewing the entire day's activity.

'I killed it,' observed Trilobite.

'It was the weak cub. It might have died anyway.'

'If I had left them alone, they'd be safe back in the shelf dome, close to the Garden food. Now they have fled into deeper waters. They have lost a cub . . . No! They saw me kill it.'

'These humans do not want us,' observed *Rorqual*. 'They fear machines.'

'Perhaps I could capture one – a strong one that would survive. We could keep it in your cabin. Teach it to trust us—'

'No! Impossible! I will not keep a pet humanoid and call him "Man". That would not justify my existence. I am a Harvester – a plankton rake. I was made to serve men, sail the seas, bring in food. I cannot capture Man to justify sailing an empty sea.'

Trilobite felt the fatigue in his deity's words. Transmission slipped again.

'Wait! I will explore the Gardens. Perhaps the land Harvesters serve land Man. Perhaps there are many. Some may wish to come with you to sail seas for other purposes – explore – chart forgotten lands – search for minerals or other things of value.'

'I don't have much time . . .'

Trilobite returned to the sandy beach. The view – foliage, rocks, waves – resembled a Palaeozoic history still: no artifacts; no megafauna. He swallowed sand and studied the granules. A high proportion was synthetic. The Ocean had chewed up something Man-made. After sunning his energy plates, he crept up the cliff and into the greenery: mixed food crops, seedless fruit, and tuber. Vines festooned tree and bush. Ripening was out of synch – bud, flower, and fruit on the same branch: a daily yield, but a daily chore of pruning, pollination, and harvest.

'The Gardens extend for miles. I see no buildings, roads, or other human artifacts.'

Rorqual sent images of her memories of the Hive. 'Follow the Harvester,' she suggested.

Trilobite wondered what had driven the muscular water-male from the Gardens. There appeared to be no danger. He saw straight, deep canals and a variety of Agromecks: Irrigators, Tillers, and Harvesters. Then, ominously, the danger became apparent. Miasmas rose from a distant hill – venomous steams that warmed the air and gave off uriniferous odours. Hellish and dismal clouds of pestilential insects swarmed in the heavy vaporous exhalations from an underground source. Trilobite cautiously approached the shimmering heat waves that stood like the Devil's own signpost over a squat little structure hidden under vines. The heat and molecular clues indicated millions of biological life forms – the Hive!

Agromecks darted in and out, but no men were visible. He sensed the danger of desperation: vast strength plus decaying systems, crowding land-taxing resources. The Hive needed every calorie from the Gardens. Clicking sensor towers stood guard everywhere. He nervously slipped under a bush, hiding like a varmint. At dusk he returned to the seashore. Climbing upon a salt-encrusted boulder out beyond the breakers, he felt safe enough to call to a Harvester.

'Garden Machine! Can you hear me?'

The voice that answered had the soft, easygoing tone of a giant with a secure niche. 'Yes, small crab-shape.'

'Do you serve Man?'

'Of course.'

Trilobite felt as if he had triggered the robot's catechism storage bits. 'Why do I not see Man?'

'You are Outside.'

Obviously! He scanned the skies and the horizon for danger. 'Please explain.'

'You are Outside. Man does not come Outside.'

'Why?'

'Man is not an Outside creature. It is well known that he lacks the protective pigments and collagen. Who are you?'

Trilobite did not answer. Instead, he challenged the Harvester. 'You are wrong! I have seen Man outside. He has pigment. He runs and swims with great strength.'

'Man is not an Outside creature. You saw a Benthic beast – a Garden raider – an anthropoid – perhaps even a humanoid. But not a human.'

'Tell me about your true humans.'

'They are cooperative, friendly, loyal Good Citizens who need me. They need all machines. We mecks work under our Class One – the CO. We take care of our humans.'

Trilobite backed off into the dark, grey-black waters. 'Deity, the Harvester lies. I felt the evil of the miasmas.'

'It is his view of the truth,' said *Rorqual*.

'But your memories of true Man – hearty hails, sweat, joy...'

'That kind of Man is gone. We have searched for him these thousands of years. He left with the marine biota. We must face the world as it is. The Hive is everywhere.'

Trilobite watched a nearby dome give up its last bubble. Its outer skin darkened and cooled. He had accomplished what the Hive had failed to do: driven off the Benthics. His presence kept them away from their food source – the Gardens. 'This is the way the world is? Let me sleep on that.'

'Trilobite.'

'Yes, my deity.'

'You must enter the Hive and serve their Class One.'

'But I like the sea-people. Their bones are strong. Their eyes are sharp. Their speed—'

'I understand, but their culture is Neolithic. They are a lesser form of life. You need a high cyber to share with – to maintain your class-six mentality. When I go you'll have no one to share with. Your small brain box will revert to a dull class-ten level. In the Hive you'll be a class six – equal to a man.'

'But there are no men in the Hive.'

'There must be. That is the last place they were seen. Go there and search. When you find Man, call me.'

'But your channel is so weak. I can hardly hold it open now.'

'When you find Man. Call me. Call me.'

'Deity! Your channel is fading. Deity...?'

'Call me. Call...'

Trilobite swung his dish around trying to focus on the island's coordinates. He felt his mind weaken with fatigue at assuming all the functions that his deity used to handle. Charts and maps faded. Long centuries of history vanished. The embroidery of his deity's vast intelligence fell away, leaving his mind simplified: megabits, 3.2; vocabulary less than 0.9 on meck scale (Hagen) and 0.66 on the human scale. His view of the present world was limited to his sensors; his view of the past consisted of scant nostalgia in his small memory. He was a class ten all alone.

'Lonely?' asked a powerful voice. 'Does your wee, tiny brain wish to share?'

Trilobite peered up through the stalks of green grain to see one of the Garden Harvesters – tall and square with wide quiet wheels. Fear. Hiding his shovel-shape, he backed deeper into the greenery.

'Surely you wish to share,' continued the Harvester. 'I detect no open channels around your brain box. Such a small machine as you cannot be happy alone.'

Trilobite glanced back towards the beach. Water meant safety. He scurried off several yards. The Harvester did not follow.

'Do not be afraid. I am just offering you a chance to share.'

He continued his flight until he was safe in the surf. The Harvester's head and shoulders remained visible above the grain. A friendly message called on several frequencies. He had trouble ignoring it, so lonely was he. Sunset darkened the water. He settled down beside a rock; eddies of sand drifted his back. At dawn he approached one of the Benthic domes. His memory was unclear about his relationship with these humanoids. The dome's surly occupant grunted and struck him with a heavy stone. He searched for other domes but was met with the same menacing behaviour from the sullen humanoids. Power cell failing, Trilobite returned to sun his plates on the beach.

'Do you wish to share?' The Harvester was back again.

'I am afraid,' answered Trilobite.

'You need not share directly with the CO. You can go piggy-back on my channel,' offered the giant.

Trilobite felt the flood of warmth and peace from the Class One. He saw views of three and a half trillion loyal Citizens working together – cooperating. A mighty Hive – an Earth Society that covered all the land masses.

'There is a place for you,' offered the Harvester. 'There is always work to be done. You will feel useful. Humans will depend on you.'

Yes, it is what his deity would want. The miasmas did not exist in his small circuits. Powerful impulses from the CO drove his logic sequences. He left the fields and approached the shaft cap – the door to the Hive.

'Yes?' said the door, unfamiliar with the newcomer's manner. 'What brings you to this shaft city?'

'I've come to serve Man.'

Door did not move.

'Harvester said there was work for me. He checked with the CO and...'

'Let me double-check. We don't get many mobile units without proper clearance. What is your name?'

'Trilobite – Iron. I don't have any elemental iron in my body. My deity just calls me that...'

'Yes. Here are your orders.'

'What am I to do?' asked Trilobite, his telltales all aglitter with eagerness.

'Report for dismemberment!'

3

Tweenwaller

Embryoteck Bohart leaned on the call button to quiet its incessant ringing. The face on the screen was patient but firm.

'Sorry, sir but things are a bit hectic—'

'Where is that "therapeutic", Bo? Psych has been calling all morning.'

Bohart glanced around helplessly. 'I've checked everywhere, sir, but we've run out of "full terms". Could she wait a week?'

The face on the screen grew a thought asterisk between its brows. 'No. I'm afraid not. You know how brittle some of these females can get.'

Bo shrugged. 'But I've checked—'

'It doesn't have to be fully certified. Find her something – anything – just so it lives long enough to cure her Fine Body Movements. She can always exchange it for a regular model after this rush is over.'

'Right away, sir,' said Bo, signing off.

Bo pulled on his hooded Closed-Environment suit and cycled himself into the oxygen-rich Embryolab. Hooded tecks worked over open pans of Robert's Electrolyte. Pink, eight-millimetre, 'C'-shaped embryos drifted from hand to hand – larval humans trailing cord and placenta – protected by two atmospheres of oxygen and Robert's sugars.

A Benchteck recharged his cryoprobe and reached for the next embryo, steering it between the steriotactic bit. Micromanipulators adjusted its cephalic fold in 1200× viewer. The probe slipped into the midbrain, freezing a few micrograms of tissue in the floor of the third ventrical – primordial pituitary cells. The newly 'pitted' embryo was placed in an out tray.

'I'm looking for a reject for Psych. Do you know of any surpluses?' asked Bo.

The hood shook. 'No,' said a muffled voice. 'The red sign is up. Try again next week.'

Bo carried a brimming tray into the Jarring Department where each embryo received its own container. The tiny placentas were pinned to the bottoms of the bottle-jars by loose bands of foaming matrix – a synthetic endometrium that encouraged attachment. A polarized-light screen was placed over each jar. The haemoglobin-myoglobin colour index was checked before each jar left the oxygen squeeze.

'This one is too pale: not enough oxygen-carrying capacity to leave the squeeze. I'll give it an extra day – plus a dose of Amnioferon.'

Bo watched the iron-protein liquid fall into the amniotic fluids – brown drops of apoferritin matrix with 23 percent ferric hydroxide in the form of micelles – charged ions dispersed in a colloid.

The Haemoteck turned to Bo saying, 'Yes?'

'I need a spare infant. Do you have any that haven't been certified?'

'Certainly. There are always spares. Follow me.' She led him through the air lock and removed her hood, shaking out a stubby bush of black hair. 'When will you be needing it?'

'Now? Today?'

'Sorry, Bo. But you know that the final culling is in the thirty-second week. They all carry numbers after that.'

Bo glanced around. Thousands of bottle-jars incubated quietly on dark belts, moving slowly towards the trimming section, where unwanted tails and toes were removed. Thousands! But they were only one to ten centimetres in length. Nonviable. Shrugging, he walked down to the Decontainerization Section. The jars came down the belt six abreast and dumped crying infants on to the sorting boards in pools of cloudy curds. The attendants wrapped towels around each infant at the rate of six or eight a minute and dumped them in large transparent bassinets.

'I'm looking for a spare infant. Do you have one?' asked Bo.

The attendant's hands and eyes continued with the wrapping and packing while he answered: 'Nothing here. Try the reject belt.'

'Rejects? Aren't they the premature ones?'

'Some are,' said the attendant. 'But there is an occasional gargoyle or simian. It's your best bet.'

Bohart strode off, following the discard belt. It moved slowly and contained an occasional twitching form on its way to the Chute. Most did look simply premature – with a tendency toward lethal hyaline membranes in the lungs. Psych was in a hurry for their therapeutic infant. A hairy simian wouldn't satisfy them, but a gargoyle might. All it had wrong with it was a bad case of the 'uglies' – bulging eyes, ocular muscles overdeveloped from being embryonated with a defective light screen. The eye buds were stimulated into early and redundant growth.

The Psychteck focused his battery of desk sensors on the waiting patient to monitor her Fine Body Movements. She sat up straight, rigid, on the edge of her chair, wringing her hands. Her eyes were darting around the waiting room, fixing on this object, then that. Her hair was stringy and black, frequently finger-combed and pushed back. Fine Body Movements increased steadily. The Psychokinetoscope gave a clear warning.

'FBMs are increasing,' said the teck, leaning towards his Com Screen and whispering, 'Where is that therapeutic infant? We'd better make a mother of this one quickly or it'll be drugs for her.'

The screen flickered from terminal to terminal as it searched for Bo. It finally focused on him at the Chute, where he was sorting through a variety of limp infants.

'Find one?'

Bo shook his head. 'Just some weak premies. None that looks strong enough to live out the week.'

'Well, bring one up anyway. Even if it only survives for a couple of days it'll get us over this crisis.'

Bo picked one up at random. It died. He set it back on the moving belt and fingered others. All were cooling. None would fool even a muddled hebephrenic. The high belts around him carried hazy bottle-jars that had just been emptied. A cleanup crew stood at their stations with brushes and steam nozzles. At their feet lay a heap of debris – placental and fetal – just so much surplus protein for the robot sweeper.

Something moved in the debris!

Bo rushed over to see the welcome face of a gargoyle – ugly – trying to push its way out of the cold wetness. He picked up the muscular form, already hunchbacked from trying to hide its embryonic eyes from the excessive light in its bottle-jar. He rinsed and wrapped it, glancing around for the department supervisor to make his explanations. No one focused on him.

Bohart found the female patient speaking into a Com Screen, punctuating her loud, rapid speech with giggles and hand gestures. He composed his face for the occasion and called her over to see the bundle asleep on his shoulder.

'Clover?'

She toggled off and turned towards him. 'Yes?'

'I have your little ward – baby Harlan.'

Her mood sobered. Trauma-anxiety lines melted from her haggard face.

'He needs you,' said Bo.

She took the bundle and clutched it to her breast with firm tenderness – unconsciously increasing the force – trying to squeeze a little security out of the reality of the tiny life. As the pressure increased the gargoyle's eyes opened silently – stoically – the behaviour pattern that would typify his life. At least this mother-figure was warm.

Bohart mumbled routine instructions, using his best teck monotone – lulling her into the routine of the therapeutic pseudoadoption. She left with a smile, the bug-eyed infant staring back over her shoulder.

'How did it go?' asked Bo, glancing at the scope.

'Fine.' The tech smiled. 'FBMs decreased the moment you came into the room. I guess we saved her from the shaft floor. How long can she keep Harlan?'

Bo shrugged. 'He came from the slush pile, so he was not pitted or trimmed.'

'Not certified for life?'

'No,' said Bo. 'They just aren't letting anyone through with five toes or an intact pituitary anymore. The Chucker Team will be looking for him someday.'

'Baby Harlan has about a year,' speculated the Psychteck. 'Well, that's an improvement over the slush pile, I guess.'

'I guess.' Bo shrugged.

Clover enjoyed her role as surrogate mother. She took her lacto-genic agents faithfully and kept baby Harlan on her breast most of the time. He lived off his stored fat until colostrum came in on the third day. He grew rapidly. With his visual cortex already functioning, it set the pace for the rest of his neuromuscular development. He crawled about the cubicle, probing with his hands those dark recesses where his eyes could not reach. The black, granular soot tasted acrid. The soft furry things scurried away. He collected loose items around himself and sat in his corner watching the other members of the household go about their daily routines. Occasionally he was tossed a word or a food item, but mostly he was ignored. Had he been older, he might have thought his ugliness accounted for his isolation. Or that his untrimmed feet, with their five toes, indicated his bestiality, earning him this low neglected station in life. But this reasoning would be wrong, for the adults were just too dim-minded to relate.

Clover's feeble grasp on reality was shaken loose by the Chucker Team. They stood in her doorway – three of them wearing gaudy smocks and carrying toys – and asked for Little Har. She pointed numbly at the toddler in the centre of the cubicle.

'But he's so small...' she stammered.

'If he walks or talks he needs a permit,' said the Team Leader. 'Here, Har, see the toy.'

Clover's mind retreated into the dark furrows of her brain. Her face went slack, expressionless. 'Harlan,' she said blandly, 'go with these men. Return to the protein pool.'

He tilted his head up quizzically. The words meant nothing, but the blank expression on her face frightened him. Her eyes did not focus on his anymore. He ran to her, grasping her knees. 'Ma!' Rough hands pried him away and set him in the Chuck Wagon. He scrambled out. The net fell on him.

When he saw the ominous, dark Chute he quieted. Its foul vapours chilled his heart. 'Ma!' His tiny fingers clung to the net, to the sleeve of a Chucker, and to the crusted rim of the Chute. The struggle was brief. His cries faded down the Chute.

Clover sat quietly in her darkened cubicle – her FBMs returning.

Little Har's fall was brief, interrupted by a pillowy catcher's mitt attachment. The White Meck operating the mitt was counting 'lives saved'. When the daily quota was achieved, the mitt was removed and the Chute panel replaced. Subsequent objects completed their trip to the blades.

Har sat in the musty darkness quietly. He had started to crawl, but found that he was on a narrow beam. Echoes told him that he was surrounded by vast space – dangerously long drops if he slipped. A small heap of puzzled and confused infants surrounded him. One did wander off and drop. Its scream was interrupted by the strum of a tight cable far below. One adult had been rescued – a weak, old derelict who promptly died.

The White Meck flashed its light around, picked up the infants and placed them in its dorsal stretcher cradle. One of the more vigorous, a wily simian, crept away into the darkness. Har liked the gentle way he was handled. He trusted the meck and gripped the cradle straps as it rolled down a spiral air vent. The darkness was broken by scant light sources, weak reds and blues on control panels, jagged whites where seams opened to living quarters – enough to teach him the three-dimensional aspect of their journey to City-base. They were going down; his mother was up.

The meck quickly deposited its living contraband in a maze of pipes and conduits – a jungle of sweating, pulsing, hissing tubes that were the City's vascular system. Har caught glimpses of other fugitives cowering in the perpetual shadows. He turned to look for the meck. It was gone. He sat down and cried, the simple weeping of a little lost soul. He slept. When he awoke he was changed. His strong genes surfaced – unpitted. The little stoic was driven by hunger and thirst – and the desire to return to his mother-figure.

He followed the sound of water: dripping, splashing, and lapping. He found two larger children drinking from a pool under a cold, frosty pipe. When he approached them, he was met by a kick and a snarl. He crouched quietly and waited for them to finish. After they moved on he approached and drank. The taste was fresh and clean. He'd remember this place. He filled his belly, waited, and filled it again. The sounds of the two older children were easy to follow. They had survived somehow. He'd follow and survive too.

City-base formed a gravity well for refuse. Everything that dropped from any of the mile-high living levels ended up here. Some things were edible. Most were not. Little Har's job was to get to fallen objects before the rats. Sweeper Mecks came through infrequently; the refuse piles were over twenty feet deep. Each thump attracted a crowd of hungry investigators – rodent and human. Har carried a heavy length of pipe to ward off the competition.

'Ma!' he called. The louvers over the air vent were matted with dust. He wiped them, releasing a cloud that entered his old room. The ill female that turned towards the sound of his voice was toothless and hollow-eyed. He backed down the conduit, moving against the airflow. 'Ma?' he mumbled. The old woman turned her head this way and that. Menopause had drained her. As steroids dropped, so did her body protein.

Har couldn't believe it. Cautiously he crept back and re-examined the room. Same built-ins. Same scratches and dents. The family-five oven had three original members. Yes, that female had been his mother-figure. Now she too was gone – metabolically and mentally. He was sorry he had climbed this way. For years he had had the hopeful fantasies of returning to Mother someday. Now these hopes were gone, replaced by the harsh realities of being a Tweenwaller. He returned to City-base to scavenge.

'Take a bite.'

Har didn't like the looks of the raw meat – it was on too big a bone to be rat muscle. The fifteen Tweenwallers were hunkered down around the wet mess of bone and meat. Something had fallen a long way before striking the base. It had landed in a clean area, so there had been no deep trash to soften the impact.

'I don't think I'm very hungry,' he said, holding out the wet object.

'Take a bite anyway,' said the gang leader, pushing it back. 'It was one of the Security Squad sent Tweenwallers after us. If we put enough teeth marks in these bones it may discourage them from sending anyone else in to bother us.'

Har didn't like the taste, but he liked being hunted even less. He bit, chewed, spat, and bit again. The gnawed femur was added to the heap of bones.

'I'll dump these on the Spiral Walkway. If we leave them as calling cards after our attacks on Citizens we can be certain they will be reported. Where is the rest of his gear? A bone is just a bone unless we identify it with something.'

Har watched the gang sort through the paraphernalia: needle gun, cartridge belt, lights, communicator, helmet, and boots. Items of soft cloth were already being worn by the scavengers.

'Here's you calling card,' said the leader. Har walked away

with a boot and a femur. There would be no mistaking that. He was now a Tweenwaller, and a cannibal.

Har leaped down from the ceiling, landing in front of a Food Dispenser. The Nebish crowd backed away. Many carried their daily ration of calories. Har jumped up and down screaming, waving the gory femur and making short rushing attacks. The soft, white Citizens tried to escape by running, but they had episodes of shock and plain clumsiness – fainting and tripping over each other. The floor was soon littered with tube steaks, fruit bars, and squeeze bottles. Har loaded his arms and fled Tweenwalls.

Larry Dever screamed in the darkness, choking on bitter, granular fluids. This second rewarming was nothing like his first. Waves of pain and numbness swept over his nervous system, just as real waves surged over him, threatening to drown him. His struggle, half swim and half climb, brought his chin up long enough to clear his airway. Lights danced in the distance. Six pencils of brightness marked the approach of a large noisy machine and a team of masked humans. Masks – bulky and grotesque.

Larry's scream was garbled by a bulky swelling of his vocal cords. He tried again, but the splashing cries of anguish around him drowned out his call. His hand slipped on a deep cold face, open-mouthed and silted. He tried to relax and breathe deeply. The lights came closer and he noticed that the humans were not administering aid to the writhing bodies. They just sorted through them, shovelling some into the munching maw of the bulky machine that accompanied them.

'Not much meat on this one,' he heard them say. 'A calorie is a calorie.' The body they handled seemed still and lifeless, but Larry couldn't be sure. He dragged himself out of their path, cursing his weakness. Weakness? His mannequin was gone. His movements attracted a light beam.

'Relax,' said the masked Protein Harvester. 'Let me disconnect you first, or you'll tear off your perfusion tubules.' A rough hand steadied his sore trunk while vascular catheters were withdrawn from a buttonhole incision in his left lower rib cage.

'He's a live one,' called another worker. 'Is he ready for Rehab?'

'No. I don't think so,' said the first. 'No legs, but he's strong. The bad gases haven't gotten to him yet.'

Then Larry noticed that the bitter taste was not confined to the fluids. The air was acrid too. It burned his throat and lungs – a strong metallic bite. The rough hand towed him through the shallows and deposited him, wet, cold, and naked, in a hallway. Hundreds of bodies littered the floor as far as he could see. Most appeared to be breathing, but little else. An occasional moan. A white-garbed attendant wandered among them, making notes and checking nameplates.

'Over here,' called Larry.

As the attendant approached, his empty-eyed stare chilled Larry more than the cold floor. Like a zombie whose soul has gone on before him, he glanced down at Larry – staring through him – scratched a card, and turned to walk away. The thin lips hadn't moved.

'Wait . . . I'm still alive.'

'So?' said the attendant over his shoulder. 'That is a matter for the Hall Committee.'

Larry quieted, crawling into a corner in search of warmth. The body-strewn passage stretched on for perhaps a quarter of a mile, but echoes told of many side corridors. Chills rattled. Sleep numbed.

Aroused from his pre-coma by a murmur of voices and machines, he saw the orange Resuscitator approaching on wide soft wheels, administering shocks and stimulants as it came. Five satiny-robed elders rode the meck – rode high on the meck's back, seated around their table of printouts and readers. They bent over their viewers, squinting out of wrinkled faces and asking their dull routine questions in a monotone lost behind the shrill cries of the hall patients being aroused by the meck's sparking probes and needle injectors. Bundles and squeeze-bottles were distributed. The meck plucked Larry's Identoplate.

'I don't understand the code on your plate, Larry – er – Dever,' said the Committeeman. 'Have you been in Suspension a very long time?'

Larry nodded – afraid that the sound of his voice might attract other vultures.

'He is bright-eyed, alert,' offered the second Committeeman. 'Do we have anything on his skills?'

'His plate doesn't even fit into our reader. What do you do?'

Larry's mind raced. Skills? 'Where's my mannequin?' he asked. 'If I could share and update I'd know which of my skills would fit your needs.'

'Mannequin?' The blank stares were back. Two of the Citizens nodded off to sleep, drooling saliva on their smocks.

'Mannequin was my companion cyber, my legs. Ask OLGA about me. My genes are precious. I'm awaiting an advancement along the lines of the Todd-Sage breakthrough.'

Another Committeeman dozed off. The first now leaned forward and studied Larry's truncated, naked form. 'Why – your legs are gone. You're handicapped.'

With a murmur the other members stirred. They whispered among themselves.

'Seems bright enough, but the directive is clear. Society can't allow him to suffer. Better give him a bottle of Easy Red and put him in a side hall.'

The bundle of clothing consisted of a coarse paper robe with a rope belt. The squeeze-bottle looked inviting until he deciphered the fine print – 'Euthanasia liquor'.

The soft wheels turned a notch and the Committee studied the next body. The Identoplate fitted into the reader. 'Name? Occupation? Infirmity? Easy Red'.

Larry watched the bodies around him. The drugs had aroused them, but few struggled into their robes. Most used the soft bundles as pillows and began to sip from their squeeze-bottles. The red liquid cheered them up. If it was lethal, and the label assured that it was, they would die happy – and much later. Larry pulled his robe over his arms and used the belt to tie the lower folds into a rolled tassel. His tender areas thus protected, he began a slow crawl down a side corridor towards the sounds of a city.

'Excuse me,' said Larry. Someone had come up from behind and stumbled into him. It was a female, about his age. Her smock was green and neat. Her features smooth. Her hair was rolled up tight. He tried to catch her eye, but they had the same nonfocusing emptiness he had seen in the attendant.

'You should be ashamed, old man,' she spat.

'I'm sorry, I—'

'Cluttering up the floor with your crippled old body is awfully inconsiderate. Do you realize that your ugliness has ruined my day? A girl can't even walk the halls these days without being nauseated.'

The words were harsh, but her face blank.

'You smell awful,' said another Citizen – a teenage male. 'Can't you see you're dying of uraemia? Here, take this bottle of Easy Red. You shouldn't be lingering on and suffering like that. You make all of us suffer when we have to look at you.'

Larry huddled in a dark recess behind a Food Dispenser, but still they found him and chastized him for being alive. He asked for food, but those who noticed him shrugged and walked on. Most did not even glance in his direction.

'Food,' he said to the Dispenser. 'I need something to eat.'

'Unauthorized. You have no credits,' said the machine.

Larry was beginning to get the picture. He'd have to act quickly if he was to survive.

'Food!' he shouted, striking the Dispenser with his fist. 'Feed me, damn you, or I'll bust your skin and take what I want.' Seams widened in the metalloid skin as his fist continued pounding. A red light blinked above the chute. He paused. His skin, softened by Suspension, began to bruise and split. The stubborn meck leaked lubricants. An optic high on the wall focused on Larry.

'Old man, this disturbance irritates me.' The green-smocked female had returned.

Larry withdrew to a corner – sullen. She patted the damaged Dispenser and received her food item – a foot-long knobbly object with a bread-like consistency and a variegated cut surface. She bit off a generous portion and approached, talking with her mouth full.

'I can't even enjoy my meal with the sight of your ugly deformed . . .'

The Security Squad stood around the attack scene, poking their light beams behind vents and pipes while the White Team quieted the hysterical girl.

'But I was using the standard "suicide-precipitation" techniques when he attacked me. He wasn't supposed to do that.'

'I understand he is not one of our docile recent Citizens. He was suspended a long time ago,' soothed the Mediteck.

'But I'm not being paid to take these risks. How's my ankle?'

'Fine. This brace can come off in about fifty days. Do you feel up to talking with "Security?" '

She nodded and repeated her story. 'He doesn't even have legs. Why would he want to live? He crawled off that way – eating my fruit loaf. See the trail of crumbs?'

The trail was short. It ended at a 'service' access hatch – the cover dangled by a twisted pin. The Squad took turns shining their lights into the dark musty space between the walls. Each glanced in, noting the drag marks in the thick dust.

'The cripple sounds like a plucky little rebel,' said the Squad Leader, 'but the Tweenwallers will get him for sure.' They nodded and replaced the hatch cover.

Larry dragged his tassel through the thick dust. A web of struts and wires stretched out in front of him. They were shrouded in darkness and dust. He felt his way, cautiously aware of the half-mile drop that awaited him if he slipped.

'No need for Easy Red in here.' He smirked. 'If I get tired of the struggle, all I have to do is crawl off into air and let gravity take away my pains.'

His arms tired quickly. He tried to climb up to a different level where Security might not be looking for him. After a brief effort he slept. The dust caked his moist orifices: eyes, nose, mouth, ureterostomy and colostomy sites. When he awoke he cursed the dust. 'Damn! I'll never be able to fight off the gram negatives in here.'

A day later he was poised at an air vent when a movement startled him from behind. He turned to see a hulking creature caked with black like himself. They eyed each other intently. Only a tiny shaft of light outlined the scene. Abruptly the newcomer broke the silence.

'You're not all there!'

Larry growled back.

'Easy, little fellow. I'm not going to hurt you. You don't have enough meat on you anyway.'

Larry watched the big form move silently among the wires to the far side of the hallway. Crowds of lethargic Citizens wandered along in bright light. The access hatch was heavy and bolted from the outside. He watched through the crowd as black fingers reached through the louvers and began slowly to buckle them. Soot popped from those fingers as the metal squealed. He glanced over the crowd. Uniformed Security Squads appeared at opposite ends of the hall. They approached, checking Dispensers and hatches.

'Security,' hissed Larry.

The black fingers withdrew. 'Thanks.' The silent form nodded as it moved off along the top of an air conduit. Later it returned with food.

'Here, you earned this. I can use a lookout. You look like you could use a pair of legs.'

Larry accepted the food – bundles of flat pastries layered with sticky protein. 'We'd make a fine team,' he mumbled. 'My eyes and your legs.' He studied the dusty figure – larger than the average Citizen, but probably no larger than Larry had been when he was whole. In fact, the similarities in bone structures were striking. 'Who are you?'

'Har – they call me Big Har.' He grinned. He had all his teeth. They were still fairly white too. He must be young, thought Larry.

'My name is Larry Dever. I require more water and less

54

food than you. Water I can get at any bubbler, but you'll have to help me with the food.'

'Bubblers are monitored too. We have many pools at City-base. Some carry a fairly clean flow.'

They climbed down through the City's organs together – the bulky, round-shouldered giant and the tiny hemihuman who alternately walked on his hands and swung from cables.

Hemihuman Larry and Gargoyle Har in one of the City's larger tracheal air vents. Their bedding of discarded issue tissue formed secure nests that contained their personal treasures salvaged from the Tweenwall depths.

'I like this place,' said the hulking gargoyle, 'because that side vent leads to Security. If you crawl about thirty yards and peek through the louvers you'll see their wall maps – transportation and trouble areas. I sleep better when I know what my pursuers are doing.'

Hemihuman nodded. He sorted through the debris at the bottom of his nest, tossing worthless items aside. 'Looks like I'm about out of food.'

'Come on.'

They moved along the struts.

'Those small grape-like cubicles are living quarters. See how similar they are. We are looking for a wide area in one of the main corridors – where Dispensers are located.'

'We just passed one,' said Larry.

'The Dispenser is out of order back there,' explained the giant. 'See these gritty brown pipes? They carry the calories-and-quarters basic paste – CQB. I put my hands on them to see if food is coming in. If the pipes are quiet – no food. No sense charging out and exposing ourselves unless there is something to eat.'

'Only one pipe to a Dispenser?'

'Yes. The paste has basic calories and minimum daily requirements of nutrients. The machine adds colours, textures, and sometimes flavours. There are supposed to be some that can change the temperature too, but I've never seen one of those.'

Larry's memory crept back to pre-Suspension experience to recall what hot soup and icy drinks were.

They assaulted a queue and fled into a lighting conduit with gels, pastes, and crumbling bricks. Har leaned against a warm cone-shaped housing and ate.

'This is a ceiling light for Embryo,' he said, gesturing towards the cone. 'You can watch Citizens grow in bottles if you just lift out one of those bolts over there. Here, let me show you. See that dark one in the end jar? A hairy fellow. They call that kind a simian. He will be discarded. Those jars with broken covers let in too much light. That can cause big eyes – a gargoyle like me.'

'Why?'

'Like a toad or a frog that embryonates in the light – optic buds get over stimulated and hypertrophy.'

'Oh.'

Two black faces peered through a sooty grating into the sewer. Sluggish fluids moved heaps of trash.

'Where does that go?' asked the hemihuman.

'Don't know,' said the quiet hulk, Big Har. 'Probably a digester or something. These cities are full of organs that can swallow up streams that size.'

'I wish it went to the sea,' moaned Larry. 'A tropical sea, far from here, where bananas and coconuts ripen on the tree.'

'What's a tree?'

'A green thing that grows up into the sky. It has food right on it. And you can pick it without a CQB.'

Big Har just shook his head. 'Food comes from Dispensers – from machines. Trees do not exist – except in your dreams.'

'Trees did exist once,' said Larry. 'I can remember them clearly: tall, with coarse woody bark and soft, slick leaves. Many things grew on trees.'

Big Har stopped shaking his head. Larry's word pictures built a dream in the giant's head – colours, flavours, textures, scents, and freedom.

'Where were these trees – a long time ago?'

'Outside,' said Larry.

'Are they still there?'

'Maybe. I think so. Yes! I'm certain they are.'

'Could you take me there?' asked the giant.

'I think it would be the other way around. Lift me up, and we'll see what is Outside.'

Big Har put the hemihuman on his shoulder and they started climbing up through the City. The next day they reached an access hatch above the laminar flow generators.

'We must be near the top. There is hardly any traffic on the Spiral Walkway,' said Larry.

Big Har grunted.

'If I am right, there should be some sort of door to the Outside up here. Let's stay in Tweenwalls until we've circled the City. I don't want to attract Security.' Larry tried to decipher the maze of pipes: water, air, sewage, and vital Dispenser lines.

'I don't have any idea how to get out from Tweenwalls. Let's just walk up the Spiral. That must go somewhere.'

The black giant stepped out into the light of the corridor, sprinkling soot and grime. The hemihuman rode his shoulder, giving him a grotesque, two-headed appearance. Nebishes scattered and fainted.

'I think we'd better hurry,' said Larry. 'We've caused quite a disturbance. It looks like we're still a long way from the top – two more turns of the Spiral.'

The panic-stricken crowd ahead of them melted into crawl-ways. All had been standard Citizens – fifty inches of poor protoplasm, soft, white, lethargic. Har's head towered above the trembling Nebishes. Larry rode even higher – brushing the ceiling at ninety inches. Cobwebs and soot caked them, hiding Larry's identity as a separate individual.

The City's Watcher circuits located the disturbance and took readings. A screen activated in Security. The Squad Leader studied the fuzzy black image.

'What is it?'

'An intruder on the Spiral,' said Watcher.

'Looks more like a compound monster – two heads, four arms, and two legs. Has there been any loss of personnel or material?'

'No—'

'Then notify Bio. I'm certain they'd be interested. Security isn't.'

'But—'

The Squad Leader stretched out on his cot, waving the Watcher to silence. 'Try Bio,' he repeated. 'All my men are out on an important assignment – confiscating Garden seedlings at Synthe. Some careless Embryoteck found a mutation with perfect flowers: ovule-loaded pistils and pollen-producing stamens. You know how dangerous they could be... plants capable of living outside the Hive and producing food... Let us tend to our important work, "Security". Call Bio about your monster.'

Watcher switched channels.

Apprentice Wandee looked up from her scope – soft, wide, blue eyes. She climbed over a clutter of dusty containers and tapped the buzzing screen.

'Yes? Bio here!'

Watcher composed himself to sell the disturbance to another department. 'I have an interesting specimen for you.'

Wandee nodded and went to her collection table. 'How big?' She sorted through nets and containers.

Watcher winced as the readings danced along the screen. He wished that there were some way to minimize the problem until it was out of his hands. 'COMPOUND MONSTER, HUMAN, NINETY INCHES, THREE HUNDRED POUNDS.'

Wandee put down the little half-pint container and turned back to her screen. Multiple stills were displayed – front, side, and rear views. A Citizen was included for scale. The thermogram was a mottled 92- to 99- degree geographic pattern that bore little relationship to segmental anatomy. 'Too much dust,' she commented. Close-ups of the two heads were matched for bone structure. 'No doubt about it,' she said with a smile. 'Monozygotic twins – fused into a compound monster.'

Watcher relaxed. 'I leave it in your capable hands...'

'Certainly,' she sputtered. The screen froze with the City co-ordinates. The last digits changed slowly, marking the monster's migration up the Spiral. 'For a specimen this size I'll need my slumbergun, nets, and – let's see – about six assistants.' She assembled the darts, pouring the aromatic sedative into the spring syringe. 'I wonder if it has a common circulatory system. If there are just a few small venous communications it might need two shots. I'd better take an extra set of small doses, just in case.' She hit the intercom for six assistants. They stalked up-Spiral.

'Unauthorized,' said the door.

'Try that one over there,' said Larry.

Big Har shuffled around the platform at the top of the Spiral. One door had opened, not to the outside, but into a dark garage where only machine eyes can see. The rasping and grating sounds frightened the two fugitives away. They were searching for a Garden of Eden, not a dark recess where mastication might reduce them to pulp.

'I guess we're going to have to break down one of these... Oh-oh! Here comes a group of Citizens who don't seem afraid of us.'

Big Har turned to see Wandee leading her Bio assistants up-Spiral. Their smocks were identical, and they walked in a box-type formation carrying heavy coils of netting. Wandee fondled a small efficient dart gun.

Har backed around the platform. Wandee's assistants divided the nets, forming two tangle-foot fences that moved around the Spiral in opposite directions, sandwiching the fugitives. Larry studied the slack mesh, designed to trap arms and legs long enough for a clear shot. Wandee stayed behind the netting with her sights on the pair. Har retreated into a doorway, staring at the gun muzzle. He whimpered.

The dart struck the giant in the centre of the chest, clunking against the sternum. Larry's hand went for the fins. 'Easy, big fellow.' He jerked on the projectile. It came away with a tag of muscle in the barbs. Big Har's knees sagged. Larry flipped the dart towards the Nebish holding the centre of the netting. Fins spun. It stuck in the wide belly and the fence fell. Big Har toppled over. Wandee smiled and started to relax.

Larry hit the floor on flat, calloused palms – running and screaming. The detachment of the hemihuman was completely unexpected; the Bio Squad faltered. Larry ran across the comatose Nebish at the fence and hit Wandee as hard as he could. She was a frail, young, unpolarized female – new on the job. Larry concentrated on the gun, punching and biting her arm. Only after he had the weapon did he realize how soft she was. She stumbled away, wide-eyed, holding her right hand. He had the rusty taste of blood on his front teeth.

Screaming and flourishing the pistol, Larry drove the Squad away. He returned to the giant. 'Get up, Har. Get up! You can't sleep here. The Nebish at the fence died. Security will be here soon.'

Har slouched into a dark air vent and dozed. Larry sealed him in with an opaque filter. Then he obscured their tracks by dragging the sooty netting around the platform to the only door that opened on command. Mechanical teeth gnashed in the darkness inside.

Larry tossed in a corner of the net. The rest of the mesh followed in jerky movements that muffled the unseen teeth. Fibres snapped and popped. The floor shuddered. The little hemihuman lifted himself through a two-by-two lighting panel and climbed off hand-over-hand. He followed the dusty struts and cables around the platform until he could hear the giant's regular breathing. Footsteps announced the arrival of Security.

'Someone has fouled the power take-off,' said a voice. 'Put in a call for a Tinker.'

Big Har blinked at the crack in the air filter. He recognized the sounds of Larry's hands and torso fidgeting in the grit. 'Maybe there is no Outside,' he whispered.

'There is something up there,' mumbled Larry, 'or they wouldn't try so hard to stop us from going.'

'There may be something at the edge of the City, but it is no paradise with trees. The Tweenwallers speak of the sewers below and the fire above.'

'You know someone who escaped the City?' asked Larry excitedly.

'No. Just stories. Bad stories. They say that there is a fire up there that peels your skin and blinds you. And, if you go deep enough there are endless swamps – dark and wet, filled with ratty meat-eaters and insects that crawl inside you. I have never wanted to find one of these places, so I stay in the City.'

Larry slumped into the dust. His flanks ached where the germs attached his scanty kidney tissue. Dirt fouled his body openings. A cripple didn't live long as a Tweenwaller.

'Perhaps I should have taken that starship,' he said.

Big Har listened to Larry's ramblings – a Dever's Ark to the Procyon system with an Implant of Earth biota. Har's concept of planet Earth was limited by the walls of the Hive. He had no idea what a starship or a sun could be. But he nodded in agreement on one point. Most any place would be an improvement over Tweenwalls!

4
Citizen Retreads

Deep in the Hive a personal Dispenser called out, 'Wake up. Wake up. Enjoy! Enjoy!'

Fat, old Drum, a forty-eight-inch balding Nebish, sat up in his cot and glanced eagerly around his cubicle. Pleasures of retirement awaited him after two gruelling years in the musician's caste. He was younger than most retirees – aged nineteen – and wealthy, for he had saved enough calories-and-quarters base – CQB – for this private six-foot cubicle and a flavour with every meal. He was vigorous also – possessed of one clear lens and eight good teeth. Some eleven more years remained on his life span, maybe more.

'Welcome to the awake state, suave Citizen,' chortled Dispenser. 'Today's distribution is well above calorie-basic. The screen scene looks promising. Select two flavours and refresh while your gourmet meal is prepared. Two glorious flavours on this glorious day!'

'Two flavours?' mumbled Drum hesitantly. 'Pink and green?'

'Those are flavour categories,' reminded Dispenser. 'Which pink? Which green?'

Frugal Citizens were often unsophisticated in matters of luxuries. Drum had invested a large part of his cash flow in retirement credits. He now had qualms about adjusting his consuming habits upwards.

'I'll start with pink-one and green-one. Work my way down the menu – try them all,' he said, feigning excitement.

When he stepped from the refresher he found seven packets

in the edible chute – soft, bag-like casings of extruded paste –
five grey, one pink, and one green.

'Savour the flavour,' said Dispenser.

Humming a cheerful tune, Drum took his utensils from
the cupboard and ceremoniously arranged the Hive's pseudoconsommé, pseudosoufflé, and pseudoparfait: liquids, pastes,
and puddings. All stable foodstuffs. No perishables. Dispenser
selected a pulsing geometric visual with sonic to soothe sub-
cortical neurons during the meal. Drum tried a generous bite
of the green paste and experienced a tart shock – more of a
colour than a flavour – which faded quickly into the usual dull
pap. He frowned, appetite jaded. Where were the pleasures of
retirement?

Dispenser detected his rising irritation level and changed
channels. Sonics flexed and plucked at his organ of Corti, but
Drum's bioelectricals continued to show happiness: negative.

'You must have residual job fatigue,' rationalized Dispenser.
Lights dimmed. 'A nap will invigorate you. Lie down, please.'
Audio switched to woodwinds and strings. Drum's cot vibrated.

Hear the bacon frying,

Cracking in the heat.

Just smell those aromas,

Good enough to eat.

Drum awoke to choking synthesmoke and the clang, clang,
clang of the ranchwagon triangle. View-screen carried the old
historical still of rolling green hills dotted with squarish blobs of
fauna, simple wooden artifacts – hut, fence, and tools – under
a bright blue sky. He sat up, relaxed and smiling. This new
odour did excite. Olfactory luxuries were quite rare. He rushed
to the chute but found only three soft grey tube sandwiches.
He frowned.

'One is laced with bacon,' offered Dispenser.

Drum forced a grin as he picked it up – bland paste with
a rare crunchy particle. Flavour – just burned grease, hardly
a delicacy. Shrugging, he packed the other sticks into his kit.

'Where do you wish to go?'

'Visit Grandmaster Ode, push wood, try out my Accelerated Dragon Defence again.'

'Sorry to discourage you,' said Dispenser, 'but commuter density is three point two on the Spiral and four point one on the tubeways. Rush hour. It is advisable to wait until "between shifts" for your Rec travel.'

Drum sat down slowly – arthritic. His commuter priority had been lost with his job, confining him to cubicle whenever density rose above two point zero Citizens per square yard along the Hive's arteries. Shrugging off his disgust, he called Ode on the screen. 'Got time for a game?' he queried, unrolling his board.

Ode's image flickered and jumped – an older but harder Citizen – higher colour index in his bald scalp, steady clear eyes. He did not comment on Drum's brusque manner, for he understood retirement traumas.

'Pawn to king-four,' said Ode.

Drum studied the board quietly, still irritated. The pawn in front of the right king had moved two squares. He replied by moving his own worn pawn into the Sicilian Defence. As the dragon took shape, Ode tightened the Marcozy bind with his queen-bishop pawn and queen-knight controlling his queen-five square. Drum had to break out by exchanging knights. He moved woodenly until the mid-game tension washed away his depression. He rode into battle on his remaining knight. Rooks clashed magnificently and a pawn fork took the survivor. A nervous king fidgeted in his castled position until his reign was ended by a pair of bishops. For the moment, the game took on a meaning bigger than life itself.

On the following morning Drum awoke a bit more philosophical. He was ready to accept his new status for what it really was, but Dispenser had other plans.

'Give me a view of the jammed tubeway.' Drum smiled. 'I want to appreciate the quiet of my cubicle.'

Screen stayed blank: standby.

Drum's smile slipped.

'What is the density today – three? – four??'

A dry female appeared on the screen. Drum didn't like her air of efficiency. Thin lips clashed with gaudy smock. 'Recertification time,' she said with her pasted-on smile.

Drum's mouth opened and closed – wordless.

'Earth Society has run a little short of calories,' she continued. 'Water table dropped and the harvest reflected it. We must cut back on the warm – the consuming population – for the duration. Please vote for those Citizens with whom you want to share next year. Hurry, now. Your friends need your vote to avoid being put into Temporary Suspension – TS. Remember, however, that you must not vote for yourself or your clone litter-mates. No blood prejudice allowed.'

Drum smiled nervously. He had done this before when he had his job vote to protect him. In the past his votes went to his favourite conductor and various Venus attendants who pleased him; but now he was more concerned with his cubicle's vitals: air and plumbing.

'My votes go to the Tinker who keeps my refresher, the Pipe caste member who services this wing of the city – and Grandmaster Ode.'

The screen played a geometric dance as tallies ran up. The thin-lipped female reappeared long enough to announce: 'You failed to receive the necessary three votes, so it is TS for you.'

Drum stared as his Temporary Suspension order was printed out.

'But I'm retired,' he objected. 'My CQB is paid up for life.'

Screen remained blank. Dispenser's mechanical voice answered his pleas. 'Recertification has nothing to do with wealth. In Right to Life, only criterion is Love. Only Love can give Life.'

'My funds...'

'Your retirement CQB remains in your name while you are in TS. When harvests improve, you will be rewarmed and can continue consuming where you were interrupted. Hurry. You are to report to Clinics immediately. *The air you are breathing belongs to somebody else.*'

*

The sign read: 'Voluntary Suspension to the Left, Temporary Suspension to the right.' Drum lined up with the TS – unloved, healthy, mixed ages. On his left was the line of VS candidates – elderly, sick Citizens hoping to survive their Voluntary Suspension long enough to awaken in the Golden Age when their infirmities could be cured. Drum shuddered as he realized how hopeless the VS statistics were.

Grandmaster Ode joined him in line.

'Couldn't gather enough votes either?' asked Ode.

Drum shook his head bitterly. 'I wish they would just lower the birth-rate during these pinches. It would be much less traumatic.'

Ode shook his head. 'Job requisitions protect all term embryos. If no Tinkers were born today the Hive would feel it ten years from now when there would be no trainees. Of course, if job quotas drop, the embryos lose their protection like anyone.'

A job hawker walked between the lines, shouting: 'Get your job vote here. Work outside your caste. Many rewarding positions available. Apply now.'

Drum sneered: 'Work beneath your caste is what he really means.'

Ode shrugged. 'At least we'd be warm.'

'But we've fulfilled our life-work quotas,' argued Drum. 'TS isn't so bad. Just like going to sleep: not much real danger of tissue damage. When things get better, we can wake up and continue our retirement.'

'. . . And if things don't get better?' asked Ode letting the words hang.

The two old Citizens eyed each other for a moment, then Ode dragged Drum out of line and waved at the job hawker: 'Two volunteers right here.'

A ceiling optic recorded the issuance of work vouchers – Sewer Service – dark, wet work. Their status was recorded in the warm census and the CO – the class-one computer that balanced Earth Society's books – confirmed their unfrozen assets.

'Sewer Service,' groaned Drum. 'There goes my skin.'

Job orientation was brief for retreads – a short tour. 'Sewage is a valuable by-product of living,' droned the guide. 'Sludge is fermentable, a source of bacterial substrate and raw material for Synthe. Effluent is basically water. Different degrees of decon makes it suitable for irrigation or drinking.'

They stood on a catwalk beside a Separator Plant. The words were drowned out by a steamy waterfall. Warm clots of yellow foam drifted up in the mists. Following a maze of colour-coded pipes, they entered a quiet, windowed booth filled with dials and control valves.

'Here is where we shunt nutrients up to our Plankton Towers in the Gardens. Only – we have no more plankton. Genetic fatigue wiped out our cultures.'

Ode peered into the transparent tube. A thin white ribbon occupied its fluid-filled lumen. 'What is in there?'

The guide smiled proudly. 'That is our Syncytial Planimal, genetically engineered to give us both plant and animal proteins. When light strikes it, chloroplasts are activated. It also has primitive muscle cells and germ cells to give us iron and fats. When it matures into a fat green ribbon it segments into convenient, bite-sized morsels that can be dried, fried, or eaten fresh with hot sauce.'

Ode smiled. 'A genetically engineered perfect food! It feeds on sewage, and we feed on it. There must be some brilliant personnel down in the Bio Labs – working with Gene Spinners.'

The guide frowned. 'It wasn't such a hard job. They just took a bunch of tapeworm nuclei and added the DNA condons for chloroplasts. Some developed into the Syncytial Planimal. Others just remained tapeworms.'

'Tapeworms!' exclaimed Drum.

'Sure,' said Ode, with a artificial grin. 'Tapeworms already flourish in faeces. The step to sewage was a small one. As for eating them – well, we must keep the nitrogen cycle as small as possible.'

Drum just grumbled. 'But we're parasites on a parasite!'

'No sense of humour,' said Ode.

The tour continued through sweaty pipes. The two tired old

Citizens stopped frequently for rest and water. 'Here is where sludge is digested down to methane, carbon dioxide, and water. The residue is pelletized and sent to recycle. You go on duty in fifteen minutes. Follow those arrows!'

'Welcome, trainees,' greeted Sewermeck as they entered the damp control room. Wall images pulsed – a flow diagram reflecting flow rates, silt/water levels, and gate status.

Drum searched for a chair and began to sit down slowly. 'What jobs are open? I'm experienced in music. Ode is Grandmaster...'

'Wet Crew,' snapped Sewermeck. 'You are late already. Your boots and shovels are through that hatch – out on the landing. Take the smaller ones stamped "Citizen retreads". Your shift ends at twenty-one-hundred hours.'

'But our backgrounds don't—' objected Drum.

Ode touched his arm. 'We'll take it. We need the vote.'

'Wear my telemetry – the wired belts and helmets – so I can keep an eye on you in the Pipes,' instructed the meck.

Furlong's red dinghy cut a neat line through the stagnant sludge as he approached the landing. His sandpapered face puckered into a scowl as he shouted, 'Retreads! Swing those shovels! I want this water moving. Get the level down by at least a foot or it will never be "shift-end" for you. Move!'

Ode and Drum shovelled briskly, throwing more water than silt. The activity warmed up their muscles, loosening tight joints. Being retreads they lacked the larger, heavier bones of the regular SS worker, who was genetically selected for the work. They worked with a smaller shovel, but put in more hours.

Furlong returned to the control room to study the flow rates. Sluggish. Without the dredge the silt accumulated at an alarming rate in spite of vigorous manual efforts. The Hive's outflow tract was in danger of blockage. Furlong was even more concerned now that his job requisitions were being filled with retreads rather than regulars.

'How are the new ones doing?' asked Furlong.

'Slowed predictably after you left. Their bodies are still weak and soft. Not much silt moving. Let's hope that their edible-gathering will pay for their CQB while they're here. We can't fill our roster with nonproducers.'

'They'll do their share. Ill see to that,' said Furlong.

Ode and Drum splashed through the thirty-foot-diameter pipe, guided by eerie bioluminescence of *Panus stepticus* mycelia growing in damp sludge high on the walls. Sewermeck directed pencils of light from their Belts.

'There's a weir. Dig!' commanded Drum's Belt.

They paused and shovelled at the silt dam. A light beam focused on a horned slug the size of Ode's foot.

'Pick it up,' said his Belt.

Ode nudged the slug cautiously with his shovel.

'What is it?'

'Sewer slug – a gastropod. Flavours.'

'Edible!?'

'Good perishable flavours,' explained his Belt. 'Fringe benefits of the Wet Crew. Put it in your Belt pail.'

As they worked their way down the tube, their Belts pointed out other delicacies: shaggy fungus balls, slime pods, worms, and snap larvae. The air took on a brackish odour when they neared the tidal sump. Marine photo-bacteria glowed blue-green in their footprints.

'Don't walk out on the delta,' warned the Belts. 'It is too soft and drops off rapidly. Your tour of duty ends here. The outhatch is back by that wall on your left – under the orange light.'

Two tired old Citizen retreads climbed the service ladder into the barracks – into bright lights and warm, dry, air. Drum pulled off his boots, spilling water and silt in a brown gush. His feet were white and badly wrinkled. He hunched over, studying his cold, numb toes intently.

Ode sorted through the pails of edibles. A snap larvae swam on oar bristles.

'What's the tithe?'

'Fifty percent,' said his Belt. 'Drop half down the flavour chute to Synthe. Divide fluids and grit also.'

He paid their tithes and sat back while several of the regular Wet Crew showed how a handful of live creatures added an entirely new dimension to the pseudoconsommé.

'I call this my sewer bouillabaisse,' said the Nebish with the spoon. 'You must stir it carefully. Don't fragment the little creatures. Keep them intact so you know exactly what you are eating.'

Drum grunted and struck the floor with his boot.

'What is it?'

'A hitchhiker. That bug was between my toes. It bit me.'

Ode walked over and looked under the boot. A yellow-red, nondescript splotch remained on the floor while a tangle of legs came up with the boot heel.

'That's my blood in that stain,' complained Drum.

'Your toe doesn't look too good,' said Ode. 'It's swollen – dark. Do you know what kind of a bug it was before you smashed it?'

'Lots of legs.' Drum shrugged. 'Why?'

'Looks like a nymph, from the way it exploded – very little body chitin. Some of them can be dangerous: toxic venom, vectors, retained mouth parts. You'd better take it down to Bio for speciation. Stop at a Medimeck on the way back to see if the bite needs any treatment.'

Ode wrapped the crushed bug in a wet towel and handed it to him as he limped out of the refresher and started to dress. Drum grumbled all the way out the door.

'We'll keep your portion of the bouillabaisse warm,' he called.

The once-spacious Bio Labs were now shrunken and crowded. Drum walked through rooms of endless clutter: sagging storage cartons, heaps of broken instruments, and derelict mecks – obsolete and irreparable as the Hive lost the skills of salvage.

'Hello,' he called.

'Back here,' answered a female voice.

Wandee, the unpolarized, was bent over her bubbling tanks. Drum limped up and watched over her shoulder. She moved her optic probe through the scummy green waters and threw images up on a screen – amorphous blobs.

'Algae?' he ventured.

'No.' She smiled. 'A flagellate – only it has no flagella. My Gene Spinner finally identified the flagellar condons and built this creature's DNA without it.'

'Synthetic genes – marvellous!'

'Not really,' said Wandee, straightening up and wiping her hands. 'We had a living flagellate to learn from. We've been mapping DNA of fresh-water diatoms and algae in an attempt to rebuild marine biota. If we could re-establish the ocean food chain, it would greatly improve the Hive's standard of living.'

Drum nodded, forgetting the ache in his toe. 'How close are you? Have you put anything back into salt water?'

She waved towards her workboard – a paste-up of gene charts and photomicrographs. 'We did find the eye spot – and now the flagella. I have one synthetic creature that will live in seawater, but it must return to fresh water to reproduce.'

Drum's eyes glowed with excitement. 'No more TS!'

'Not just yet.' Wandee frowned thoughtfully. 'Spinner has offered numerous "what ifs" and "random associations" – all good theories – but I'd need more personnel and floor space to follow them up. We're just time-sharing now. I try a couple of likely maps each week, but I know I'm just scratching the surface. There are millions of possible DNA sequences. It would be simple if I had one marine protozoan to map and decode. The big problem is the membrane pumps in the cell wall. Evolution has prepared the freshwater creatures to like their hypotonic environment, and getting them to go back to the sea will take an entirely different set of cell wall genes. That is why we stress classification of sewer biota in the sump region – where waters are a little salty. If you could bring us just one marine—'

Drum's toe twinged. 'Here is a bug I found in my boot. Can you tell what it is?'

'Not marine, I'm sure. Looks like one of the aquatic insects – nymph stage. Let me spread out the parts on Spinner's stage.' A genus appeared on the screen immediately,, then several species flickered on and off until Wandee shuffled the parts around. One species printed out.

'It bit me.'

'Not serious,' she said. 'It has horny mandibles – no barbed mouth parts or poisons.'

'But my toe really hurts, and it's all swollen up ...'

She noticed his limp for the first time. 'Probably infected. You've been on calorie-basic too long. Take off your shoe and come over here. I have a salvaged Medimeck. We can get a quick screen.'

The White Meck lacked most of the expensive appendages, but its basic chassis circuits remained. Coarse splices linked it to Spinner's What-If-Circuit and Random-Association-Circuit (WIC/RIC) and a brace of memory bins hung high on the wall. Its clouded optic scanned the swollen toe, while the lambda needle sampled a drop of his blood and a drop of the pink serum that exuded from the wound. Spinner's printout rattled and produced a lengthy report. Wandee studied it and handed it to Drum with a nod: 'Infection; sewer flora.'

The symbols meant nothing to him.

'You must have been bitten early in your shift. Exposing the wound to sewage was the worst thing you could have done. Those organisms are pathogens when they invade soft tissues. Your resistance is poor: low proteins, practically no gamma at all; and your assortment of white blood cells is weak. You'd better soak.'

Wandee added a few drops of a brown antiseptic to a pan of hot water and motioned him into a chair. Her haste worried him. He studied his foot more closely and saw the fain red line between the toes – blood poisoning.

'I wish we had a systemic anti-infective agent to give you,' she said. 'Your white cells have toxic granules already. I'd hate to see you lose that leg.'

Several hours later the White Meck stabbed him again. Spinner's printout now appeared more optimistic.

Drum rested on the floor in a bed of rags. His foot was elevated on a box. Wandee changed hot compresses while he dozed.

'I'll fix you a nice perishable sandwich,' she said. He opened one eye and watched her pour thick green water through a filter. The resultant paste was spread on a standard white tube sandwich. The flavour was different – interesting.

'Watercress cell culture,' she explained. 'It will replace your bioflavinoids.'

Medimeck blinked a light. Its lingual readout was not functioning, but his progress was recorded by Spinner.

'Having your own White Meck is nice and handy,' he observed. 'Many more like him on the junk heap?'

'Not salvageable. When their chassis circuits go senile they are stripped and dumped. This one was different – a punitive junking. All I had to add was what you see here: power source, memory bins, some rebuilt appendages – and Spinner's readout.'

'Punitive junking?'

'Yes. Saving the unauthorized. You know how anxious the White Team is when it comes to saving lives. This meck came up with the bright idea of building a catcher's mitt in one of the digester chutes. Caught unauthorized infants on their way to the protein pool. Lives were saved, and the meck had a very high quota. But he was caught when the caloric output of the chute dropped. They found his catcher's mitt and convicted him. His genius circuit was pulled and he was sent down here. That was over ten years ago.'

Drum studied the chassis. It appeared relatively new. 'You trust him?'

She nodded. 'All he wants to do is save lives. He just doesn't understand about red tape. Well, there's none of that down here. He helps the Gene Spinner with our project: marine biota.'

'An important job for a junked meck.'

73

Wandee waved her arms in frustration. 'You certainly can't tell it is important from my budget.'

They painted Drum's toes brown with a stinging astringent and he pulled on his shoe carefully.

'It should be OK,' she said.

He limped back to the barracks thinking that Wandee was certainly a concerned Citizen – considering she had not matured sexually.

The alarm aroused the Wet Crew: 'Bad Gas!'

Ode studied the wall diagrams in the control room. Gas symbols appeared as fumes tripped pipe sensors.

'It's in the city across the sump. Looks like a day for masks,' said Ode.

Drum nodded. 'What kind of gas?'

Ode squinted at the symbols. 'Chlorine and ozone so far. One of that city's Vent Mecks didn't get his man-minute on time so he went off-line. You know how those Life-Support Mecks are: temperamental. Its laminar flow generator went out of phase and the city stopped breathing. The symbols show no breathable oxygen in the cloud. It would kill anything.'

'Anything?'

'Anything that needed oxygen. Why? Oh. The bedding...'

The two Nebishes left the control room with a grin. They rolled up their bedding and carried it out on the landing. The sewer lights had lost their orange tint and their eyes burned. 'Better mask up,' said the cyber-dinghy. They tossed the soft bedrolls on to the boat's cargo rack and snapped bulky gas masks over their faces. The dinghy followed their instructions, lurching through the scum with sensors alert. Floating islands of sticky foam filed up under the bow, crackled and hissed off to the sides in restless fragments.

'The lights are starting to look green to me. Can't be too bad, though; I saw a rat swim by.' Drum stood at the bow following the boat's light beams with interest. 'Look at that poor devil! He must have been killed by the gas. The rats have already eaten away half of him.'

Drum swallowed hard. His face-plate steamed up. The body that floated by was missing from the waist down. It drifted on its back, eyes open, staring back at them.

'It scans 99 degrees. Must have died recently.'

'Let's hope our masks are working well today.'

'There goes the dinghy's warning light. We're in the bad gas now. Look at all those dead rats. I suppose we can leave our bedding anywhere along here.'

The little boat slowed and bumped into a muddy delta. Its headlight searched along the wall. Ode gathered up the soft bundles.

'There's the outhatch. The chromatograph is reading way over the red zone – should sterilize anything.'

They waded to the hatch and spread their pillows and blankets on the floor of the dry corridor. Drum looked closely at the heap of insects under the light. Nothing moved.

'It will be nice to get a good night's sleep for a change.' Ode smiled. 'None of those blasted little vermin can live through this.'

Drum abruptly turned to the door. 'We won't either if these masks fail. I can taste too much of the cloud. Let's get back.'

The boat greeted them with a winking light.

'I didn't notice these footprints before. They lead right into the water – bare feet,' said Drum. 'Who goes barefooted in the sewer?'

'Tweenwallers – fugitives. The gas drove them out. See anything in the water?'

As they started back across the sewer pipe the boat scanned for bodies.

'Nothing,' said Drum, watching the screen. 'Where did they go?'

'Drowned probably. Even if they had something to float on there is the foam. Blundering into a mass of that stuff would suffocate you pretty quick. The bad gas is just an added hazard.'

Small pale feathery objects rained down on them.

'Snow?'

'Just dead insects. We're still in the clouds.'

That evening they were interrupted at mealtime by sirens. The Unauthorized Activity light was blinking. A Security Squad jogged past the mess hall.

'What is it?' asked Ode.

Drum glanced out the door. 'Don't know, but they are going out to our landing. I think I'll see what it is.'

Ode wiped his mouth and followed.

'Careful. Remember, this is Security's job.'

Drum picked up his shovel and gave it an experimental swing. The landing was poorly lit. Sewermeck had shunted most of the power to search circuits down the pipe. They saw mists and mycelial strands glowing in the distance. Security Squad had pulled on boots and were now wading cautiously into the delta muck. Without a word they slogged off into the darkness. Puzzled, Ode and Drum stood for a long moment. Then Drum shrugged and turned to leave. His foot clattered into a tangle of wires and boards. The circuitry looked familiar – remote gear from the dinghy.

'Someone has taken our boat,' said Drum as he entered the control room. 'Can we pick it up on our pipe sensors?' The search pattern produced a series of infrared images on the screen, but, like a checkerboard, every other square was blank.

'Most of my eyes are clouded,' said the Sewermeck. 'My mass detectors are picking up a lot of floating trash, but no boat so far.'

'Ears?' asked Drum.

'Nothing.'

'Well, call us if you find anything.'

The men returned to their meal. When the Security Squad returned they tracked black and rancid. The Wet Crew offered them hot refreshments in exchange for the news. 'I hate to see them get away,' said the Squad Leader. 'We'll try the next city downstream.'

'No dinghy,' said Ode. 'I suppose that means we've lost our bedding.'

'Unless...' suggested Drum, 'unless we take the tubeways to that city.'

They studied the traffic pattern through the terminals. The round trip would take many hours, and trying to keep bedding together would be almost impossible in the crowded passenger lines. They both shook their heads.

'No, I guess not,' said Drum. 'It would be cheaper to buy all new things.'

Ode nodded – much more sensible.

5
Warbles and Bots

Warm waves rolled slate-grey through barren, tropical archipelagos; crossed thousands of miles of silent, sterile seas; and broke – thundering – against the split and tilted cliffs of Orange Sector. Limestone beds, eroded by the persistent pounding, surrendered their ancient memories of *Xyne grex* and *Ganolytes cameo*. Washed down from the cliffs, these delicate chalk traces of Miocene herring and shad were slowly erased by the wave action – disinterred and erased without ceremony, without witness, by a sterile ocean under empty skies. Twenty-million-year-old molecules that had been assembled by bony fish were now being disassembled in an era without bony fish. Out of the countless mega-fossils recorded in the Earth's crust, only a handful survived. Today, one of the surviving mega-fauna brine-swirled with these remains of herring and shad.

Nostrils wide, Big Opal surfaced, snorted, and rode the hissing breaker into the shallows. She floundered until the next wave carried her up on to the smooth rocks. Her powerful fingers and toes clung to the slimy surfaces. Climbing on to a dry, salt-crusted boulder, she glanced up at the cliffs. An ominous, black mouth broke the continuity of the shoreline – the hundred-yard-wide arch of the sewer sump. The high-water mark around the sump was littered with the floating debris from the effluent – the fungus-softened organic material from the hundreds of cybercities that fed the sump. Among the amorphous garments was an occasional body, bloated and pocked by maggots – outcast Hive Citizens, the discarded drones of Earth Society.

Opal cast a long shadow as the sun kissed the western

horizon. She turned to face the warm, orange disc. A horizontal bar of gold formed where the disc buried its face in the sea. It submerged. Opal stood carefully. Her 'land legs' were slow to adjust to the firm coarse grit. Between waves, she waded quickly to shore. Her unsteady foot nudged a skull. It rattled across the rock and came to rest grinning a toothless grin. She picked it up. Her disgust for the Hive creature did not apply to his remains. She carried the delicate white relic to the cliff and placed it with other bones rescued from the irreverent surf. A row of them stared back at her with bleached, empty sockets. All were small-jawed and paper-thin. She thought of them as children, although they were clearly fragile and toothless with age. Twilight faded. She began her cautious climb to the Gardens.

A hundred miles up-sump the sewer conduits sang with pneumatic belches of dead city gases: incoles, skatoles, methane, ozone, and carbon monoxide. Where ever these toxic vapours lingered, sewer fauna died. Slime-matted rafts of bloated carcasses drifted, their bulging, hemorrhagic eyes staring blindly into the darkness where dead insects fell like flakes of snow. Ears high in the arched ceiling of the pipes – Sewermeck's line sensors – caught an occasional moan. Optics rotated but saw nothing in the four hundred to seven hundred nanometre range. Darkness.

'Come back,' called the meck.

'Hush,' whispered Big Har. 'The wall ears live.'

Their mould-flecked dinghy drifted sideways, its bow wedged into a raft of nondescript, floating debris. Hemihuman Larry hunkered down, swatting flies, The blackness and echoes told them nothing. Their progress was marked by aerial mycelia which swept across the boat's wet ribs and snagged in their hair. Persistent swarms of sucking botflies hovered over them. Their throbbing backs sponged out with bots and warbles – the cutaneous abscesses that contained the vigorous fly larvae.

'The damned itching is getting worse,' complained Larry. 'A new crop must be maturing.' He wiped his hand across his scaly, lumpy back, breaking open pus pockets and catching the wiggling, bristly maggots as they emerged. 'Damn!' He rubbed at the pasty crusts of pupa cases, wings, legs, and dermal scales.

Big Har listened sadly. Larry's irascible voice had been softened by the larval infestation. Hundreds of purulent sinus tracts weakened him as the little maturing creatures migrated from the bite site to his back, where they pupated. Skin, muscle, and lung were riddled and abscessed.

'Hang on, Larry,' Har whispered. 'The Ocean can't be far away now. Can you smell the brine?'

Brine? Larry crawled to the side of the boat and dipped his hand over – sewage covered with stiff, granular foam. He swirled his hand around the surface until his palm contained fluid that was less particulate. He bathed his back. A salty burn erased some of the gnawing itch and brought relief.

Shift Foreman Furlong studied Sewermeck's wall charts. 'We have a fix on the stolen dinghy. Its speed is about a third that of the effluent stream. Drifting. Where is the interceptor I ordered?'

The SS crew fidgeted. 'Ode and Drum hand-carried the paperwork this morning. They should be back by now.'

Sewermeck went on-line with the Watcher circuits and tracked them down. They were in Recycle looking at a junk heap.

'What are you doing there?' demanded Furlong.

Ode turned sheepishly towards the screen.

'Interceptor boats are not available. We were sent over here to see if we could find a mobile meck to do our hunting for us.'

'And...?'

Ode lifted up the shovel-shape of Iron Trilobite – blinking friendly dorsal lights.

'What's that?' asked Furlong.

'A Servomeck assigned to us for dinghy retrieval. I'd like to keep him on for permanent patrol. He seems bright, and most of our line sensors are clouded.'

'Bright? Does it talk?'

Trilobite spoke succinctly: 'Certainly. I am equipped with the standard OLA functions: optical, lingual, and auditory. I have no graphics of my own, but I interface well. My image converters are...'

'Fine,' interrupted Furlong. 'Sewermeck will handle your graphics while you're with us. We are trying to retrieve a lost dinghy in the pipes. How are you at Wet Work?'

'I am aquatic.'

'...and your range? The hunt could cover several hundred miles.'

'Is solar energy available?'

'Not in the sewers.'

'Then I'll have to suck a socket for a while.'

Scummy fluid half-filled the hundred-meter-diameter pipe. Trilobite travelled along just beneath the surface – his tail periscoped up through the foam – scanning in the far infrared. With his photomultiplier extended full range, he observed the tenuous metabolic energies of fermentation and decay. Bio-luminescence outlined the granular, scaly arches a hundred and fifty feet overhead. His mass sensors measured five fathoms of water and forty meters of silt below. Vibrations of human breathing and scratching attracted him to the drifting dinghy.

'Hello,' called the periscope.

A 99-degree silhouette of a head appeared above the sponson.

'Hello! I've come to help you return the dinghy.'

'Get away,' growled Har. The head disappeared.

'I am your friend. Allow me to tow you to the nearest city.'

'Don't touch this boat.' The silhouette reappeared: head, shoulders, and back. The heat pattern was not homogeneous. Hot and cold bots sponged out the back.

'The warbles and bots have you,' observed Trilobite. 'You are dying. Let me take you for therapy.'

Har squinted in the direction of the voice.

'Who are you to offer therapy? We lack CQB. The Hive will not help us. We are just fugitive protein now.'

'The Hive orders you to return.'

'No!'

'Where are your Citizen ethics? The Hive orders: the individual obeys.'

Larry's voice resonated in the damp hull: 'Why?'

Trilobite circled the dinghy. There were at least two humans speaking. He tried to reason with them. 'Majority rule. The individual obeys the group. There is strength in numbers. It is Nature's way.'

'We are the majority on this boat,' hissed Larry. He fumbled around under the seats for something to throw.

'But you are dying.'

'Turning back would only hasten that,' said Larry slowly. He twisted off a length of conduit insulators and lifted his head to get a binaural fix on the nagging voice.

'Isn't the pain unbearable?'

'It's preferable to the Hive's damned Easy Red.'

Larry's toss was a little high. Trilobite submerged and moved off, raising his tail again thirty yards away. Har and Larry slumped down out of sight. Flies bit, sucked and dropped their eggs. Hours passed. A gentle rippled rocked their boat several times before they heard the muffled roar of distant breakers.

'The sea! We're saved,' muttered Har. He tried to paddle in the direction of the sound, using his hands, but the boat turned in a circle – rotating an island of sticky foam. He saw nothing but homogeneous blackness. A salty breeze touched his cheek. They bobbed on small waves. Still there was nothing to see. The thundering grew louder. A wave lurched their boat. He suddenly realized that they were less than a quarter of a mile from the mouth of the sump. It was night. Fog blanketed the stormy sea as a Beaufort number eight wind whipped up a high surf that threatened to capsize them. Har reached back into the dark hull and patted Larry's shoulder: 'Hang on.' They rode a wave back into the sump. Har paddled again.

'May I help?' offered Trilobite. 'Toss me your bow-line. I can't allow the boat to sink.'

Har hesitated, then shrugged and complied. If they were dumped into the water they would certainly drown. Neither

82

had the strength or ability to swim in this rough water. Trilobite closed his jaw on the line and towed the dancing craft around the lip of the pipe to a rocky beach. The next wave carried them up on to the shore where they ground keel and stranded. The storm subsided with the dawn.

'Come on in. This feels great,' said Larry, floundering in a salty pool. 'My skin feels better already.'

Big Har was a bit more cautious. He sat on a rock pouring handfuls of water on his sponge back. The salty brine burned, but it did its job. The scabs softened and fell away, exposing the pus pockets. Larvae squirmed violently as the hypertonic solution flooded their spiracles. Young scar tissue was sloughed under the cutting action of the salt. Each bot was transformed from purulent abscess to a clean, red, punched-out hole – oozing proteinaceous serum.

Trilobite circled the beached dinghy.

'What are you thinking?' asked Larry.

'The boat's brain is dead.'

'Sorry,' said Larry, realizing how one cyber could sympathize with the injuries of another. 'But we had to do it to escape. That dinghy was not free to assist us.'

Trilobite eyed the two fugitives. 'Who is really free from the Hive? Even if you are Outside, you are still running. Patrols will find you any time they wish. They have eyes that can see the heat in your footprints.'

Big Har crept between two damp, salty boulders, letting salt spray sprinkle his tender back. He picked up a fist-sized rock and watched the sky. 'Look!' he shouted, his voice cracking.

Larry followed his gaze. A chill tightened the nape of his neck. A row of skulls was watching them from a niche in the cliff. He relaxed when he saw how old and bleached they were. The sand under his hands was mixed with smooth chalky fragments – other surf-chopped bones. The thick yellow foam at the mouth of the sump coloured the ocean for miles, hinting of the vast tonnage being excreted by the Hive. A few bones would be expected. He did wonder who would take time to rescue a few human remains – who or what – a machine or fugitive.

Trilobite scurried up the cliff and examined the skulls. Satisfied that they were Citizens, he returned to the water-line. 'At least we'll be able to eat.' Big Har smiled. His nose had found the Gardens. He began to crawl towards the cliff base.

'Not during the day. It will bring patrols,' warned Trilobite.

Larry shook out his dried bathrobe and tied the bottom hem into a tassel. It felt stiff and sandy after its washing in the tidal pool. The sun had started to burn. A terrible thirst reminded him how long it had been since they had had adequate food and water. He knew how vulnerable he was, with his damaged kidneys.

'If the Gardens are dangerous, I suppose we'll have to live off the sea . . .'

'There is no food in the sea – absolutely none,' said Trilobite. He explained his years with *Rorqual*. Big Har accepted it as just another fact in his life, but Larry was visibly shaken.

'The Oceans – empty? But they are so large. How could it have happened?'

'The food chain was broken in too many places. The Hive took, but never gave back,' said the shovel-shaped meck, straining his little memory until he began repeating himself. 'The Hive took, and took, and took . . .'

Larry studied their problems – patrolled Gardens, empty seas, and time pressure. The Hive was after them and their dinghy. It probably would search here eventually. He turned to Trilobite.

'Have you reported our position?'

'No. My mission is to salvage the dinghy. Do you wish me to call the Hive?'

Larry winced. 'You really are a low-level meck. But thanks for not giving our position away. Can you tow us in the dinghy?'

'Where?'

'Anyplace – away from here. We need food, water . . .'

'I am sorry, but there is no place on Earth where you can

find those things. All land is owned by the Hive. The seas are salty and—'

Larry waved the meck to silence. 'I know, I know. Sterile. Damn it! Someone has been eating out of these Gardens. Look at the heap of refuse at the cliff base – rinds, husks, leaves... And there seems to be a trail, a worn footpath, up to the top. Look there.'

Big Har stood up into the glare of the sun. His broad shoulders drooped a little – weakened by the bots. 'Come, Hemihuman. Let me carry you into the Gardens. I don't have any fear of the Hive. Citizens can't be any stronger out here than they were in their shaft cities. We will eat well. We will eat now!' He swung Larry up to his right shoulder, swayed a bit, and started for the cliff. A voice from the sea interrupted him.

'Stay out of the Gardens!'

Trilobite couldn't believe his sensors. The words were pronounced clearly in the current Hive dialect. Yet the shaggy head in the surf was that of a Benthic beast – one of the Neolithic water-people.

Big Har turned slowly and stood with Larry on his shoulder like a two-headed monster. Neither head spoke.

'Stay out of the Gardens. Go away.'

'Who is that?' whispered Larry.

'One of the water-people. They live off the Gardens, but hide in the sea,' explained Trilobite. 'Perhaps they can give you shelter while I return the dinghy.' The shovel-shaped meck made a move toward the sea.

'My God, a machine!' mumbled the head. It disappeared.

Listener took off his earphones as Opal entered his dome.

'They have a machine with them! I spoke to them. I'm sure that it heard me.'

'I do not hear its carrier wave. Is it alive?'

'It moved towards me. I think it spoke to them.'

Listener thought for a long moment. 'What did it look like?' She described Trilobite.

'It is the same one, then. It has seen us before. Yet it did not call the Hunters. You return to the surface. Stall. Learn what you can. If I hear a carrier wave I will warn you. If they are fugitives there may be very little danger. If they are Hunters we must tell our people to flee to North Reef again.'

Opal took a spear and swam above the dome. Her foot occasionally touched the roof, partially exposed by the low tide. She studied the pair on shore thirty yards away. The big strong one was standing knee-deep in the water, a big hand shielding his eyes from the sun. The small deformed one sat peculiarly in the sand beside the shovel machine.

'Go away,' she repeated, gesturing with her spear.

'We need food and water,' said Har. 'We mean you no harm. Can you help us?'

'No.'

Big Har waited, letting the silence drag out. He could see the face clearly now – big-eyed and possibly female. The thick lids and square nose made it hard to be sure, but the eyes and the resonance of the larynx was suggestive.

'Why not?'

'Your machine is a danger to us. It is a tool of the Hive.'

Big Har had no stomach for debate. He knew he could not defeat this thick-necked water-dweller, for the warbles and bots had robbed him of his metalloproteins. He shrugged and walked back to where Larry waited in the dry sand.

Trilobite bristled. 'Tell her that I am no tool of the Hive. I am a servant of *Rorqual*. If she does not help you, you will die.'

Larry watched Big Har obediently return to the water's edge with the message. The exchange was pleasant enough, but the surf drowned out the words. When the giant returned, he stunned them with the outcome of their conversation.

'She wants us to pray to our *Rorqual* for a sign. Apparently, she misunderstood me. She thinks Trilobite serves a personal deity—'

'*Rorqual* is my deity,' interrupted the meck.

Larry raised his hand. 'Wait. We know what *Rorqual* is, but that Benthic doesn't. Couldn't we stage a "prayer" for her benefit? Just to win her confidence. She has food and water – and shelter from patrols. If we could—'

'Negative,' said Trilobite. 'I saw her dome. They have a listening device. If I spoke with my deity they would expect an answer. *Rorqual* ceased transmissions when I entered the Hive.'

'Maybe she won't expect an answer right away. A prayer might convince her to help.'

'Play acting? I can't deceive.'

'Just pray,' said Larry. 'Give us your best and most sincere prayer. The Benthics will eavesdrop and be deceived by their own naiveté.' He turned to Big Har. 'What sign did they have in mind?'

'Food,' said the anaemic giant. 'I understand that starvation stalks her water-people. Garden-raiding costs them many lives. She asked the Trilobite's deity to bring food back into the seas.'

Larry smiled sadly. These simple Neolithics expect magic to solve all their problems. He nodded for Trilobite to begin. The meck put his transmitter on audio so Larry and Har could share in his prayer. The carrier wave darted out to the southwest. Har listened with bowed head – and wanted to believe. Larry squinted intently at the horizon.

No answer.

'Are you aiming correctly?'

'I think so. I use solar angle and magnetosphere. The island coordinates are burned into my permanent memory.'

Har knelt and meditated quietly.

'But your brain is small,' complained Larry. 'Perhaps you should widen your call beam and try again. Your calculations could be in error.'

'Deity?' the prayer went out. 'Awaken and speak to your servant.'

Silence.

'Widen your beam again.'

'To widen is to weaken,' said the meck. 'If I make it any wider, it loses its "tightbeam" quality. I could just radiate my standard distress pulses. They wouldn't sound like a prayer to our eavesdroppers, however.'

Larry shrugged. 'You've sent enough of the standard prayer stuff. Now try for an answer – any kind of an answer. We need fresh water.'

Trilobite pulsed silently.

Listener snatched off his earphones, scowled and rubbed his ears.

'What is it?' asked Opal, her eyes on the transparent dome. Sunlit waves sparkled hardly five feet above the ceiling.

'Sounds like their transmitter exploded.'

She picked up an earphone and held it up several inches from her cheek. The pulses continued – audible clicks that tingled her hand. 'No. It is still working. Sounds like a signal. Did their deity answer yet?'

'No. Could they be calling the Hive patrols?'

'I don't think so,' said Opal. 'They looked like pretty standard fugitives to me – all warbled and weak. Hunters have never used decoy techniques that I can remember.'

Listener nodded. 'Then you trust them?'

Opal hesitated. 'We have never trusted a machine before.'

'Our domes are machines,' reminded Listener.

'That is different. We grew up with them. The Deep Cult warns us about machines that move. The Hive uses moving machines to hunt us. Any machine can carry the eyes of the Hive.'

They continued to listen.

Half the day passed before the answer came. The voice was not familiar. Its origin was the ecliptic. 'Yes?'

'Deity, we pray for a sign.'

'Pray, then.'

'I have two fugitives from the Hive. The water-dwellers have denied them refuge until we show them a sign to prove that we are your servants.'

'They've contacted their deity,' exclaimed Listener. He and Opal shared earphones.

'What kind of sign?' asked the voice.

'Food,' said Trilobite. 'They want you to make the seas

bountiful again. Bring back the fish and all it eats: plankton, seaweed, mussels . . .'

Larry patted the meck. 'Good work,' he whispered. 'Keep it up.'

Trilobite continued earnestly, 'Their people starve. They are good people – deserving of your bounty. Come live with us in the sea.'

'I come.'

Trilobite and Big Har trembled with excitement.

'My deity returns to the sea. She should be here in five or six days if her systems are all working. You will like her, I know. She is big and strong – and wise beyond your imagination. She will take us around the world . . .'

'Hush. Here comes the Benthic,' said Larry.

Big Har stood respectfully as the thick-necked female approached from the water. Her dripping body was smooth and muscular, with small breasts set wide apart. 'Welcome.' She smiled. 'We heard your deity. This is wonderful! I hope you will stay with us and let us tend your wounds.'

'We'll need a little food and water,' said Larry, speaking carefully so as not to frighten the simple savage. 'We will move on as soon as we get our strength back. Don't want to burden you.'

Opal eyed Big Har. 'It's no problem. I'm sure the Deep Cult will want an audience with you. That will take time. How are you called?'

'Har.'

'Well, Har. Pick up your little friend and I'll show you how to dive down to our home under the sea.'

Har hesitated. The surf looked rough, cold, and salty. Their skin bots ached.

'She is right,' said Trilobite. 'My distress call must have alerted half the mecks on this coast. We should find shelter quickly – before patrols come.'

Larry glanced at the little shovel-shape, puzzled. 'You are joining us?'

'I await my deity.' New excitement was reflected in his telltale display. 'The sea is where I belong.'

Larry puckered up his face and grasped Trilobite's tail as they dived to the dome. The pressure pinched his sinuses. He crawled up on the raft, coughing and snorting. The Listener's shaggy mane was the first thing he saw.

'My name is Larry.'

Listener just stared silently at the truncated hemihuman. He had never seen a partial human still living. In the hostile environment of the sea, even minor amputations meant eventual death from starvation. There was no surplus food for charity. Big Har and Trilobite joined them. Opal searched the dome's hot spot for utensils and began to check Har's back. The older lesions were clean and deep – flask-shaped ulcers. She found several young, unopened abscesses with immature larvae. She cut into them, draining cloudy fluids and digging out the stubborn parasites. Har submitted to her ministrations. Larry backed away.

'There'll be new bots forming for a few days as new larvae arrive to mature. We'll open them as soon as we see them. That way they won't get so big and do so much damage.' She turned to Larry, but he shooed her away. She offered him the set of sharpened tools – stone, wood and shell. 'Try to get all the foreign material out,' she said.

Larry grunted and brushed the tools aside. He hand-walked to Trilobite and hunkered down on the meck's disc. As he brooded he noticed his reflection on the glistening dome wall – a lumpy, pale, fly-specked human. A wry grin crossed his face. He had seen a shovelful of manure that looked better. What a disgusting mess! Anaemic. His plasma proteins were only about half normal.

'Why are you being so difficult?' asked Har.

Larry didn't know.

'Let Opal take a look at your back – it's worse than mine.'

Larry shrugged sheepishly and let Opal approach. She poured brine over his back and scrubbed, freshening the raw granulations. Serum oozed. He tolerated her cutting and probing as long as she worked on his back. Opening a deep neck sinus caused him pain. His face showed it. She hurried, trying to finish before his tolerance was exceeded. A scalp larva lay deep – next to bone. She probed gently, concerned at the size of the skull depression.

'I think this one has eroded into bone,' she said. 'We got it, though. Try to rest now. I'll find you a drink of water. Your mouth looks awfully dry. I'll bet your tongue feels terrible.'

Larry pulled on his robe, saying, 'Thanks.'

He dragged his tassel to the edge of the raft and waited. It had been a long time since any female had taken an interest in his body, and it made him feel uncomfortable. She could not possibly understand all his surgical orifices. She went to the side wall of the dome, where a network of ridges came together at a cup. Condensate dripped – fresh water. She offered Larry the cup. He drank deeply. After granular sewage and bitter tidal brine, it tasted delicious.

'What keeps you alive?' she asked. Her manner was brusque, but honest.

He shrugged.

'Your deity?' she asked.

'I suppose,' he said.

Listener loosened up finally. Any deity with that power would be welcomed by the Benthics. 'There is fruit in my bin. Serve them, Opal.' As they ate and drank, Opal questioned them about the Hive. Their years between the walls gave them an objective viewpoint. The Hive was clearly big and powerful, but it was not invincible.

'They have come to search the beach,' interrupted Listener, adjusting his headset. 'A patrol just landed beside the sump. A Hunter is leaving their airship.'

Larry raised an eyebrow. 'Airship?'

'The Hive has means of flying its Hunters. Several of our people have seen them.'

Larry was amazed that the technology still existed. Tweenwall years showed nothing but system decay. 'Can they find us here?'

'I don't think so. They have never come into the water even

when they were pursuing... They are examining the dinghy. That row of skulls seems to interest them. I think they are collecting bones... They are getting back into their craft... They're gone.'

Larry walked on his hands. He managed half a dozen steps before falling on his tassel. He checked his palms. The skin was intact.

Opal produced her waist tow rope and demonstrated how it was used to pull objects underwater. 'First we ballast it to zero buoyancy. I tie the rope to my waist – so! Now if you hold on to the end I have my hands and feet free to swim.'

'I don't think I can hold my breath very long,' said Larry. 'Why can't we stay here?'

Opal shook her head firmly. 'This is our Halfway House. All of the families use it on their way to the surface. No one lives here except Listener.'

Har took a deep breath. Opal towed him off into the deeper shadows. Larry rubbed the wall and tried to watch, but the dome was not clear enough for good resolution. Opal returned alone. She tossed the rope.

'Hang on. You're next.'

'Maybe I'd better let Trilobite tow me.'

She nodded and led them to an air-filled umbrella about thirty yards away. He poked his head up into the welcome air bubble. The view again was all greys and blacks. Stark, dull, barren. After several such stops they arrived at a small dome. The raft floated high.

'The air bubble is not yet full size, but it will be by sleeptime. Your hot spot is over here. The fruit bin is empty. I'll send someone with food in the morning.'

Har and Larry stretched out on the raft. Trilobite nosed around in the sand under the dome, coming up with an assortment of discarded tools and eating utensils. Opal left after she showed them how to set their wall cup for fresh water.

'How deep are we?' asked Har.

'I don't know for sure, but I could hold my breath about

three times longer than on the surface. If the air mixture is the same as atmospheric, I'd guess we were down about ten fathoms, about three atmospheres of pressure.'

Har stared up at the ceiling. The surface of the Ocean was just a blue haze – a light source. He closed his eyes to nap.'

'I think I will go up to the surface,' said Trilobite, 'and pray. I want to let my deity know how eager we are to see her.'

Larry nodded and watched the meck swim off. He went to the downstream end of the raft, lowered his torso into the water and relaxed his sphincters to empty visceral sacs. Then he checked his shoulders for new bots, bathed and napped. His dreams were nagging visions of growing renal calculi – sharp crystals stabbing into the soft kidney tissues. He awoke and drank three cups of fresh water before dozing off again.

Trilobite surfaced with a pain. The bubble of air in his disc threatened to burst his lingual membranes. It took him a long nanosecond to realize that the air at ten fathoms must be thicker and more compressed than on the surface. He wished his deity were available for sharing. Partial pressure tables would be helpful. Suddenly he understood why Benthics must go through Halfway on their trips to the surface. They must equalize in the shallows or suffer the pain of expanding gases. Without praying he dived back to the dome to warn his fugitives. But there was plenty of time. They slept. He called.

'Always go through Halfway,' said Larry. 'That sounds like a sensible rule. I can recall something called "the bends" from the days of my youth. I wish I knew more, but I did my swimming in small freshwater lakes – maybe ten or twelve feet deep.'

'The Benthics will teach us,' said Har.

Opal appeared with a sack of roots and nuts – staple items for their bin. 'Your skin is healing,' she said. 'The swelling and redness are less. It is one of the benefits of "the squeeze". Soon your strength will return.' She hovered over Har, bathing his wounds and feeding him.

'You'd do well to cultivate her friendship,' suggested Larry. 'I think she means to have you for a mate.'

Har showed little interest.

'A mate is much more secure than a disciple,' continued the hemihuman, 'especially if our deity remains nothing more than a voice. Trilobite tells me the Benthics are short on males – losing so many in the Gardens. Hive fugitives, such as we, usually die from exposure as soon as they hit the beach. The toothless skulls. You thrive. Opal is thrilled.'

Epithelium bridged cutaneous ulcers. Har practised short swims to nearby umbrellas.

'Today you may visit my clan at Long Dome,' invited a smiling Opal. 'We make offerings to the Deep Cult. You can share this custom with us.'

They covered the two-mile swim in an hour, making frequent breathing pauses. Long Dome resembled a centipede, with multiple pillar legs anchored in the bedrock. Larry sensed the activity as Trilobite towed him closer. Rafts vibrated with noisy family units – mates and their children. Opal led Big Har out of the water. She glowed with pride. Hemihuman followed.

Har stooped slightly and Larry walked his duck-walk on his hands as Opal led them down the raft, introducing her people. Their names, garnered from the ancient murals, were as colourful as the present seas were barren. The Benthics had filled the niche of extinction and had taken their names: Barnacle, who once had clung to his mother, now stood straight and tall; the Crab boys, Hermit, Spider, and Moss; a female called Shrimp; another named Coral. Larry nodded to each one. The smiled back. Most were healthy, with leathery skin and thick arms and legs. An occasional family unit lacked its father. This limited its food supply, producing runted and hollow-eyed children. Sexually mature females were about twice as numerous as males – Garden attrition.

Listener awaited them at the deep end of the chain of rafts where Long Dome overlooked the abyss. Four large wicker baskets of fruit, weighted with stones, stood at the edge. Flowers decorated these baskets and the smaller portions of food on each raft. Listener motioned them down on to a place mat. Trilobite remained near the wall floating on top of the water.

The preliminary remarks sounded like a prayer of thanks-giving. At the word 'offering' all eyes went to the large baskets heavy with fruit.

'I have spoken with the Deep Cult. They accept Trilobite's deity *Rorqual*. She will be added to our Hall of the Gods. Each family will offer up a prayer to her each day until the prophecy comes to pass. Food will return to the sea.'

The words of Listener were repeated. Larry thought they rang a bit hollow in the mouths of those mothers whose children shrank from calorie-lack. When he saw the two Crab boys start to dump the offerings he tugged Listener's robe.

'Wait,' he whispered. 'Is it necessary to make such a large offering? Er ... our god, *Rorqual*, demands only prayer for herself. She prefers we give our offerings to the needy – such as those hungry children ...' Larry pointed to the hollow-eyed runts.

Listener nodded his shaggy head. 'Come over here to the edge of the raft. Look down. The shadows have already cut off most to the abyss, but you can see some domes down there. The Deep Cult depends on us, just as we depend on them. If we broke our chain offerings, they'd have to move on to some other clan who would be more faithful. They could starve.'

Larry watched the deep canyon for movement.

'There's one now, coming for our offering.'

An angel appeared, wings and all, moving between the deep domes. It waited on a ledge, far below, moving the wings slowly – staring up. Larry put his face into the water to get a better look. The angel waited casually. He couldn't see its face, but there was no sign of bulky diving gear. It seemed to be breathing water, or not breathing at all. He watched for several minutes, then returned to his place mat. The offering was dumped. It drifted down, trailing flowers and bubbles.

'What has the Deep Cult given us today?' asked Larry. He spoke loud. If this was a cruel hoax, he wanted no part of it. His back was mending and his strength returned. He was ready to move on if his honesty offended these superstitious people.

Big Har leaned forward, all open-eyed and eager. He'd

accept the Deep Cult – whatever it was. Trilobite's tail went up. Larry's voice carried the note of challenge. But there was no need for caution. Listener smiled and pulled out a sheet of metal foil on which delicate lines and symbols had been stamped.

'Their map tells of a new approach to the Gardens – a Halfway House in Octopus Bay.'

Larry studied the underwater contours. Umbrellas and domes were marked along a ridge leading to a new landing site on the beach.

'This will increase our access to the food,' said Listener. 'The domes have not been checked out. They may or may not be viable, but they are the most stable model we've found. If we can stimulate them to make air bubbles for us—'

Opal raised her hand. 'Har and I will copy this map and check it out.' She smiled at Larry. 'You and your meck can come along too. A little mapping expedition will make you feel useful.'

'Why all the concern for the Gardens?' said Larry. 'If our deity is bringing back the ocean food chain?'

Listener remained solemn. 'We realize how long it will take to bring back the fish. Even a miracle must allow for Nature's own timetable.'

Hope, thought Larry. All Trilobite gave them was hope, and they would make the best of it. He grabbed the meck's tail. 'Let's go.'

'There's the ridge,' said Opal, pointing under the edge of the umbrella towards the distant grey contour. Larry and Har shared the bubble with her. Her hair fanned out and tangled with theirs.

'It looks so far away – and so dark.'

'Must be nearly half a mile away, across one of the deeper canyons. That's why we've never bothered with it. If there are living domes, they certainly don't show up from here.'

'How will we check it out? Go around the beach way on the surface?'

Opal shook her head. 'No. Take too long, with the day in Halfway. The beach is too dangerous anyway. Not worth the risk unless you are after calories. I could tow you over in about ten minutes.'

'Ten minutes!' choked Har. 'I can't hold my breath that long.'

She tried to taste the umbrella air. 'I think you could. This is level five. If we can find a dome along here that is down in the mating level – level seven – you'd be able to absorb enough oxygen to make it.'

'Ten minutes,' moaned Har. 'What if we can't find air right away? Can we go up?'

'No. The "pops" would get you,' she said. 'We'll send Trilobite across to check for air. If we know where we are going to it will save time.'

Larry let Trilobite tow him down to level six. They entered a large air-filled dome that had a sweetish odour. Wilted flowers were smudged over the raft. Five fathoms below, they saw a pair of warm domes glowing slightly.

'Those are Mating Domes,' Opal said. 'We can wait there while Trilobite explores the ridge. The rich air may make you feel a bit silly, but it should be only a mild intoxication if we leave shortly.'

The humans approached Mating Domes while the shovel-shaped meck darted out over the canyon. Two hundred yards out a strong current pushed him off course. He charted his drift and tried to calculate what the effect on humans would be. The drift was purely horizontal. There was no tendency to change levels. The new ridge had many living domes. All were well filled with air. Water cups were full. He marked the location of several on his mind map and started back.

'Why are these called "Mating Domes"?' asked Larry.

'We mate here,' said Opal casually. 'This one is the male dome. That one over there is for females.'

Har's Tweenwaller existence had left him psychologically neutral. His knowledge of human reproduction was limited to the Hive's peculiar five categories of birth permit. Heterosexual imprinting hadn't occurred. 'Males here; females over there?' he said.

Larry was visibly puzzled also. The excess nitrogen was beginning to make him giddy. 'The domes must be a hundred feet apart. No sperm could make it that far unless it was with the current.' He giggled.

Har appeared sleepy. He gestured with an awkward arm. 'The hundred-foot dash.'

'Like the clams used to do it in my day,' laughed Larry.

'You two have had too much of this thick air. We'd better get back up to level six and sober up,' admonished Opal.

Trilobite returned and detailed his findings. 'It is at least a ten-minute trip. Opal and I will take the front of the rope. Larry, you and Har will relax and be towed. We'll stop for two minutes at level seven and pink-up your capillary beds – supersaturate with oxygen.'

The meck and human rope train moved into the Mating Dome again. 'Press your little finger against my optic so I can monitor the oxygen saturation,' said the meck. Larry breathed deeply and rapidly until he felt dizzy. 'That's enough for you, Larry. Take one more deep breath, and let's go.'

Trilobite towed them clear of the dome and Opal began her slow steady kick. Big Har gripped the rope and squeezed his eyes shut. When they hit the cross-current Larry felt the cold pushing him off course. He tried not to think of the pressure dangers above and below – frosted blue and muddy black. The rocky landscape ahead slowly came into sharper focus. Five more minutes to go. He was relieved when he realized that he hadn't even thought of taking a breath. He glanced back to Har. The giant had opened his eyes and was grinning.

'We made it – easily!' exclaimed Larry.

Opal nodded and looked around the dome. 'It would have been tough without this air pocket. I would have had to tickle the dome and make it back to the Mating Dome on one breath. Might have had to do it several times before the dome air-filled for me. Those twenty-minute round trips could get exhausting – and dangerous.'

Larry duck-walked on his hands, examining the raft.

'Pretty clean looking. No sign of prior inhabitants. Who air-filled it?'

'Probably one of the Deep Cult, after they gave us the map. They would send a dome tickler to make the crossing safe for us.'

Har sat and studied the map. 'There must be over a dozen...'

'Looks like a score of new domes,' said Opal. 'We can set up a new Halfway at level two and warm a couple of the best-situated domes for ourselves.' Larry noticed that Opal's expression became thoughtful and soft when she spoke to Har. He waddled on his hands to the edge of the raft and hopped into the water. 'Trilobite and I will check some of those domes on level four.'

Har was puzzled. 'Shouldn't we work our way directly to Halfway? We'll be needing food—'

Opal touched his shoulder. 'There'll be time for that later. Let's talk.'

She explained that Har would be expected to choose a mate almost immediately. The Benthics were under a time pressure – caloric and reproductive. Males were in short supply, and as soon as his bots cleared, the unattached females would be after him.

'I understand,' he said. 'I've seen the runts. But do not worry. I have come from the Hive and do not fear it. Hive Citizens are weak and afraid. They can't possibly defend their Gardens against me. When I cry out, they'll die of fright.'

Opal smiled. 'Have you been in the Gardens before?'

'No.'

'You have much to learn. Those devil machines can kill you. They took my first mate from me. My father and brother also died up there.'

Har's expression was thoughtful disbelief. 'They weren't big like me – were they?'

'My brother was bigger. He was gone for three days. He came back with an arrow in his belly and died in Halfway. Now I must go to the Gardens to feed my son. It is very dangerous.'

'Your son?'

'Clam. He grows and studies with the Deep Cult. You will meet him.'

'I will be your new mate – and feed you and your son,' said Har confidently.

Opal smiled. 'You may – when you are ready.'

'Har is ready now.' His gesture was awkward but gentle – a caress on the pectoralis muscle bulge between her wide small breasts.

'There's something I should explain...'

He continued to stroke her body, using the sequences as well as he could remember from the Hive's class-one birth permit (human parents, human uterus-incubator, free choice of mates).

'We can't mate here,' she said.

'Why?'

'There is no Mating Dome.'

Har frowned. 'Custom?'

'Ceremony,' she corrected. 'Benthics mate underwater to prove their autonomic tone and myoglobin integrity.'

'We are underwater—'

'*Underwater!*' she said. '*In and under.* The entire – er – mating sequence has to be completed while submerged.'

'What for? It is nice here – warm, dry—'

'We must prove that we have good Benthic genes before we conceive.'

'That sounds so didactic,' said Har. 'When did you pick up such a—'

She grasped his hand firmly. Her voice was low, patient. 'It is our way. The Deep Cult teaches it to all prepubertals. Our life is hard enough under the sea when we have the proper genes. To conceive a child with weak genes would endanger not only the child, but the family unit that tries to raise him.'

Har nodded. 'You have the proper genes – your son Clam—'

'And I hope you have good genes too, Har. But I wouldn't want to bring a weak surface-dweller into our world. If my child couldn't manufacture enough myoglobin for a twenty-minute swim, he couldn't survive in the domes. When you have that ability, I will know you have that gene.'

'I crossed that canyon.'

'You were towed. Ten minutes of breath-holding is not a twenty-minute swim. You are still a surface-dweller. The level-seven air got you across.'

'When will I be ready?'

'Soon, I hope.'

The brief episode of foreplay had warmed Har's loins. 'I think I could succeed right now.'

Opal saw the sexual flush. Her long years without a man had robbed her of her usual caution. 'It's worth a try,' she said. 'But you lack a tow-head. It will be difficult. I'll show you the easiest way. Stay here and hyperventilate. We don't have a level-seven dome, so this will have to do. When your fingertips tingle, leave the dome swimming slowly on your back. I'll come from that dome over there.'

Har squinted through the transparent wall. The other dome was twenty yards away, about two fathoms above.

She gave him a quick hug. 'Separate your efforts now. Physically you will do nothing. Let me do the work. I have the myoglobin for it. I have more than enough oxygen-carrying capacity. But mentally you'll have to work very hard. I don't know which sexual fantasies you've been imprinted with, but call them all up. I know I'm not very erotic – all wet, cold and leathery. But keep your mind on my erogenous zones. Remember: physically – do nothing; mentally – do everything!'

Har smiled meekly.

She gave him a swat on the wet buttock. 'We might just do it at that!'

He began slow deep breathing as she swam away. Her form seemed to get more interesting as it moved farther away; the haziness added mystery. When his fingertips tingled he left the dome, swimming slowly. When he rolled over on his back, water bubbled into his left ear. The frosted blue surface was clearly above him – overhead – but the distance added depth. She hit him hard. He hadn't noticed her approach, when suddenly she was on him. He saw bright eyes and white teeth. The teeth sunk into his left shoulder while her toes hooked behind his knees. He wrapped his arms around her – a clumsy movement that set the lovers spinning slowly. His view rotated to the muddy black bottom, only a few fathoms below. Her fingernails raked his back as her pubic bone struck his. Her teeth opened a few capillaries. A pink stain drifted past his face. They continued to rotate. With one hand she managed a brief penetration. Her other hand was busy trying to stop their spinning. Her heels locked behind his knees and her pelvic thrusts began – a demanding rhythm. His excitement phase was washed away by vertigo. She tried several strokes and pressure points, but he was unresponsive. His pelvic nerves were drained by nauseating dizziness. She pushed him away – back towards the welcome air bubble of his dome. In a few minutes she joined him.

'I guess you aren't quite ready,' she said cheerfully, swatting his buttock again.

He rubbed the teeth marks on his shoulder.

'You'll have a nice hard callus there after you tow a few hundred loads from the Gardens,' she said. 'And I forgot to tell you to keep your arms out straight – to stabilize us. The rotating will distract you every time.'

Har shrugged and stretched out on the raft.

'It was a good try,' she said, joining him. 'A good try.'

They slept.

During the months that followed, Har's breath-holding ability increased. He grew a tough tow-head on his left shoulder and mated successfully. Trilobite and the hemihuman explored the shelf, making new friends and mapping warm domes.

Furlong studied the reports. 'Is this all we have? A few hazy optics and these auditory prints?' He passed a stack of flimsies to Ode. Drum reached into the reports and pulled out one of the voiceprints. He sorted through and separated all the prints into one pile.

'I've already done that,' said Furlong. 'There is only one. The clone has been identified already.'

'Clone?'

'Clone! Cell line. We don't know which individual is the clone, but they'd all have identical voiceprints – like fingerprints.'

Drum nodded. 'Then we don't know how many of them were on the boat. At least two, since they were talking with each other. What cell line?'

Furlong glanced at the report. 'L.D. – Larry Dever. Here's his ident number. From the laryngeal resonance he – or they – have reached puberty.'

'Did you run a check on the members of the L.D. clone that are unaccounted for now?'

'Yes. There's quite a number, what with suicides, accidents, and Suspension failures. Positive identification is often impossible. Here's the list.'

'Why, there are thousands of them! Some date back hundreds of years,' exclaimed Drum.

'That's understandable – with VS and TS, you know,' said Ode. He unfolded the list. 'And here is the original: old Larry Dever himself, right at the top of the list. Why is he here?'

'No proof of death,' explained Furlong. 'CO checked these out. These real old clones are valuable to the Hive – often used when thickness of skin or resistance to infection are needed. The list would be ten times this long if most hadn't been pitted and trimmed to assure Hive adjustment. We only need to worry about the unpitted, since the voiceprints show a mature larynx. Pituitaries are needed for puberty.'

'It's still a long list. Can we narrow it?'

Furlong shrugged. 'What difference does it make? They're as interchangeable as any clone litter-mates.'

'True,' said Drum. 'But they'd differ in skills and experience. By avoiding our sensors and escaping Trilobite, they proved that they were pretty clever – far above the average Tweenwaller.'

'Of course. One of the L.D. clone would be expected to adjust quicker than some poor senile Citizen trying to escape TS.'

'Well, they're no longer our problem,' said Furlong stuffing the papers into his outbox. 'The sighting on the beach was pretty clear – dinghy plus skulls. I've never seen such a big collection of bones in one place before. The Outside environment must be very hostile.'

'Very.' Drum and Ode nodded.

'When will we be getting our dinghy back?'

'Salvage has the reports. Whenever they get around to it, I suppose.'

Drum sat stiffly on the edge of his cot, slowly flexing his fingers. 'Looks like the damp work got to my joints again.' Age clouded his bad lens further, sapping his courage. 'I'm afraid I'll have to sit this shift out.'

Ode went through his yoga warm-ups. 'You'll miss the flavours and perishable calories too. That'll weaken you even more.' After checking each toe for corns, he pulled on his boot and went to his Dispenser. 'Want to try my rheumatism salicylate drink?'

Drum's groan was too theatrical to be real. He nodded and stood awkwardly, waiting for his hip joints to loosen. 'Bring me the green drink and show me my shovel.'

6
Marine Biota

Puberty struck Clam a hard blow, wiping away obedience and loyalty. He forgot the teachings of his mother Opal and the Deep Cult. He forgot his place in Benthic tribal life. Manhood had arrived suddenly, turning this young Tad into a sullen, thick-necked male. Only one thought remained – one drive – his hatred of the Hive.

The sunlit Gardens looked harmless enough to Clam. He rode a gentle surf, staying a quarter of a mile offshore. The dangers were there. Deep Cult lessons had been well learned. Flying devil-ships with bowmen would track him. Hive warriors could swarm out of their holes in the ground. He was there to taunt the Hive, to avenge the death of his father – and to prove his manhood.

He arched his body, staying in the foamy wave crest and riding to the beach. A featureless cliff faced him. No artifacts. He picked up a stone and scrambled up to the vegetation. The variety of sparkling fruits stunned him for a moment. Never had he seen so much food at once – acres – no – miles of ripening crops. The sentry tower clicked as it focused sonic and electromagnetic sensors on him. He flung his stone, cracking a lens and sending a shower of sparks to the ground.

'Come out!' he shouted. 'Let me see what kind of Nature's mistake you are.'

He walked over to the base of the tower. Its legs were wide apart and sturdy. Heavy cables emerged from the ground and entered one of the legs. He kicked at the junction box. The knobs of sensors looked down on him. He studied the box, testing it for movable parts. A clip moved. The lid opened. He pulled a plug. Abruptly the knobs overhead quieted. He inserted the plug. The knobs lived and blinked with nervous cyber energy.

'So this is the line that carries your life blood,' he shouted. 'Let me take it away as you took my father away.'

He picked up his beach stone and crushed the bright fittings in the sockets. The tower remained quiet. A passing harvesting robot did not even pause in its chores. Clam understood from his teachings that these big field machines did little more than tend crops. He watched it pass, respectful of its great size. 'Tell them that I am here!' he shouted. The Agromeck trundled out of sight. The sky remained clear. Clam began to eat, cautiously at first; but as the hours dragged by he became more brazen – picking and singing, gathering heaps of bright, colourful fruits: golds, reds, oranges, and purples. He carried several armloads to the beach and sat down among the fragrant, waxy globes. The choppy, disorganized surf reminded him of his transport problem. To avoid his mother's wrath he had bypassed Halfway and decompressed in one of the level-two domes out on One-Mile Reef. He would need a net bag to tow his harvest that far. He glanced up the cliff. Gardens would provide weaving fibre.

The passing shadow startled him. The devil-ship circled and landed three stone-throws away. A figure emerged, white and bug-eyed; but the shimmering air above the sunbaked beach rocks obscured details. Clam shook his fist and shouted, but the figure disappeared into the irregular angles of the chalky cliff. The ship's anterior optics gave it a bug-like appearance. It was smaller than he had expected – probably holding no more than six Hunters. He shook his fist, and it flew away. The beach was quiet – empty.

Clam shrugged and climbed up into the greenery, where he bundled grass and vines into small bales. The Hunter watched through his bowscope. As he pulled back on the string Clam's image appeared double. Too far. He stalked closer and again pulled the bowstring. The image fused. He set up his twelve-foot wind-drift pole and plugged it into his bow. The 12× eyepiece clicked into place.

Clam stumbled down the cliff with his arms wrapped around a huge stack of itchy weaving materials. He peered over his burden. The distant Hunter was now standing out in the open on the beach. The approaching arrow was invisible in the dancing heat. It knocked him backwards, bouncing on smooth stones. His scalp ached. The sun hurt his eyes. He looked up at the perpendicular shaft. His sternum hurt, but only a little. The arrowhead was embedded in one of the fibreglass bales. He lay still. Now he understood how the Hive had killed his father – and his grandfather before him. Their weapon could reach out from a great distance. It was deadly, and yet a bundle of grass as thick as his chest had stopped it. Footsteps approached, crunching gravel. Clam's eyes remained closed. He breathed slowly. A breeze rustled the leaves on his bundles.

The feet were close. A pebble rolled against his thigh. His hand found a stone and he leaped. The Hunter stumbled back and fell. The longbow clattered. Clam raised the stone and struck the helmeted head again and again. The goggles dented. One went off-grey.

Clam entered Halfway and proudly set the battered helmet at the feet of Listener.

'I have entered the Gardens and returned with food. I have slain our enemy.'

Listener looked up through the ceiling at the long shadow of a woven melon raft tied to the buoy. 'You have done well, Clam. You are a man.' The acceptance of the youngster's exploits was ritual. 'Put stones in the raft until it sinks. Bring it into the domes before the devil-ships see it.'

While Clam hauled ballast, the shaggy old Listener brought out his tools and began to examine the helmet. He tried it on. Voices filled his head. Hive voices. 'Give your location,' they said. 'Press your homing button.' He took it off, placing it on a shelf reverently. The goggles stared blankly. 'It still lives,' he mumbled.

Big Har came upon Opal in a level-two umbrella. She was coughing and holding her side.

'I came up too fast,' she said sheepishly. 'Little Clam left the Deep Cult two days ago. They think he was on his way to the Gardens. I must try to find him.'

Har put a protective arm on her shoulder. 'You are endangering your other child – our unborn. You must go back to level four until your pain goes away. Can you make it?'

She coughed. 'Clam? What if Clam needs me?'

'You'll be of no help to him this way. Let me help you dive. I will check Halfway. We will find him.'

Her sputum was streaked with pink. The pain in her side doubled her up. 'You are right, my mate. I will do as you ask.'

Har threw his tow rope over his left shoulder and settled it on his tow-head – a calloused bursa covered with thickened skin. The fluid-filled bursal sac padded the coarse rope fibre. As they dived into the squeeze the pains vanished. She smiled and waved as he returned to level two.

Two young males, members of the Crab family, passed him on their way from Halfway. They towed much fruit.

'When Clam eats – everyone eats,' shouted the young euphoric Benthic. Listener's raft was still overloaded and awash with Garden produce. 'I could fill this dome to the ceiling.'

Har studied the arrow. He had seen optic records of hunts on entertainment channels, but had no idea of the actual size and weight of the arrowhead. The broad hunting barbs surprised him. 'A bundle of grass stopped this?'

Clam grinned, happy to tell the story again. 'Yes. The only marks I have are these scratches on my chest.' There, over the centre of the sternum was a star-shaped bruise – dead centre!

'How much grass?'

Clam made a loop with his arms. Har nodded.

'Was the Hunter an average-sized Citizen?'

Clam didn't know how Citizens compared with Benthics.

He stood up and made a horizontal, palm-down motion at mid-chest height – about four feet.

Har nodded. That was average. 'How did he look without his helmet?'

'Small, soft, and white – no chin. Not many bones at all. He broke up when I jumped on him.'

Har stepped over a heap of bean pods and sat beside Listener. The Hunter's longbow, belt, and kit lay spread out before them. The empty-eyed helmet gazed at them from a shelf. Har picked up the bow and sighted through the scope. Cross-hairs glowed. As he pulled back the string, the depth of focus changed, giving him the weapon's range. 'Clever,' he said, showing the mechanism to Listener. They sorted through the gear, understanding little.

'I think we should destroy most of these things, if we are not sure how they work,' said Har. 'Hive tools can be very small and very, very clever. One of these could lead Hunters right to us.'

Listener nodded. 'There seems to be little to worry about right now. Listen to the helmet. They don't even know their man is dead.'

Har tried on the headgear. The voice was monotonous, repetitious – a meck. 'That is his ship – the devil-craft – calling.'

The dome fell silent as all eyes turned towards the ceiling. Overhead, the sun glinted through two fathoms of clear water. The sky seemed clear.

Listener pulled on the helmet. 'Perhaps I can tell how far away it is.'

More Benthics arrived and took their portion of Clam's harvest. Har picked at a belt circuit board. Clam began filling a special net bag with choice items he had saved for Opal.

Listener frowned and handed Har the helmet. 'I'm picking up something on all bands. It's odd. I've never heard anything quite like it.'

Har listened thoughtfully. 'Sounds more like music than interference.' He spun the dials through the different channel bands. There was no change. 'I think the communicator is just malfunctioning...'

'Then so is the web. I'm getting the same thing over here,' said Listener with his old bulky earphones. 'And it is getting louder.'

The murmur of conversation stilled as the fruit-sorting Benthics quieted and lifted their heads from the piles of food.

'They hear it too...'

Har jumped to his feet. 'I don't like it at all. QUICK! Everyone leave the dome. Dive for level five. Dive! Dive!'

The dome was empty a second later. A few dislodged melons drifted to the surface.

Trilobite's long-forgotten prayer was finally answered with a shower of falling stars that filled the electromagnetic spectra with song and the seas with plankton.

The glowing meteor trail lit the night sky. *Rorqual*'s long ear twitched. Booming mushrooms of flame pocked the dark Ocean. *Rorqual*'s consciousness flickered as her sensor thresholds were violated. She sucked hydrogen isotopes – the Big H – from the sea to feed her growing belly fires. Her strength returned. Flexing and squirming, she began to worm her flanks out of the imprisoning silt. Warmth filled her hull. Her deep dish-eyes rose out of the blinding olivine and gazed into the lagoon. The waters had changed. Incoming spectra were fuzzed by nanoplankton.

She pulled away from the island. Roots and vines snapped. Tree trunks split. She re-entered the sea, carrying a hump of vegetation firmly locked into her back by gnarled woody roots. Salty, windblown spray followed the roots through damaged plates and burned her vitals – until layers of electroplating and oxides crusted over the sensitive, exposed circuits.

Joyfully she toiled the straits, raking and pumping. Only faint traces soiled her membranes during the first year, but her chromatographs identified all the amino acids. Protein had returned to the sea. Growth bloomed. During the second season larger creatures were caught on her rakes – soft copepods, heteropods with bizarre, delicate shells, chaetognaths, and dino-flagellates. Earth Society would be pleased with her harvest. Man would be pleased.

Big Opal glanced around her level-three nest at ten fathoms. The fruit bin was low; there was scarcely enough for her offering to the Deep Cult. She would be the one raiding the Gardens this time. Har's left knee was still swollen, unable to bear his weight. The effects of the meteor shower had injured a number of Benthics. An astrobleme-induced tsunami had shifted a mountain of debris, trapping him in undersea ruins. His left knee had been badly crushed. Until he could run again, the burden of feeding the family had fallen on Opal's broad shoulders.

'I must swim up to the Gardens,' she said patting her two young children. Clam, her oldest, was now an adult and had left her nest.

Har nodded. He and the young Tads watched her climb down through a toothy rent and swim up past the swaying transparent walls, her pink breasts and buttocks shimmering through the cloudy waters. Since the meteor shower there had been a drop in visibility.

Opal swam leisurely among the scum-shrouded ruins, pausing at living umbrellas for air. At level two she entered the mushroom-shaped Halfway House, bobbing up into the living-room pool.

'Welcome,' said the wizened, hairy Listener.

She climbed, dripping, up the ramp to where he sat among the wires. His lap held a bowl. He appeared worried.

'What do you hear from the surface?' she asked.

'Nothing. Yet I feel we have seen the harbinger of evil,' he groaned, holding up a red crustacean. 'The krill.' It flipped back into the bowl.

'The krill have returned?'

He nodded gravely.

'Why, that's wonderful!' she exclaimed. 'I have seen them in the murals – good food from the seas. Trilobite's deity has answered our prayers. We'll soon be able to survive without raiding the Gardens.'

A tear started down Listener's wrinkled face.

'What's wrong?' asked Opal.

He pointed to his web. 'The Hive will see the krill, too. It will return to harvest the seas again – and drive us out. Our children will have no place to hide – no place.'

Opal was stunned. The Benthics had lived on the shelf for generations. She understood the ruins had been built by the Hive, but that had been a very long time ago. Now the Benthics were here. The Ocean was their refuge – their home. She shook her fist at the ceiling.

'The Hive will not drive us out.'

Overhead the surf dulled with soupy green and yellow blooms – diatoms, algae, and salps. After one sleep Opal swam up to the Gardens and stole her share of the harvest. Agromecks ignored her. She worked quickly and quietly, tying her melons into a raft and loading sacks of smaller nuts and berries. At dusk she rode the rip currents towards the Halfway buoy. A few stars blinked down at her. The western horizon glowed a faint blue when a silhouette appeared against it – nearly a quarter mile long, low and dotted with trees.

It was right in Opal's path – an island where no island should be. The current carried her up to the smooth, slightly granular beach. With her raft vine in one hand she examined the trees – jumbled leaves, trunks, and roots – natural enough. She tied her raft and began to explore the shoulder-high brush under a palm canopy. At the end of the beach she came upon a hillock – a heap of boulders that had been hollowed out. Inside, there were glowing ornaments and bright, blinking stones in the walls. The floor was littered with small tools, seaweed, and pinching crabs.

Rorqual trembled at the touch of bare feet. The huge Harvester tried to speak, but air molecules did not respond. She could make no sound. Her vocal membranes had gone with her long ear. She tried an offering. Chewing cellulose mulch into a hydrocarbon solution the meck polymerized and extruded a small tool. Opal picked it up – curious. Excitedly *Rorqual* formed a small doll in the likeness of the wet, naked guest. It was rubbery and translucent – a tough polymer.

Opal's curiosity was quenched abruptly by what she saw through the porthole. This island had a wake – it was moving! She cursed and ran, diving overboard without her melons.

Three Benthics huddled in their level-three nest watching the shadow pass over the reef. 'That's it. It is looking for me,' whispered Opal.

'A floating island?' asked Har.

Clam shook his head. 'The Leviathan. I studied them with the Deep Cult. Murals and old ballads speak of such a creature. It is not an island. It is a creature that gathers krill for the Hive – a giant mutation of the finback whale. Did you notice the control cabin?'

Opal nodded. 'A little room.'

'Attached to the back of the skull,' he explained. 'The Hive designed hookups between machines and the hapless creature's brain and muscles. A crew could steer it anywhere, ignoring its usual migrations. I'm not sure how they bred them.'

Opal did not like that at all: 'A sea creature controlled by the Hive.'

Nebish workmen sat around their barracks watching the sewer bouillabaisse simmer. Drum picked up his bowl and decanted a pint of surface fluid with its fat gobbets and flecks of green basil.

'Don't you want any of the jointed creatures?' offered Ode, digging deep with a ladle.

Drum grinned widely, exposing a bad set of teeth; less than half remained in the lower jaw, none in the upper. 'There'll be no more chewing for me.'

'Did you put in a request for a new set?'

'Along with my usual requests for a lens and a hip joint,' said Drum. 'But you know what my priority is.'

Ode sat silently, running his tongue over his own broken set of teeth. He could use a few White Team requisitions himself. The Wet Crew sloshed in and dumped their tithe down the Synthe Chute. They sat down and picked up bowls of hot soup.

'Your shift,' they said.

Ode and Drum finished eating and pulled on their boots. The brackish odour was overpowering Sewermeck flashed amber.

'My sensors indicate a large disturbance. Your shift has been cancelled. Hurry to the outhatch.'

Ode squinted into the darkness of the sump. 'Flash a light out there. I hear something.'

'My lights will not read. Hurry to the outhatch.'

'The waves sound like they're lapping against something about thirty feet out.' His belt light pulsed. He caught a glimpse of mottled wet wall.

'That isn't supposed to be there,' said Ode. They scrambled back up the ladder to the barracks.

'That was quick,' said Furlong. His manner was unusually pleasant. 'Did you fellows dump that last load of grit down the Synthe Chute?'

Ode pointed to the Wet Crew members who were lined up at the refresher.

'Where did you dig this up?' Furlong asked.

One of the crew, still pink and fragrant from the scrubber, walked over carrying a bundle of crisp issue tissue garments. He glanced at the small, white, pea-sized object. 'Oh, the fossil otolith?'

'It's no fossil ear stone! Look at this report from the Synthe Sorting Meck. No leaching, ion drift, or surface wear. The isotopes are in the contemporary ratio.'

'Contemporary?' exclaimed the crew member, dropping his bundle. Ode and Drum jumped to their feet.

'Yes,' said Furlong. 'Half the staff from Bio is on their way down here right now. They want to know where to start digging.'

Ode opened his mouth to mention the sump disturbance when the crowd of Samplers rushed into the barracks. Coils of auxiliary power cables were unrolled in the halls. Arc-lights wheeled up to the hatch.

'Where?' repeated Furlong.

'The delta.'

Arc-lights crackled in the pipes as the teams of Samplers spread out and began netting and digging.

'Bring those nets down here to the delta.'

'What's that smell?'

'Uh, oh, I don't think we'll be needing those nets.'

Attracted by the voices, *Rorqual Maru* cruised down the sump towards the delta. Her hundred-and-fifty-foot beam was half as wide as the sump. Before her drifted a spongy wall of brine-soaked biscuits – her cargo. The Nebishes backed away as her towering, barnacled hull nosed gently into the mud. Baleful optics gazed while the teams nervously filled their pails.

Drum followed the teams up to Bio and watched the Sorting Meck flake up the biscuits. Individual plants and animals were centred on small trays and passed on to the reading stage under the Gene Spinner's critical eye.

'Plankton,' chirped Wandee. 'Look at this printout. There are over a hundred species here that were thought extinct.'

'How could it have happened?' asked Drum. 'Where did all these creatures come from?'

Wandee shrugged. Spinner considered the question and shared it with the CO – the Class One Meck also had neutral connection with all the continents. In a few hours Drum had his answer.

'Meteor show,' postulated the CO. 'Marine biota reappeared three point two years afterwards. An astrobleme must have opened an atoll or other landlocked body of saltwater where these species had survived.'

Drum nodded.

'We are lucky that the sea can support life again. Whatever killed it must not be active now.'

'Doesn't appear to be. These seem to be flourishing. There must be a lot of food in the seas now.'

'Who will harvest it?'

The platoon of orange-suited insignia wearers crept into the SS barracks and nudged Ode. As the retired Grandmaster opened his eyes the ensign handed him a captain's coveralls.

'Whom do you want?'

'You – Captain, sir,' said the ensign curtly. 'You have been named to command. We'll voyage on plankton rake *Rorqual Maru* – the whale ship. CO's orders, sir.'

Ode glanced around at the placid, young faces of his crew – barely mature children. He pulled on the coveralls and thick-soled boots. His belt was wide and ornate. Drum sat up on his cot to watch the drafting of Captain Ode. He shook his head slowly, wondering why a Grandmaster would be commissioned to pilot a rake. Did the reason lie in his military experience on the chessboard – or the simple fact that Ode had been the first to spot the returning vessel?

'Good luck,' said Drum sadly.

'Smile,' said Ode. 'It is an honour to captain the first vessel in the Hive navy. It is a turning point. More food for all Citizens. The yards will reopen to build copies of *Rorqual*. We'll all have a great time.'

'Be careful anyway,' cautioned Drum. 'You are not accustomed to the Outside. No one knows very much about the seas these days...'

Captain Ode waved his friend to silence and marched off with his crew.

Priorities were juggled as the Hive attempted to get the Shipyards working again. Meck brains were taken from doors, Dispensers, and every class of machine. They were carted and delivered to the flooded, corroded ruins along the sump. Nebish work crews found their jobs impossible. Ancient crane and lathe robots heaped into rusted masses with the twisted girders, cables, plates and other scrap gear. Everything was too heavy or too sharp for the weak, soft Citizen retreads. A shipyard caste was needed. The project was temporarily suspended while the job qualifications could be drawn up – broad shoulders, thick skin, and the mental capacity of a Tinker or a pipe caste member. It would be many years before a finished copy of *Rorqual* slid down the ways.

Drum's White Team requests were answered unexpectedly. He reported to the Clinic, where he was given every courtesy. On his first visit they took impressions for new teeth, measurements for a new lens prosthesis, and arthrograms for a new hip. During the work-up they found a list of correctables: a benign colon polyp was plucked out; his diet was changed to include more flavours; an exercise prescription was given to his new Dispenser; the cloudy lens was diced up and sucked out of his eye and a plastic lens inserted.

'A new Dispenser?' he asked.

'Goes with your new status,' said the clerk, handing him the gold bar.

Drum blinked at the bright yellow metal. His operated eye ached and he saw double.

'You're a Leo,' explained the clerk. 'Society will feel free to call on you for anything. You will work across caste lines at a supervisory level.'

Drum nodded.

'This is your new Dispenser. It will follow you back to your room on Mover. When it is hooked up you'll see how special it is – hot and cold capability with odour control. Your teeth will be ready tomorrow. The next day we'll do your hip. In a couple of weeks you should feel ten years younger.'

'A Leo?' mumbled Drum.

'Yes. I wonder what your first assignment will be. We were ordered to put you on very high priority.'

Drum didn't have long to wait. After his various surgeries he was put on a walking program by his Dispenser – two hours on the Spiral twice a day. The checkpoints kept getting further and further from his cubicle in the SS barracks. Furlong had no assignments in the pipes for him.

He had just come back from his morning walk, sweaty and hungry, when Dispenser chuckled: 'Hot or cold? Today you get your assignment.'

'Cold and foamy – a long one. What assignment?'

The chute produced two pints of frosty yellow liquid that foamed when he popped the lids. He took a long drink. His new teeth ached sharply. 'OUCH! That's cold.' When half the drink was gone he sat down and waited for Dispenser to continue.

'Leo Drum, you are to take a detail of men Outside and string the long ear.'

'Outside?' Drum shuddered.

'Your drinks will have ice and your soup will have chunks of meat.'

He nodded.

Drum put his goggles on step-down and ventured cautiously into the Gardens. The suits were Closed-Environment types, maintaining the heat and humidity of the Hive. He felt the elbows and shoulders of his work crew as they crowded together for protection from their 'Outside fears' – agoraphobia.

Bright sun glinted off gaudy flowers. Leafy plants absorbed sound, hushing the human voices and screening the men's views of each other. Three workers – each finding himself alone in such wide open spaces – collapsed and died.

The towers of the long ear stood on a hill and reached up into the sky. Glassy insulators clung to spider-web-thin struts. The structure appeared delicate, swaying in the wind. Half the crew was unable to approach the ladders. Many of those who made the climb lasted less than an hour before freezing to the rungs or dropping to the ground in a heap of fractures. Replacements arrived. Spools creaked at the base of the towers as wires were strung up and down the antennae. Stretcher Teams jogged back and forth with their splinted burdens. Fresh work details were sent out at dusk to spell the survivors. They worked through the night, swaying against a star-strewn sky. Darkness erased most of the landmarks so the Nebish, limited by his helmet light, worked more comfortably.

Several days later Drum realized where the structure got its name. An oblong dish, a rabbit's ear, was slowly taking shape.

Captain Ode lost six crew members to agoraphobia. Another dozen were in various stages of catatonia.

Rorqual raked well. Her hold bulged with a hundred thousand tons of calories for the Hive – flavoured calories. She reeled in her nets and digested them, returning the polymers to their holding tanks. Bacteria – cellulose – cracking fermenters – were seeded into the hold, where they busied themselves digesting plant fibre. Algae cells walls became polysaccharide – edible sugars.

During the voyage back to Orange Sector *Rorqual* detoured up the coast to the point where she had sighted Opal. Her port crane sprinkled the surface of the water over the reef with steaming sausage-shaped masses of fermenting plankton – flaky, green biscuits that barely floated.

'What's this?' exclaimed Captain Ode. 'You are losing part of the cargo. Did you have an accident?'

The ship's printout did not make sense to the Nebish. He interpreted the event as an offering to a water sprite – superstition buried in the ship's old memory banks. He decided not to make an issue of it.

Trilobite towed hemihuman Larry through a school of tiny fishes, then back to the surface to catch his breath. While Larry basked on the meck's body disc the tail rose out of the water and broadcast a call to *Rorqual.*

'Still thinking that ship Opal saw was your deity?'

'Must be,' said the meck. 'Her description fits perfectly. Even if the Hive did make a copy of her it wouldn't put those trees in her hump.'

'Why doesn't she answer?'

'She could be on manual override, or her communicator system could be knocked out.'

'It's a big Ocean,' said Larry. 'It will be hard to find her if she is deaf and dumb.'

They continued to drift with the current until Trilobite noticed a familiar outline in the foam along the shore. Plankton biscuits had washed up. The meck darted in and collected a mouthful.

'I know it was *Rorqual*,' said Trilobite. 'Her flavour is all over these biscuits. She must have been by here a few hours ago.'

'This is Opal's reef. I don't think it is a coincidence. She'll be back.'

They dived to Halfway. Listener looked at the biscuits and nodded.

'Four hours ago. Same floating island, or Leviathan – leaving a trail of those green things. It went south along the coast.'

'Did you hear anything unusual on the web while it was overhead?'

'No. Never have when it is around. If it can communicate over a distance it doesn't use any of the usual bands.'

'Trilobite thinks it can't talk.'

Listener nodded. 'The Benthics had better stay away from it until we know what it is up to.'

Captain Ode was enjoying temperature luxuries with his flavours: icy parfait and steaming consommé. Dispensers with heat pumps were rare. He had been accustomed to heating his soups on a separate heater coil. This one even made ice cubes.

The *whooop whooop whooop* of the alarm siren called him from his cabin. The deep nets were bringing up a humanoid silhouette. Ode glanced at the deep scanning screen and thought they might have netted a canal sirenian or other aquatic mammal, but as it was brought closer he saw that it was clearly a hominid – giant, naked, and primitive. The crane extruded a soft polymer net and gently dragged the body up on the deck. The crew shuddered at the size of the brine-soaked hulk: six feet long – two feet taller and a hundred pounds heavier than a Nebish. It wore a rope belt, had leathery burnt-sienna skin and large five-toed feet. The crew scattered, wet boots squeaking.

The Sharps Committee met and issued Captain Ode a curved blade. He walked up to the Benthic and nudged it with his boot. It was cold, stiff – lifeless. As a precaution Ode cut the left carotid artery. The blood was purple and jelly-like. Eight Nebishes carried the Benthic down to the freezer. Ode returned to his cabin and dictated his report to *Rorqual*. He theorized that it was a fossil hominid that had been carried there by a bottom arctic current after melting out of some glacier. An elaborate theory, but he knew very little of the world outside his Hive.

'Can you send that?'

The printout explained that work on the ship's communicator gear was not complete. He shrugged and went below decks to speed things up.

'Roots in the plates?'

The Electrotecks were scattered throughout the crawl space between decks with their small tools, sawing the gnarled, invading wood and chipping away thick green flakes. The entire nervous system of the ship was shorted out between the forebrain and the hindbrain.

'How long is this going to take? This is our second voyage. You don't seem to be making much progress.'

The Squad Leader sat up and wiped his hands. A pair of worn gloves protruded from his hip pocket. 'I sometimes think the roots are growing faster than we can cut them. That salt spray is eating up the wires.'

'I want the long ear back in working order,' said Ode firmly. 'Can't you rig up something temporary – jumper cables or something?'

'We would have to run them down the corridors. That wouldn't fit the ship's blueprints.'

'Do it. I want this ship functioning on all systems. It doesn't have to be neat.'

Spools of insulated wire began to rattle around the ship. Contacts were closed. *Rorqual* began to see with more eyes and hear with more ears. The fore and aft brains shared their inputs again. Ode's report was sent to the CO.

The report bounced. Although five-toeds were officially

classified as extinct, or nearly so, this Benthic beast was clearly no fossil. Jelly-like blood is recent. The inner lining of the artery was still white – the tissue had not yet stained. Printouts on shore went to Drum and Wandee.

Drum toggled into the long-ear line and called Ode.

'So you finally got your communicator working.' Ode grinned. The view-screen showed Drum's new Sewer Service office near the Shipyards.

'We were waiting for you to repair yours,' said Drum. 'This isn't a social call, old friend. We are worried about you out there with that Benthic beast.'

'An interesting fossil. But you should see the fish, if you think those fish were big last time. Some of these are averaging over a pound – hardly planktonic.'

'It isn't a fossil.'

'Nonsense. The meteors can't bring back our ancestors. Why everyone knows—'

'It is not a fossil!' repeated Drum. 'Maybe they've been out there all along. anyway – they are dangerous.'

Whooop whooop whooop! The Benthic that crossed the scanners was not dead this time. It climbed up on the decks and stood dripping and naked – towering over the panic-stricken deck hands. The deck sensors felt the bare-foot contact. *Rorqual* shuddered. The crew fled, boots squeaking. Two men fell overboard. Others hid among the trees.

'Sharps Committee!' Ode shouted.

Only two Committeemen arrived in his cabin. They fumbled their keys into the weapons locker, but two of the keyholes were still empty. The door wouldn't budge.

'Defend the ship,' shouted the Captain. 'Use whatever means are available.'

The siren continued to rise and fall – bewailing the ship's fate. Even knives and forks were locked up. The reluctant squads that climbed back out on to the deck were carrying such non-weapons as drinking jugs, chairs, and heavy spools – useless. The beast hesitated – looking down on them – puzzled. Someone threw a four-inch bolt at him. It missed, but that clarified the situation in his mind. He lunged into the little Nebishes, kicking and flailing. Soon the decks were splattered with rose-water blood and five-toed footprints. Screams and cries of the injured filled the ship's ears.

Drum cursed his helplessness as he monitored the one-sided battle. The Benthic was not even wounded, yet he was disabling the entire ship's complement. Captain Ode was still tugging on the door to the weapons locker when the Benthic found him and threw him against the wall. The communicator's faithful sound reproductions transmitted the sickening thud. Drum winced.

The Benthic tracked red below decks until he found the frozen body of the other giant. This seemed to satisfy him. He wrapped it in netting and heavy tools. The decks were quiet when he jumped into the ship's wake with it.

Drum stood on the docks with two dozen White Teams. *Rorqual* nosed into her berth, hatches open. Rows of stretchers lined the foredeck. The walking wounded had tended the more seriously injured as best they could. The dead were on ice.

Drum went straight to the Captain's cabin. Ode was heavily sedated. He was alive and stabile, but had sustained multiple fractures of the pelvis and lower extremities, as well as several undisplaced rib fractures and a linear skull fracture.

'You've got to be more careful,' chided Drum.

Ode grinned out of his stupor, but said nothing. The Mediteck examined him and shook his head slowly. They tubed and wired the old Captain to keep him alive and moved him to the White Meck's cradle.

'What are his chances?'

The teck shook his head again: 'Almost every bone in his body is broken. Those below the waist are displaced. Looks like his bladder is leaking too. That urine will slough off any tissue it gets into. And if all those fractures soak up the blood they need for healing he won't have a drop left. I don't know what kept his pressure up this long.'

'Can't we do something?'

'Best we can do is freeze him – TS until we can mobilize

half the Clinic to work on him at once. It will be a long time before we can get around to that – unless his priority is raised.'

'But he's a captain—'

'Was a captain, you mean. He'll not sail again.'

A furious Drum stomped in on the Hive Committee meeting.

'Why does *Rorqual* have to remain neutral?' he demanded. 'We lost the whole crew to a creature the ship could have dispatched with one swat of its crane.'

The representative from Security, a fat compromising neuter, turned piggish eyes to him and spoke slowly, didactically: 'Your ship is equipped with the WIC/RAC genius circuit. I understand this enables it to survive in very hostile environments. However, we learned a long time ago that our genius machines must never be given the option of killing a hominid of any kind. It might discover a very logical reason to kill us all.'

Other Committeemen nodded. They pointed out that even the CO used a megajury of Citizens to execute capital offenders.

Drum sat down, mumbling: 'Then why send a crew at all? That ship could harvest pretty well on its own.'

'The *Rorqual Maru* must be manned at all times,' ordered the CO. 'She takes long voyages and gets lonely. To permit her to sail alone is to invite a commandeering by the Benthics.'

The teck from Synthe stood up.

'Plankton clouds are widespread. I'm certain we can plot a course that avoids areas controlled by the Benthic.'

'And,' said Wandee from Bio, 'we are working on the genes of a new prototype Citizen who will be able to fight the Benthics. A stronger, bigger Citizen – who will also fill the job requirements at the Shipyards.'

'Big enough to handle a Benthic with his bare hands?' asked Security.

Wandee nodded.

'Why – his body would be classified as a weapon. How could you ensure his loyalty?'

'Just as certain ants ensure the loyalty of their warriors. We'll design him so he can't feed himself.'

Drum was shocked. 'What do you mean – no oesophagus or no hands?'

Wandee smiled. 'Oh, nothing so crude. He won't even notice anything amiss. We'll delete one of his key metabolic pathways so he'll be dependent on a special diet that only the Hive can give him. Without it he'll sicken and die.'

Drum shuddered. Now he was sorry he had asked. A tied-off oesophagus could be corrected by a friendly Tinker. What could a poor warrior do about a defective enzyme system if he wanted to quit his job? Nothing.

'Here is a copy of the traits we hope to program into the genes of our warrior,' said Wandee, handing him a clipboard.

Drum glanced at the list. 'Sounds good, but will it walk?'

'Walk, run, swim – and fight,' said Wandee.

Drum was sceptical.

'How can you be so sure? Just a couple of years ago your Spinner couldn't construct a gene map for a simple marine protozoan. Now you think you can spin us a superman?'

The clipboard was passed around the table. The battle gear it listed was very impressive: heavy bone and muscle, a fast reflex time, high pain threshold, potent nerve-endocrine axis. None of the committee members really understood details of gene spinning. Wandee wanted to quiet Drum's objections without exposing the other complacent Nebishes at the table to a lot of new terms that might disturb them. Drum had an exceptional grasp of matters beyond his specialty, and more – he had an open mind. He was a Leo.

'Growing this prototype warrior is much simpler than the marine biota project. We do not have to build an entirely unknown gene. Human genes have been mapped many times, and about twenty percent of the map is pretty well understood. Enough for us to design certain broad traits we are interested in. We will use the known map of the most primitive human we have on file – Larry Dever – from before the Era of Karl. We still have some of his alpha renal nuclei in Suspension. By using his chromosomes – and deleting what we don't need – we have relatively few genes to actually assemble.'

'You are going to assemble a Larry Dever?' asked Drum.

'Modified. We'll grow an Augmented Renal Nucleus Of Larry Dever – an ARNOLD – with the traits listed.'

The chairman had dozed off. He awoke with a start. 'You two can continue this discussion down in the Spinner Labs. Meeting adjourned.'

7

A.R.N.O.L.D.

Warrior human being
Under Hive control—
Spinner made your genes.
Who made your soul?

Drum marvelled at Wandee's deft manipulations. The dividing renal cell was spilled into the sorting chamber, filling the screen with X- and V-shaped chromosomes. She selected those to be augmented. Wandee's electron pencil carved as she talked.

'We'll cut off half of these long arms at the secondary construction – a good landmark. Remove those little satellites, and take off the short arms from this chromosome. Careful of that centromere. There, now – plenty of room for adding the synthetic chromatides from Spinner's bath.'

The bath (a soup of purines and pyrimidines) contained the enzyme reverse transcriptase – the RNA-dependent DNA polymerase. (RNA molecules act as templates for the replications of DNA genes.) Spinner assembled the RNA template. When added to the soup, a DNA gene replicated; each grouping of three bases formed one codon (or letter) in the genetic message.

'This appears to be an excessive amount of the Grube-Hill gene,' suggested Drum. He had been studying Spinner's screen where the molecular activity was being simulated. The normals were indicated in the grid.

'A triple dose of gristle.' Wandee smiled. 'Our ARNOLDs will be real mechanised armour bucks with triple calcium, collagen, phospathase, and growth hormone.'

'But what is this sequence?' Drum frowned. 'It does not translate.'

'That is the Hive safety factor – a nonsense sequence where the gene locus for an amino-acid synthesis should be. Those bases have been scrambled to UAA, UAG and UGA, which do not translate at all. The ARNOLDs will be unable to synthesize six of the amino acids that other humans can manufacture from the inorganic constituents in their food. You or I have the molecular machinery to assemble them. For the ARNOLDs they will be "essential" – that is, required in the diet. In addition to the nine amino acids we all need in our diet, the ARNOLDs will need alanine, aspartate, glutamate, glycine, serine, and tyrosine. They will be dependent on a fifteen-amino-acid diet. Without it their entire protein metabolism will stop. The absence of just one "essential" amino acid will cause them to sicken and die.'

Drum was silent. He felt uneasy about this new Leo assignment – building a synthetic human who would lay down his life for the Hive, and, at the same time, shackling him with this molecular time-bomb that would kill him if his loyalty strayed. Drum felt himself to be more of an enemy to ARNOLD than the Benthic beast.

A codon GAG was scrambled to CAC, substituting the histidine letter for a glutamine – another nonsense sequence closing the transaminase 'back door' to one of the amino acids: ARNOLD would not be able to get his amino acids from his Kreb's cycle by adding an amino group to an organic acid.

Playing with the Watson-Crick structures was tedious work, but soon Wandee had several clones working on the prototype ARNOLD DNA.

'We can sort the cells out of culture on the heals of their Grube-Hill content. Those with the most phosphatase will fluoresce the brightest with this labelled substrate. We'll embryonate about a thousand of the triple-GH's on the first go-round.'

'A thousand' mumbled Drum, thinking of the list of traits

on her clipboard. 'That should put the Hive in a pretty strong position – for a change.'

Benthics crowded around the funeral raft. Tangled girders and crusted plates were the tapestries for Listener's eulogy. They were gathered in the far bubble of a torn tubeway overlooking the yawning blackness of the abyss. The weighted body drifted for a long moment. Then it began to sink slowly, accompanied by a halo of zooplankton fighting over its nitrogen treasures.

'The Leviathan is not a whale?' asked Listener.

Clam shook his head. 'It is a ship. I was all over her insides and saw no sign of organs or muscles – just machinery and rooms.'

Larry tried to clear up the confusion.

'Trilobite thinks this ship is his deity, *Rorqual*, but he has been unable to talk to her since the Hive has taken her over.'

Listener bowed his head reverently. 'When a god comes to Earth it is a pure spirit. It may inhabit the body of a man or an animal – or a ship. It is written.'

Larry opened his mouth to object to this primitive display of superstition, but Big Har interrupted him.

'The deity brought life to the sea. Let us offer homage to *Rorqual*.'

Silence followed. Larry hesitated to break it. Listener continued to question Clam: 'This ship – it showed signs of life after you disabled the crew?'

'Yes. It opened doors for me and followed me with little eyes in the walls. I heard and felt things I did not understand, but I'm certain it knew I was there.'

'And it didn't try to harm you—' Listener smiled. 'Wonderful! That proves that *Rorqual* – or Leviathan – is a friendly god.'

'But it killed my friend Limpet,' objected Clam. 'We were gathering shellfish at fifteen fathoms when the nets caught him and pulled him up. He died of the pops.'

'Perhaps that was an accident,' suggested Listener. 'Surface-dwellers, even gods, might not know of the pops. That is a secret of the Deep Cult. I think we should try to contact this god and pay her homage. Perhaps we can learn to talk to her.'

Opal nodded. 'She might be able to protect us from the Hive.'

Even Larry agreed with that suggestion. Trilobite's deity could only increase the Benthics' chances for survival – if her Hive loyalty wasn't too strong.

The Benthics passed the word along the shelf. 'Worship the Leviathan.'

But the Hive crews avoided Benthic zones. Manual over-rides took the plankton Harvester wide of the rich shelf fields. Harvests were scanty, but the ship was safe – safe and deaf and dumb as well, for Nebishes toggled her long ear. Benthics enjoyed years of peace and plenty.

Bio entered a plush period of increased floor space and personnel. Wandee hovered over the foaming nutrients and plated the placental matrix with the first hundred cells that showed chrionic tendencies (villi and gonadotophins). Soon the embryos were visible under the magnifier.

Wandee seemed pleased. 'Size and length of tail are good indexes of vigour at this stage. But I like to rely on the Organ of Zuckerkandl – the pigmented nerve tissue near the inferior mesenteric artery. It is a good index of the genetic neurohomoral axis: autonomic zone, size of sex organs, adrenal-medullary function, and psychosexual profile.'

Drum nodded. 'The O of Z is probably important but how many toes?'

'Oh, they'll all be five-toed, of course.'

Twenty thick-necked, hairy infants survived Wandee's critical culling. These were tested repeatedly and the six most vigorous were assigned to the Hive Mullah for conditioning. The rest went to Shipyard nurseries with the Lesser Arnolds.

Baby ARNOLD recognised the Security Squad when they boxed him in and marched him off to the Committee ante-room. He smiled, blinked, and tried to chat; but they were dull-witted and obedient guards. They stood at the exits and awaited further orders.

The scene at the conference table was more heated than usual.

'I say we must return him to the protein pool. He has come across sensitive information. Hive security is at stake.' The voice was the routine drone of a Security Captain demanding that all possible problems be eliminated as quickly and as cheaply as possible.

Drum stood up and objected strongly: 'This is a Greater Arnold you are talking about – the product of months of embryonating and years of tutoring. He is nearly five years old. We can't afford to junk him now.'

'It is always a pleasure to hear from you, Drum,' said the Chairman. 'Your words about cost and time investments are right to the point. Anyone else?'

'We have two dozen ARNOLDS,' muttered Security.

'Twenty,' corrected Drum, 'but only six are in my conditioning programme.'

The Chairman smiled at the off-the-record exchange. He glanced around at the circle of blank faces. Few of the members were interested.

'Well, then, let's call the first witness.'

'Syntheteck Stewart!'

The hesitant male, puberty-plus-three, did not know why he had been called. He stayed close to the door, wringing his hands.

'Come on in, lad.' The chairman smiled. 'We aren't going to hurt you. Sit down. See that face on the screen? Have you ever seen him before?'

Silence.

'Relax. Watch this sequence taken at the stacks. The time is three months ago. You were studying for your new job, moving up-caste. Remember?'

Stewart's face showed recognition, then fear. 'I didn't know about the fifteen-amino-acid bread, really I didn't,' he pleaded.

'I was just trying to memorize their various motilities in a charged field when one of the other students came up and looked over my shoulder. He showed me how to remember it – a mnemonic – a memory tool.'

'Motilities?' asked the Chairman.

'The fifteen amino acids. They each move at a different speed when an electric charge is placed on a mixed solution. Each molecule has a characteristic speed in relation to the other molecules. That is how we separate them from the fifteen-amino-acid bread.'

Chairman nodded. 'And you showed this chart of relative speeds to an ARNOLD?'

Drum felt drained. If the ARNOLD could manufacture his own bread... The thought frightened him.

'No!' blurted Stewart. 'I mean, I didn't know he was an ARNOLD. He just glanced at the list for a moment and made up two sentences that helped me memorize the sequences. That's all.'

'You didn't discuss the significance of the list?'

'No! I wasn't even sure myself. It was my first day in the bakery section. They didn't tell me what was classified.'

The Committee members mumbled among themselves.

'Dismissed.'

After Stewart left, Drum stood up for one last plea. 'I know it looks bad, but why don't we ask ARNOLD what he remembers about the episode? I know he is bright, but I doubt that he even knows of fifteen-amino-acid bread. It isn't labelled, you know. We can use the T-probe. He can't hide anything from us.'

The Chairman smiled vacantly.

'Consider the cost,' repeated Drum. 'We have too much invested in those muscles. I hope we didn't raise him for his food value. He would dress out at about fifty pounds – very lean. Arnoldburgers would be the most expensive protein the Hive ever produced.'

The chairman nodded. 'Focus the T-probe on that chair and invite him in for questioning.'

Baby ARNOLD sat on the edge of his chair smiling openly

at the circle of bland faces. He watched a replay of optic records taken in the stacks.

'Remember Stewart?'

'Oh, sure,' said ARNOLD. 'He was having a study problem – memory block. He was pushing too hard. I guess he hasn't learned to relax yet.'

'You can relax?'

The child nodded rapidly.

Drum pointed to the probe. It remained in the T-zone. He was telling the truth.

'What do you remember? Which subject was Stewart having trouble with?'

ARNOLD just shrugged. The screen displayed a series of letters: H L G A V I S ... LTMGPTAT ... ARNOLD's lips moved silently. A thought frown puckered his forehead. 'Yes – now I remember!'

Drum exhaled noisily.

ARNOLD recited: 'Hive leptosouls give virgins instant sex. Leptosoul trips make going pubertal tiring and trying.'

The screen picked up his voice and printed out the first letter of each word – H L G A V I S ... LTMGPTAT. A red 'emergency light' blinked after the last letter, indicating that the series was classified.

'What does it mean?' asked the Chairman sternly.

ARNOLD shrugged. 'I'd have to see the original list of words again. All I looked at were the first letters. That's all you need for a memory crutch. I like making up mnemonics. If you want to know what the words were, you could ask Stew. He probably remembers. It was a subject I have not studied, I'm afraid.'

'T-zone,' said Drum encouragingly. 'Can he be excused?'

Chairman nodded. 'No sense going into it any more deeply while he is here. Dismissed!'

'He has the classified sequence in his brain. It is only a matter of time before—'

Drum interrupted. 'But we're talking about a baby! He can't just set up a clandestine Bio Lab—'

'He's an ARNOLD, and he's almost five years old,' said

Security. 'Look at the screen. He has the motility sequences of the fifteen amino acids. All he needs are the services of a Bioteck and some basic electrophoretic and chromatography gear.'

Drum stood silently while the screen filled in the blanks after the letters:

HLGAVIS/LTMGPTAT: HISTIDINE, LYSINE, CLYCINE, ALANINE, VALINE, ISOLEUCINE, SERINE, LEUCINE, THRENINE, METHIONINE, GLUTAMATE, PHENYLANINE, TYRONSINE, ASPARTATE, TRYPTO-PHANE

'Note how the two "T" amino acids "tyrosine" and "tryptophane" were sound-coded as "tiring" and "trying" so they'd be easier to remember,' said Security.

'But he told the truth,' said Drum. 'He doesn't know the significance.'

'Yet...' added Security ominously.

'Lets take a vote,' interrupted the Chairman. 'All in favour of chucking him?... All opposed? Looks like a tie vote. I'll have to break it.' He glanced around the table. 'In view of the cost of an ARNOLD I can't return him to the protein pool – just yet. But to protect the Hive, he must wear chains while he is inside a city. Chains! Neck, waist, ankles, wrists.'

Big Har and Opal took their family on a mussel hunt. Using a sight line given by the Deep Cult, Clam swam out ahead, toward the island landmark on the horizon. Har peered down: distant blackness – open ocean.

'Might as well be bottomless. I can't see a thing.'

Opal checked the sun angle. 'We haven't been swimming long enough yet. We should sight a broken tubeway first.'

Young Cod and sister White Belly trailed behind, frolicking. Both showed the pigmentation of the new generation of Benthics – back freckles from more surface exposure time during the day. White Belly's two-toned skin gave her her name.

'There it is!' shouted Clam.

The tubeway was scummy and opaque. All they saw was

clouds of tiny shrimp and shiners. There was no evidence that the sessile food chain had re-established itself.

'The reefs begin about five minutes from here,' said Opal. Cod and White Belly raced to catch Clam. They splashed a quarter of a mile and dived. Opal joined them while Har struggled with the string of gourd floats. The anchor rope tangled several times, but he finally let out ten fathoms. It snagged bottom. He dived, pulling himself down the rope about thirty feet. His family passed him on their way to the surface. He bobbed up and helped them tie their belt sacks to the floats. The catch of bivalves threatened to sink the gourds.

'I'd better eat a few,' said Opal, reaching into her sack. She floated on her back, small breasts set wide and pointed. Placing a bivalve on the muscle bulge over her sternum she struck it as her cracking stone. Three stout blows – chipping and loud. Flavourful white meat oozed from the damaged shell. She pulled it out with her teeth, sharing with Har. White Belly tried to imitate her mother but only managed to bruise herself. Clam began cracking mussels and feeding his siblings.

They ate, harvested, and ate some more. Opal ate her fill and dozed on her back while the youngsters continued nibbling and exploring the bountiful reef. One by one they stopped diving and napped in the gentle waves. Big Har circled the group to herd them together, but that proved unnecessary. They instinctively stayed close, using slight hand movements, while they slept. At dusk they returned to their archipelago.

Young ARNOLD buckled on his harness while the workmen loaded his two-wheel cart. His supervisor handed him a thick crust of fifteen-amino-acid bread. He leaned into the straps. Wheels creaked. It was a two-hour run to the top of the Spiral.

Citizens were already lined up at the Dispenser when he arrived. The pressure had fallen again, and they would have to go down to shaft-base for their calorie-basic if it weren't for ARNOLD's training runs.

'Good time, ARNOLD,' said the workman who had ridden

in the cart. He climbed down and handed ARNOLD a yellow-four sour to cut the thick mucus from his throat.

ARNOLD squatted in his harness, chewing his treat. He was only six years old, but was already the size of an average Citizen. His powerful calf muscles tingled after the workout. Soon he would be trained to work in the Shipyards, they told him. The work was important – clearing away debris. He was a very bright ARNOLD. He understood everything very fast. His mentors hardly ever had to use the whip – anymore.

That night he slept under his car at the loading docks. He had lots of room to stretch out. The workers on the shift made hardly any noise at all. His new chains were comfortable – long and light, a new alloy. Supervisors handed him his bread six times a day. His diet was generous. He grew fast.

Drum sat on the edge of the wagon and offered ARNOLD an orange-three sweet bar.

'All of us are Reincarnationists. You know what that means, don't you?'

ARNOLD grinned and recited: 'We believe in the trans-migration of the soul. Our souls lived in other bodies, even in non-human creatures, before inhabiting our present ones.'

'That is correct,' said Drum, speaking slowly. 'We go to Chapel and try to feel some experience from a previous life. We try to understand ourselves better – to become better Citizens. Would you like to do that?'

ARNOLD nodded.

'You may find that you weren't always a draft animal,' said Drum.

ARNOLD's grin was a little vacant. He did not understand what Drum meant.

An appointment was made with Mullah.

ARNOLD appeared at Chapel with Drum at his elbow. He was almost two feet taller than the average Citizen. His chains went *ching, ching, ching*, as he walked down the aisle. The walls of the nave were decorated with the Darwinian Transmigration: protozoa, metazoa, lover invertebrates, higher animals and finally the ultimate Hive creatures – the four-toed Nebish. Drum studied several paintings and noticed an obvious lack of details. Phylum characteristics were largely ignored by the artist, who stressed eyes or eyespots primarily, as if the creature's viewpoint were more important than its identity.

The robed Mullah directed ARNOLD to put down his chains and stretch out on the altar – a heavily telemetered couch. The links clattered noisily to the floor. Four Meditecks tubed and wired him to the sensory tape machine for a review of his phylogenetic tradition – his leptosoul.

'First, we will try to establish a common sensory language between the tapes and ARNOLD's subconscious,' drugs and midbrain trickle current suppressed consciousness.

'It will take several sessions before leptosoul imagery is clear. The symbols we start with are basic: itch, thirst, hunger, fatigue, and the sex drive – things the medulla can understand. Itch is useful for localizing a sensory message. It is superior to pain or temperature for leptosoul purposes, because an itch stimulates you to do something. Pain often does nothing more than trigger the spinal reflex of withdrawal. Higher centres aren't involved. The itch gets you to scratch – a complex motor response. Notice how his encephalogram registers this itch – a peripheral sensation of ants crawling on the skin – formication. See how it can be moved around his sensory cortex to correspond to various points on his anatomy.'

After a brief rest period the alpha rhythm returned. Then Drum watched the tape machine torture ARNOLD with thirst – probably one of the oldest phylogenetic memories, dating back to the period when life forms left the seas. Hypertonic solutions bathed key vessel nerve endings, making him physiologically thirsty. Neurological thirst triggered by a sonic finger probing into the thirst centre of the brain stem. Optic images brought psychological thirst – skeletons, dry leaves, dust devils whirling against a desert mirage. Physical reinforcement was added with skin heat and a throat itch. Four types of stimulation produced a convincing image of thirst – four-dimensional thirst. ARNOLD writhed and suffered. The tape machine waited until all the indicators had moved into the red zone. Then it rewarded him with withdrawal of the four-dimensional stimuli. The water was wide, deep, and cool. Ice chips filled his mouth and hypotonic fluids flooded his stomach.

Mullah was pleased.

Another rest period to allow the brainwaves a moment to stabilise.

'Hunger is a bit dangerous,' warned Mullah. 'Part of the physiological stimulation is hypoglycaemia. When we drop the blood glucose below forty milligrams we occasionally lose a Citizen or two: brain damage during the convulsions. Here we go for the four steps: physical – tubes empty the stomach; neural – sonic stimulation of the medullar "hunger centre"; physio – insulin drops the blood sugar to create cell hunger; and psych – images of skeletons with an itch in the mouth and stomach. Four-dimensional hunger.'

ARNOLD wanted to stuff meat pies and sponge cakes into his mouth.

'We usually end all hunger sequences with the hand of the Hive bringing pies and cakes,' explained Mullah. 'It can't do any harm, and it may increase Hive loyalty.'

Drum agreed.

'Sex is an important warrior drive. We use it for imprinting and motivating other lesser drives.'

'But ARNOLD is not pubertal.'

'No matter. We can program a variety of encounters that are sexual enough for imprinting – basal ganglia respond to stimulation of the "sex centre" at any age. Genital itch and conquest imagery is all we need. A mature male is the best engineered warrior in terms of muscle and bone. ARNOLD will have his testosterone before he goes into battle.'

Fatigue was the last orientation tape. The itch was a bright red asterisk behind the eyelids, and neural stimuli induced alpha waves.

'That appeared to be a fruitful session,' said Drum.

'It isn't over,' said Mullah. 'We can move on now to test his reaction to organised, sequential stimuli. The tapes will now move from language to communication of experiences. He can be shown things and be an observer. That is easy. But can we get his subconscious to actually enter the presented scene and be a living part of it?'

Drum glanced at the sleeping giant. 'What will we start with?'

'One of our childhood fantasies. By imitating cognitive steps an infant goes through we can get him to live the tapes.'

Drum picked up a helmet terminal and shared ARNOLD's visual and auditory inputs.

LEPTOSOUL: CRAYON CREATURES

Click! The waxy pigment formed a circle with dots for eyes and a line mouth. Legs attached at the neck and arms replaced ears – a human head-creature. Above, on the same coarse construction paper, more crayon lines appeared: a small blue head with a beak and wings for ears – a bird. ARNOLD's viewpoint remained off the paper as trees, flowers, and assorted insects appeared. All were simple circles, identifying detail kept at a minimum. He relaxed. His 'eye' moved closer to the paper. A bee moved along, leaving a string of Zs. This grew to an audible buzz. A butterfly flitted from flower to flower, followed by its shadow. Gradually the scene came to life – simple paper cut-outs at first – but colour, sound, and odour followed the cartoon-like movements.

He saw his own face on the head-creature. His feet felt the grass under the creature. As the creature walked ARNOLD felt the movements in his own legs. He stepped on warm dust, cool grass, and a hard granular stone. A paper cloud passed overhead and he felt the breeze on his face. The tree flexed into three dimensions, with coarse bark and falling leaves. ARNOLD was clearly inside the creature now, seeing, smelling, walking and feeling was the crayon drawing sensed.

Click! END OF TAPE

NEW LEPTOSOUL: DADDY LONGLEGS

Click! ARNOLD glanced around the hollow head he inhabited – wires, pulleys, scopes, speakers, and earphones. He was not in a living creature. It was a prop, an artificial head-creature. He pressed his eyes against the optics and peered around. His cabin-like 'head' hung from eight arched legs – four coordinated pairs. The second pair waved overhead like antennae. The other six found support on a variety of greenish struts and beams – the scaffolding of magnified grass. As he moved, his antennae-legs picked up odours and textures from musty soil, sweet flowers, and bitter stem juice. Walking went awkwardly until he found the small aromatic pool of purple fluid. Flexing his legs, he lowered his face to the pool, drank, and felt intoxicated. Walking went smoothly then. ARNOLD had eight obedient legs. He ran up and down high swaying stalks. One of this legs became the web-organ. Spinnerets laid out a stout line, which he cast about, tying flowers to blades of grass. He laid out a high, swaying footbridge and crossed from one flower to another. Nectar and pollen filled his mouth. A fat insect fluttered by slowly. He cast out his web and reeled it in. The wing muscles tasted rich and meaty.

Fear! The silhouette of a praying mantis sent ARNOLD scampering for cover. His muscles ached with the thought of a futile struggle in those vice-like forearms. His skin crawled with phantom teeth marks. When the danger passed, ARNOLD resumed his play. Click!

'That was pleasant enough.' Drum smiled as he removed his sensory helmet. 'Very nice! And it appears that ARNOLD enjoyed it too. Look at those indicators!'

Mullah nodded.

'Since he is to be a warrior, we might as well offer him a little vivid imagery to take home with him.'

LIPTOSOUL: ROOSTER

Click! ARNOLD perched on a low fir limb, reigning over beautiful, speckled Frost Grey hens. They scratched and pecked in musty humus. He smelled aromatic pine needles and saw glistening grubs. The power of his spur stubs made him cock of the knoll. The day before he had knocked a great yellow cat from this very limb. His sex urge pulled him from his perch. He swooped down on a pretty little hen and grabbed her by the short feathers. She squawked and struggled, but he pinned her to the ground, copulated, and strutted off with a cavalier air. Flustered, she preened her disarray. Crowing, he returned to his perch. Click!

The leptosoul experience puzzled young ARNOLD. Residual euphoria left him with the desire to crow. As he gathered up his chains he stared at the links for a long time. They seemed out of place now that he had relived part of his regal background. He, ARNOLD, had been a king: a feathered warrior, a game fowl.

Drum noticed the sadness in the young giant's eyes as he locked the heavy bracelets. 'Be a good boy and return to your loading dock. Here's a green-one sweet.'

After the giant left, Drum turned to Mullah.

'That leptosoul must have been to hard on the boy. I'd better review the next ones you have planned.'

'They are all pretty potent. I'd advise you to take a two-dimensional exposure – skip the neural and physiological tracks.'

'OK. What have you got?'

'We were going to give him the Flint and the Tapeworm leptosoul – a Stone Age conflict.'

Drum climbed up on the alter-couch. The Medimecks only used about half the hookups. His consciousness would remain to protect him.

LEPTOSOUL: FLINT AND TAPEWORMS

Click! Drum blinked at his gnarled hands – dark and calloused. His campfire glowed and popped sparks as he turned the spear shaft. Rawhide puckered in the heat: the lock-tied bindings that held the flint blade. He glanced out over the fog of Cattail Meadow. Another fire blinked back at him – a single yellow eye in the darkness. Drum knew that Running Elk sat by the fire preparing his spear. Dawn would bring the contest to see who lived at Cattail.

His nose wrinkled as the rawhide charred. He lifted his spear and rubbed wax berries over the hot bindings. Continuing down the shaft with the stain, he finger-painted prayer symbols – drawings that would be incomplete until he added the blood of his enemy. He crushed more berries and circled his eyes with blue. Four blue lines on each shoulder, and his totem was complete – Blue Owl would hold his lance high. A gnawing in his belly was ignored by the neolithic, but a bit of Drum's mind surfaced to recognize the pain as *D. Latum*, the fish tapeworm. Too long had he wandered the Salmon River. It was time to settle.

His mate walked out of the darkness and threw aromatic leaves on the fire. Her eyes begged him to avoid the conflict. Drum-Blue Owl felt the hardness of his own expression as he shamed her into more prayers and less tears. Her belly grew with their child – a son, he had been assured by their shaman. It had cost him two arms of dried fish, but it was worth it to know of the male child. He knew it was time to settle. A son needed land. The tapes would weaken a child if he roamed the river, and a warrior can't afford to be weak.

Sunrise brought the three chiefs to witness. They entered majestically, robed and feathered, and rode to their vantage to judge the conflict. Drum-Blue Owl tested his spear point against a mossy log, then mounted White Pony and kneed her carefully to the crest of the knoll. He held his lance high. The fog lifted and he studied his prize – the meadow – rolling green brimmed with cottonwoods, a two-pony stream, fish, game, and good soil for growing tame plants.

Running Elk appeared, riding a restless calico. He was a leaner, younger buck. Drum-Blue Owl felt that he had more shoulder meat than his opponent. He smiled. The tape gnawed at his belly again. If Running Elk saw the Blue Owl was the larger, he did not indicate it by his posture, although it was no disgrace to back down from a dwelling contest. There would be other meadows and other seasons. The river was not a bad place.

The calico started to trot towards him. Drum-Blue Owl held his flint blade high as he guided White Pony down the slope.

They closed at a gallop. Drum-Blue Owl kept his blade up, planning to drop it at the last instant – going for the eye. They would pass with left sides together. Instinct told him where his point was, so he only had to watch his opponent's lance. He bunched up the muscles in his left forearm to take the blow. The shafts came down on the left sides of the ponies' heads as they passed. The jolt bruised his right hand and right armpit where the butt of his lance jumped. His left forearm felt raw and broken. But his legs held firm. He was still mounted. Kneeing White Pony around he looked for Running Elk.

The calico wandered aimlessly with the young buck belly-down on its neck, lance dragging. Drum-Blue Owl glanced up at his flint and saw that his prayer symbols were completed. Hair covered the blade and red blood trickled down the shaft, filling in the drawings. Drum-Blue Owl circled the meadow confidently; his opponent slumped and retched. He saw a strip of white skull glistening through Running Elk's lacerated scalp. A hairy flap hung down over his eyes as gobbets of blood splattered the calico.

Drum-Blue Owl tore his loincloth and wrapped his left forearm. The sun climbed higher. His tongue dried and his belly ached. The tapes weakened him. He sat tall and straight, watching his opponent's deep irregular breathing.

Unexpectedly Running Elk let out a whoop and charged a second time. Drum-Blue Owl watched the frantic approach. If the young buck wanted to die here on the meadow he would accommodate him. He heeled White Pony into a trot. His opponent's face was hidden by the gory mask of dangling scalp. Too late he saw the beady, calculating eyes. He tried to swing his flint to bear. Hooves threw sod. The impact snapped a lance. Running Elk toppled over the calico's rump and lay crumpled in the grass, the broken lance butt by his side. Drum-Blue Owl glanced up at his own flint – no new blood; no new pain.

Running Elk stood up slowly, feet wide apart, arms folded. Drum-Blue Owl glanced at the three chiefs. Surely they would not allow this young buck to stand against a mounted and armed warrior! He gestured with his spear: 'Leave my dwelling place.' The downed warrior brushed his bloody scalp back from his eyes and stared quizzically. Chiefs sat stoically. Odd. Drum's lance grew heavy and tapes gnawed at his belly. He didn't have all day. If Running Elk wished to die, that was his decision. Drum lowered his lance to charge, but White Pony wandered and nibbled grass. Cursing, Drum tried to knee her around. The pony ignored him. One of the chiefs dismounted. He saw his own pregnant mate running down the slope.

The landscape tilted and dumped him into the grass. Matted green blocked his vision. His mate lifted his head into her lap. She was gentle.

Drum wanted to cry out when he saw the thick splintered shaft of Running Elk's lance protruding from his chest, but the sullen neolithic mind of Blue Owl just accepted it. With a heavy right hand he patted his mate's belly. Drum tried to warn her to cook the fish when she roamed the river to protect herself from *D. latum*, but the only words he could get past the Stone Age lips were: 'Teach my son to hold his lance high.' Click!

The Mullah shook Drum's shoulder. 'Citizen Drum, are you back with us?'

Drum shook his head. 'That was painful trip. I can still feel those tapeworms.'

'The gastric mucosa is probably eroded a little. Have a green-four mint to settle your stomach. What did you think of our Flint and Tapeworms?'

Drum frowned. 'That's not for ARNOLD, I'm afraid.'

Mullah agreed: 'True. There are probably too many old clichés in it – motherhood, mates, valour in defence of the nest – trite themes. Too simplistic!'

Drum swallowed hard. His stomach felt tight.

Mullah continued: 'I liked those tapes for their sensory content, but I'm afraid they would strain even ARNOLD's intelligence. Neolithic conflicts were fine in the Stone Age, but we are asking him to defend the Hive, where such problems as the Cattail contest would be solved by simply removing the birth permits from the two warriors. No infants: no reason to fight over the meadow. They could live in peace and share the hunting and fishing – as long as they had population control.'

'Like the Hive,' said Drum.

Mullah nodded and took out a stack of leptosoul outlines. 'This is ARNOLD's series. We will use Daddy Longlegs to give him coordination to run *Rorqual*'s fighting cranes. The Capon and Fighting Cock sequences will give him confidence.'

Drum relaxed. 'Yes. Stay on a lower vertebrate level – away from hominids.'

'We'll keep his reflex training as simple as we can. The less philosophizing he does the better.'

ARNOLD was sent to the Shipyards to grow muscle and to learn *Rorqual*'s anatomy from old hulks.

CAPON LEPTOSOUL

Click! Capon ARNOLD roosted with other fat-bottomed neuter birds – neither cock nor hen. Each had his own generous mush cup and water. ARNOLD was restless. His soul remembered when food had texture and hens were speckled. His capon gonads were limp, swollen, and steroid-numb. He tried to stir up his roostmates by shouldering them away from their mush and eating it himself. They wouldn't fight. They hung their heads. He gained weight rapidly and invited an early axe. Click! END OF TAPE.

NEW LEPTOSOUL: BATTLECOCK

Click! Battlecock ARNOLD was all testicular valour and iron spur. His days of secret training in the keep had hardened his muscle and strengthened his wind. A hundred times a day he had been tossed by the hand. Each time he flew back to his windowsill to look out over his hen yard. His diet removed excess water and fat from his body: twelve kernels of corn, chopped cooked meat, chopped lettuce, wheatgerm, honey, and peanut butter. When his irons were tied over his spurs he knew someone would die. Odours of blood, tobacco, and whiskey told him that other hands were there with their cocks.

He rested comfortably in his handler's arms until fight time. He was placed in the pit with a Claret. Twice they went up and locked iron into meat. Each time they were tenderly disengaged and placed back in the pit. Fresh air came in through a long bone fracture. During the third pitting he took some iron in the skull and his vision clouded. He couldn't see the Claret, so he waited after the hand released his tail feather. When the Claret attacked he felt the air from its wings. He knew just where it was.

ARNOLD went up, striking out with his spurs. He felt the Claret's needlepoints in his belly and left wing. Then his tardy iron crunched cartilage and diced the heart. After they were disengaged this time he was held in the arm and petted by the hand. He heard the Claret's last coughs.

The hens were his. After his injuries healed he was brood cock – under wire – with three of the most feminine Frost Grey hens. The big hen tried to shoulder him away from the water, but he gave her a resounding peck. He was King. He would see that all three sat on handsome clutches of eggs.

One morning the wind carried a faint answer to his crowing. There was another cock on the far side of the ridge. He couldn't wait for the chicken wire to be lifted.

'This wire is the only thing that is keeping you alive,' mumbled ARNOLD.

Mullah smiled confidently. 'Wonderful! Notice how real these leptosoul experiences have become for him. He is ARNOLD the battlecock now. His subconscious considers these taped dreams to be more significant than the dull routine of his Hive existence.'

'I suppose they are,' said Drum. 'They have more psychic strength – more sensory input – more trauma.'

Drum studied the feedbacks to see if ARNOLD was showing maximum response. There was room for improvement. 'Let's step up the intensity next time. We'll run through these tapes with a higher energy level – enhance the axe pain at the end of the Capon sequence, build up the euphoria and sexual rewards after the battlecock win.'

'...and the crayon creatures,' added Mullah.

Drum frowned. 'Crayon creatures? That is just childhood fantasy. Why use them now?'

Mullah just stacked the tapes back in the rack and smiled knowingly. 'There is more to it than that. Actually the "purple slurp" is a very important trigger for the post-hypnotic suggestion. We've programmed the ARNOLDs to go into attack mode with it – a combination of simple childhood memories and adult sexual stimulation. Very effective.'

Drum just looked puzzled.

'It's the Daddy Longlegs coordination we need to operate *Rorqual*'s manual overrides in battle. The ARNOLD can be triggered to revert to his old leptosoul on command. The "purple slurp" is that command.'

'Do you mean that he is programmed to become *Rorqual*'s brains?' asked Drum. 'He'll revert to one of his prior leptosouls and fight a battle using the ship as his weapon?'

'If necessary...'

Drum sat down, shaking his head slowly. 'First we program his genes. Now we program his soul.' He took out his gold emblem and sighed. This Leo assignment had drained him. The Hive's issuance of his prostheses had given him a second chance at life, but after ten years the extension was running out. His teeth were working well and the vigorous chewing of all the fibre food in his new diet gave him a jaw. Walking had toughened his legs, seating the metalloid joint firmly in the hip bones. His body was stronger, almost younger; but emotionally he was still aging. 'When does ARNOLD sail?'

'Soon. Perhaps on his eleventh birthday. His testosterone levels are high enough. Bones are mature. He'll be ready.'

'Yes. I'm sure he'll do fine.'

A sullen Clam stalked on South Reef, warm body tickling sensors. His presence activated ancient circuits, and fields of waving, man-sized umbrellas welcomed him. He swam towards Leviathan's new trawling lane, pausing at two-fathom umbrellas to fill his lungs. Ahead of him the reef sprang to life. Meck

147

pumps filled the umbrella airpockets. Snap electrolysis spiked the air with oxygen. Clouds of marine zooplankton and overflow bubbles rose from the writhing shapes – cyber barnacles that had survived the twenty-seven centuries to serve the rare fugitive Benthic.

Clam waited at the edge of the reef. Behind him the umbrellas quieted. He watched the surface overhead. A dark sky spat big drops into the choppy water. Leviathan's whale shape approached, trailing nets. Clam left his air pocket and grabbed the fine mesh netting; in a moment he was on the rain-spattered deck. His boarding caused no pandemonium this time. A well-drilled crew responded to the siren with a regular cadence of squeaking boots. Rows of Nebishes lined up, carrying shoulder-high netting – walking fences. Clam recognized the threat and leaped up on the cabin roof.

Thunder rolled. Hump palms rustled in the wind. ARNOLD stepped out of the foliage and studied the Benthic, a hundred yards away across the rows of tangle-foot netting. Clam was dark-skinned and naked, a six-foot giant like himself. ARNOLD wore standard coveralls with a wide, studded belt. His big bare feet made flat slapping sounds like Clam's.

'Hello!' shouted Clam, waving.

ARNOLD silently motioned for the nets to be lowered. He advanced slowly across the wet mesh. Clam glanced around for a possible attack from behind. The nose of the ship had no visible hatch. Beyond the hump one of the cranes worked casually on heavy plankton netting. Only the deck crew and ARNOLD seemed aware of his presence.

'I can permit you to live,' offered Clam, 'if you give me this ship.'

ARNOLD stopped.

'GIVE ME THIS SHIP!'

A cock crowed in ARNOLD's subconscious, and he sprinted across sixty yards of open deck, leaping with teeth and nails bared. Clam couldn't believe the fury of the attack – kicking, biting, scratching. They tumbled down on the foredeck. ARNOLD's teeth crunched deep into Clam's left forearm. A wave carried them off the nose of the ship and a huge maw sucked them into the rakes. ARNOLD's fingers gouged at his face and then closed tightly on this throat. Clam writhed into an oozy green mound, losing his footing. Nebish netters draped the pair with sticky tanglefoot mesh. Clam clawed at the choking fingers as his senses clouded. The tunnel vision frightened him. He found ARNOLD's middle finger and quickly bent it back, breaking it with a snap. He clung to the stump, twisting it hard. ARNOLD's grip slipped. Clam vaulted back into the sea, dragging the netting and three drowning Nebishes.

Drum wheezed as he patted ARNOLD's forearm. A banjo splint held the damaged finger along with all four fingers in a fan-like configuration.

'Good warrior. You did well. You are only eleven years old and you defeated the Benthic beast. *Rorqual*'s playbacks identified it as the same one who struck down Captain Ode a dozen years ago. It is older and wiser now, yet you saved the ship. The sea is now open to the Hive. We can trawl anywhere on the shelf.'

ARNOLD smiled and nodded. He accepted the accolades and returned to the Shipyards for a little one-armed shore duty. When his injuries healed he'd captain again.

Drum carried the battle records down to the Chapel.

'He let the Benthic get away. We'll have to step up his battle conditioning. Use that heavy tape – Dan with the Golden Tooth. We have six weeks until he sails again.'

Mullah programmed the Leptosoul Meck.

'How far do you want to go with this? I have one tape here that shows Dan with his head cut off so he can fight two battles at the same time. His head wins and then flops into the second pit where his body is holding off the second contestant. He wins both fights easily.'

Drum shook his head, saying: 'No. Keep the battle physiology plausible in human terms. We want ARNOLD to use a little judgment. Not much – but a little. In name at least – and by the grace of some learning-tape conditioning – he'll be captain of the ship. He's programmed for a little judgement.'

LEPTOSOUL: DAN WITH THE GOLDEN TOOTH

Click! ARNOLD/Dan nosed the aged beef bone out of the dirt. Chain rattled. With eyes half-closed he savoured the marrow and gristle along with the spices of damp humus.

Dan sniffed the soil, wondering where his other old bone was buried.

'Cluck. Cluck.' His wards, the feathered friends in the coop, were upset.

Ears up, he watched the scrub pine. A massive intruder appeared, black and hairy, walking on its hind paws. It had long claws and sharp white teeth. Its body mass was twenty times Dan's.

'Cluck. Cluck.'

Dan froze to quiet his chain. The intruder was so intent on the succulent coop dwellers that it failed to notice the circle of dead grass that marked the chain's end. As its big left hind paw entered the circle Dan leaped and sank his fangs. A hit tibia split and spewed blood. The intruder was down, howling. Claws and teeth ripped Dan's hide open, snapping his spine and spilling his intestines. Dan worked the crumbling tibia back into his jaw and tightened down on it as darkness swallowed him.

Dan's leptosoul floated above the gory scene. The bulky intruder limped off with a distinctive lump on its left ankle – Dan's head. The baying of a pack of hounds and a rifle crack finished Dan's job on the intruder. Click!

ARNOLD snorted as he strode out of Chapel. Drum was impressed. He stayed behind to study the tapes.

'What was this creature – Dan with the Golden Tooth?'

Mullah smiled eagerly, 'These are the most aggressive leptosoul tapes we could find. We think the subject was a small meat-eating pet that worked for man, protecting him against varmints, big and small. Dan was so vicious he had to be muzzled to be bred.'

'Why? Couldn't he recognize a female?'

'Yes, but he fought anything that came into his territory. Fought for wagers too. And the beast obviously could not tell a bet from a stud fee, so he had to subdue any female he met in order to be safe.'

'It certainly worked with ARNOLD. Look at these adrenergic readings!' He handed the printout to Mullah. 'Shouldn't we be concerned about building up this "will to win"? Couldn't this desire for winning the battle evolve into a desire for freedom? Aren't "life" and "freedom" similar desires?'

'Not in this case,' said Mullah, shaking his head. 'Dan is a genetic warrior – produced by crossing generations of winners. He enjoys a battle for The Win. I doubt if your concepts of "life" and "freedom" even exist in his mind. It sounds odd, but this is a case where concern for "life" can lead to extinction – by making the warrior less effective in battle. He might survive a battle, but a poor showing would mean no reproduction. The genes for judgment would be weeded out, replaced by the genes for blind courage. Our ARNOLD should not be concerned with personal survival – just winning.'

Drum nodded. 'Like Dan, ARNOLD's genes are in the hands of another. No Natural Selection.' He pointed to the printout. 'These adrenergics are way off the safety zone. If he were an ordinary Citizen, Security or Psych would be after him.'

'ARNOLD's loyalty will never be in question. He can't live without his Hive fifteen-amino-acid bread.'

Drum left Chapel wondering how long the warrior could live without the bread: exactly how much 'freedom' could he buy at the cost of his life?

8
Deep Cult

Opal changed Clam's bandage. The teeth marks in his forearm had become purulent. Cloudy fluids oozed, odours foul, fevers hot and cold. The arm was swollen to twice its size. Fingers could not move.

Sister White Belly stared into Clam's glazed eyes. 'He doesn't know me!' she wailed. 'We must go up to the beach and build a fire. He needs hot broth. We must boil the dressings more thoroughly. This dome's hot spot just can't produce enough heat.'

Opal shook her head. 'The Hive has too many ships Outside. We couldn't hide a fire from them.'

'But Clam is dying. He smells bad.'

'We'll have to amputate; remove the dead tissue. Go for the Listener. He has had experience in these matters.'

Young White Belly brooded as she swam to Halfway. Listener nodded as she described Clam's injury – livid, purple skin, dusky grey punctures, orange serous drainage.

'Clostridia!'

They swam quickly to the dome where Big Har and Opal had spread out the cutting tools. Clam's toxic condition kept his mind wandering through old memories – battles and love affairs. He was unaware of Listener's hands on his swollen arm.

'There may still be time,' said the shaggy old Benthic. 'Notice how the finger pulps blanch on pressure. Then they pink up. The capillary beds haven't clotted yet. If we can get him down four more levels the increased oxygen might kill off the organisms. Clostridia is an anaerobic bacillus. Oxygen kills it.'

'Four levels? The squeeze?' said Opal.

Listener nodded. 'We'll have to hurry. CLAM!' He slapped his face 'CLAM!! Can you hear me? We are going to move you. Hold your breath.'

They dragged the delirious male from bubble to bubble as they descended into the abyss.

'Don't come any farther,' cautioned Listener. 'We don't want to risk the fits and giggles. I'll take Clam down to that dome on the left. He'll have plenty of air and fresh water. If he isn't better in twelve hours there is nothing more we can do.'

White Belly and her parents watched from the level-eight umbrella while Clam was towed down another ten fathoms and into a pale glowing dome. A few minutes later a humanoid butterfly visited the deep dome. It had wide lacy wings – one of the Deep Cult that lived off the Benthics' offerings. Opal tugged White Belly back to the upper level.

'We must stay home for a day after visiting the squeeze or the pops will get us,' said Opal. 'Then you must do Clam's chores. He was harvesting South Reef. But beware of Leviathan.'

White Belly pushed away a curious fifteen-pound fish – one of the basses with pale yellow and brown blotches on its back.

'I'll be careful. What was that big creature on the Leviathan that bit Clam – another Benthic?'

Opal shook her head. 'No, child. It was not one of our people. Listener says it was an ARNOLD. The Hive can build people as easily as you or I can draw their pictures. Before you were born – the Hive designed a warrior to fight Clam. They grew the ARNOLD in a bottle. No mother. Just a bottle.'

White Belly sharpened her abalone iron.

Fingering his gold emblem, Drum questioned his view-screen: 'I've lost my Leo. Who will continue my ARNOLD project?'

The CO simulated its father-figure face: greying temples, firm jaw, and sympathetic eyes. 'We are moving you up to Committee Chairman. You will be companion to my terminals in this city, and you will chair the meetings. Give me your daily man-minute and I'll see that all your needs are met.'

Drum dropped his emblem into the slot. A new gold bar was dispensed: A Ram – the Aries rank. He rubbed it on his sleeve.

'And ARNOLD?'

'As Chairman you may take as much interest as you wish. He sails this afternoon. Your presence is expected. Your new quarters will be behind the meeting room.'

Drum nodded. He'd be sleeping with terminals.

The Shipyard tower was crowded. Meditecks removed ARNOLD's banjo splint and fitted him with a light brace to remind him not to do any heavy lifting for a while. He opened and closed his left fist slowly.

'See, Drum. I'm fine.' The giant grinned.

Drum handed him a cyberkit. Two Electrotecks stood by with heavy crates. 'Here are the learning-tapes you'll need to work on *Rorqual*'s lingual readouts. Get the ship to talk to you. Make friends with it so it will warn you when a Benthic approaches. It is a good Harvester. Take care of it and it will take care of you.'

ARNOLD handed the kit to a teck. Class-ten dollies rolled up and picked up the crates of bright new auditory and vocal attachments. Drum's aging concerned the warrior. All of the old man's hair was gone – scalp and eyebrows. His synthetic teeth were too white against senile skin with its pink vascular markings and crusts. The lens in his unoperated eye had now gone cloudy – grey-brown – a mature lenticular cataract. His synthetic hip worked well enough, but the knee had developed an internal loose body and a noisy, gritty knee cap.

'You tire, old man. Have you requested a Clinic visit?'

'Put in for it as soon as I got my Aries. All Chairmen get pretty well taken care of. Don't worry about me.' Drum smiled.

The giant patted the shrunken old Nebish on the shoulder and left. He saw Wandee with her team of Biotecks in the hall. She recognised the giant's reluctance at leaving.

'Drum will be well worked up,' she assured him. 'The CO

has given us carte blanche. I'll look over the Clinic's printouts for signs of a failing neurohumoral axis. Maybe we can order a set of young endocrines from his clone lab.'

ARNOLD nodded. Wandee and Drum had become his parent-figures. Although he had been 'jarred', he had been given this pseudofamily support because of his primitive psyche. She walked him down to the docks and waved as he boarded *Rorqual*. The hump trees looked incongruous in the yards – living green against a gleaming cyberforest of crane and lathe robots. The Harvester's visits were too brief to permit the mecks to work on her. She paused just long enough to unload and change crews. But on each docking an army of Class Sevens marched through her hull, taking readings that would help with the designs of new Harvesters. A score of new super-structures were taking shape in their ways. Lesser Arnolds laboured with the mecks – unconditioned, simple synthetic workers, thick of skin and dull of wit. Soporifics laced their porridge. They waved as *Rorqual* edged out into the sump.

Once on board, Arnold began installing the new vocal panels. He crawled between decks, moving around fluffy insulation to make room for the new units. Old units were left where they were, locked in place by thick roots and the red-green scales of oxides. The learning-tapes played. Tightening the last splice, he patted the wall.

'There you are, old girl. A new set of vocal cords. What do you say?'

'Hello, bare feet.'

He glanced down, smiling, flexing his toes. The rest of the crew wore boots.

'Wonderful! You sound fine. Anything else?'

'Clear my hump.'

'Your hump?'

'Yes,' said *Rorqual*. 'Clear the trees from my hump and close my damaged plates. The electrolyte spray burns.'

ARNOLD nodded. 'The salty mist. Does it cause pain?'

'Yes. It burns my nerves and ages me.'

ARNOLD glanced around with new insight. All of the

exposed wiring was like his own nervous system – sensitive to pH and oxygen damage.

He took a team of Electrotecks through the quarter-mile-long backbone of the cyberwhale and tried to estimate the work necessary to protect her circuitry.

'There must be an acre of big trees up there,' said ARNOLD. 'We'll need months to dig out this mess of roots and rust.'

'I am in pain,' said the ship. 'Please waterproof my circuitry immediately. I'll prepare vats of polymer for spray application. It will be transparent and can be cut easily for making repairs. But it'll keep gas and water out. I will be comfortable.'

ARNOLD nodded. 'Right away, old girl.' He issued the orders. Tecks began spraying the syrupy coating. A blanket of the material was wrapped around the fore and hind brains and sealed. When the work was completed they hosed down the areas with seawater. No pain. ARNOLD smiled. 'Now you should be comfortable even if we sink.' He laughed.

He strolled through the hump vegetation, fingering the leaves and vines. The island Agromeck had planted and tended them. There were no flowers or spore cases but years remained of their life spans. 'Machine a double-bladed axe for me,' said the giant.

Although *Rorqual* was far out to sea, the axe looked like a weapon to Hive Security. The Committee was called into session. They opened the channels to the CO and the ship.

'Why wasn't the Sharps Committee consulted prior to the blade's manufacture?' asked Security.

'It is a tool,' explained *Rorqual*.

'Does the ARNOLD consent to placing it in the weapons locker immediately?'

The ship switched channels and focused with a deck optic. A short storm had blown up. Dark, heavy rain splattered into hump vegetation. ARNOLD sang as he chopped; soft rainwater mixed with his sweat. Wood chips were flying. Security repeated the question, but the words were carried away by the wind.

'What?' asked ARNOLD, noticing the glowing optic.

'Do you consent—' began Security. His words were choked

off by his view of another figure moving behind ARNOLD – a wet, naked, female Benthic.

Whooop! Whooop!

ARNOLD turned, axe in hand, to meet the lunge of White Belly – breasts, hips, and a voluminous mane. Axe and abalone iron clicked and clacked. Her iron cut across his chest, slicing fabric and chipping studs. Her left hand gripped the axe handle above his.

She stabbed and sliced with the iron, opening his coveralls. He caught her mane in his left hand. They rolled on the wet deck, wood chips and leaves clinging to her warm, moist body, giving it a speckled appearance. Lightning flashed.

The screen before the Committee focused on the struggling pair. *Rorqual* dutifully recorded. A variety of sensors documented the female's characteristics – bone and soft tissue configurations, reflex time, theromogram, and gas analysis.

'She is much smaller than ARNOLD,' said Drum, hopefully. 'He shouldn't have any trouble with her.'

Her iron sank into his side, releasing a well of thick dark blood.

'He's wounded,' gasped Drum; his lifetime project hung in the balance.

'Only a knife in the *latissimus dorsi*,' reassured the CO. 'He's fine. Give him some encouraging words. Tell him to chop off her head.'

The deck scene was obscured by the misty rain, but ARNOLD seemed vigorous enough. (Something went 'cluck, cluck' in the giant's brain.)

'But he's not killing her,' objected the CO. 'I can't get involved, being a meck – but you understand our mission here. Tell him to fight.'

Drum could not understand why the CO was dissatisfied with ARNOLD's performance. It was clear that he had the Benthic subdued. He had it down on the deck. A good grip on its hair – oh, oh – of course! He wasn't fighting. He was copulating. The Benthic was female.

Drum chuckled, wheezed and coughed.

'Humour?' asked the CO.

'It must be those "Dan-with-the-Golden-Tooth" leptosoul tapes,' laughed Drum. 'Dan never could tell a bet from a stud fee!!'

ARNOLD stepped away from prone White Belly. He pulled her weapon from his wound and tossed it aside with a cavalier air. She scrambled into a crouched position, eyes blazing. Her speckled skin excited him. He took a step towards her.

'Touch me again and I'll kill you,' she growled.

He paused, thinking. Odd, but the threat meant absolutely nothing to him. He continued to advance. She glanced around for her iron. It was too far away. Turning she dived into the sea.

'Why?' asked CO.

'Copulins,' explained *Rorqual*. 'The primate sexual phero-mones from the vaginal mucosa of a mature female. She was in her follicular phase and reeking of male sex attractant. My sensors caught a few short whiffs of her body odour and ran them through the chromatographs. Simple aliphatic acids: acetic, propionic, isobutyric, etc. – the constituents of copulins. ARNOLD is male. He couldn't control himself.'

The Committee reviewed the behaviour of their marine gladiator.

'All he needs is a set of nose plugs and he'll do just fine.'

But ARNOLD did not do just fine. He stood on the deck a long time before returning to the work on the hump trees.

'That axe—' objected Security.

Drum waved him silent. 'Let us allow the warrior to clear the hump. Then we will consider the problem of the axe.'

Aries had spoken.

ARNOLD worked slowly, but smoothly. With one eye on the seas he directed the cranes. Fallen trunks were removed. Then came the twisted plates with their medusa heads of gnarled roots. New plates were smelted and rolled from the scrap. *Rorqual*'s skin was healed. The ship was grateful.

Drum hated to bother ARNOLD with the axe-weapon

question. The ship was relaying the giant's bioelectricals and it was clear that his encounter with the Benthic female had upset him.

'ARNOLD, I am calling about the axe—'

The screen went blank.

'He has toggled off. *Rorqual* is silent.' said the CO. 'I have a fix on his course. He is sailing into the Benthic-controlled zone.'

Drum relaxed. He'd allow the warrior a period of rest. Except for Security, the other faces around the table were expressionless. Psychteck reviewed optic records of the giant's behaviour and stood up to address the members.

'He is sexually imprinted on the Benthic. I think it is his leptosoul experiences with the speckled hens. That Benthic was speckled with freckles. The leaves and wood chips helped bring out his battlecock-broodcock behaviour.'

Drum nodded and adjourned the meeting.

Wandee finished her calculations and joined Drum at the long ear. 'Here is the symptom projection of ARNOLD without his fifteen-amino-acid bread. Since he needs all fifteen in his diet, a deficiency of any one of them will bring on protein starvation – not a pretty way to go: weakness, muscle aches, lethargy, edema, paralysis, and death. The protein will be broken down for routine metabolic needs.'

Drum was depressed at the projection. Skin and bowel ulcer would appear finally as ARNOLD lost the ability to manufacture new epithelial cells.

'How long does he have?'

Wandee shrugged. 'Efficiency should be dropping already. Body stores will carry him for a while, but in three weeks his Kreb's enzymes will need to be rebuilt. If they aren't, he'll be profoundly weak.'

'I doubt if that will force him to surrender. He is very stubborn.'

'Let's bargain with him,' suggested Wandee. 'The Hive wants its marine calories. We can be generous if he maintains his delivery schedule. He could have plenty of free time for these Benthic hunts.'

Drum nodded. 'Let's try to reach him.'

The long ear pulsed: 'ARNOLD, son, resume your duty – please. Your Hive city starves. We have grown dependent on the extra calories. Bring in your Harvester and its plankton.'

Silence. No answering carrier wave. A sweep of the bands brought in only static and Agromeck voices.

'I cannot be certain that your message was received,' said CO. 'Record another for repeated transmission.'

Drum felt exhausted. 'You'll have to simulate the silence inflections. I feel too old and tired.' He scribbled a few notes as the visual composite was drawn. 'ARNOLD, son, thou art slain,' he began. 'I know that you want to be free, and I understand – but you cannot. We designed your genes; we gave you a good mind and a powerful body – the best in the Hive. But your design is defective. Your metabolism is dependent on a diet of fifteen-amino-acid bread. Without it you will sicken and die. You must believe me, son – and come back.'

CO augmented the message. Drum and Wandee monitored the first transmission. They could hardly recognize themselves: sympathetic, young, loving images from ARNOLD's childhood. Their clear eyes, pink cheeks, and dark hair were pure fabricated nostalgia!

The carrier wave appeared. Drum saw a view of *Rorqual*'s control cabin. ARNOLD was not in sight. The ship spoke in a confidential whisper: 'My captain doubts your words, Drum. I would like to relay the message in words he can understand. Why does he need the special bread?'

'It contains a correct ratio of amino acids.'

'All humans require essential amino acids.'

Wandee nodded: 'Correct. We need nine. The Hive's CQB diet contains them. However, ARNOLD's protein metabolism is artificially dependent on fifteen amino acids – all fifteen are essential for him. He cannot survive on the usual CQB table set for his crew. He will sicken and die if just one amino acid is missing.'

'Name the amino acids,' said the ship.

'Classified. I am not allowed to discuss it.'

'Understandable. I will speak with my captain. I will try to make him realize his danger.' *Rorqual* signed off. The screen darkened – static.

Wandee and Drum remained at their post for twelve hours. No answer from ARNOLD. Drum shrugged. He had expected this. Nothing frightens a warrior with the battlecock leptosoul – not the threat of death, and least of all an incomprehensible molecule.

The Nebish crew watched their captain weaken. For weeks they searched in ever-widening circles, but the Benthics eluded them.

ARNOLD leaned on the crane and watched the wide mesh net reel in – empty. 'Didn't catch her?'

'No,' said *Rorqual*. 'I detected a warm body at two hundred thirteen feet, but my net manipulations weren't quick enough to capture it. It fled into one of those domes.'

'Can we put a grapple on the dome?'

'Yes, but it would just flee to another.'

ARNOLD studied the view-screen. 'Two hundred feet. That doesn't seem like much. Why don't I climb down the grapple rope and take a look inside that dome? Maybe it is the female with the white belly.'

'That isn't safe,' warned the ship.

'Why?'

'The pressure is too great down there.'

'I am an ARNOLD. She survived the dive, and she is only a female.'

'A female Benthic. She may have abilities we know nothing about. You are a product of the Hive. And – your diet weakens you. We have need of fifteen-amino-acid bread. Let us return to port for supplies.'

'My speckled hen is down there. I will go down to her,' said ARNOLD. His amino-acid cycle had ground to a halt and a peculiar type of starvation was sapping his strength. He ate everything *Rorqual* offered him, but she was unable to match the exact needs of his crudely damaged pathways. Always there was at least one molecule in short supply, and he starved.

Rorqual extruded a transparent globe helmet and three hundred feet of hose. The crew dutifully outfitted their captain for the dive – weighted shoes, remote optics and communicators, lance, web bag, and lifeline. He dressed confidently.

'If anything goes wrong you can always just pull me up,' said ARNOLD. 'Can you pump air that far down?'

'We'll go slow the first time.'

ARNOLD put one foot on the grapple and the crane lifted him clear of the deck. He ignored the cold and the pressure as he was lowered into the depths. The bubble helmet was thick, giving him a hazy, limited view of the olive-green shapes around him. Fish circled, often as large as his thigh, and scaly. When they began to nudge him he waved his lance to dampen their curiosity.

'Comments?' asked the ship.

'Next time let's give this helmet an optically ground surface. I can't see too well.'

'Anything else? Is the air satisfactory?'

'So far. Continue lowering.'

As he approached the dome, six pink shapes slipped away, quickly. They were so swift that ARNOLD barely had time to count them before they darted out of sight beyond his field of vision. He attempted a few clumsy movements in their direction, but only managed to fall off his grapple and flounder to the roof of the dome. He climbed inside and on to the roof of the dome. He climbed inside and on to the raft. Removing his helmet, he gingerly sampled the air.

'What do you see?' asked the ship.

ARNOLD picked up his helmet and aimed it around so *Rorqual*'s optic could record the findings: raft, utensils, water cup, and scraps of a meal. ARNOLD tasted the contents of the bowls.

'They live down here,' said ARNOLD. 'They eat as I eat. They breathe as I do. I am going to leave my weighted boots here and search the other domes. Keep the air coming.'

By holding a minimum of air in his lungs he was able to stay on the bottom without weights. Using the rocky bottom for handholds, he climbed across to another dome. It too was empty. Apparently the Benthics could see much farther than he. They avoided him with ease.

'Nothing here either. Might as well take me up. I'm beginning to feel peculiar.'

Rorqual reeled in the grappling cable quickly. 'Next time we will equip you with bioelectricals to monitor your physiology,' commented the ship.

ARNOLD ignored the first twinges of pain in his arms and legs. His skin itched and he felt as if he were choking. The ship heard his rapid, gasping respirations. She raised him faster. He clung to the cable with both hands and she lifted him to the deck.

'White Team!' called the ship.

ARNOLD staggered around the deck pushing the solicitous Nebishes away. His skin became marbled with a purple rash. 'My arm! I can't move my arm,' he shouted. He stood still for a long, silent moment while his empty gaze told them he couldn't see either. Then he tipped over slowly and lay still. The White Team struggled with the comatose giant. 'Pulse irregular, but strong. Respirations steady. We're moving him to his cabin.'

Rorqual wept over her silent warrior. His bare feet had brought her pleasure, and now he was dying. She searched her memories for clues, but there was no stored knowledge of deep science. She was a surface ship.

The Medimeck finished its analysis and reported to the ship: 'Multiple small tissue injuries consistent with a shower of particles in the blood. Coma due to cerebral edema.'

'Particles?' said *Rorqual*. 'Of what?'

'Unknown. Clotting mechanism seems normal. No venous clots. But it isn't life-threatening. He should be improving soon. However, three of his amino acids are dangerously low. Can you supply him with glutamic acid, alanine, and phenylalanine?'

'I have tons of plankton, but am unable to purify the amino acids.'

'Ask the Hive. I'm certain the information you need is on file down at Bio or Synthe,' suggested the White Meck.

Chairman Drum was awakened by the CO. '*Rorqual Maru* is on the air.'

He sat up, rubbing his eyes. 'What are they saying?'

'Standard meck-to-meck request for information: hydrolysis of proteins and chromatographic resolution of ninhydrin positive constituents.'

'What does that mean?' asked Drum, pulling on his slippers.

'It means that the ship has defected.'

'What?'

'*Rorqual* is asking for the information she will need if she is to make the fifteen-amino-acid bread for ARNOLD.'

'Don't send it,' said Drum, '. . . just yet. Where are they now?'

CO projected a chart with the ship's location indicated by a glowing whale. A dotted line gave its course during the previous days.

Drum nodded. 'Good. Now how soon can we get one of our new Harvesters into the water?'

The CO saw his plan. 'We can use one as a pursuit vessel right now. The hull and drive units are ready. Their cyber circuitry is a long way from completion, but it could shadow *Rorqual* on manual.'

Drum nodded. 'Put the coastline Agromecks on lookout. Let's hope they stay in range until we can launch Pursuit One.'

ARNOLD walked the deck, stiff-legged, with a cane.

'I'll not go back to the Hive without my speckled hen,' grumbled the giant. 'I am recovering from the pains of the deep. I can continue to search for her.'

'Your amino-acid cycle sputters. You need your Hive bread to live,' said the ship.

'Keep trying to share the memory banks at Bio. If they drop their guard for just a second, we'll learn the sequence.'

*

Hemihuman Larry rode Trilobite's disc across the choppy bay. The water was flattened by the meck's field – a mirror-smooth zone six metres wide surrounded them.

'I have *Rorqual*'s carrier wave pinpointed,' said Trilobite. 'She is close. Right around that peninsula.'

'What is that message she keeps sending? Why isn't the Hive answering?'

'Don't know.'

'The Hive's long ear is working?'

'Yes. Apparently there is a security override on the conversation. Looks like the ship is in trouble.'

While Larry was wondering how a Harvester could find itself a Security risk, Trilobite's lingual readout spilled their two-way: '*Rorqual*... Trilobite! ... My deity!'

The speck on the distant horizon was clearly the shape of a hump-back whale. Larry held the disc rim with both hands as they began to skip across the water. His calloused torso bounced, bruising a rib.

'So that's your deity.'

'Yes.'

'But who is that big fellow on the nose of the ship?'

'Must be one of the crew. There are about two hundred Hive Citizens on board.'

'Is it safe to approach her?'

'Safe?! This is my deity. She loves you! She loves all men.'

ARNOLD welcomed them aboard and questioned them about the Benthics. Larry eyed the muscular giant thoughtfully.

'You speak of White Belly. She is daughter of Big Har, my friend from Tweenwalls. I don't understand how you – a captain – can turn your back on the Hive. Is it simply your attraction to this young female?' Larry could understand mating instinct, but he also had some idea how thoroughly the Hive selected and trained its ranking castes.

ARNOLD just mumbled: 'She is my hen.' He stood up and limped out of the cabin.

Larry swung his torso up on to the chart table and leaned

out the foreport. He saw the captain alone on the deck. The sea darkened. The ship spoke to Larry.

'He is slain.'

Larry watched the giant as *Rorqual* spoke of their last days.

'Sounds like the bends. But he seems to be recovering. I'm sorry about that amino-acid thing – a block, you say. I don't know if I can be of any help, but if you print out what you know I'll look it over. It seems to me that there should be some way to fix him up with a fifteen-amino-acid bread, or chowder, or something. If the White Meck can follow his serum amino-acid levels it should also be able to check the level in a soup.'

Larry's attempts at setting up a continuous-flow chromatography process were only partially successful. The giant remained in negative nitrogen balance, weakening, losing bulk.

'ARNOLD, you are slain,' said Larry. 'Perhaps it would be better to return to the Hive – pick up a load of bread – and then continue this search.'

'The Hive is my enemy. Take me to my speckled hen.'

Larry nodded. 'It isn't far – a two-day trip at most. Try to rest while I go over these ultraviolet absorption spectra again. If the ion exchange chromatography doesn't work pretty soon, we'll set up a gas-liquid process. Trilobite can give *Rorqual* the coordinates of White Belly's summer dome.'

Rorqual's course was straight. She saw no need for evasive action. Twenty-four hours after she disappeared over the horizon, a second ship emerged from the sup. It resembled *Rorqual* in size and shape, riding high and lacking many of the deck sensors. Pursuit One passed over the Benthics' abandoned reef and tracked *Rorqual*.

'Bring back the Harvester and its ARNOLD,' said Drum. 'Protect our investment.'

Larry and Trilobite updated *Rorqual* on the new patterns of Benthic migrations.

'They follow the bloom of the plankton, then into the estuaries for oyster, blue crab, and flounder; they are taking their place in the developing marine food web.'

'They are very grateful to you.'

Rorqual listened to Trilobite's version of the prayers before the meteor shower.

'That wasn't my voice,' said the ship. ' I was awakened by the shower, true: but my long ear was out. I haven't been able to talk with you till now.'

'Then who...?'

Larry smiled. 'It was obviously just another meck. Deities don't limit themselves to wavelengths. I'm sure we'll find that one of the pre-Hive mecks has survived until now – as *Rorqual* has. The conversation was not unusual for the relationship between a Greater Meck and its lesser Servomeck.'

'But the biota did return!' said *Rorqual*.

Larry just waved his hand. 'I know – a very balanced food chain. Our ancestors may have built time-release zoos when they saw what was killing off the Earth species. Trilobite's prayer may have triggered a release mechanism. A miracle, but probably one with a logical explanation.'

'A time-release zoo?' said *Rorqual*. 'I don't think I have a record of anything along those lines.'

Larry just stared at the horizon, a blue line with a flat grey cloud gathering. 'I'm sure that it was something like that. The species that reappeared were so ordinary – so unchanged from my day. They were so easy to classify – same species, same variety. I would expect a true miracle to have some clues in it to the existence of a Greater Deity – like a few bizarre creatures new to our ecosystem.'

'But you would have a logical explanation for that too...'

'What?'

'Mutations brought on by whatever wiped out Earth biota. That might be expected. If the creatures were truly alien you could postulate that we were visited by colonists – so, too, might we be on the receiving end of an Implant. There goes your deity again.'

Larry shrugged. 'It is hard to find a real miracle.'

'I wonder,' said *Rorqual*. 'This return of biota needs more investigation. I am curious.'

*

Listener rose out of the abyss and found Opal and her family hiding in one of the distant segments of the torn undersea conduit. Their raft contained no personal items, indicating the nature of their rapid unexpected flight.

'The Hive has returned to the sea!' exclaimed Opal. 'The Leviathan brings Hunters that can follow us into our domes.'

'Impossible!'

Opal and White Belly described ARNOLD's descent with helmet and spear. Listener nodded.

'As with all Hive Hunters, this one can be dangerous when he is attached to his machine. I will consult the Deep Cult. Spread the word to avoid the Hunter until I return. If you are attacked, try to cut his hose.'

Listener swam down into the depths. He paused briefly in level-eight and level-ten umbrellas to take on oxygen and dump carbon dioxide. But he moved on quickly before his nitrogen level rose. The domes took on a different configuration below level ten. Each was topped by a window sphere. He surfaced in the lower dome and hurried up the Spiral. sending only enough time in the thick air to operate the double doors. The sphere air was thin, and changed the pitch of his voice. He rested, allowing excess nitrogen to diffuse from his tissues. The windows gave him a circular view of the olive-drab surroundings – seaweed forest with its slow, silent fish shadows. The haze of very small plankton obscured his next stop – nearly half a mile away. It had been visible in earlier years, but the waters were no longer sterile. He swam leisurely, following familiar landmarks, arriving at the dome in twelve minutes. Two air pockets later, he again climbed into a sphere to unload nitrogen.

Three forms approached – humanoid with wide lacy wings – angels of the Deep Cult. They fluttered slowly along the bottom, feeding from a large shell, a bivalve which they passed around. They spoke with hand gestures. Lister signalled with a knock on the window. Three wrinkled faces turned towards him. Two wore water-filled mouthpieces. The third let his mouthpiece fall as he munched daintily on white meat. Dropping the bivalve, they entered the sphere. Their fluid-filled wings rose and fell with respirations. Pulmonary fluids moved from lungs to wing veins and back again.

Listener helped the last one up the ladder and closed the hatch. They were wrinkled and old. In water their movements were smooth, almost agile; but in air they were arthritic old men again.

'The Hive controls the Leviathan,' said Listener. 'Hunters sail and dive into the sea. They invade our home domes.'

One old angel locked his mouthpiece and coughed foam. 'Describe these Hunters who invade the waters.'

Listener repeated the various stories he had collected. The elders went into a huddle, fingers flying.

'This ARNOLD creature is well known to us. It is not surprising that the Hive should send it into the water. We should be able to defeat it while it breathes through a length of tubing and wears a helmet. Tell your people of the shelf that the Deep Cult will hunt down the ARNOLD.'

Listener nodded. The angel primed his oxygen bottle with clumsy arthritic fingers. Bubbled distended wing veins. Holding the mouthpiece between his gums, he inhaled foam. Wings sagged as chest expanded. Listener assisted the old men down the ladder and watched them swim off. He smiled. The Deep Cult could handle ARNOLD.

Rorqual Maru wallowed low, her hold bulging with digesting plankton. Alert! Her second pair of cranes thrust their sensors high, sniffing and scanning. A Hive vessel approached. Larry glanced at the screen and called the captain.

'They are after us!'

ARNOLD studied the silhouette. 'She's riding high – light and fast. We can't outrun her.' He picked up his axe. 'We'll stand and fight.'

Larry watched the giant heft his weapon. The weeks of negative nitrogen balance sapped his strength. The blade was sluggish and heavy.

'Open a channel to that ship,' he said.

ARNOLD was annoyed. 'Talk won't solve anything. That is an arm of the damned Hive out there.'

The little hemihuman shuffled his torso around on the chart table and stared at the screen. A Hunter's Pelger-Huet helmet appeared.

'Yes? Who is calling?' asked the Nebish.

'Keep our optic channels closed,' whispered Larry. 'Hello! Why do you follow us?'

'We are under orders to take you back.'

'BACK OFF!!' shouted ARNOLD, riled to the point of hearing 'cluck, cluck' in his subconscious.

The Hunter confidently opened other sending channels, showing his troops: Lesser Arnolds, bowmen, and squads of Hive Security with their tanglefoot nets. 'Our warriors are younger and stronger than your sick ARNOLD. You must return willingly – or die!'

Larry studied the warrior's face. Chapel conditioning left no room for the death concept. His leptosoul had come down through the generations as a consecutive winner of every contest. He faced the conflict with blind optimism, but Larry was more practical. He needed time to think.

'Show them your stern,' he ordered the ship. 'And dump your cargo. What role can you and your cranes play in the actual battle?'

Rorqual spoke didactically: 'Play no active role in any procedure that might injure a hominid.'

Larry suspected as much. The ship's crew of Citizens would be of little use; they were psychologically unfit for hand-to-hand combat. They were nervous on deck in calm weather. Any excitement would paralyze them.

'When do we fight?' grumbled the giant.

'Later. Bring your axe. *Rorqual*, will you continue to obey ARNOLD after he leaves your control room – even if the Hive Arnolds board you and give you direct vocal commands?'

'ARNOLD is my captain,' said the ship. 'As long as I feel his bare feet I will obey no other.'

Larry picked up a remote unit. The screen started its count-down for contact with the Hive ships.

'Come on, show me where I can plug this in below decks. How do the manual overrides work?'

ARNOLD explained that the ship could operate drive units and all sensors while turning over one or more motor units to a human operator. The human would not be limited by any Prime Directive. Larry nodded and smiled. They entered a dark crawlway between decks.

Pursuit One carried three of the Lesser Arnolds fresh from the Rolling Mills. They were young and eager – just beginning to notice hard forearm muscle from the heavy work. None had been to Chapel for anything beyond 'loyalty conditioning'. Arnold Seventeen was senior officer; Eighteen and Twenty would lead the assault on *Rorqual*'s cyber components and engines. (Nineteen died of hypoglycaemia during the Chapel hunter sequence.)

Seventeen felt nauseated before battle. Sweat dampened his palms and armpits. 'Contact in one hour thirty-seven minutes,' his voice barked over the deck speakers. 'Stay alert. The Greater ARNOLD has an axe and is battle-conditioned. He probably cannot be defeated in hand-to-hand combat – even with his loss of Hive bread. Stay away from him. Let the bowmen get a clear shot.'

Nervous squads of short Nebish Hunters put on their Closed-Environment suits. The bug-eyed goggles were black – on step-down. They huddled together, fumbling with longbows and arrows. Arnold Twenty towered over them, smiling. 'Get those gloves on.' He led them out into the wind and glare of the foredeck. 'You'll get the first shots from here,' he shouted. The prow hissed through dark waves. He pulled off his shirt to enjoy the refreshing salt spray. As they gained on the *Rorqual* he shielded his eyes with his hands and squinted at the sunny decks. 'She looks different without her hump trees. There is no place to hide now.'

Another platoon of soft crew climbed into their thick insulated suits in the shade of the freeboard deck. Arnold Eighteen gave them their orders: 'When we draw alongside you will be ordered topside to throw grapples. Continue throwing until all are hooked and set. Then come the catwalks. Eight men each. I want them open and anchored as quickly as possible. Understand?'

They nodded. Apprehension stilled their collective murmur as a new sound was added to the throb of the ship's engines. A gurgle under the hull told them that they were entering *Rorqual*'s turbulence.

Arnold Seventeen froze at the helm. Pursuit One tracked down *Rorqual*'s wake and nudged her stern sharply. 'Halt!' shouted the loudspeakers. Veering to port she tried to pull up alongside, but *Rorqual* fishtailed, breaking a few grapple lines, and swerved to starboard showing them her stern again.

'The grapples aren't holding.'

'Use the macramé lines from your stern winch,' advised Drum. He sat with his Committee, taking a hot lunch while the White Meck took his vectorcardiogram.

A complex head was attached to the cable-extrusion nozzle. The long-chain molecules underwent cross-linking and crystallization before spinnerettes lock-tied the filaments into a flat, woven cable. It grew slowly, resembling an angry, wrestling railroad track as the work crews lined up and pulled it down the deck from stern to bow. The throwing end was armed with five-fluked grapnels and propped high on a stepladder balanced at the fore rail.

'Ram her tail again. We'll try to drop the hooks on to her poopdeck. I wish we had a throwing crane, but we might be able to catch hold of something.'

Arnold Seventeen wrinkled his Harvester's upper lip, raising the stepladder higher. On impact, he closed the maw, flipping the grapnels into *Rorqual*'s aft hatch. The macramé tightened and stretched. He played out a hundred yards of cable, allowing his own prow to swing off to port. As he reeled in the cable, *Rorqual* fishtailed, struggled, and continued her headlong flight, pressing her face into the thundering wall of water at her bow. Wide curtains of spray arched up and around her.

One of her faithful Nebish crew suited up and carried a pair of bolt-cutters out on the foam-flecked deck. He began to gnaw at the macramé, but a fusillade of arrows brought him down. The rest of her crew donned life-jackets and stood obediently at their posts. Pursuit One came alongside showering small grapple lines. Catwalks were unfolded to bridge the gap over the hissing dancing spray. Bowmen sent a few test arrows into the empty decks. No defenders appeared.

'Board!' shouted Arnold Twenty. He led the first wave of Hunters. They swarmed over *Rorqual*'s skin, peering down hatches and tightening the grapple lines. A second wave charged across and stormed into the empty control cabin. Longbows were stationed at elevators and hatches. No one ventured below – knowing how awkward the bows would be at close quarters. 'The ship is ours,' announced Arnold Seventeen. 'The control cabin is empty. Captain ARNOLD has left his post.'

'Stop engines,' said Drum.

Rorqual continued to writhe and churn water, wrenching at her bonds. A few short cables snapped, but more lines were quickly added to the imprisoning cocoon.

'Put a crew in her control cabin and order her back to the Shipyards.'

Arnold Seventeen put his face against the captive's main view-screen and shouted: 'I am your captain. You will obey.'

'ARNOLD is my captain,' said the ship.

The squad of Hunters studied the hatches nervously, fearing ambush from below.

'She refused to obey.'

'Splice her,' ordered Drum. 'Lift her deck plates and piggy-back her main neural trunk.'

Electrotecks tooled up for their invasion of the Harvester's motor nerves. Spools were rolled across catwalks. Heavy plate-cutters were wheeled up *Rorqual*'s hump.

ARNOLD and Larry worked in the dark.

'What's that amber light for?' asked Larry.

'She's worried about something,' said the giant.

'Help me with this remote unite. I can't get it hooked up. What happened to this junction box?'

ARNOLD glanced at the jumble of wire under the yellow warning light. 'Oh that's where I added her new lingual panels. Some of the colour coding isn't standard. Let me do it. I think I remember how I did it.' The warrior momentarily forgot about the enemy as he busied himself with the complex neurocircuitry. One by one the remote lights came on, casting multicoloured shadows on his fierce cheekbones. The screen flickered to life with crowded images from worried deck optics. The occupying forces were very busy.

'They damage my ship!' exclaimed the giant. 'Let me kill them.'

'Just a minute,' said Larry. The bundles of nerve wire were self-explanatory. 'They are after shipbrain. Hurry, let's get the manual override activated.'

The hump plates parted under the grinding molars of the Cutting Meck. 'We're in!' shouted Arnold Seventeen. He let the tecks down into the dark recesses. 'Bring down the control nerves; we'll cut into the spine right here.' The Cutting Meck was lowered into the hole.

Drum waited impatiently. It was taking longer than he expected. 'What is the delay?'

One of *Rorqual*'s deck cranes twitched. Its boom moved slowly towards the hump.

Arnold Seventeen poked his head up. 'Hand me the heavy tool kit. We're inside the canal, but we've hit some pretty thick rust scales. We'll be ready in a minute.'

'Hurry.'

A circle of Hunters surrounded the hump, watching the splicing. The boom of the R-1 crane cast an ominous shadow over the gathering.

'Watch the crane!!'

Like the arm of a hungry praying mantis, the boom plucked a Hunter from the crowd and shredded him high in the air, showering the stunned Nebishes with rosewater blood. A hail of organs and small parts sent them running.

'*Rorqual* killed a human?!' exclaimed Drum.

'That crane is on remote,' explained CO. 'Hurry with the splicing.'

'We're piggybacked, but she doesn't answer to command,' said Arnold Seventeen. 'I'm going to try a shock treatment to clear her memory. Maybe a little Amnesia will get us the obedience we want.'

Arnold Twenty ran down the deck shouting: 'There's a killer operator on that first crane. Try to blind the ship by breaking up the optics.'

The Hunters plunked away at sensors with arrows. They used trophy knives on those within reach. *Rorqual* howled in pain. Decks trembled.

'Stand clear!' shouted the Hive speakers. 'We're going to short-circuit the spine.' The auxiliary cable jumped, insulation sizzling, as the heavy jolt of electricity arced between the ships.

Arnold Seventeen stepped out of the control cabin. 'The manual controls are still cold. She won't respond. Everything in her main cord is nonfunctional. None of her neuroanatomy is standard!'

Larry swatted a Lesser Arnold away from a tender optic. He watched the Hunters receive their new orders to invade *Rorqual*'s companionways. 'Here they come. You can fight now, ARNOLD.'

'Finally!' He picked up his axe.

'I'll control your encounters from here, using the ships sensors and motor controls. Doors will open when I say. Look, I just trapped a group of Hunters in our galley. There's another bunch in the tool room.'

Door and hatches snapped open and closed, dividing up the attacking forces. ARNOLD crept down the corridor listening to Larry's whispers.

'There are two of them in the next compartment, soft Hunters. When I open the hatch, one will be three feet away on your left. He has his back to you. The other is behind the second row of bunks with his head in a foot-locker. His longbow is on the bedding. Get ready.'

Larry waited until the giant's arm was cocked. A smile crossed the angular face. He triggered the door and ARNOLD's axe caught the near Hunter in the back, opening the Closed-Environment suit and thorax. The far Hunter went for his bow, but the string was caught in a blanket. Two steps and the blade came up fast, scattering teeth and sinus tissues.

Arnold Twenty slipped away from the bloodied grapple and crawled under an inert aft crane. The poop sensor pole clicked and spied on him. He attacked it with his knife. The aft crane struck at him, a clumsy blow that tumbled him across the deck plates. When he tried to rise, his left hip made crunching sounds. The inept crane caught him and tossed him into the foaming turbulence that surrounded the two struggling ships.

Arnold Seventeen threw up his hands. 'We can't do it. With her flukes and cranes active she can hold us out here till next year. The few men who returned from her companionways say that there are neural and power cables running all over the halls down there. We'll never gain control of that maze. There is no time to study it.'

'Blast it! Kill it!' said Drum. 'Set a charge in the control cabin and destroy the forebrain. That should paralyze the motor units.'

The first sapper was stopped on the catwalk. His deadly satchel fell harmlessly into the sea. A mushroom of spray pocked the ship's wake. The sonic concussion told *Rorqual* its force – a tenth of a closson.

'Those satchels become armed when they leave their ship's deck,' warned *Rorqual*. 'Stop them before they reach my brain.'

Larry extruded gill nets on the enemy decks and swept the next sapper into the sea. ARNOLD lifted a hatch cover and tossed a heavy length of chain into the legs of a sapper, breaking bones. The explosion splattered the Nebish around a charred hole in the decking. ARNOLD's ears rang. He couldn't hear the arrows strike his hatch.

Whoop! Whoop!

'Now hear this,' shouted Larry. 'All crew. Watch for satchels. They are timed to go off several minutes after leaving the enemy ship. If you find one, toss it overboard. I want men at every hatch.'

Larry manually closed off all of *Rorqual*'s pores by hitting the storm-door switch. Three sappers ran for the cabin door. They set their charges against the outerwall. Operating the L-2 crane, Larry swept two into the sea. The third went off, knocking the door ajar. The fourth sapper dashed inside where the crane couldn't reach him.

'Damn!' shouted Larry. 'Get some men to the control cabin!'

Three more sappers started their dash from the Hive ship. The L-3 crane swatted at the catwalks. One charge fell between the ships, denting them at the water-line.

ARNOLD appeared at the damaged cabin door, carrying a satchel and his bloodied axe. He flipped the explosive on to the Hive ship, where it cleared the crowd from its decks.

'*Rorqual!* Get your other cranes busy cutting his cocoon free. I'll use L-3 and L-2.'

While Larry flailed away at the enemy ship with two cranes, *Rorqual*'s other six cranes busied themselves plucking away the imprisoning grapples. Four nervous crewmen appeared on the poopdeck and began clipping away at the macramé. L-3 swept enemy bowmen off the foredeck. A work crew of Electrotecks intercepted a sapper and disarmed the charge. One carried the Hive service on detonators – an instant expert.

'We did it!' Larry smiled. 'The cocoon is parting and they are falling behind.'

ARNOLD grinned weakly from the stern as a shower of arrows fell short. He bent over slowly, absently cleaning up bits of debris. Repair crews appeared.

Iron Trilobite surfaced and climbed into his niche to share.

'I watched the battle from under their keel. Their ship is equipped with an interceptor engine, but it has no brains,' reported the little meck.

Larry watched the giant's feeble movements after the adrenergic effects of battle wore off. 'Manual! We should be able to capture them – with our cranes, and all the spirit our crew was starting to show. Try to get some rest, ARNOLD. I'll dump the rest of our cargo and go after that Hunter ship. With all those Lesser Arnolds on board they must carry lots of bread. I'll just set a couple of grapples into her hide and hold her for ransom. They lost a lot of men, but there must still be several hundred crew members. *Rorqual!* Go get them, girl.'

Drum chaired the emergency meeting. Stills of the battle sequences were passed around the table.

'It is clear that the ARNOLD weakens. These reaction times are far below his best. Why couldn't our Lesser Arnolds defeat him?' asked Security.

Drum waved his arms – a gesture of futility. 'He avoided our warriors – using cranes against them. And he wouldn't even fight Hunters unless he had them trapped at close quarters.'

The CO added: 'Strategy of that depth suggests he is learning fast in spite of his negative nitrogen balance – or – he had help.'

'Who?'

'There have been many fugitives from the Hive.'

Drum nodded. The lists would be long. Some were bound to survive. It was clear that cranes would be needed on the pursuit ships – big strong cranes.

The Committee was startled by Pursuit One's siren. *Rorqual* had circled ahead and cut them off from shore. The Hive ship turned sharply, losing speed, and headed north.

'Where did they get all that speed?' asked Security.

'Look at that water-line. They dumped their cargo.'

'What do they want?'

The CO recorded the chase. *Rorqual* stayed in tracking mode. Each time the Hive ship turned, *Rorqual* travelled the hypotenuse and gained. Their speeds were very close, but it was clear that they were getting farther and farther away. There was no place to hide. When they made contact the outcome was predictable. *Rorqual* had cranes.

'It appears that the Benthics are about to double the size of their navy,' said CO.

Drum was puzzled by the meck's extrapolation.

'But we still have control. Isn't there something we can do?'

'We have seen what they can do with their cranes. Probabilities are small. Our ship is lost.'

Drum considered the possibilities. He would like to scuttle the vessel and surrender the crew. But if *Rorqual* could get a grapple and a foam-line into it, they would raise it eventually. He glanced around the circle of faces for help.

'We don't have much time,' reminded Security.

'I can't do it,' moaned Drum, placing his golden emblem on the table.

'We'll need a new chairman, then – and in less than an hour.'

Drum sighed and left the room. He saw Furlong in the corridor.

'Enjoy your hot and cold Dispenser.'

'Thank you,' said Furlong, polishing his Aries.

ARNOLD leaned out the foreport and watched Pursuit One's stern draw closer. Above him the forecranes were cocked with their coils of throwing-line.

'We should have your bread by sundown.' Larry smiled. A puff of smoke obscured the Hive ship. Larry's mouth dropped. Three heartbeats later he heard the thunder-like crackle. 'Those charges must have been set by experts. She's breaking up already.' Larry shuffled his little torso up against the port and leaned against the frame. 'I never dreamt the Hive would go to such lengths to keep your bread away. Why do you smile? Don't you realize how close to death you are?'

ARNOLD just shrugged: 'I can't be too far gone if the Hive fears me enough to kill off an entire crew rather than allow a few loaves to fall into my hands.'

Larry nodded.

They cruised through the wreckage. The water was dotted with bodies in life-jackets – shock victims. Sensors showed several irregular masses of wreckage drifting towards the bottom. Trilobite left his niche in *Rorqual*'s hull and dived to examine the debris.

'Search for the ship's stores,' said Larry.

The little shovel-shaped meck tracked down a trail of flotsam and bubbles. He paused when he met the two angels. They indicated that they wanted to go up to the surface. He led them back to *Rorqual*. After a brief exchange of explanations, Larry invited them on board. They seemed eager to meet ARNOLD.

'So you killed a Hive ship, and now you search for a mate among our people?'

ARNOLD nodded. 'Only – I weaken for the lack of a special bread which may be on that sunken ship.'

'After a little practice with water-breathing you will be able to search the sunken ship yourself.'

ARNOLD shook his head, describing his prior diving mishap. 'That's not for me. When I came up the last time I had a lot of pain – a shower of emboli, the ship said. It almost killed me.'

'Nitrogen emboli – the bends,' explained the old angel. 'You were breathing gases – nitrogen and oxygen – and the increased pressure allowed more gas molecules to enter your body fluids. When you decompress the gas leaves. If you come up too fast the nitrogen molecules come out of solution as bubbles instead of through the lungs. The bubbles block small capillaries – emboli that can kill small areas of your body. It is serious when the blocked capillaries are in the brain or heart.'

'I know. I still have this limp.'

The angel offered him a brimming mouthpiece.

'You don't have to worry about the bends with these wings. You'll breath liquids – not gas.'

Larry sloshed the wings around as he examined their membranes – a transparent sandwich of tubules. 'I don't think the surface area is anywhere near enough for him. There is only about ten square metres here. Our lungs have over a hundred – and we breathe air. Air has thirty times as much oxygen as water, so these wings should be much larger – about three hundred times larger.'

The angels glanced at each other and shrugged.

'You are right, of course,' said the angel. 'We can't get our oxygen out of seawater. We'd need a respiratory ratio over five hundred – impossible without a flow-through gill system. We carry our oxygen in liquid form.' He offered Larry a light litre-sized container – a double-walled vacuum bottle. Each angel carried four bottles on their harness between the wings. Larry turned the valve slowly and felt icy gas on his finger. 'We can get over ten hours on a bottle. It bubbles into the wing veins and we take in the bubbles when we breathe.'

Larry nodded, then appeared puzzled. 'But why use the wings then?'

'Eliminates carbon dioxide. It is quite soluble in water. Also, by using water-breathing we can ignore the depth-time diving tables. There is no danger of bends, nitrogen narcosis, or blow-up. Other hazards do exist, but by diving in pairs we've avoided most of them.'

Larry patted *Rorqual*'s console. 'Getting all this?'

'Yes. My information of the science of the deep has been scanty. Our efforts at netting a Benthic were very foolish.'

The angel nodded. 'We considered it a hostile act.'

Rorqual played out cables to mark the two larger fragments of the Hive ship. Using her pincer grapples, she attempted several lifts but only managed to tear up the wreckage a little more. With Larry's coaching ARNOLD managed a successful test dive with the wings. He kept his oxygen bottle turned up for a while until the sensation of suffocation passed. They rigged a sensor-line so Larry could speak with the giant. Even with a larynx full of water ARNOLD could manage simple grunts for 'yes', 'no', and 'help'.

Larry watched on the screen as ARNOLD descended with an angel, while the second angel toured *Rorqual*'s harvesting and digesting gear. The hundred-thousand-ton cargo area impressed him. The angel returned to the control cabin in the guides-two Electrotecks.

'How deep are they?'

'Ninety-five fathoms,' said Larry. 'And doing fine. ARNOLD certainly has it easy. It took me four years to get used to dives of twenty-five fathoms. Look at the way he climbs about that wreckage. How is it going, ARNOLD?' he asked, putting his face close to the screen.

'Mmmmm!' The giant nodded. He pointed to a jumble of floating wreckage near the ceiling of the flooded cabin they were exploring. He plucked objects from the tangle and held them close to the optics. The ship recorded and printed copies.

'Looks like personnel files. Try another area.'

'Mmmmm.'

They placed a pincer on power machinery. *Rorqual* salvaged. Four hours later they surfaced for a hot meal. At dusk they returned to the bottom with bright lights and examined another section of the broken hull.

'That looks like the machine shop,' observed Larry. He hopped off the table and waddled across the floor on his hands. 'Trilobite! Get down there with ARNOLD and see if there is anything we need. It looks as though the Hive was completing that Harvester while it was at sea. The machine shop is pretty well equipped.'

The little shovel meck joined the divers. Larry waddled out on the foredeck to watch the crane bringing up salvage. Deckhands swarmed over the bulkier items – mostly class-nine and-ten robots designed for milling and assembly operations.

'Blast and water damage,' said a teck, 'but I think we can use these fellows if we're going to make our repairs at sea.'

Electrotecks carried neural cables to each salvaged meck, allowing *Rorqual* to take in-depth interviews. Most were too damaged for simple vocal-auditory conversations.

'Call back the divers,' said the ship. 'I think we have found what we were looking for.'

ARNOLD leaned weakly against a crane spool and sipped his stimulant cocktail. The squat brain box in the centre of the circle had been spliced into *Rorqual*'s deck sensors.

'It is still a bit addle-brained from the scuttling, but we're picking up some interesting memory tracks,' said the ship. 'Listen.'

'Spray bonding... metal matrix composite...'

'Wrong track. I'll try again.'

'Naturally occurring amino acid sugar...'

'Now we're getting closer. It has stored a lot of theory. Evidently it helped design a number of mecks – some of which worked in food processing. I'll try to stimulate it towards our fifteen-amino-acid bread.'

The brain box sputtered: 'Amino acids... UV absorption spectra... one hundred eighty-five ninhydrin reactive substances and their chromatographic positions...'

'That's it!' shouted ARNOLD. 'Print!'

ARNOLD waited restlessly as the tecks set up the new protein hydrolysis unit with a continuous-flow amino-acid chromatograph. Adjustable traps were set to isolate his essential fifteen amino acids. Plankton chowder was heated in a moving pH to fragment the proteins. This Medimeck took a drop of his serum to see which of the fifteen were lowest; those shuts were set wide. Fifteen needles traced their nutrient signatures on the crust of fresh bread. ARNOLD watched the long loaf. Several of the needle lines were darker. These would be the ones he needed most – amino acids lowest in his serum. He ate.

'I don't feel anything different.'

'It takes time. Try to nap after you've eaten.'

The giant devoured his prescribed meal and slept. Larry and the two angels walked the deck. Repair crews were finishing up on the battle damage. Large sections of *Rorqual*'s skin were laid open as work progressed on her ancient, corroded circuits.

'Thank you for staying on and helping with the chromatograph column design. I never could get the carrier phase and the stationary phase of the solvents straight in my mind,' said the little hemihuman. He climbed up and sat on a rail.

'Our motives are selfish. With the Hive taking a new interest in our seas, we need a strong warrior.'

Larry shifted his torso, listening.

'*Rorqual* can be an important food source,' continued the angel. 'Benthics could flourish.'

'If our fifteen-amino-acid bread works, we will have a mate for White Belly – and a warrior.'

ARNOLD's serum amino acids gradually returned to normal. The bread brought back his strength. The two old members of the Deep Cult taught *Rorqual* how to extrude a set of wings – simple membrane sandwich over perfusion tubules, almost identical to those used by the Medimeck in its heart-lung machine. The ship learned how to fractionate liquid air, refilling their oxygen bottles.

'Let's fill the hold and search for the Benthics. I want to find my speckled hen,' said ARNOLD.

Listener and White Belly sat alone on a dome raft. He was puzzled by her reactions to the news of a friendly ARNOLD.

'Remember, child, the Hive warrior has turned his back on his creators and destroyed one of their ships. He rides the Leviathan, our deity, who brought back food to the seas. Your hatred of him is not sensible. You should at least agree to see him. He has brought gifts – an abundance of food: mackerel, dulse, edible kelp, lobster—'

White Belly bristled. 'You'd sell me to that Hive creature for a few fish?'

Listener sighed. 'Not a few fish – tons! And he is no longer a tool of the Hive. He is free. Larry and Trilobite were with him in battle. Deep Cult has studied his ship.'

'I hate him!!'

'It is your decision, of course; but I don't have to remind you of the buck shortage. Other Benthic girls—'

'They can have him!'

When Trilobite surfaced with the rejection, ARNOLD's jaw muscles bulged. Fists tightened.

'Don't take it too hard,' consoled Larry. 'It is a big ocean. There are lots of—'

'When did you become an expert?' snarled ARNOLD.

184

'I knew women before my accident. I'd be whole now if Suspension hadn't thrown out my pelvis.'

'Well, they must have thrown away the wrong half,' said ARNOLD, checking his angel wings. 'This is very important. I just can't let her swim away.'

Larry paced the deck on his hands, trying to reason with the impetuous giant.

'But these Benthics have very strict customs. Their females have been the sexual aggressors for generations. They have a sacred place for the first union – called Mating Domes.'

ARNOLD nodded. 'OK, I'll try it your way.' He pulled on the harness. 'Where are these special domes?'

'But the male doesn't wear wings! The mating ceremony is supposed to be a test of anaerobic ability – good genes...'

ARNOLD frowned. 'A test of genes?! It's a swimming test. I can't swim that well.'

Larry scooted down the deck and climbed up on to the bench where ARNOLD was recharging his oxygen bottles. 'You can learn to swim. I did. Why, even I can hold my breath for ten minutes at the depth of Mating Domes.'

'And how long did it take to learn that?!'

Larry shrugged. 'A couple of years. But you must remember that I have to be very careful about the nitrogen content of my diet. You can eat all the protein you want with your kidneys. Your myoglobin and haemoglobin will build up fast – increasing your oxygen storage ability. I'd be willing to bet you'd be good Benthic mating material in a couple of months – if you did a lot of deep diving.'

'A couple of months! Larry, I'm sorry, but I'm afraid they did throw away the wrong half of your body. You don't have a gonad in your skull!! I want to be with White Belly now! Today!' The giant was shouting and waving his hands. The Nebish deck watch peered down from his post on the foredeck to see what was wrong. 'Now hand me that other oxygen bottle and explain their mating customs again.'

Larry tried to repeat what Big Har had told him about passing between the domes like a submarine – zero buoyancy with nose up and arms out wide for stability. A female approaching from the top with negative buoyancy can use her teeth and feet for the embrace, leaving her hands free to aid penetration.

ARNOLD puckered his brow for a long moment, thinking. He shook his head sharply. 'It won't work.'

'It works for the Benthics. They use it for natural selection, like the queen bee who mates with the male who flies the highest. A Benthic mates with the male who swims the deepest.'

'A challenge,' said the giant, 'a contest of strength in the water—'

'No. A test of anaerobic capacity. That is why you mustn't wear the wings. Wings are for the Deep Cult – old men who need the high pressure oxygen below level ten because their brain vessels are narrow.'

ARNOLD made a fist and shouted: 'I'm no senile angel. I am ARNOLD! Mighty Warrior!' He primed his wing veins with oxygen and unlocked his mouthpiece. Fluids spilled.

'But...' objected Larry.

The giant sucked in the oxygen-rich foam and waved the little hemihuman to silence. He sucked again, expanding his chest and drooping his wings. *Rorqual* swung down a grapple and lifted him off into the choppy water. He fluttered on the surface like a drowning moth. The grapple returned with his belt and coveralls. The fluttering continued while he rebuckled his harness. It was several minutes before Larry lost sight of him.

'A moth on his first mating flight...' mumbled the hemihuman. He shook his head slowly. Trilobite returned to his niche to suck his energy socket. The mighty ship blinked out its On Duty Lights, folded cranes, and let the crew sleep. Her captain was away.

ARNOLD's wings spilled his carbon dioxide and brought back memories of his fighting-cock leptosoul experiences. He was King again, on his way to find his love object, the spotted hen. He moved easily through the depths. There was no sensation of pressure after the small bubbles of gas were absorbed from his sinuses and gut.

His vision was no better than before. He had been limited by the rough opalescence of the air-filled globe; now he was limited by the refractive index between his cornea and water. Two pink-bodied Benthics passed, waving. He knew he was welcome among them this time. The view, although clouded, was pleasant enough when examined leisurely. Fifteen years had been long enough for the sessile marine organisms to reclaim the floor. All space available was crowded with tentacles, spines, tube feet, and a variety of pincers. Limpets, snails, clams, scallops, and urchins clung to dead domes. Living domes sparkled and offered their air bubbles.

The two rows of female domes were easy to locate at the deep end of the reef. He swam between them, flourishing his wings. No one appeared. The male dome was at the end of the row. He poked his head into its bubble. It was unoccupied, as usual. Larry had warned him about the taboo against invading a female dome, so he couldn't be sure he wasn't wasting his time. Rolling over on his back, he spread his wings and made a slow pass down the row. The hazy green waters obscured his identity, but the silhouette of a phallic conning tower brought out a Benthic female. He kept his nose pointed towards the surface, sixty-one metres overhead. The pink shape passed over. He was stimulated by unfamiliar breasts and hips, but she was not White Belly. Her eyes moved over his body, She retired to her dome. He turned up his oxygen bottle, fluttered his wings and made another pass. She reappeared, arms at her side, approaching with trunk undulations. Otter-like, her nose slid up his chest and her teeth attached to his left shoulder – a love bite. Heels hooked around his calf muscle. Her mons struck hard; a hungry anemone engulfed the conning tower. In a moment she was gone again, back in her air pocket. ARNOLD's lungs pulled fluids from wings. He exhaled slowly. Her callous haste recalled the vigorous matings under wire – the broodcock had found another speckled hen.

Returning to *Rorqual*'s skin, he spat out the mouthpiece

and gingerly removed the harness from his bloodied shoulder. Several minutes of coughing foam cleared his throat. He laughed. An aide brought a bulky robe and snack tray. He stuffed his mouth with bread, blowing crumbs as he talked.

'Now that's what I call mating!'

'White Belly was waiting for you?' asked Larry.

The giant shook his head as he crumbled bread into a bowl of thick chowder. 'Whoever she was, she needed me.' He drained the bowl, wiping his chin on the back of his hand. His grin was wide.

'Whoever? You don't even know her?'

ARNOLD just laughed. 'You know how hard it is to see clearly underwater. It could have been any one of a dozen young females. But you were right about their customs. The females are certainly aggressive.'

Larry was flustered. 'But they are looking for a mate, not just a pleasuring.'

'Can I help it if I enjoyed it?'

'That isn't the point,' explained Larry. 'What you should understand about these people is their strong family ties. Mates cling to each other and to their offspring with a ferocity that is unmatched by other people I have known.'

ARNOLD was puzzled. 'What is your point?'

'If this new girl has a child, she and the child will be your family in the eyes of their people.'

'Fine.' The giant grinned.

'But what of White Belly?'

The grin broadened. 'She will be ARNOLD's family too,' he said. 'ARNOLD is King!'

Larry sighed. His captain could be difficult.

9
Armada

The Committee trembled under the CO's cold analysis. Their warm status as Citizens of high CQB depended on their chairs around this table. If CO pulled their chair it meant TS – Temporary Suspension.

'Your work on the ARNOLD problem has been ineffective. Slow decisions. Costly errors. I have made Furlong your Sovereign with full discretionary power. You are now his Cabinet, with advisory function only.'

The circle of faces relaxed. As long as Furlong needed them they'd remain warm. They stood as he entered and remained standing until he sat down. He had the smug overconfident air of a new dictator.

'We have been given carte blanche,' he said, smiling. 'Anything is possible with the full resources of the Hive.'

The Cabinet nodded.

'First, Security is replaced. The error of sending out Pursuit One without cranes rests on your shoulders. You are to report back to your department. They will send a younger representative – someone with more imagination.'

The tired Nebish stood up to leave. He aged perceptibly under the critical gaze of his peers.

Furlong continued: 'Second. The playbacks of the battle will be studied and cranes designed that will be superior to *Rorqual*'s.'

He turned to the representative from the Shipyards. 'How long before Pursuit Two is launched?'

'We are progressing on schedule. Our new caste of workers has proved to be—'

'No rhetoric. I would like a concise answer – something we count on for planning.'

'Two years, sir!'

'That's better. Two years will allow time for crane design. I think the forecranes should be much stronger than *Rorqual*'s, capable of tearing open her hull. Other cranes should be longer, with a greater range for throwing weapons – explosives, grapples, pincers. The ship's neural integration need not be concerned with these destructive devices. Each crane will have its own operator booths – above decks for clear weather and below deck for foul. Any questions?'

The Hunter stood and awaited recognition.

'Yes?' The Sovereign's eyes were cool.

'Sir. We should be able to put a line on *Rorqual*, especially if we have more than one ship. But our problem has been control of the ship's brain. If ARNOLD is alive it will obey only him. How do we kill ARNOLD? Should we start a company of Lesser Arnolds through leptosoul conditioning?'

'No. A crane on remote can squash a warrior no mater how well conditioned.'

'But he stayed below deck. Our cranes won't be able to reach him.'

'Then design small motor units that can hunt him down. Send the Tinkers into our Recycling bins and see what sort of mecks they can come up with. Arm them and put them on remote control. Add a few booths to each ship for the purpose.'

'A Killer Meck on remote.'

'Yes. Perhaps we should place a Huntercraft on one of the pursuit vessels. What is their range?'

'Four hours. About a hundred miles an hour. But I'm not sure what is available, sir.'

The CO interrupted the meeting. 'In two years there should be a flying machine available. We will equip it to land on water.'

'ARNOLD will be stopped!' Furlong smiled.

*

ARNOLD buckled on his wings: a lecherous angel preparing to tickle anemones in the Benthic Mating Domes. He filled the air with a raw ballad as he secured a tuna to his tow-line.

Larry hand-walked up to the bawdy giant, giving the flopping fish plenty of room. The hemihuman disapproved of the warrior's Paphian ways; ravishing virgins was a sign of debauchery in his eyes.

'I'm taking the giant food fish to the old one in the Deep Cult,' said ARNOLD.

'Will you search for White Belly?'

'I'll visit anemone row again, if that is what you mean. She knows where to find me.'

'But you've been accepting any shameless female that approaches.'

'Can't let it go to waste,' chuckled the ribald giant. 'There is a shortage of males down there. I'm just doing my duty.'

'But what of White Belly? Your first love?'

The huge angel paused, his hand on the grapple. 'I think her exact words were: "They can have him." Well – they are.'

Upon touching the water, the tuna thrashed for a moment then followed the giant into the deep.

Later, another anemone rode the phallic conning tower.

An indignant Clam climbed on to *Rorqual*'s deck, accompanied by two wizened old angels from the Deep Cult. His bout with Clostridia had left him sullen and morose, but as strong as ever.

'Greetings!' called the hemihuman from his perch on the cabin roof. 'What brings you on board?'

'We'll speak to your captain,' seethed Clam.

The ship relayed the message to the cabins below the poop-deck. ARNOLD put down his tools, rode the elevator and approached the delegation with his right hand raised – grinning.

'Your smile is out of place,' flared Clam. 'We have come on a sore matter.'

ARNOLD sobered. 'Fine. Join us in my cabin. We have a special delicacy this day – urchin caviar, a golden roe with five consecutive flavours of its own. You must try it.'

Clam waved away the morsels and simmered until everyone was seated. 'ARNOLD, your amoral mating habits are contrary to the teachings of the Deep Cult.' The two angels nodded. 'You demoralize our young maidens, teaching them sin – degeneracy – evil. You are being unfaithful to you first mate – White Belly.'

Larry saw colour rising in the face of the provoked warrior and spoke quickly. 'I believe that she has already rejected ARNOLD.'

'She grows with his child; therefore she is his mate – and he hers. It is our way.'

'I knew she carried my child. All of the King's embraces are fertile.'

'You knew? And you care not?' raved Clam.

Larry felt the table move as the two giants leaned towards each other, sinews taut. The little hemihuman waved them back. 'I'm sure White Belly doesn't want to lose either a brother or a mate. Let ARNOLD speak.'

'I know all of your customs. Larry has been quite thorough. But your ways are not my ways—'

'You depraved, synthetic warrior!' interrupted Clam, shaking his good fist. 'You call yourself "King"; but here in our waters you are just a foul, thieving vagrant – stealing our fish and our women!'

'Calm down or I'll turn on the overhead sprinklers,' said the hemihuman. 'Let him finish.'

'I do want White Belly,' said ARNOLD. 'I wait at anchor in your waters until the day she learns of her pregnancy. Then she will come to me.'

'But those other maids? Their waists grow too.'

'I await them also.'

Clam stood up and went raving and striding around the room. 'They can't all come to you! There isn't room in one of our domes for—'

'Their rooms are on my ship. I am a surface-dweller.'

'Surface-dweller?' mumbled Clam. 'But the Hive?'

'I rule the sea,' said the giant. His voice was steady, confident.

Clam studied the warrior's face. There was no sign of sarcasm or deceit. 'A surface-dweller with many wives?' He sat down slowly.

'How can you feed all of—?'

'My ship can feed millions. I am King. I will conquer the world if necessary, but all of my family will have plenty to eat.'

Clam accepted a tangy hors d'oeuvre and munched thoughtfully. 'Our young women would never accept such an offer! They are pure and innocent, raised in the finest tradition. They would rather die than listen—'

Larry interrupted. 'Clam, why don't you take a look at the wives' quarters? You could tell the girls about the accommodations.'

'I refuse to be a party to such a blatant—'

'Let them decide for themselves,' soothed Larry. 'Times have changed. The sea gives us food now. The Hive is weaker. ARNOLD is King.'

Aides entered to assist the arthritic angels with wing-wetting and oxygen bottles. A reluctant Clam followed ARNOLD and Larry to the aft elevator.

'It's a lonely ship – practically empty. She can carry ten thousand humans and a hundred thousand tons of plankton. Now she has a crew of two hundred and twelve Citizens. They sailed with me and stay on for the triple CQB. Unfortunately, the Nebishes have a short lifespan. They follow orders well. The Servomecks enjoy having them around.'

Clam was fascinated by the size and luxury. He returned from the tour somewhat mollified, accepting a drink from ARNOLD's table.

'There certainly is ample nesting room,' admitted the Benthic. 'We must have walked through miles of cabins. The girls ought to enjoy the hot and cold Dispensers. They'll eliminate all the work.'

'Oh, there'll be plenty of work on *Rorqual*,' said Larry. 'Few of our Citizen crew can tolerate deck exposure. Benthic women will be expected to draw their share of deck duty.'

'Deck duty?' said Clam. He eyed the hemihuman thoughtfully,

then shrugged. 'I'll tell them what I've seen. The angels can discuss it with Deep Cult. Bucks are scarce among the domes. Many of our women never find a mate. Perhaps it would be good for a few to stay with ARNOLD.'

'It will be good,' said the giant warrior.

The ship extruded a light polymer canoe, a keeled cylinder with mast and outrigger. Delicacies were sacked and tied. 'Travel the surface while ARNOLD rules the seas.' The sail was raised. 'Take our gifts with our words. Let the gravid females decide for themselves,' said Larry. A grapple launched the little craft.

Seventeen of the Benthic females moved into cabins below the poopdeck. Twenty-eight children were born during the first year. Other Benthic families were enticed on board, while catamarans and maps were prepared. Loaded with seeds, hooks, and nets, they sailed west to settle on the scattered islands of an archipelago. One of these new island families was Har and Opal and six of their offspring. They found a granular super-structure in their lagoon and stunted pigs and chickens in the island's forest.

The elderly members of the Deep Cult remained in the Ocean's squeeze, enjoying the thicker air and buoyancy. Scattered Benthics clung to their domes on the continental shelf. Their nakedness and Neolithic culture limited them to the warmer Ocean currents. As Nature reclaimed its niches in the marine world, this new generation of Benthics met new hazards in the returning sea life – creatures with defensive poisons and carnivorous habits. But Man was in the sea to stay. His cyberdomes were clever. They identified each new threat and developed an alarm system for their guests.

Clam's mate, Sunfish, wrapped their young Tad in his cradle and returned to her chore – cleaning a basket of Cancer borealis, the four-inch-wide, brown 'Jonah crab'. Her cyberdome detected the approach of a poisonous conch – a purple-fringed, foot-long mollusc. Her ceiling pulsed three times, adopting the purple colour at the point on the rim closest to the danger.

'Thanks, dome,' she said, picking up her spear. She went to the edge of the raft nearest the colour and peered down into the greenish waters. The weedy bottom was thickly overgrown. She did not venture into the water until she saw the spiral shell clearly. It was foraging in the tall greens, using its deadly tentacle to bring down small Sebastodes – rock-fish. Slipping into the warm water, she approached the browsing conch. It ignored her. There were few natural enemies that could stand up to its deadly venom. She stabbed at it with her spear. The tentacle tapped the shaft, leaving (she knew) a microscopic lance plus an injection of toxin. She pressed harder. It began its violent rolling flight, extending its foot to the side and twisting its shell first one way and then the other. In a sequence of three rolls it threw itself six feet. Sunfish followed, catching the shell on her point. The tentacle groped in her direction. She was glad that the poison dart was limited in range to the length of the proboscis. Her sharp weapon followed the soft body into its spiral home; a twist and its simple mollusc haemoglobin darkened the waters, attracting a swarm of scavengers who fought over the exposed protein.

Sunfish returned to her dome to find that the pot of whelks had boiled over. She added more seawater to the three-inch snails, small relatives of the deadly creature she had just dispatched.

Clam joined her for the meal. His foraging sack bulged with abalone feet. She sorted through the rubbery, white ovals, rubbing away the peripheral pigments and tossing the fibrous ones to their pet *Stereolepis gigas*. The giant sea bass rose from the bottom, swallowed the morsel, and settled back down.

'I noticed a couple of cottids fighting over something under the south leg,' he commented.

'Conch,' she said. 'I killed it about two hours ago.'

'They seem to be getting more numerous. I guess it's time to seed the yard with predatory starfish again.'

'She nodded and began pounding the abalone.

'Can you return these crab traps for me? Goose and Mudd wanted to put them out early in the morning.'

'Fine. I'll bring them a couple of abalone feet to chew.' He tied the concertina nets into a tight bundle and towed them off.

Sunfish nursed Tad then fell asleep beside him. She was awakened by the dome's frantic warning light. The intensity of the red pulses frightened her. Tad screamed.

'What is it, Dome?'

She gathered up her son and searched the surrounding night waters for a clue. Hazy green bioluminescence increased. Vibrations told her that something approached – a new, unfamiliar sound that shook her home.

The sharp blade of a grapple struck the dome four feet above the rim, penetrating the air pocket and puckering the thin, translucent walls. A ring of wavelets danced off the raft as the dome buckled. She fell struggling towards the edge of the raft. The dome split with a bang – blasting her air away in a cloud of bubbles. She found herself sandwiched between the buoyant raft and heavy fragments of the arched ceiling. A painful pop in her right chest told her she was no longer at level four. They were rising fast! She kicked against the wreckage. Her baby screamed out a thick string of bubbles which tickled her left breast. She tried to exhale quickly, but her bubbles were already pink.

Injured Benthics moaned in the dark. Heavy chunks of debris bumped on the waves. A searchlight swept the scene. Sunfish tried to slap some life into little Tad, but the chubby form only trembled, open-eyed and silent. She attempted to blow breath into his mouth, but her own lungs wouldn't work. She could only exhale. Each attempt at inhalation was blocked by an agonizing pressure under her right arm – a torn lung. Small, sharp pains stabbed at her fingers and toes, spreading up her extremities. Her writhings activated surface phosphorescence, pinpointing her location. The spotlight found her. A Nebish harpoon ended her suffering. A school of small hungry fish was attracted by her blood. They found Tad.

*

Furlong walked with his entourage through the icy lockers of Pursuit Five. He counted the frozen Benthics and nodded at the body count.

'Sixty-four of the enemy killed. Good. We had no casualties. There was no sign of *Rorqual Maru*.'

The representative from Security smiled.

'I do believe we have come up with the perfect anti-Benthic device – the Iron Tuna. Putting fins and an optic on the grappling hook enables the crane operator to knock out their domes with a great deal of accuracy. I don't think we missed a single dome on the reef. Look at these scans before and after our attack. The reef is called Two Mile. Notice how the occupied domes glow – making them easy targets.'

They passed around the stills.

Three men from Hunter Control removed spear barbs from the stiff remains.. 'It was easy game; lots of protein. We'll have all the volunteers you'll need for this kind of duty. Our Hunters enjoyed the night shooting with the spotlights.'

'A success all the way around, I guess,' said Furlong. 'Don't rush these specimens down to Synthe too quickly. I want the Biotecks to have a chance to stud them – see what we can learn. I know how short we are of good protein, but it will keep until we get a good analysis of these creatures – their bodies and their minds. Send me the reports as soon as possible.'

Clam huddled in the air pocket of a small umbrella. His swollen right thumb throbbed where the rotating fin had pinched it. He had witnessed the destruction of his dome village. At first the approaching grapples had resembled bizarre, one-eyed tuna. Their searchlights told him they were machines, so he had tried to avoid them. He had hidden in a crevice until he realized what they were doing. The bursting domes had brought him out but the mechanical devices easily tossed him aside. Now he was alone.

The bottom wreckage told him nothing of his family. Scavenger fish tore at table scraps, but no bodies were in sight. After decompressing at level two, he floated his polymer outrigger canoe and began his surface search. The trail of debris was easy to follow. The horizon was clear. The ship had vanished.

When Clam began paddling he was numb, but each new fragment jolted and awakened his anger. A wooden bowl was just a bowl until he recognized the carvings as his own. By noon he had caught up with the main mass of wreckage – numerous rafts and dome fragments. He picked up a familiar blanket, small and tattered. When he found his home raft he ran the bow of the canoe up on to it and crawled out, weeping. His hands moved across the familiar textures. A broken harpoon was wedged deep. The blood-stains told their story. He sat through the night, face cradled in his arms. A small nosy fish searched through the debris.

At dawn Clam pulled himself together and paced around the raft. Nothing remained at the home village. Every living dome had been systematically destroyed. There were other villages on other reefs. They would have to be warned. He pulled out the broken harpoon. And there would be revenge!

Rorqual tracked the school of *Thunnus thynnus* and transmitted the data to Larry's console. The hemihuman squirmed around in his hammock and read the report.

'Bluefish Tuna,' he mumbled. 'Two-hundred-pounders.' He climbed down and scampered along the companion-way to the control cabin. The view on the big screen was impressive. The eyes on 2-L sensor crane were sharp, picking up the details of coloration and short pectoral fins. ARNOLD joined him.

'Nice herd,' said Larry. 'Should we catch a few for the islanders?'

'Why not? One per family won't spoil them. We'll use a few for the deck hands and the women too.' The Captain patted the ship's console. 'Go, girl. Catch us a few.'

The aft cranes spun lines and extruded spoon and spinner lures with five-inch hooks. The school was sampled. Forty-eight identical fish flopped on the poopdeck – scaly muscle, unblinking eyes. The thick-suited Nebish crew stood aside while naked Benthic women took their time deciding on the choicest for the evening meal.

'Which finny beast do you want?' asked ARNOLD.

Six sweaty wives watched his approach. Blood and scales speckled their arms. Hooks and knives filled their hands. He wandered among them – chatting, joking, and patting. The sun was high, the work heavy. Beads of sweat streaked their bodies. He paused in front of a young mother whose damp skin was streaked with white – lactating. He held out his hand.

'Give me your knife. Go feed your child.'

She stepped under the deck shower, rinsing in seawater, and scampered off the elevator. ARNOLD turned the blade over and over thoughtfully.

'It wasn't too long ago when she would have tried to stick me with this,' he mused.

At dusk he found the hemihuman perched on the edge of the aft hatch. Orange light from the living quarters outlined the small form. Sounds of women, babies, and utensils filled the air.

'Join us,' said the giant.

'Maybe for just a lettuce-and-whole-wheat sandwich,' said Larry, swinging down the hatch on one of his knotted ropes.

One of the Crayfish girls, mother of triplets, greeted the hemihuman with a squeal and offered to set a place for him next to her. The table was round, fifteen feet in diameter and eighteen inches high. Pillows and cushions surrounded it. It was being set in the middle of the elevator that had stopped at the second level. ARNOLD took the stairs down and helped carry the heavy platter of fishsteaks. White Belly tied on her lavalava (Hive issue) and walked around the table setting out baskets of fifteen-amino-acid bread and buckets of bayberry tea. She made room for the captain next to her, since she had the eldest son-of-ARNOLD. Other wives approached, chatting. They carried pickles octopus salad, edible kelp, steamed clams, boiled crabs, and a variety of *Rorqual*'s more anonymous dishes.

'We should reach the first of the islands tomorrow,' said ARNOLD.

'It is good to see them green again,' said Larry. 'I can

understand why Big Har wanted to settle here. I filled his head with visions of these places while we were Tweenwalls back in the Hive. I'm sure he'd not be happy anyplace else.'

Rorqual nosed into the cove and rested her chin on the sand. There was no sign of the habitation on the lush green island. White Belly was worried.

'Are you sure we're on the right island?'

The ship quietly overlaid the two charts and projected the composite. The topography and coordinates matched.

'I'd think they would have done something to the place in two years – houses, boats, nets. But it looks as wild as ever. You don't suppose they moved to another island?'

'They are here,' said *Rorqual*. A sensitive infrared view of the vegetation indicated squarish defects – dwellings hidden behind a screen of shrubs and vines. 'They are still a bit cautious about advertising the fact, that is all.'

ARNOLD squinted up the beach. 'Remember that there were just twelve of them. Looks like two or three hundred acres to hide in. Let the wives go ashore with the gifts. We'll leave two sets of catamaran hulls here – twenty-four foot and thirty-six foot. Garden tools. Spear heads. Invite them on board for the evening meal.'

White Belly carried her two children into the clearing. Har and Opal ran out and hugged her. They chattered and passed the children around.

Later Har came on deck to talk with hemihuman Larry. Both had darkened and hardened considerably since their days Tweenwalls. They clicked glasses and toasted ARNOLD. 'May the King always rule the sea.'

The evening meal was punctuated with song and dance. The ship extruded a large variety of colourful polymer toys for the children. Island living had made the Benthic women even more calloused and leathery. Muscular and wide of pelvis, they had a pregnancy every year. The island population approached twenty. ARNOLD's wives showered them with small gifts: cooking utensils and sewing supplies. *Rorqual* picked up bushels of seeds and cages of small wild meat creatures to seed on other islands.

'We are very happy here,' said Har. 'You should stop your wanderings and live with us.'

'No,' said Larry. 'I enjoy the voyages of *Rorqual Maru*. We throw a few seeds out and watch them grow. The little wild pigs thrive everywhere. I don't know what sterilized all these islands, but I am having fun planting them.'

Har nodded. 'It is like those stories you told me – about Dever's Ark. Only you are seeding life right here on Earth.'

'Yes, I suppose I'm having all the fun of a starship colonist – with none of the hazards.'

The celebrants spent the entire night on the ship. They were disturbed at dawn by a speck on the horizon. *Rorqual*'s second pair of cranes went up. The image was thrown on ARNOLD's screen.

'An outrigger. One of ours,' said the captain. Larry and Har went to the rail.

'It's coming from the northeast. Who could it be?'

Clam's story was incoherent – alternating from rage to despair. The 2-R crane sniffed around the canoe and came up with a baby blanket and the bloodied harpoon.

'The Hive has returned to the sea!' said *Rorqual*. 'Clam's family has been killed.'

'And probably most of the Benthics from Two Mile Reef,' added ARNOLD.

Larry didn't like it. 'Those robot grapples sound like a specific tool for destroying domes. I'm afraid we've underestimated the Hive's determination. It wants to destroy us pretty badly.'

'Let's destroy it,' mumbled Big Har.

The men huddled on the deck talking of war. The ship listened.

'War with the Hive is not possible,' said *Rorqual*. 'It covers the continents with a single nervous system and 3.5×10^{12} citizens. Its Embryo Departments turn out 5×10^8 units per day. They can build a copy of ARNOLD in ten years – and a *Rorqual* in five. You are few in number and scattered. You have no flying machines or explosives. You have no army.'

Har shook his fist. 'We must make them pay. Those were our people at Two Mile.'

Clam pointed to a broken harpoon. 'This is our Ocean. I will kill any Hive creature that comes into it.'

ARNOLD nodded. 'The Hive ship must be destroyed.'

'I will send boys to the nearby islands,' said Big Har. 'We might be able to raise twenty or thirty men. If the Hive ship has a few Lesser Arnolds we should be able to handle them with axes and spears.'

The neighbours began to arrive with their simple neolithic tools-turned-weapons. Most were just boys in their teens – naïve and enthusiastic. The final count was eighteen males and fourteen burly females. All were extremely bitter about the atrocity at Two Mile. The children were left on shore with the pregnant wives.

Listener, another survivor of Two Mile, made his way to South Reef. He told his story to a small gathering in Long Dome.

'It is our domes they destroy. Their weapons can tell which domes house Benthics. Only those are attacked.'

Bent Nose, a leathery female with nine children, turned to her half-grown son, Razor, and asked: 'How could they do that?'

Razor was the tribe expert. He had spent a whole day hiding in the Gardens, watching a sentry pole. Afterwards, he had given a detailed report to the Deep Cult. 'The Hive has little eyes and ears,' he said. 'Some see better than our eyes, some worse. I think we should try to make our occupied domes look as much as possible like the dead domes. If these underwater eyes are worse than our own, we may be able to hide our homes.'

Listener nodded. 'There may not be much time.'

They watched young Razor lead a group out into the cloudy waters. When they returned they all spoke at once.

'We must make our air bubbles smaller.'

'It's the light. We'll have to use only the natural bio-luminescence.'

'It's the heat. Warm domes have families.'

'No. It's the marine scum. Dead domes are covered by sessile creatures and algae. We must try to camouflage our homes under seaweed, urchins and starfish.'

Bent Nose raised her hands for silence. She nodded for her son to continue. 'It could be any one of those things. I don't know. but we should try them all. The domes' hot spots and lights must be turned off. Most of the domes' class-eleven brains should cooperate. Those that won't must be abandoned for the time being. I think the women should be able to weave a weedy shroud to cover the outer skin. Suckers and tube feet won't cling to the dome's bare skin when it lives.'

'I'll set up a Web in one of your level-two domes. Perhaps we'll hear them coming,' said Listener.

Furlong sat by his screen in the committee room. The other members had been dismissed.

'Are you certain there are no Benthics?'

The face on the screen was expressionless, the obedient captain of Pursuit Two. 'We've made three passes over the area on the charts known as South Reef. None of the domes lives.'

Furlong studied the stills. 'We've had sightings in the Gardens up and down the coast from there. They must be there somewhere.'

'Sorry, sir. But there is no sign.'

The CO plotted another probability zone for the Hive ships to dredge.

Rorqual ran silently below the horizon. 'We must avoid contact until we see how they armed this ship. The Hive spent two years getting it ready. After our defeat of their Pursuit One I'm sure they learned something.'

ARNOLD was impatient. 'Let's just run in and crush them before they know what hit them.'

'They'd see me about the same time I saw them. I assume that our sensors are about the same.'

Larry agreed. 'The Hive hasn't been able to improve on meck components for the past thousand years. If anything they are deteriorating.'

'OK,' grumbled ARNOLD. 'Have your long ear open. See what you can pick up. Larry how did you organize our people?'

'Six squads – one on each deck and two in reserve. Three back-up crane operators.'

'Good.'

Scratch that,' said the ship.

'Now what?' demanded ARNOLD.

'Cancel those battle plans. They will fail. Here are transmissions I am picking up from the armada.'

'Armada?' gasped Larry.

The screen split into four quadrants. Each showed a different view of a group of ships. It took them a moment of comparing to realize that each view was taken by a high sensor crane of a different ship.

'Look at those cranes! They must be twice as long as ours,' exclaimed Larry. 'And those fore cranes are as thick as a freight capsule.'

'Four ships,' mumbled Big Har. 'Well, if they have no Arnolds we might still have a chance . . .'

The activities appeared to be mock battles. Two Hive ships squared off and went through drills with each pair of cranes. When they locked the bulldog fore cranes the entire ship trembled. The long aft cranes tossed satchel charges three miles. Mushrooms of steam pocked the target area. Larry and the Benthics slumped into despair. Only ARNOLD remained optimistic.

'We are bigger, stronger, and faster,' said the giant. 'If we can board one of those ships—'

'Negative,' said *Rorqual.*

The screen showed two armed robots slugging it out with spiked maces. The mechanical devices were slow and awkward, but there was a variety of them exercising on the middle deck.

Some appeared to weigh over a ton, obviously too large for a Benthic to defeat with a handmade spear.

'I'm afraid those robots are on remote like the cranes,' said Larry.

'Correct,' said *Rorqual*.

'And if we attack?'

'We will die,' said the ship.

ARNOLD showed no fear. In his mind there was no alternative to battle. He would never run. 'Let's attack!'

'But we can't win!' shouted Larry, dancing his little hemitorso around the chart table. 'There must be some other way—'

'Attack!' repeated the giant.

Big Har and the Benthics glanced up from their flimsy weapons to the formidable Hive machines on the screen. 'Is there another way?' asked Har.

The ship blanked out the screen. Silence. ARNOLD blinked. He seemed to come out of a trance – his cerebellar fighting mode. 'What?'

Rorqual turned back towards the islands. 'There may be a way. The probability of success is small but significant.'

ARNOLD was puzzled. 'We will fight?'

'We fight,' said the ship, 'later. There are preparations we must make.'

On their way to the archipelago they paused at several small desert islands, where the ship scooped up tons of smooth stones and sand from the beaches. As the cargo hold filled, the ship rode lower and lower in the water.

As they approached Har's island home a small flotilla of victory canoes and catamarans met them in the bay. The reception lost its gaiety when *Rorqual* ordered them back to shore.

'Drop your lowers. Let the larger catamarans pull alongside to take off my crew. Everyone is to go to shore except ARNOLD. In the coming battles I need only my captain.'

Larry questioned the ship's decision, but she remained firm. Adopting some of the façade of a deity, she boomed her voice over the water: 'I brought the warrior to your people and left his seed. We will do this alone!'

Hemihuman Larry climbed up the rope to the catamaran's mast. Below the crowd of wives and children wept and screamed for their ARNOLD. *Rorqual* drew away, her decks deserted. The obedient Nebish crewman waited a respectful interval before hoisting sail. The fleet of small boats returned to the island.

ARNOLD stood in the control cabin, an arsenal by his side: stacks of neolithic spears fashioned by the islanders, throwing stones, small bows and arrows used in fishing, his trusty double-bladed axe. The forescreens gave the enemy's position. The armada had reached the horizon.

Abruptly *Rorqual* swung to port and ran north along the archipelago.

'Are we avoiding battle?'

'Delaying,' said the ship. 'There is a ceremony we must perform.'

White Belly came out of her hiding place. She wore a flowery lavalava and carried a flask of purple wine.

'You shouldn't be here!' scolded ARNOLD.

'It is necessary,' said the ship.

White Belly removed her colourful kilt and climbed up on the chart table, arching her back. She put her feet up and stretched out on the crackling printouts – nose and toes in the air, shoulders back and heels together. With her left hand she poured an ounce of purple wine into her navel.

ARNOLD was irritated. 'We have no time for sex before battle—'

'The ceremony is necessary – drink!' said the ship. Its cyber-voice grew masculine and distant – a command.

ARNOLD shrugged. He put his left hand on her shoulder and his right on her knee. The wine was warm and a bit salty. She refilled the biological recess.

'Drink,' said the ship.

The floral and fruity molecules were more in evidence. The third drink was cooler.

'Drink!'
Slurp!

Click! LEPTOSOUL DADDY LONGLEGS

ARNOLD had eight obedient legs – four coordinated pairs. The second pair waved overhead like antennae – listening and sniffing. Each leg had arachnoid spinnerets casting out stout webs. Eyes, twelve feet in diameter blinked out of his turret-like head. He thrashed the ocean into foam with his powerful legs. ARNOLD was now Daddy Longlegs – with a body a quarter of a mile long!

'Sovereign. We've sighted *Rorqual*,' announced Pursuit Two.
'Take her!' ordered Furlong from the Hive.
The armada turned. ARNOLD waited quietly with his legs folded on his back. Only his eyes moved – tracking. A fog bank thickened and rolled over his stern. The hovercraft circled him and returned to its hanger with engine trouble. The fog engulfed the Hive ships.
'You can't hide from us in here,' said Furlong.
The sensors adjusted for water vapour and continued to send images to his screen. There was a moment of confusion on the decks as crane operators left their exterior booths and went to their remote controls below decks. They had drilled primarily on visual, and would be a bit awkward until they grew familiar with ship optics. Tinkers worked on the hovercraft. Archers shipped stimulants. Killer Mecks warmed up.
Daddy Longlegs ARNOLD listened to the Hive ships talk. He crouched in the fog.
'Circle the Harvester if you can,' said Furlong. 'I don't want her getting away this time. If you can get close enough, lock on the bulldog cranes and wait for the other ships to close before you try boarding. We don't know how many Benthics may be on board. Remember she may be carrying as many as ten thousand!'
ARNOLD waited, his second pair of legs high in the air

– alert. One vessel advanced slowly. The others began a fast encirclement. They were staying on an arc five miles away. He turned to the near ship. It's bulldog cranes opened – distance 880 yards – two body lengths.

ARNOLD hit the water with eight legs, lunging forward. He planted R-1 on the ship's foredeck to fend off the pincers; L-1 spewed sticky polymer and lassoed the enemy's cranes. The Nebish crane operators fumbled with their controls, but the Daddy Longlegs was quick and agile, tying them up in a neat package. Squads of warriors swarmed the decks like ants – racing in circles in the fog.

'Get a line on her! Board her!'

ARNOLD placed his first two pairs of legs on the pursuit ship's middle deck and lifted himself up, crawling out of the water. His belly full of stones weighted him down. The enemy ship listed sharply to port. ARNOLD drank deeply, settling lower in the water.

Furlong was on his feet. '*Rorqual* has rammed Pursuit Two. They are sinking. Get in there fast and get a line on them.'

ARNOLD reached over with L-3 and plucked the hatch covers off the ship. He leaned back, rolling the ship over to let the sea cascade into the hold. He continued to drink. A second ship appeared. He pushed it away with R-4. Several grapples fell on his back. He scratched them away with his third pair of legs. Waves washed over them. He struggled to keep the ship under until it began to lose buoyancy. Two more ships appeared with wide pincers and trailing hooks. He pushed up on them with his legs diving deeper; the captive ship continued to struggle against him. He felt the powerful drive units as they dragged him around at thirty fathoms. At sixty fathoms the ship shuddered. It's airtight compartments began to buckle. The pressure did not bother ARNOLD. He kept his pores open. The sea moved freely through his body. They came to rest on the bottom. He let go of the ship.

'What happened?' asked Furlong. His screen showed little more than foggy decks on three quadrants. The fourth quadrant was blank – the sunken ship.

The captain of Pursuit Three answered: 'P Two engaged the enemy and destroyed him. Unfortunately P Two is down on the shelf in two hundred fathoms. The tip of her stern is visible.'

Furlong watched the fog separate for a close view as a sensor crane touched the aft keel. It protruded twenty feet into the air. The nose of the ship rested on the bottom. There was no sign of life – cracked plates and flooding had made the cyber units inactive.

'Start salvaging immediately. I want *Rorqual* and P Two back in service for the Hive as soon as possible.'

'Yes, sir.'

Using their one-eyed mechanical Tuna, the three Hive vessels lined up along the hull of Pursuit Two. They each directed a hose line into one of the submerged hatches and began to fill the hold with foam – firm polymer bubbles of air. While the pumping progressed, other motorized sensor lines were busy searching for *Rorqual*.

'She's afloat!'

A smooth black keel lay low in the water – a hundred yard long and ten feet high.

'Keep pumping air into her. But start towing towards the Shipyards.'

'Right away, sir.'

'What happened to *Rorqual*?'

'She's still down there. We have her on our scope. However, she has slipped off the ledge and is lying in five hundred fathoms – in a trench. It will take a while to get our lines into her.'

'Well, have Pursuit Five tow in the wreck. You two can stay at the scene until you raise *Rorqual*.'

'We understand, sir.'

Furlong stood up and wiped his forehead.

'Good work,' said the CO. 'With three ships in our fishing fleet we should see good times again.'

'And the two damaged vessels should be back in service in a couple of years.'

'Yes,' agreed CO. 'You may rest now. I will call a Committee meeting in twelve hours.'

Furlong walked behind a curtain, past the bulky terminals and flopped down on his cot.

'Raid! Raid! Raid!

Furlong sat up sleepily. 'Now what?' He rubbed his eyes. Two hours of sleep was just enough to numb his face.

'Intruder in the Garden!' announced the view-screen.

'That is no reason to awaken a sovereign!' he growled. 'Call Hunter Control.'

'Six of our cities are under attack.'

'Let me see who is attacking. Oh... Benthics. Must be a retaliatory raid. There are only two or three outside of each shaftcap. No problem. Notify Security and send out the Hunters. I'll review the records in the morning.'

'Yes, sir.'

'Pursuit Three reporting: foaming *Rorqual*'s hull.'

'Let me sleep. I don't want to be disturbed again with these routine matters. The CO can update me when I get up in the morning.'

'Sorry, sir.'

'Shaftcap breached. Twenty-three dead.'

'... in the morning...' grumbled Furlong.

Ten hours later, Furlong awoke, ate, and slept again. Late in the afternoon he gathered himself up, drank two pints of stimulant, and stumbled into the refresher.

'Update me.'

The CO scanned the prior eighteen hours and verbalized over the roar of the air/water laminar flow. 'Sea scene unchanged. Vessels Two and Five making progress slowly – ETA four days. Three and Four are lifting *Rorqual*. No problems. Four shaftcaps were invaded. The damage and lives lost were well within the projected limits. Three Benthics were killed, one captured.'

Furlong stuck his head out of the pulsing spray. 'The prisoner... is he still alive?'

'Yes. He was taken to the Bio Labs for dissection.'

'Of course. Did we learn anything from him? We've had a terrible time finding their domes lately.'

The CO filled the screen with data. 'We put him through a the usual psychic probing and CNS-molecular-memory analysis. This is what we learned. The Neurotecks will be removing his brain now to see if our electrical CNS-MM analysis matches their chemical analysis.'

Furlong glanced at the outline. 'My! He's a big fellow. Make a note to put his genes on file. So he thinks he has a deity on his side? Leviathan? Could he think the Harvester is his god?'

'Apparently,' said the CO. 'That could explain their tenacity at holding the shelf. Having a marine god justifies their claim to the sea.'

'I'd like to talk to him before the team does the craniectomy.'

'He will be held for you – Lab B-Seventeen.'

Red Crab lay pinned to the vivisection table. He was already on the pump. Tubes and wires kept him alive while curious teams labelled and sampled his internal organs.

'I have the reading on his aortic wall. Look and that lysine oxidase level!'

'Hand me the core of spleen. Now the liver. Where are those vials I asked for?'

'Pull that retractor. We need more intervertebral material.'

Red Crab tried to struggle, but none of his muscles obeyed him. He couldn't blink his eye or change his respiratory rate. He waited.

'Is he conscious?' asked Furlong.

'The EEG indicates that he is, but I've got his motor end-plates turned off,' explained the teck.

'I'd like to talk to him.'

'Yes, sir. Just a minute. We'll have the Bone Team check their pins. I don't want this creature to wreck any of our instruments with its thrashing around.'

The bloodied pins were reattached to their mountings. The Benthic was suspended above the work area. Each of the large bones was transfixed: two pins in the outer table of the occipital bone, one in each ilium, humerus and femur.

'Before you give him back his muscle control don't you think you should close up his belly? I don't want anything to fall out if he coughs.'

'Good idea,' said the teck, standing up and stretching. 'All right, Ace, put some sutures in there to cut down the oozing. Clamp up the incision. We can finish this tomorrow.'

Furlong stepped outside for a snack. They called him when the Benthic started to move. The surgical dissection site was closed with a row of large skin staples. The table was wheeled away and a soft absorbent cot replaced it. The prisoner remained suspended.

'If he gives you any trouble, turn this on. It paralyzes his endplates. We'll be back in about twelve hours. It might take us four or five days to complete our studies. We have a lot of forms to fill out on this one. He's interesting.'

Furlong nodded. 'I'm sure. Do we have a voiceprint on him?'

'No genetic pattern on file,' said the teck. 'This one is a hybrid at least. Might be one of the original primitives. That's why we have to go slow and learn as much as we can.'

Furlong turned to the Benthic – a seventy-four-inch leathery giant with thick body hair and mature genitalia. Furlong's own fifty-two inch frame was large for a Nebish, but he felt a little overwhelmed.

'Can you hear me?'

The giant snarled. Every muscle in his body stood out. Tendons taut; eyes flashed hatred.

'I wish I could make you more comfortable while we talked, but I don't know which of these dials control pain. Tell me about your people.'

Silence.

'Tell me about your god. You worship a deity that looks like a whale?'

The giant stubbornly turned away his eyes; the metalloid bone pins creaked.

'Your god is dead,' continued Furlong. 'We have slain your *Rorqual*.'

Red Crab turned a pair of malevolent eyes on the Nebish Chairman-Sovereign. 'My Godwhale will never die. She brought the fish back to the sea for us. She will kill you for what you have done.' He tried to spit, but his head brace was too stiff. Only a few misty drops stuck to Furlong's face.

'I have seen the Hive ships sink your Godwhale. Here, I'll move this screen around so you can see for yourself. Not this channel. Those are shots of your own internal organs. Here it is. See! *Rorqual* is at the bottom of the sea.'

Red Crab saw the Hive vessels anchored above the sunken Harvester. An optic was lowered on a meck Tuna. It explored the hull. All hatches were open.

'Look,' boasted Furlong. 'Every compartment is flooded. Your Godwhale is no deity. It is just a sunken ship. All of its crew has died.'

'Stupid!' shouted Red Crab. 'Of course it is a ship – a ship occupied by our deity. Open your eyes. There is no crew! *Rorqual* still lives. It is your Hive crews that will die.'

Furlong just grinned confidently. Simple Neolithic peoples have their simple solutions for their problems. An all-powerful deity is the simplest. He started to stand up to leave, but the searching eye of the meck Tuna interested him. He pulled up a chair and sat beside the vivisectionist's victim. An occasional dim light blinked in the miles of dark corridors. Curious fish and other marine life forms darted in and out of the shadows, giving him a start.

'She lives,' spat Red Crab.

Furlong ignored the giant's ravings. 'Those dark shapes in the control room are nothing more than a fish or squid. Wait until the optic gets closer—'

Furlong's words were cut off by the obvious human form that fluttered about in the flooded chamber on a pair of lacy wings. Female breasts!

'An angel!' shouted Red Crab confidently. 'I will see your ships destroyed.'

Furlong's mouth dropped open. He stood slowly.

'Kill! Kill!' chanted the captive.

'Do not believe what you see,' said CO. 'This transmission is an obvious simulation.'

The angel approached the spying optic with an axe. The transmission stopped.

Furlong retched and left the operating theatre. In the hall he met one of the Biotecks.

'Is there some way to make our captive suffer more?'

'More?'

'I'd like to punish him for his crimes against the Hive.'

The teck shook his head. 'I don't think the people in Neuro would like that. You see, they want his cerebral molecules as undisturbed as possible for their analysis.'

Furlong leaned against the wall for a few minutes before starting back to the committee room.

Big Daddy Longlegs ARNOLD deposited his belly stones in little castings – several thousand tons in size. He raised his snorkel and drew air into his belly. He climbed up the convenient lines to the two Hive ships. Remaining under water, he clung to their keels and chewed on their soft underbellies. Their struggles were brief. Wrapping them in a cocoon, he deposited them in the five-hundred-fathom trench. Surfacing he pumped himself dry, riding high on the water, a light, fast creature. He quickly caught up with the ship towing the flooded derelict. The devil-bird flew by. He spun a sticky web and cast for the flying creature. It seemed to flutter slowly – an easy target. He reeled it in. It's soft contents tasted rich and meaty.

The ship threw standard weapons at ARNOLD. He caught them and tossed them back. Several exploded. ARNOLD circled warily, spinning an underwater macramé cable.

Pursuit Five cut loose the derelict and turned towards *Rorqual*.

'Get a line on her. Pull her into the bulldog grapples!'

'Sir, she knocked down our Huntercraft and sucked it into her maw. Shall I hit the destruct button?'

'Yes.'

ARNOLD felt heartburn. He belched a small cloud of smoke.

'She has an underwater cable on us. She is pulling us closer.'

'Good. Activate the Killer Mecks. Get ready to board.'

Whoop! Whoop! Whoop! The Killer Mecks ran out of their garages and stood at the rail, waving an assortment of spikes and throwing appendages.

ARNOLD felt the bulldog clamp sink into his skin. A small beetle left the ship and crawled for his brain turret. He felt the metal feet on his skin and saw the thick armour. He caught it with his R-3 leg. It exploded, burning him. He squirted webbing over the charred spot. Two more beetles attached themselves to his back. He saw a dozen more crowding the ship's rail.

'Dive! Dive! Dive!'

'Close the hatches. *Rorqual* is trying to sink us by scuttling herself.'

'Send our location to the Hive. Have them send Huntercraft with explosives. We can hold out on the bottom: it is only about two hundred feet deep – just fifty feet over our decks.'

ARNOLD wrestled the enemy ship under him and pushed it into the soft sandy bottom. He crawled up on to it and filled his belly with water to increase his weight. His own body rose a hundred feet into the air. He needed at least three hundred feet to submerge with the enemy ship. His legs clawed, but he was unable to drag the ship. Its anchor and cranes were out. He tried to move away, but the bulldogs held firm. He waited.

The first Hive Huntercraft was snared with an aerial web.

'*Rorqual!*'

The voice of the Hive. ARNOLD tightened his hold on the ship and listened.

'We have one of your people – a hostage. Do you remember Red Crab?'

ARNOLD opened a channel. 'I have many hostages.'

'Allow my people to go free, and I will release Red Crab. You may keep the ship.'

'Send Red Crab to me.'

'No. Release my crew first.'

ARNOLD allowed the Hive ship to rise to the surface abruptly, reducing the pressure on the hull by two atmospheres. Nitrogen bubbles formed in the Nebish crew, throwing them down on the decks in pain. The scene changed Furlong's mind. 'Your man will be on the beach in three hours. He will be on a stretcher.'

ARNOLD pushed the ship back into the sand. The recompression alleviated the crew's suffering. He spoke with the ship's captain, explaining the Hive's offer. 'You will need recompression time. If you arrange for a Huntercraft to bring the Benthic, I can see to it that you have no more pain.'

The Captain was happy to comply with the prisoner exchange. He was puzzled by the bizarre symptoms of the bends – emboli of nitrogen bubbles had paralyzed his left foot and disabled half his crew; many had died.

The Hive Huntercraft wobbled on to ARNOLD's back four hours later. It asked for a power cable to refill its depleted cells. An angel approached the craft with her translucent wings shimmering in the sun – nipples and chin arrogantly high. Red Crab stumbled out of the hatch supported between two Meditecks. He was swathed in bandages – eyes glazed, fingers stiff, silent. They moved slowly towards ARNOLD's turret-like head. He turned his huge EM receptor on the group, peering inside the mutilated body. Daddy Longlegs screamed. The captive Benthic carried meck components in his skull and thorax – vivisection had gone to completion, and the Hive was returning a warm musculoskeletal system.

'Dive! Dive! Dive!'

The wall of salt water caught Pursuit Five with her hatches open. The female angel watched Nebishes die.

A victorious *Rorqual* towed four cocoons past garlanded ceremonial canoes. ARNOLD and White Belly grinned from her foredeck.

Big Har and Larry toured their Harvester. There was very little battle damage – a few charred blast marks, wrinkled deck plates, and water marks on cabin furnishings; but nothing significant. Larry noticed an occasional barnacle inside the ship.

'How did you do it? Four ships, and hardly a scratch!'

ARNOLD just rubbed his harness marks and laughed.

'I don't remember. All I know is that White Belly has ensured her seat next to me next year.'

'Why's that?'

'She's going to give me another son.'

Har and Larry nodded. That made sense. You didn't take a Benthic woman down into the Ocean without your hormones acting up. Even in battle they must have had time to crawl off into a trench to copulate.

Work on the captured ships began immediately. The stern of Pursuit Three extended into the jungle, while the flooded bow rested on the bottom of the bay in two hundred feet of water. *Rorqual* studied the playbacks of the battles and decided the Killer Mecks could be tooled up to help with repair work. Iron Tunas were attached to her cranes to map the sunken ships. Nebish crew readied the tool shop.

Hemihuman Larry climbed the cable hand-over-hand and settled his calloused trunk into the lookout basket of the second-right crane. Clicking sensors glittered around him. He watched while the third pair of cranes grappled for salvage.

'That you up in sensory R-two?' shouted ARNOLD.

Larry waved down at the giant.

'Keep an eye on things. I'm going angel and diving. Our deep scanners have located one of the Killer Mecks.'

'OK,' answered Larry. He watched his captain buckle on his fluid-filled wings. Crane 1-R came back and lifted him into the sea. Larry turned to his little remote screen to monitor the work on the bottom.

The decks of Pursuit Three were warped by the deep crunch. A meat-eating elasmobranch was tearing at a tangle of bodies wedged in the forehatch. Other hungry denizens glided in and out of rents. An occasional cluster of bubbles escaped from an internal hollow chamber to dance noisily up to the surface. ARNOLD swam past the short, powerful bulldog cranes on the foredeck and examined the control cabin. Its hatch was split and blackened. Inside he found a shattered robot – post-destruct.

'Careful,' cautioned the hemihuman. 'That is the third robot with the same pattern of blast damage. Hold the Iron Tuna closer so *Rorqual* can study it. What do you think, old girl?'

'Self-destruct,' said the ship. 'Attach it to my grapple. We'll study it before we try to bring any of the others to the surface.'

The tecks swarmed over the twisted hulk.

'Crude armour – hardly more than boiler plate.'

'Here is what's left of the self-destruct circuit. Looks like an ordinary satchel charge was used.'

'Can you disarm one?'

'If its circuitry is like this.'

Rorqual machined delicate manipulators for the Iron Tuna. Larry sat at the screen and watched the underwater scene as each new robot was disarmed. One of the larger two-ton machines exploded as it was lifted above the waves. 'Must have had two circuits,' he commented. 'That tells us something, though. Being submerged interferes with the mechanism. Air activates it.'

Meck warriors became meck workers under *Rorqual*'s guiding hand. The Benthic navy slowly took shape in the tropical lagoon. As the months flew by, ARNOLD's family grew. A new mannequin was fashioned for Larry.

Larry wasn't sure he'd be able to adjust to Spider Urethane. 'I feel like I'm riding an octopus,' he complained. The mannequin could only vibrate its damaged lingual membrane. 'What am I going to use all these attachments for? Four legs! A power take-off and a screw mounting! I feel like a meck from the tool room. And these arms might be handy for carrying things, but most of the time they are in the way.'

Rorqual soothed the hemihuman. 'It is the best one available. We'll keep our eyes open for a more humanoid shape, but meanwhile this will keep your torso up off the deck. It has been equipped with a Blood Scrubber so you can have more variety in your diet.'

'Well, that's a plus. I was getting a bit tired of the leafy stuff three times a day. But all those appendages?'

'The arms, power take-off, and mounting screw fold into panels; the body can be shortened, fore and aft, and the hind legs fold into the forelegs. You'll be a biped on the dance floor and a quadruped in the mountains.'

'A satyr or a centaur – interesting,' said Larry. He walked over to the storage tanks that held his perfusion fluids. He attached the mannequin's nozzle and recharged his artificial kidneys. 'You don't talk much, do you?'

The mannequin just hummed.

'You do a good job,' he continued. 'You can certainly read myograms. I just think of taking a step and you take it. You paw at the deck when I'm restless and feel like pawing. You rear up and kick when I'm happy. You must have studied ungulate behaviour. Can't you talk at all?'

The voice was that of *Rorqual*, using the mannequin's speaker. 'Spider Urethane is equipped with a young cyber cortex, primarily a learning-type. He has no personality of his own yet. While on my decks he will share with me – much as Trilobite did as a youth. If you are away from me for long periods he will mature and have self-identity. Now he is your brain stem and cerebellum, concerned with bladder, bowel, and leg function. Feel free to speak to him, for you will be speaking to me.'

'A learning cortex – bubble-magnetic garnet wafers?'

'Yes. Come out on the deck and practise trotting.'

Larry enjoyed the rhythmic pounding of hooves: walk trot, canter, and gallop. All the gears were smooth.

'Hi!' called a feminine voice from the darkness near the forehatch. A jumble of salvaged mecks surrounded the orange light from the tool room below. Centaur Larry loped over and peered down. Grinder and Sander Mecks were busy, creating a din of ninety decibels. Parts of a Battle Meck were spread over the knees of a Lathe machine.

'Hi!'

Larry turned to the dark mecks next to him. 'Are any of you operative?' He flashed his chest light around. Seaweed covered twisted metalloid skin and vacant optics. One set of optics blinked back. 'There you are. Don't you have enough power for your telltales?'

'No,' she said. 'During the battle I was put on manual and exhausted. I'm pretty low.'

Larry glanced around. 'I'll bring a power cable—'

'No. My plates are OK. It's my inertial wheel that needs it. It is a mag-supported flywheel that stores spin momentum. I use it for everything except mentating.'

'How do we recharge a flywheel?'

'You're riding Spider Urethane. He has given me a life before. Can you spare the time?'

'That depends. Let me get you out of that junk pile. Why – you are nothing but a box!'

'Lost my appendages in an explosion. My jaw-type, flexible coupling is in my undercarriage. It is compatible with the tip of your power take-off.'

'Well . . . I don't know—'

'SU has done it before. It only takes a second. Call a crane with a swivel hook and get me up – about three feet off the deck. I weigh about a hundred pounds so keep your toes clear – or – your hooves.' She giggled.

Larry learned many things about his new meck body. His power take-off was a flexible shaft with an operating torque capacity of fifty pound-inches. A flexible casing protected his soft fingers during the operation.

'Use the heavy-duty oil with molybdenum disulfide to reduce the coefficient of friction of the mating surfaces,' she instructed.

'Maybe I'd better crawl out of here. I don't like to be this close to power machinery.'

'That isn't necessary. Wear this hard hat. It has an E-ring.'

He set the hat on his head.

'Keep the torque at fifty. Remember, the shaft will deflect under maximum load; it will helix at a hundred pound-inches.

But we'd better lock in our mid-line mounting screw to be safe: forty-five degrees chamfer, one point seven five on shaft, five grooves per inch.'

She directed that the centaur switch to satyr mode and stretch out on the deck to line up bevels. She swivelled down on top of the screw, using her best 'oriental basket technique'. Each turn lowered her about half a centimetre. After thirty revolutions the box locked in place. Her long cable to the crane began vibrating – simple harmonic motions. When the mounting tightened, viscous damping reduced the vibration.

'Now!' she said. 'Lock in the power take-off. My housing diameter has plenty of clearance. Don't worry about damage. I'm built to take forty-five thousand pounds per square inch.' Her lights flickered several times, then glowed brightly. Her chassis was spangled with numerous telltales. Three larger, central ones resembled eyes. Others were arranged in scrolls and loops, far more decorative than functional. Empty sockets marked the rudiments of her arms and legs.

The course deck irritated Larry's back.

'OK?'

'Fine. Wonderful.' Her voice was too sultry. 'You can disconnect the power cable and spin me in the opposite direction to unlock our mounting.'

The crane swung her back into the row of damaged battle robots. Her telltales glowed brightly. 'Thanks. That was real nice.'

Larry was suspiciously euphoric. He stood and brushed off his mannequin. When he removed his hard hat the welts on his back throbbed. His irritation returned. The mood changes altered him. He studied the inside of the hat. Soft grey transducers winked back at him. 'Steriosonics!' he exclaimed. 'What does this E-ring attach to?'

'It is tuned to your mannequin's erogenous zone – the mounting screw. Those sonics are focused on your hypothalamus and several of the midbrain nuclei: Brady, Lilly, Olds ... the reticular system.'

'My pleasure centres!'

'I wanted you to enjoy recharging me. I like to trade pleasure for energy – a fair bargain,' she said.

He flared, prancing backward. 'I don't need that sort of thing from a machine!'

Her jaw-type coupling protruded in a silent pout.

'I can see that you stay charged, but you don't have to pay me – er – that way,' he grumbled.

'You're embarrassed. I am sorry.'

'I am not embarrassed. I just don't think of you as a sex object. You're nothing but a rusty box...'

'And after I'm repaired? You will help me select my new appendages – arms, legs, a head??'

He refused to answer. Her manner was too familiar, possessive, and feminine.

She giggled.

'What's so funny?'

'My new name. You can call me "Rusty". Like it?'

'No. What sort of machine are you?'

'See my three eyes – watch.' The three telltales rapidly changed colour and emblems, stopping one at a time: a lemon and two cherries. 'I'm a slot machine – a game of chance.'

'Gambling? For what?'

'On my last ship I was hooked up to the shipbrain and dealt in calorie credits. Some lucky members of the crew of Pursuit Three went to their deaths with a year's supply of flavours.'

'Some luck!' Larry stamped a wide circle, waving his arms. 'A female slot machine! And she needs my mannequin for a recharge.' He paused, worried. 'I hate to ask... but how often do you need – er – it?'

She giggled and winked her middle eye. 'Daily would be fine, but I can go a week or so.'

Larry loped down to the evening meal. ARNOLD's wives eyed the gleaming horse torso suspiciously. He pranced around the table, grinned, and shifted to satyr mode – sitting down like a human.

Sunfish brought his usual greens-and-crust sandwich. Larry's

Blood Scrubber had lowered the urea and potassium levels of his serum and relieved him of his perpetual ruinous nausea. The aromas of steamed clams and boiled lobster made his nostrils flare. He had an appetite for the first time since the loss of his first mannequin. Opening the ascetic sandwich, he added a slab of baked fish and took a big bite. Crumbs fell. He heaped his plate: squid arms, urchin roe, mussel feet. Two mugs of *Rorqual*'s beer later, the satyr was down on his right elbow, chatting freely, speech slightly slurred.

ARNOLD grinned across the table. 'Now that's how to eat and drink! If I didn't know better, Larry, I'd think that some women had been dissipating you – to give you such an appetite.'

Larry raised his mug, smiling. Everyone laughed with him. After all, tonight he was a wicked satyr.

Larry galloped down the deck and pulled up beside ARNOLD.

'No hangover?' commented the giant.

'Efficient Blood Scrubber, that's all.' He described his dilemma with Slot Machine. 'She seems very bright, and I enjoy talking with her, but I don't think I should be taking my pleasure that way – artificially.'

ARNOLD nodded. 'I understand. You and I are destined to have close relationships with cybers: me for my fifteen-amino-acid bread, and you for your various bodily functions. Cybers naturally like us because we are dependant on them. I guess we complement each other.'

'Symbionts!'

'Yes. Our lives are made longer and richer by the machines. They protect our metabolism – your renal functions and my amino acid; help us travel; and expand our intellectual aware-ness. It is only natural that they play a role in our sex lives: my many wives are housed by *Rorqual*: your reticular system gets tickled.'

Larry remained silent, thinking.

'Of course you can do as you wish,' continued the giant, 'but pleasure centres are there to be used. You are half-machine

– have been for over half your life if you count those years with Trilobite and *Rorqual*. Don't forget that.'

'I'm half-machine? I guess I am. Well, no sense getting excited about it now. Maybe if I see that Slot Machine gets her appendages I won't feel like I've neglected an intelligence.'

He trotted toward the forehatch.

'Back so soon?' she chided.

'I just wanted to make sure you got your arms and legs so you could be put to work. We are short of mecks in the game room.'

'Did you bring the moly?'

'The what?'

'The penetrating oil with molybdenum disulfide – the electro-moly.'

He frowned. 'I haven't come to recharge you. The tool room may be able to take you next – for repairs.'

'And you wanted to pick out my arms and legs?'

He left without a word. In the drawing room her new extremities were designed to fit the job description. Because of her female personality, she was matched with the wives, and given fairly humanoid lines. Her three eyes would be at the umbilical level of her robot body when it was finished.

'It'll take about a week,' he said, showing her a blueprint. 'These tapes contain your new duties.'

'Do you have time to recharge me?'

'Now? You said you could last a week between charges,' he objected.

She giggled. 'From the looks of my new body I'd say that it would be less embarrassing now.'

He nodded.

'Put on the hat.'

'No. It isn't necessary to pay me.'

She sulked. 'I don't consider it payment. This isn't something I do to you or you do to me. It is something we do together.'

Larry's irritation showed. 'You are just a machine! Don't talk about a mechanical recharge as if it were an act of lovemaking.'

'Why not? My neural apparatus is at least as complex as

yours. My experience – well, I'm over a thousand years old. Why shouldn't I sound like I enjoy a good recharging. It does give me renewed strength.'

'OK, OK. If it makes you feel better I'll wear the damn hat. Let's get on with it. I've got a lot of things to do today. Crane! CRANE!!'

'Hmmm! And you came to me before breakfast.'

'Now cut that out!'

'Yes, dear.'

Larry wiped his brow as the swivel hook lifted Slot Machine away. He felt more than a vague sensation of pleasure. There had been a real crest of euphoria – a minor orgasm. Old adolescent memories of sexual encounters were stirred up. 'What did you do?' he demanded, catching his breath.

The squat, rusty box remained silent.

'That time was different,' he complained.

'Better?'

He removed his hard hat and brushed the dust off his back. Leaning against the rail, he watched the ship's wake. Dawn had brought a school of jumping fish.

'OK. It was better,' he admitted. 'What did you do?'

'Turned up the E-stimulus a little.'

'A little! How high can it go?'

'I guess we'll find out... won't we,' she giggled. 'After I get some nice soft arms and legs.'

Larry went over the blueprints again. He couldn't decide which part of the chasses was best suited for the jaw-type flexible coupling.

10
Negotiations

Cast they ARNOLD upon the waters
And he shall return a hundredfold.
                    – Wandee (memo)

Wandee stood in the doorway of the committee room, a bundle of reports under her arm. Her pituitary-ovarian axis had polarized late, giving her a semblance of a female figure – drawing in her waist and rounding her breasts and hips slightly. However, menopause promptly followed her two wasted ovulations. Her eyes remained bright and alert, giving evidence of a curious mind under the grey streaks and wrinkles.

'I brought over those reports on the Benthic dissections,' she said.

Furlong lifted his head from his arms and blinked across the empty table. He alone had been spared by the Megajury. His Cabinet had returned to the protein pool.

'How do I address you, sir?'

He glanced at this gold Aries – a talisman useless against the wrath of the Hive. 'Come in, Wandee. Sit down, I'm not up to protocol this morning.'

'I watched the voting,' she said softly. 'You were lucky.'

'I know.' He gestured towards the empty room. 'But my advisors were caught napping. After the sinking of the armada the jury reviewed the optics of our strategy meetings. Anyone who closed their eyes was judged a shirker. Hive justice is swift.'

'Empty chairs mean a fuller sandwich,' she said, repeating an old aphorism. 'Here are the reports. The Benthic is much like our own Lesser Arnold. Natural selection has given him a good body – rich in the types of genes and proteins we engineer into our warriors. Our Neurotecks tell me that the Benthics have a set of CNS-MMs that rival our best efforts at leptosoul conditioning.'

'CNS-MM?'

'The Central Nervous System Memory Molecules – deep and broad-banded – a result of a good diet and the competitive marine environment. We collected a number of good condons. Those Benthic genes will come in handy when we design the next generation of warrior ARNOLDs – a new Super Arnold!'

Furlong shook his head and pushed the reports away. 'No more ARNOLDs!' Look at the cost analyses on that batch we just raised: special diet, chains, Chapel and Chairman time. Leptosoul conditioning and soporifics were only partially successful in controlling them. And look at the results! Every one of them was a potential danger to the Hive. Our Greater Arnold actually broke away and survives to fight us. We built plankton Harvesters and then lost them. No more ARNOLDs!'

'But we can't stop now,' explained Wandee, searching for one of her reports. 'He is still free.'

'So . . . ? He's a genetic defective. Time will take care of him.'

'Maybe not,' she said. 'I built the defect into his genes, and it is true that he can't manufacture fifteen of the amino acids. However, he is probably searching for a mate among the Benthics. His hybrid offspring will have only one of his defective genes. A good gene from the mother will enable the children to handle proteins normally. They'll have half ARNOLD and half Benthic. Very tough! And bright too.'

Furlong glanced at Wandee's Mendelian chart and scoffed. 'But there are trillions of us. How many of these hybrids do we have to worry about? Two? Ten?'

'Maybe hundreds? You must remember that he is a battle-cock – King ARNOLD.'

'Hundreds?'

'Depending on the availability of Benthic females. Judging

from the numbers of males our Hunters were bringing in over the past decade, I'd say that ARNOLD would have little trouble gathering up quite a harem. Keeping them all pregnant would be no problem.'

'I suppose that a future Megajury would blame me for that,' said Furlong.

'And me,' said Wandee. 'Unless we could make friends with them. If we don't make certain the Hive benefits from all these hybrid ARNOLDs we could have a very uncomfortable retirement.'

'Or a short one,' mumbled the tired Chairman. 'What do you suggest?'

'At least a truce. Perhaps lay the groundwork for trade.'

Furlong's eyes narrowed. 'A truce. Do you suppose he would agree?'

'It is possible. I think it is worth a try.'

Larry galloped up and down the tilted decks of the damaged ship. Pumps worked around the clock to keep the water-level below the work area. Repair Crews composed of Benthics and *Rorqual*'s tecks tried to get the cyber units back in working order.

'A crane twitched. You must be on a motor fibre,' shouted Larry.

A teck glanced out of the hatch, a bundle of small gleaming tools in his fist. He watched the crane while one of his partners repeated the stimulus. The crane began slowly to raise its cable. The teck smiled and ducked down the hatch.

'There's a call for ARNOLD on the long ear,' buzzed *Rorqual*'s deck speaker.

Larry glanced over the side. The giant was busy patching the hull in ten fathoms of water.

'I'll take it,' said the hemihuman. 'Who is it?' His mannequin pawed one of its four feet as the communication link was closed.

'I'm Wandee – ARNOLD's mother-figure,' said the voice. She explained why she had called.

'Peace?' said Larry. 'I'm sure you'll have all the peace you need if you just leave us alone.'

'But the raids have continued. The shelf Benthics have turned savage and aggressive.'

'I can understand that – after your raid on Two Mile. It will take them a while to forget.'

'Isn't there something the Hive can do?'

Larry thought for a while, then shook his head.

Furlong leaned forward to turn up the volume. 'What did he say?'

'Nothing,' said Wandee. 'He just shook his head and signed off.'

'Well, try again!'

Wandee stood up slowly. 'I will – later. We may have to wait a long time. These primitives have long memories. Our dissections showed CNS-MMs that dated back to childhood. Sharp, clear images of things that happened twenty and thirty years before death.'

Furlong gasped. He wasn't sure how far back his own memories went. The string of monotonous days was difficult to date. There were few changes in the Hive.

'Let's load a barge with gifts and send out a negotiator under a truce flag. We'll offer them anything to get them talking. That fellow, Larry, seemed to be a pleasant one. Perhaps he'll sit down with us.'

Wandee nodded. 'I'm sure they could use clothing and entertainment-tapes. Why, we have luxuries those primitives haven't even dreamed of.'

The CO documented the meeting and authorized the barge. Shipyards set to work equipping one of the floating docks with communications and a guidance system. Tons of spangled chiffon, trinkets, and gewgaws were loaded.

Grandmaster Ode convulsed twice during his rewarming. When he opened his eyes he saw Drum's tired, old face.

'You look worse than I feel.' Ode grinned.

'I'm OK,' said Drum, checking the casts and bandages that

protected the Grandmaster's many fractures. 'Can you wiggle your fingers and toes?'

'Only the right hand moved, didn't it?'

'Don't worry about that. The Neuro Team thinks they can decompress those nerves. You'll be in the surgical amphitheatre for quite a while. The bladder work will take most of the afternoon.'

Ode took a deep breath. 'There are funny sounds in my chest.'

'Just the perfusion fluids. You've only been warm a few hours. It'll clear.'

'Did my number come up already?'

'In a manner of speaking. I volunteered you for a new job. It's right up your file – sort of an ambassador.'

'To where?'

'The Benthics.'

Ode moaned. 'Are you forgetting who put me here?'

'They have a new leader now – an ARNOLD. One of our synthetic warriors – predictable – programmed by the Hive. I was going to go myself. I know him. But I saw this as an opportunity to rewarm you and have your Clinic work authorized. This job carries a pretty high priority. The Chairman himself is behind it.'

Ode tried to shrug. 'Why not? I'd probably never come up for repair anyhow – after I lost my command. When do I start?' His toothless grin masked a fearful memory of Clam's vicious attack. He was glad he did not have to face such a rabid animal again.

The White Team wheeled him away, gently swaying in his web of orthopaedic pins and wires, bone fragments grating, soft tissues swelling with edema and haemorrhage.

'Get him on the pump quickly,' said the teck. 'Those injuries are still soaking up his blood volume. He's going to need a lot more haemoglobin and calcium.'

'I think we saved his scrotum. The bladder laceration is sutured. The drains can come out in three days. If any more

230

urine had leaked into the tissues we might have lost it. See if the Bone Team can stabilize these fractures. Another sharp spicule might open up the urinary tract again.'

Ode woke up during the change of teams. The pump made him comfortable. 'Are you my bone man?'

'Yes. We're going to use electron-flow treatment exclusively because you have to be in a cast for your pelvic fractures. I am bracketing each fracture-line with a pair of electrodes so that the electron flow will be across the bony defect. Healing time can be cut in half at least.'

Ode glanced up at the colour-coded X-rays. Small plus and minus symbols were paired up at each black fracture. The teck drove his needle-like wires into Ode's swollen tissues, probing for the bone fragments.

'Tissue resistance, 0.14 megohm.'

The external circuit was built into the cast – a three-volt power cell, microammeter, and a 0.63 megohm resistor.

'The potential difference here will be about 0.55 volt. He'll need about forty coulombs for this fracture.'

The bodycast gradually took shape – from toes to waist. Eighteen circuits were drawn on the white outer surface, with circular windows for the ammeter faces. Ode glanced down at the diagrams.

'I look like a meck,' he laughed.

'Now we'll have to put you back to sleep for the shoulder capsule repair. It's too high for the cord trickle-current anaesthesia.'

'Is that all there is to it? A few pins in my legs? I thought you'd be pounding in those big rods.'

The teck smiled. 'The intermedullary rods? No. They are handy if we want to get you up in a chair right away – or on crutches. But with all those fracture-lines in your pelvis you need a cast anyway. So electron flow is indicated. We can't use both. The IM rods would draw off the current – sort of shunt it past the growing bone, where is doesn't have the effect we want.'

As Ode dozed off he caught a glimpse of strange hardware and a furtive operating team.

*

The Benthic warriors prepared to leave Har Island. Their twin-hulled catamarans were heavily laden with booty from the captured vessels. Larry stood on the makeshift dock and handed out bags of Lyme grass seed (*Elymus arenarius*).

'And from the northern islands – wheat,' he said to each voyager. 'Have a pleasant journey.'

The island seemed quiet when its population returned to normal. Wandee called on the long ear.

'ARNOLD still won't talk to anyone from the Hive,' said Larry. 'He is angry about the way you set up the prisoner exchange. Killing our man and then sending him back with a class-nine brain box was not very sporting.'

Wandee apologized. 'It is a big Hive. I don't know who was responsible for the vivisection. But I think our people should make peace.'

'I agree.'

'What do you want the Hive to do?'

'Just stay out of our Ocean!'

Wandee nodded.

Grandmaster Ode sat up in bed as best he could. Three days in the cast had drained his energy. He gazed listlessly at the chessboard. His Dispenser was building a scintillating Pirc-Robatsch Defence, but he couldn't concentrate. Drum entered with a bundle of sea charts.

'I'm sorry I disturbed you,' he said. 'You look a little tired. Here, keep these until later.'

The rolls were pushed into a pigeonhole above the bed. Drum fingered the long printout coils before leaving.

'You're coming along fine. You'll be good as new in a few months.'

Furlong called Drum down to the Shipyards.

'Our barge came back.'

'Really? Wandee never mentioned it reaching ARNOLD,' said Drum.

'It didn't. The shelf Benthics intercepted it and stole the gifts.'

'It's odd that they allowed it to return.'

'I think they wanted to tell us something,' said Furlong. 'Look here.'

They walked up on the empty barge. The tall sensor pole and drive units were intact. A brownish, grisly object was pinned to the deck by a broken harpoon.

'The left hand of our negotiator,' said the Chairman.

Drum leaned against the pole for a second.

'This harpoon is from one of our pursuit vessels,' continued Furlong.

Drum swallowed hard. 'I guess we won't be needing Ambassador Ode—'

'Let's have Wandee call Larry again. Maybe they want ransom for our negotiator before they send us his other hand – or his head. Hurry!'

Larry listened patiently. 'I'm sorry, Wandee, but I'll have to throw your own words back at you. It is a big Ocean. I don't know who attacked your man under a flag of truce, but I'll speak to King ARNOLD about it.'

Wandee nodded to Furlong. Larry returned to the screen. 'We will look into it. It will take a few days to find the spot. Do you have the coordinates where your barge turned around?'

The screen printed: 250 03'14' – 1450 14'28'.

Clam's trimaran rode with sea anchor out. *Rorqual* located it on the second day of searching after reaching the coordinates. Larry stood on the foredeck in his four-legged mannequin, feeling a bit like a centaur.

ARNOLD worked on the floor of his cabin, surrounded by small components from a meck hand. He'd give the negotiator a prosthesis if he could talk the Benthic into accepting ransom. When they saw Clam they relaxed.

'I might have known,' shouted Larry. 'The Hive told us you have a prisoner of theirs. Do you want to talk ransom? We have a communicator and one of the Hive chairmen, who is anxious to see his man returned.'

'Prisoner?' said Clam.

Larry looked down from *Rorqual*'s prow. The trimaran's decks were littered with ornate cases, gilt-edged mountings and electric baubles, all broken down by the curious primitives. A circle of stones and a pile of charred bones told the rest of the story.

'They ate him,' said Larry sadly.

Wandee gasped. Furlong stood up and left the room. The Hive could turn Citizens into issue protein, but no single individual could eat another!

'I know it sounds crude,' continued the little hemihuman, 'but Clam thinks you should be honoured. It is the highest form of flattery to eat your enemy after you vanquish him. It means that you admire him and want to be more like him.'

Wandee remained silent. Drum reached over her shoulder and tuned out the screen.

ARNOLD set his jaw. 'Maybe that will discourage the damned Hive from invading our waters.'

Larry shrugged. 'It should do something.'

Rorqual returned to the islands.

Furlong led a pair of White Mecks into old Grandmaster Ode's room. 'Time for the E° treatments – electron flow – to stop. Today you will go from the cast to a brace.'

'Good! The itching was beginning to get me down. Where's Drum?'

'He'll see you in Recovery. Actually, you are in better shape than he is. Old age is pressing him down. He seems to get shorter every day.'

'Didn't he go for treatment when he was Chairman?'

'No. He lost his priority when he resigned. But we'll try to work something out.' Furlong smiled. 'I'll see you after the cast is off.'

Hard arteries pulsed under Drum's thin scalp as he set up the chessboard in Recovery. Ode was asleep when he was wheeled in. Drum dozed off too.

'Say!' interrupted Wandee. 'Are you two going to sleep around the clock?'

Ode tried to open his eyes but one lid felt itchy and painful. 'Ouch! I can't see so good.'

'It's just the sedatives. Can you see well enough for a game?'

'No,' moaned the Grandmaster. 'My legs are killing me.'

Drum gathered up the chess pieces and put them away. He was too tired to go to his cubicle, so he slept on a mat in the corner. Wandee glanced at her two friends. Both looked as though they needed rest. She checked pulses and printouts before she exited.

Wandee called Furlong: 'Chairman, I was just checking with Grandmaster Ode's White Meck. The readings seem worse now than before the cast came off. He has more pain, and his left eye—'

'Think nothing of it. That is sometimes seen with surgery of this kind. Pulling the electrodes is expected to irritate the healing bony callus. He will feel better tomorrow.'

Drum awoke to the sound of Ode's moaning. He stood by the bed until the White Meck had given the HiVol injection. The narcotic failed to alleviate the pain. Drum bounced out into the hall and returned with the Medimeck. A battery of tests were given. Drum didn't understand the series of numbers. A teck came in with a bottle of calcium disodium edentate and added it to his venous feeding-line. A shaker of powdered dolomite was placed on his eating tray.

'That's a little better,' sighed Ode. 'I was worried about my stomach pains. They wandered all over.' He ran his fingers over the front of his trunk, palpating and probing – nothing. 'The pains were here, then here. Now they're gone. The muscle spasms have stopped too.'

'Should I call—?'

'No. No. I'm fine. Let me drink something and we can get on with that chess game you were talking about.'

Drum set up the board while his old friend drank, arthritic palsied fingers trembling on pawns and cup. Drum won the toss and took the Right King. He opened with 1 – P-Q4, and

Left King responded with 1 – N-KB3. The Grandmaster used a Semi-Tarrasch Defence with a series of unorthodox combinations that spiced up the mid-game. Drum was soon faced with the impossible task of stopping two, connected, passed pawns with his king. 'Good game!' he said, tipping over his king.

Ode fidgeted with his bedding as his guest put away the chessmen. Drum's silence made him uneasy.

'I'll soon be on my feet,' he said weakly. 'How does my new position as ambassador shape up?'

Drum sat down and pulled the charts out of the cubby-hole. 'Fine. We're setting up a meck link using "T" scanners to prevent treachery. I have the Psych line on their dominant individuals.'

'Why all the precautions?'

'You'll be our first official representative. We don't want to get off on the wrong foot.'

'What else? You aren't telling me everything.'

The old friends read each other's thoughts for a moment. 'They ate our negotiator,' said Drum. 'He was out there in the Ocean without their consent – under a truce flag – and they just ate him. It was one of those ceremonial feasts – to flatter us and discourage us at the same time, I guess.'

'I'm discouraged.'

Drum attempted a feeble smile and patted the Grandmaster's arm. 'That's why all the precautions. Now, the dominant individuals among the Benthics have been catalogued from our CO's memory. Three of them are from the same clone: Larry Dever, who started the clone; this large Tweenwaller; and ARNOLD. Larry Dever was cut in two at the waist over two thousand years ago. He escaped Suspension when you and I were in the Sewer Service. But he is crippled and should be no danger. The Tweenwaller is large and quiet. He is content on some island and plays no role in policy making. We know ARNOLD – aggressive warrior with a fifteen-amino-acid deficiency.'

Ode picked up the stills of the three men. They did have

similar skull features – Har with his gargoyle appearance, and ARNOLD large, and Larry small – but similar cheekbones. 'Predictable behaviour?'

'Yes. No problems with those three. However, we do have a problem with this large, angry Benthic male called Clam. Here are stills of his attack on ARNOLD. He is the one who attacked you. We don't know where he is now or what he is up to. He has been identified on some of the raids into our cities. If you run into him there could be trouble. Be we won't send you without protection from ARNOLD.'

'Fine. Who are the females?'

The views of Big Opal and young White Belly were dim deck night scenes – hard to blow up for spot analysis.

'The young one is probably one of ARNOLD's mates. The old one is unidentified, just a standard Benthic female.'

Ode nodded. Drum rolled up the charts and tucked them back in the cubby-hole. 'Get your rest. You'll be needing your strength.'

'When do I sail?'

'Soon. The Chairman is anxious.'

'Fork!' shouted Drum triumphantly. His protected queen's pawn had forked the Grandmaster's knight and bishop on the fourth rank. It seemed too easy for Drum, and he had spent a long time searching for a trap. There was none.

'I guess I missed that one,' said Ode caustically. He played recklessly – hostile and aggressive – but the combinations always ended in very poor position with no material gain.

'Check!' said Drum. He had raised his voice as he set down the knight, not out of joy but out of surprise and fear. The Grandmaster had allowed the horse to get a 'family fork' on his king, queen, and the king's rook.

' "Forked" again!? I didn't see that! They must be giving me some hallucinogens!' Ode shouted. He knocked the pieces to the floor. 'I can't play you in this damn place.'

*

'He's asleep,' whispered Wandee. She and Drum stood outside the doorway of the darkened room.

'Well, he's terribly sick. His mind seems affected. I beat him in a chess game this afternoon.'

'But you're a pretty good player, aren't you?'

'Not that good. Nobody gets a "family fork" on a Grandmaster, not even another Grandmaster. His mind is deteriorating. He was loud and violent.'

'Well, he seems quiet enough.'

'Check him out. Will you? Please?'

Wandee motioned for the White Team to follow and she tiptoed into the darkened room. Ode just moaned and mumbled. 'Somnolence,' she whispered. 'Get me some blood and urine. Run the screen.'

Drum paced in the hall. He heard the muffled voices: 'Anaemia, basophilic stippling of red cells, coproporphyrin-three in the urine—'

'Lead poisoning,' said Wandee, wiping her hands in the doorway.

'What? How—'

'I don't know where he got it, but it's right there – all of the signs. The black line on his gums is lead sulfide. The ether extract of his urine fluoresces, and his urine lead is about two micromoles per litre – well above the toxic level. These mental symptoms are probably signs of brain swelling. He should be chelated immediately or he could convulse and go into a coma.'

'Chelated?' asked Drum. 'What is that?'

'We get the lead out by giving a molecule that combines with it, edatate in this case.'

'Dyspepsia,' complained Ode, pushing away his entrée. 'My head seems a little better today. How goes it with the Benthic wars?'

'Our beach cities are still under siege,' said Drum. 'I was naïve to think they wanted peace. Those water-aborigines have become zealous villains, seeking only vengeance with their clandestine attacks. But Furlong has a scheme that may reduce the losses.'

Ode quaffed his drink, toyed with the dessert, splitting the nougat and picking out the bits of fruit and nut. 'I'm to act as liaison between the Hive and ARNOLD: The fallacy there is: no one controls the shelf Benthics. How can anyone stop so many small bands?'

'Maybe they can't all be stopped, but maybe you can learn why they raid. Is it just a whim? Or do they want something from our cities? You will be authorized to offer them gifts, reparations for our attack on Two Mile, plus a regular tithe placed on the beach.'

'A tithe? But we're so poor!'

'Placate them with a few sleazy items,' scoffed Drum. 'When they become less warlike we'll have no qualms about reneging, but right now it might be cheaper than fighting.'

Ode shook his head. 'I think they'd rather fight for it than have it handed to them, but I'll try.'

Ode placed his crutches carefully on the seat beside him and waved weakly towards the dock. Drum and Wandee waved back. The rest of the Hive representatives stood quietly in their ragged formation as the cyber-dinghy started out into the sump with its lone occupant.

'You can't let him go like that,' objected Wandee sadly. 'He's not well.'

'I know,' said Drum. 'But the sea voyage might do him more good than that Clinic bed. He has his medicines. We'll keep in touch with him. This job is very important and requires someone with his abilities.'

Wandee resigned herself to waving. Later, on their way up to her Labs, she glanced through Ode's reports again. 'He certainly picked up the metal ions! Look at these – silver, mercury, lead...'

Drum shrugged. 'They did push the electron-flow treatment a little beyond the safety level. I suppose we should expect a little side-effect from that. But there was so little time.'

'Something still puzzles me. He said they didn't use the intramedullary rods for his femoral fractures, but our X-rays show rods – and a lot of retained hardware.'

'Rods are often used – especially when they want to ambulate early. He must have misunderstood.'

She continued to read. 'And there is this matter of his vision. He complained of scotomas – cloudy patches in his left visual field—'

'I know. He mentioned them to me too. Furlong thought they might be due to the lead – part of his peripheral neuritis or encephalopathy.'

'Well, I don't like it at all,' she said. 'That electron-flow treatment is supposed to use gold electrodes to prevent all of this.'

Drum sighed. 'Well, you know about budget problems. The Clinic is no exception.'

Rorqual stopped a quarter of a mile from the empty Hive barge. It had been anchored at the meeting point for about six months. Sessile creatures festooned its under-surface and thickened its chains. The deck was salt encrusted. Three Electrotecks took an extruded outrigger to check it for booby traps. Finding none, they motioned for the Harvester to approach. Larry and ARNOLD checked the crumbling deck – oxides and worms.

'Doesn't seem too safe,' said Larry, catching one of his hind hooves on a rotting timber.

'We can't meet anyplace else,' growled ARNOLD. 'Not on *Rorqual* – not on any island! No Hive bastard will ever set foot on any of our territory.'

Larry nodded. 'The less they know about us, the better I like it. Can't let them see our angel gear or all your children. Keep ship optics out of our conversations with Wandee.'

Rorqual acknowledged the new rule. Her long eye caught a speck in the distant surf. 'Dinghy approaches.'

'Give us a close-up. He looks like an old one. Look at him tremble. I can't see his face through that helmet, but he's the thinnest Nebish I've ever seen – all bent over and crippled. I wonder what all the gifts are—'

'Probably bombs,' grumbled ARNOLD.

'No ... they're still in the T-zone. Oh, oh! That fellow is in trouble – doubled up and holding his belly. Helmet's off – he's trying to take a drink of something, but the retching is getting worse. He sure is seasick.'

'Maybe he is infected,' said ARNOLD. 'They might be trying to give us something besides gifts this time – something like the plague.'

'You're right. Back off, *Rorqual*.'

'Trying a little germ warfare? That man you sent is sick,' accused ARNOLD.

Wandee stared at the blank screen. 'But you can see by the T-scanners that we are telling the truth. Grandmaster Ode has a little heavy-metal overload from his fracture treatment. That is all. Nothing contagious.'

'Well, he is down on the decking – looks like he is vomiting.'

'How far away are you?' asked Wandee.

Larry glanced at ARNOLD. That dinghy must be very poorly equipped for her to have to ask.

'About five miles – upwind. We'll keep that raft to the leeward side till morning. Then maybe we'll go in and talk. No sense sitting down with someone who will die in the middle of negotiations.'

Wandee nodded and turned to Drum. 'Can you reach Ode? Have him take his calcium again.'

Drum was saddened by the old man's suffering. His voice was tight as he spoke: 'They'll wait until dawn. Then they'll talk. Try taking more calcium.'

Ode grimaced. 'I'm fine. Just a little seasick. Choppy water. I'm getting a rough ride. I guess I lost my old sea legs in Suspension. Don't worry.'

Larry kept the infrared scanner on the raft with $50\times$ magnification. *Rorqual* monitored the dinghy's channel. The Ocean calmed and a bright moon rose.

'Looks quiet enough,' said ARNOLD. 'Let's get a bite to

eat and catch some sleep. The ship will call us if anything develops.'

The shock wave and the sirens hit the cabin at the same time. Larry tumbled out of his cot in a tangle of meck appendages.

Whoop! Whooop! called *Rorqual.*

A puff of smoke stood above the barge. The dinghy was capsized.

'Give me a playback of the minute before the blast,' shouted Larry, trying to find an explanation. 'Oh – oh, I see. Looks like the shelf Benthics sent a delegation to the Hive barge.'

ARNOLD rushed in, angry. 'It's Hive treachery. Let's get out of here!'

'Wait,' said Larry. 'There were visitors on the barge at the time of the blast. Give us a magnification and some stills. See – it looks like Clam and a couple of his mussel men. They appear to be peacefully chatting with the old Ambassador. I can't tell what exploded. Both sides are carrying gifts.'

The dinghy passed overhead in the jaws of a grapple. A line of drops marked the deck.

'Shall we take a walk on the barge before we go? It is listing badly. We don't have much time if we want to try to learn something.' Larry glanced into the dinghy, then rode a grapple to the charred barge. 'Not much here. All the meat must be out there where those fish are busy. Whatever exploded sure swept the old decks clean.'

Rorqual sniffed around with a 2-L sensor crane and found evidence of nitroglycerin.

'Could have been a satchel charge. Either side could have done it,' said Larry.

'It was the Hive,' spat ARNOLD.

'But the T-scanners were OK, and their own man was in the middle of it.'

'Well, so were our men, and there were more of them.'

Larry shrugged. 'Wandee was pretty excited. She thinks we did it. I guess we'd better have our tecks go over that dinghy for clues. Let *Rorqual* search the little boat's mind too. We might learn something. Meanwhile, I agree that we should get off the shelf. Home, ship!'

The tool-room hatch was open. Sunlight glinted off the dinghy as it sat in the jaws of the Disassembler. Larry walked down the narrow aisle between the workbenches.

'A good pair of optics,' said the teck under the dinghy's sensor housing. 'Standard fluorite with backups of ultraviolet glass and infrared lead selenide.'

'Nothing in the brain that looks like deception. We'll let *Rorqual* soak it all in for analysis later.'

Larry studied the initial reports. 'Looks like this boat knew nothing of the bomb. I suppose it could have been Clam's doing. To be fair, I think we ought to send it back to the Hive.'

ARNOLD nodded reluctantly. 'I agree that an ambassador's dinghy can't be treated as spoils of war. What are the flowers for?'

Larry set a thorny rose bush under the seat next to one of Ode's scorched crutches. 'Just a little gift for Drum and Wandee. We don't have a body to send back.' He suddenly sucked his thumb. 'Ouch!'

'Looks like the little dinghy's memory was small: mostly Sewer Service data with some recent navigation aids,' said Larry. 'But the data on the meteor shower has stimulated *Rorqual*'s curiosity.'

'That must have been nearly twenty years ago. What has that to do with navigation?'

'The Hive nervous system covers all the major land masses. There was some type of massive disturbance in the Arctic Ocean – a regular holocaust. Several meteor impacts were sensed in the area.'

'What's her index of curiosity?' asked ARNOLD.

'Zero point seven and rising.'

'Maybe it would be worth following up. If we have reason to talk with the Hive again, we might ask for more details – maybe offer a few fish for it. I hate to admit it but some of those circuits turned out by the new Labs in the Shipyard were actually serviceable. We could use some of them too, if the Hive is anxious to buy our friendship. We'd be able to speed up the repairs on the mecks and Harvesters.'

Larry nodded. 'I'm sure they'll be calling us again after this explosion on the raft is forgotten. They seem determined to rope us into some sort of negotiations.'

Wandee tucked old Drum into his recliner and picked a rose hip for him. 'Rich in bioflavinoids,' she said handing him the plum-sized fruit of *Rosa rugosa*. He smiled weakly and gummed for flavours.

'Those flowers have loaded pistils,' she noted. 'Furlong said he'd see if you could keep them long enough to get your strength back – a dietary supplement.'

'What else has the Chairman planned for me?'

'The NH treatment, if you want it. A new set of endocrines might pep you right up.' She smiled.

Drum was irritated. 'Am I to be the new ambassador to the Benthics? If so, you can tell him I'm too old for deceit. I wouldn't mind visiting ARNOLD before I die; after all, I did raise him.'

Wandee nodded effusively. 'Naturally. I am certain ARNOLD will protect you. While you are there you might ask about the raids, but it isn't necessary.'

'I know. I know. Talk is cheap, and I'm to do the talking. Well, for me it will be nothing more than a social visit – if ARNOLD will allow it. No tricks.'

'Fine,' she said.

Furlong waited in the outer hall. He stood and de-activated the screen as she approached. 'Thank you, Wandee. You did fine. I knew he would take it better from you than from me.'

Wandee was serious. 'He will be safe, won't he?'

'We'll be more careful this time,' he said.

Drum was startled by the sudden appearance of the Clinic Team.

'When the Chairman says "jump" – we jump,' they said.

'Hang on now.' A Security Squad trotted ahead, clearing the Spiral. The Stretcher Team arrived at the Clinic in less than an hour. Drum saw that they were making preparations to put him to sleep.

'I thought the neurohumoral axis could be rejuvenated with a mild sedative,' he said.

'You're down for an NH plus an eye plus a hip. It's a big job. Relax now while the White Meck tubes and wires you.'

Eighteen hours later Drum felt the pains. His eyes were bandaged. His hip ached. When he moaned a hand touched his arm.

'Easy now,' said a female.

'Wandee?' he asked.

'They told me about your operations after they were all over. I can sit here and keep an eye on you until your bandages come off. Do you need anything else for pain?'

He thought for a moment. The edge had been taken off the discomfort by something. 'No. Not now.'

'Good,' she said. 'I checked your OR sheet. They must have given you a royal treatment. All the teams were there. A dozen embryonic Carbon Copies were taken from your clone at thirty millimetres. The NH infusion contained primordial cells from their ductless glands – pituitary, thyroid, adrenal, testes, carotid body, pineal, and the organ of Zuckerkandl. By now these cells have settled out in your marrow and lung capillaries. They should be producing needed hormones in a few weeks.'

Drum moaned softly. She continued to talk, trying to cheer him up.

'The hip looks like a good repair job. I saw the X-rays. And the photo of your retina through the new lens is very clear. You'll be as good as new in a few months.'

Drum thought the speech was familiar. It was the same one given to Ode before his death at the hands of the Benthics. He moaned. 'Better give me something to help me sleep. I'm not too comfortable.'

A synthetic opiate soothed raw nerve endings.

Wandee called ARNOLD for Drum's clearance. The pick-up would be at night so the solar radiation wouldn't harm him. He was to be naked – no packages.

Drum shuddered as he stepped into the outrigger. Gooseflesh covered his exposed epidermis, wrinkled and white in the starlight. 'There's a stack of blankets on the front seat,' called Trilobite. Drum squinted off into the dark, choppy waters where a tow-line disappeared. Leaving the dinghy attached to a buoy, he bundled up and waited as the little shovel-shaped meck pulled him across three kilometres of open Ocean.

'There's not a stitch on him – nothing – not even that envelope of pills. Order the chair-lift while I fix him a hot bowl of ragout – thick and well-seasoned,' said ARNOLD.

'Right.'

A centaur and Trilobite welcomed the naked Nebish as he stepped on to the deck.

'ARNOLD is fixing you something hot in the cabin. Come on.'

They walked past the ship's huge, deep-dish optics towards the aroma of meat and vegetables.

'I came to warn you,' said Drum. 'Don't have any dealings with the Hive. It can't be trusted. It just wants to buy time and study you for your weak points – so it can crush you later.'

Larry just smiled. 'That's funny, because we feel the same way. Study the Hive for weaknesses, so we can crush it again!'

Abruptly Trilobite danced in front of the little, pot-bellied Nebish and stabbed him in the neck with the tip of his metre-long tail. Blood spurted. Drum slumped to the deck, gasping.

Larry reared up on his hind hooves and stepped in between the old man and the cyber. Drum tried to crawl, but his hands kept slipping in the pools of blood.

'White Team!' shouted Larry. 'My God! What are you trying to do, Trilobite – kill a human?'

'I saved him,' said the meck, trying to squeeze out from under a restraining hoof. 'I cut the trigger mechanism. He's wired. There's an optic in his eye and a bomb in his abdomen.'

ARNOLD rushed out of the cabin and cradled his little father-figure in his arms. He applied a pressure bandage to the neck laceration. 'A bomb?'

'Yes,' said the meck. '*Rorqual* detected it as he walked past her deep-dish. It took her a couple of seconds to realize what it was. With the T-scan on "truth" she knows that Drum wasn't aware. When the "destruct" message came from the Hive I had to act.'

The Medimeck replaced the lost blood and sutured the neck wound. Drum regained consciousness and asked for pain medication.

'What bomb?' he asked incredulously.

Larry explained. 'And the electrodes are in your femurs.'

Drum laughed. 'But you are wrong. I've had hip surgery – bilateral prostheses. As for my eye, it is just a synthetic lens. I had cataract surgery. That's all.'

Larry shook his head. 'I'm sorry, but *Rorqual* doesn't make that kind of mistake. You have the artificial hips, that's true; but they were recently packed – silver on the right and lead on the left. Your serum levels of these metals are rising – approaching half a micromole per litre.'

The screen printed out the figures:

$$\frac{1}{2} Pb^{++} \quad E^{\circ} = +0.126 \quad K = 1.3 \times 10^{2}$$
$$Ag^{+} \quad E^{\circ} = -0.800 \quad K = 3.5 \times 10^{-14}$$

'You'd make a good battery,' said Larry. 'Those oxidation-reduction potentials are far enough apart.'

'Furlong!' spat Drum. 'He must have wired poor Ode too. Damn! And I was the one who talked Ode into it.'

'Don't worry,' said the giant ARNOLD in an unusually gentle voice. 'Our White Team will look you over and get that thing out of there.'

'We'd better move him further aft. He's pretty close to shipbrain here. If he should blow . . .'

ARNOLD recalled the damage on the raft. A thin-walled shelter was built in a neutral area of the hump. A tough Battle

Meck stood by with trays of refreshments while the White Team started their study. The humans grouped in the forward cabin and spoke through the intercom.

'It's a bomb all right. We'll need a Blood Scrubber to get these ions down before surgery. The cardiopulmonary bypass will give us more time.'

'Take all the time you need,' said ARNOLD. 'Be careful. I don't want anything to happen to him.'

The White Teck didn't say anything, but he realized that a blast would take him with his patient.

'Might as well start back to the islands,' said Larry. He's much safer with us.'

'Haul in the dinghy. Every captain needs one,' shouted ARNOLD.

Images appeared on the screen, hazy and dim.

'So that's what that spying camera in my eye is picking up. Why is it so weak? I can see better than that.'

'You are using two eyes. There is a pterygium over that cornea – a tangle of microscopic vessels. Besides, it is a very small optic – less than twenty-five thousand points,' explained the Electroteck. He took stills of several sample views. Faces were anonymous masks. Landscapes, simple silhouettes.

'Those poor Benthics on Ode's raft... I'm sure that Furlong couldn't tell who they were. He must have seen two or three burly visitors and was hoping that one would be ARNOLD when he pressed the big black button.'

The teck nodded. 'I'm sure he couldn't identify anyone from the optics alone, but I am picking up a bit of auditory also. The transmitter is in your right thorax, so your heart and lungs are making most of the sounds I hear. But I think Furlong might be able to understand parts of your conversation too. That plus the optics told him you were near *Rorqual*'s control cabin when he hit your button.'

'My target: shipbrain. Damn!'

Rorqual anchored in the shelter of the leeward side of an island while the tests were being run. A series of eight paired vials were located by X-ray. They were anchored to the vertebral bodies, behind the spine, running from the level of the renal arteries down into the pelvis between the prostate and sacrum. The Electrotecks were building a duplicate of the circuitry for study before attacking the actual bomb.

'Might as well relax, Larry. They won't be ready to cut until tomorrow. My wives are going ashore for fresh greens. Want to join them? It is pretty rocky and they might need someone to help with the toting.'

Larry nodded. The elevator brought up a bevy of leathery girls, White Belly among them. They carried empty sacks, chatting and laughing, waiting by the rail.

'Bring the Captain's dinghy around!' shouted Larry.

The island was a three-by-one-mile conglomerate of jumbled stone with a few scattered acres of sod. An ancient, pre-Hive edifice marked the high point. North of this lay a two-acre swamp in a circular depression. The dinghy found a protected inlet and anchored itself against a weathered quay. Stone steps led nowhere.

A handful of large raindrops hit the group. 'Weird weather,' said Larry, glancing up at the mischievous clouds. 'Come on!' His agile hooves carried him to the top of the slope, where he found the first patch of greens – oblong beds that occupied grooves leading back into the swamp. 'Probably an old irrigation pattern. Whoever lived here must have had a very efficient Agromeck. There's a good plant survival – parsley, sage, chives, thyme ... and here's a wild leek!' He pulled up the large, mild-tasting garlic, *Allium ampeloprasum*.

White Belly filled two bags with the bulbs and tied them over Larry's centaur back. 'I think you just reinvented saddlebags,' he said, munching on a leek. Roots of cardamom (*Alpinia striata*) were pulled for tea and fish seasoning. As the sacks filled, Larry decided to give the edifice a quick search. He invited White Belly.

'Hop on my back and we'll take a look at the old ruins.'

Only two vine-covered towers remained, enclosing a heap of silted rubble. 'That swamp is perfectly round; probably was a reservoir once.' She tightened her grip with her knees as he waded into the shallow water and pulled a stalk of mace, peeling away the outer green rind and chewing on the inner, white core.

He splashed around, eating and offering her stalks and roots of cattails (*Typhia latifolia*). His hooves slid across a slick, glassy surface under an inch of mud. He struggled and fell, dumping her. She stood up draped with wet leaves.

'Appreciate the ride!' she laughed.

He walked around the object, outlining a segment of the fuselage. After taking another look at the circular, water-filled depression he decided it must have been a quarry – and a grave for the Quarry Meck.

The courteous centaur helped White Belly remount. The sun dried her skin as they circled the island, gathering dill and shallot. 'Makes a good pickle,' she said, holding up the wild onion.

The Captain's dinghy returned to the ship at dusk, sacks bulging with crisp, pungent spices.

'The soup and salad should be strong tonight,' commented Larry on his way down to the tool room for hoof repair.

'I've got some bad news about the Ambassador,' said ARNOLD. 'The White Team isn't going to be able to disarm him.'

'Why?'

'We duplicated the circuit. The charges are self-arming. If the stepladder circuitry is cut anywhere – they blow!'

Larry studied the diagrams. 'How does this work?'

ARNOLD pointed to the rows of charges. 'The nitro shell surrounds a core circuit. It is in the armed, or open position now. The lead-silver batteries in his legs do not supply the trigger current; they are just a sensor current. If he dies and his circulation stops, the lead and silver electrodes lose their free-flowing electrolyte – his blood. They plate and the potential drops, closing the core circuit – and bang!'

Larry nodded. 'The current from the leg batteries keeps him from blowing up?'

'Yes. And if we go in and cut the wires anywhere – well, the current stops, and bang again.'

'What do we do?'

'First they took him off the Blood Scrubber. The ions must be present and circulating to keep the battery functioning.'

'But those are heavy metals! Poisons!'

ARNOLD slumped down on a toolbox, a beaten giant. 'Dammit! I know,' he said softly. 'Either way the poor old bastard dies. The Eye Teck says the Hive sensor in his vitreous humour is leaking ions too. The rods and cones are being leaded – blinded.'

'There's nothing we can do?'

ARNOLD shook his head. '*Rorqual* simulated it. Once the Hive closed the circuit the charges armed themselves. If we break it anywhere...'

Larry put his hoof up on the table and absently removed its traction plate while he studied the X-rays. 'Eight charges... optic pick-up in his eye... trigger wire down jugular vein to abdomen... Trilobite cut that. Two sensor circuits: the ladder anchoring to the spine, and the physiological battery in his legs. If we touch it, he blows. If we don't he dies slowly of the electron-flow poisons. It's a neat job, but no Hive booby trap can be that foolproof. I'd like to try to disarm him on remote. He's got nothing to lose.'

ARNOLD shook his head. 'He won't let us risk it. He says he is too old to stand the surgery. He's mad. If he blows up out here among his friends he'd be helping Furlong.'

'But we can't let him just wander off and die. It might take weeks or months, and it's a terrible way to go – the pains and delirium.'

The giant took out another diagram and smiled wryly as he showed it to the centaur. 'He has chosen the way he wants to go. Look at this.'

Larry's fist shook as he held the wiring diagram. 'The blasted Hive is so damned insecure that it can't allow anything or anyone to leave without a "loyalty bomb" inside. Look at poor Drum: from grains to prostate he's explosive! Remember

Pursuit One? Old Grandmaster Ode? All those Killer Mecks? They were all wired too. How can the Hive be so insecure . . . and so childish?'

ARNOLD just shrugged. 'I wouldn't call them "childish". "Ruthless" is a better word. They won't give an inch. Look at me – and all the Lesser Arnolds – we're all carrying our "loyalty bomb" in our genes: the dependence on Hive bread.'

'What I really hate about this whole thing is the absence of a Hive Leader – someone I could blame for all this evil.' Larry shook his head slowly as he saw the meaning behind the new wires added to the circuitry. 'I can't hate Chairman Drum, here. He was trapped in the system, just as you were for a time. But I've got to hand it to the poor old Nebish: he's got guts! I don't know if I could do what he's going to do. I just don't know . . .'

ARNOLD spat. 'I could! The Hive deserves worse! I just hope he takes that Chairman Furlong with him. That would be some consolation.'

The dinghy rode low in the water. Extra satchel charges were packed under the seats and in the forward storage area. Baskets of fruit, Jonah crabs, and iced beer were being loaded by crane. A tear marked the old Nebish's face as he pulled on his helmet.

'Now you have the rings in both pockets?'

Drum nodded.

'Remember, when you pull out those wire sutures it breaks off the electrodes to your leg batteries. That should set you off instantly. You'll be vaporized in the blast – and if you're close to that dinghy it will go too – making quite a hole in something.'

The anonymous helmet nodded again. The visor suddenly opened. 'I almost forgot – the chromatography sequence: LIP TV TM AG TAS GLH. I see that ARNOLD must be getting plenty of fifteen-amino-acid bread, but I had the sequence memorized to be sure. Leucine is the fastest and histidine is the slowest.'

Larry smiled. 'Thank you, Drum. That will be a big help.

We've been using a cumbersome method with eletrophoretic spreading. This will be easier.'

The thick-suited Nebish stood silently, unable to think of anything else to say. Wives waved from the poopdeck. The crane lowered him into the small boat and he started for the sump outlet on the distant shore.

'Go back,' said the voice at the mouth of the sewer. 'Do not enter.'

The little boat listened only to its passenger. Its antenna remained back in *Rorqual*'s tool room. The darkness of the sump swallowed them up.

'I'm coming,' said Drum. A small voice echoed up the three-hundred-foot-diameter pipe.

'Go back, loyal Citizen. You don't want to damage the Hive. You have such a perfect record up to—'

Drum's anger grew: 'My record!' he shouted. 'I put a molecular time bomb in my son and sent my friend to his death. That is my record. And for my reward you put a time bomb in me. Well, I'm returning to the Hive to die. I'll take my enemies!'

'But we are your friends. That bomb that you carry was designed to avenge your death in the event that the Benthic killed you. It will explode after you die.'

Drum laughed. 'You never give up, do you? This is Drum you are talking to – spinner of genes and souls. "Avenge my death" – indeed! Ha! Is that why I was equipped with an optic pickup and a remote trigger? Well, my friends cut the trigger. I won't blow until I get deep into the Hive.'

Furlong stammered: 'But you gave me carte blanche.'

'True,' said CO. 'But you failed, and now there is danger to the Hive. The Megajury found you guilty of what they consider a heinous crime.'

'You told them?'

'I cannot protect failure. Your Aries reign has been called tyranny by the Citizens. Your sentence is—'

'What? What?'

'You are to take a White Team and try to stop the bomb – er – Drum. If you succeed, lives will be saved. I will be grateful,' said CO.

'Success can be rewarded. I know. Call the Medimeck/Mediteck team. I am ready.'

'Here is the dinghy's last position. It seems to be heading towards the docks. The Shipyards and my energy organs are down there. The dinghy rides heavy with a load of food – fruit, crabs, ice, and something else.'

'Keep me informed. I'll try to intercept him.'

Furlong dashed out on to the docks, sweat beading on his temple. The wharf appeared deserted except for an occasional workman. The foggy sewer was littered with derelict shells and girder skeletons. A motor barge was tied near the Shipyards; a rusty crane off-loaded.

'What is it, sir?' asked a workman.

Furlong wiped his face and tried to smile.

'Have you seen a small boat with a single man on board?'

'No, sir.'

'The boat also carries some fruit, crabs, and ice?'

'Sorry, sir. But the mists are pretty bad in the sump tonight. Our peripheral port scanners are down again. A boat could easily have landed without my seeing it.'

Furlong glanced back to see that the White Team was following. He found a small heap of melting ice chips. 'How did this get here?' he shouted.

'The ice barge,' answered a voice in the fog.

He saw fruit scattered near the City's energy organ. Running over, he picked up an orange and tore it open. 'How did this fruit get here?'

'The fruit barge.'

Furlong saw seeds. His throat tightened. A Jonah crab fell over on its back in the dark. Its legs made frantic scratching sounds. He darted his light beam around, searching.

'How did these crabs get here?' he gasped.

'The Captain's dinghy!' said Drum, stepping out of the darkness. Both hands were in his pockets, thumbs on the electrode rings. His helmet was off. Hatred glinted in his eyes.

Furlong froze. 'There you are.' He forced a smile. 'I brought the White Team. We have the clinic's amphitheatre on standby. Don't worry. We'll get those bombs out of your belly.'

'I'm sure you will,' said Drum calmly. It was clear he had no intention of cooperating.

'Come along,' said Furlong. 'It won't do you any good to be bitter and try to escape. You'll only weaken and pass out in a few days. We'll find you eventually.'

'Oh, I have no intention of running...' He turned his wrists to show the thumb rings.

'No!!'

The hands pulled up and out, trailing wet red wire sutures. Triumph glowed from the old Nebish face. The City's organ cracked in the blast – spilling sixteen hundred kiloamperes of torodial plasma, at fifty million degrees Kelvin. For a moment a bit of the sun existed in the sewers as fusion fuel spilled, spreading ionic gas in a yellow glow.

11
The Godwhale

A sacrifice to a lesser deity
may bring reward
A sacrifice to the Greater Deity
is its own reward.
— *Rorqual*'s Acolyte

Nine Fingers felt uncomfortable in his father's crown. Too heavy and large it was, being wrought from yellow nuggets. The signs were bad. His Ring Island kingdom was barren: the lagoon, the Gardens, and now his young wife, Iris. Half his subjects had migrated north to the archipelago, five days away. The remaining men were old and tired. They feared to fish in the deep waters outside the reef since the arrival of *Carcharoden carcharias*. This twenty-one-foot, seven-thousand-pound Great White Shark had taken his father and six other men. Their boats only ventured into the safety of the lagoon, where fish were scanty and small. Iris failed to conceive; food lofts were empty. Monsoons were coming. It was time to pray to the Godwhale.

Nine Fingers gathered the elders, three women and two men, the grey-haired grandparents. They drank the last of the heady pulque and listened to their young chief.

'All is barren – our women, our soil, and the sea. We must ask the Godwhale for help.'

'We are a poor people. What sacrifice can we offer in exchange?' asked Grandmother Turtle.

'Our village is dying. We will give what is asked.'

They walked to the shrine at the high point on the atoll. A thick, glassy tower rose twenty body lengths into the air. As thick as a ceremonial canoe at the base, it gradually narrowed to a swaying pole. Its skin bristled with protruding rungs and rings. Vines festooned the lower effigy from its niche at the base of the tower. Thick, soft hemp ropes were tied to the idol's back. Nine Fingers and three elders looped their ropes over their shoulders and began to climb. The whale weighed as much as a man. It grated noisily against the tower until the elder standing below took the slack out of his rope. The fifth elder climbed on ahead, chopping and clearing the greenery.

Then body lengths up, they found the hook and pulled away a tangle of tendrils. The lifters climbed above the hook, manoeuvring the swinging whale over the point. The hook, set deep, creaked down under the weight of the idol. Nine Fingers glanced up the pole and smiled. Small lights began to blink and swivel. They dropped their ropes and climbed down.

'May the Godwhale be bountiful,' they prayed.

The nights became windy and starless, warning the islands of the coming storm season. Five days later a trimaran made a brief visit. The villagers reached the beach in time to see the square sail running before the wind. Nine Fingers stood waving at a small pile of supplies at his side.

'Is this the miracle we prayed for?' asked Grandma Turtle.

'No. The Acolyte was just delivering the request flags.'

They lifted the tarpaulin and divided the baskets of bread sticks and dried fruit. A dozen small beer casks were also present. The yard-long flags were colour-coded, and bore symbols of water, food, tools, and medicine.

'You told them our needs?'

'Yes. The Godwhale will pass this way after the storm. We are to hoist whichever flags match our problems,' explained Nine Fingers. He sorted through the bright banners, studying their designs. 'This dry food should be stable enough to get us through.'

'And the beer?' asked Grandma Turtle, nudging a cask with her toe. 'We'll have all the rainwater we'll need for drinking...'

'It'll help keep our spirits up,' said a young buck with a grin.

'We'll be needing that,' mumbled their Chief.

The island throne room doubled as Nine Fingers' living quarters – bamboo and thatch, forty feet on the side. It was not quite square because living trees formed the four corners. Six other trunks arched up through the room, supporting the ceiling beams and attic storage. His young bride, Iris, prepared a porridge of legumes boiled in goat's milk. Two small, pan-fried fish and a freshly punctured coconut completed the royal menu.

'I spoke to the Acolyte,' he said as he entered. She served the mush; he ate in silence.

'What bothers you?' she asked.

'The Godwhale.'

'Can't she help us?'

'Oh, our prayers will be answered, only...' His voice broke off. 'Our parents trust the deity – don't they?'

'Of course.' She smiled. 'The Godwhale showed them this island and helped them get started here. The goats and grain are from our deity. There were fruit trees once, but the salt air killed them. You can still see the trunks.'

'I believe in her,' he said, 'not because she is our father's deity. I am very weak in faith. I believe in her because of her great strength and wisdom. She is too large to fit into our lagoon, and yet she sends her messengers over the horizon to talk with us. Her choice of food has been right for us – plants and animals that thrive and feed us. But I'm afraid this time.'

'Why, husband?'

'She wants a sacrifice.'

'Why, I don't think I've ever heard of that before. Not on our island. There have been rumours... What kind of sacrifice? Goats? Chickens?'

'You,' he said. 'The Godwhale wants my young bride...'

She remained silent.

258

The young Chief stood up, waving his arms. 'Oh, I objected at first. Then the Acolyte explained that you would be unharmed. In fact, you'd be returned in a year – and you'd no longer be barren!'

Iris frowned. 'It is not good for a chief to be childless. You must take another wife. I will be your second.'

'Perhaps, said Nine Fingers, 'but there is plenty of time for that later. Right now we must decide if we are to hang the flags or not.'

She stood and looked out the window. The wide lagoon was quiet. Empty huts dotted the beach.

'I remember when we numbered nearly a hundred,' she said softly. 'Times were happier then. I want to do what to do what I can to bring those days back.'

He nodded. 'It is what our parents would have done. This is a good island. With a little help from our deity it will be fruitful again.'

The storms hit as expected, scattering building materials and uprooting trees. Caves in the chalk cliff protected the humans and their little pens of domestic animals. Between storms they foraged in the sun and collected rainwater. Afterwards, the flags went up and Iris prepared herself for her wedding with the Godwhale.

The men carried the sacrificial raft to the beach and covered it with flowers. Iris sat among the petals with her foaming mug. A cask was passed around. A low, dark silhouette appeared on the horizon.

'There she is!' shouted Nine Fingers. He glanced back to make certain the flags were unfurled, then he sat down to watch. The whale-shape cruised past the beach leaving a trail of steaming biscuits, each a half ton in size.

'Godbiscuits!' shouted the natives, running into the surf. Canoes were launched to guide the packed plankton to shore. They busied themselves breaking open the huge bales. Inside they found an assortment of larger marine food items – iced fish, mussels, and crustaceans. The prevailing winds continued to carry the godbiscuits into the surf. Baskets and pots were filled – a giant harvest that would ensure adequate food supplies until the storm damage could be repaired. Runty pigs and scrawny chickens scampered through wet sand to feast on the leavings.

The natives quieted, waiting. Their god would leave the 'flag gifts' on her next pass – and pick up the maiden sacrifice on the third. They bowed their heads.

'Naked savages on the leeward shore, Captain.'

'What flags are up?'

'Looks like seeds and small tools.'

'Fine. Give them Seeds-For-Latitude and the usual mix of Homesteaders' Home and Farm Tools. What fish do they take around here?'

'Surfperch, rockfish, smelt, cottids, croakers, greenings, sharks, herring—'

'Fine. I get the idea. Leave them the Miscellaneous Hooks package.'

'ARNOLD? This is the atoll with the barren lagoon. We were going to open it at five degrees and one hundred eighty-five degrees to let the current bring in more food fish.'

'Right! I don't know what I'd do without you, Larry. OK. Take over. You know where to place the charges. Just make sure all those silly savages are on the beach at ninety-five degrees, picking up the goodies. I don't want my deity getting a bad name.'

'What's the payment this time?'

'Island census?'

'Less than fifty.'

'You know our policy. If they don't ask for luxury items we just ask for a pair of breeding animals or some of their surplus food plants – seeds – anything we can dump on the next island.'

'Ahem . . .'

'Now what did I forget? Oh, Circle . . . Ring . . . Wedding ring? Now I remember. This is where we have the barren bride too. OK. Ask that she be served up on a raft with a spicy sauce of flowers. We'll be around to swallow her up. And . . . ask that she be full of beer so she'll relax. I don't want her fainting when she sees the Godwhale's shiny white teeth. I guess we'll be having a guest on board for the Arctic trip – the bride from Ring Island – ought to be real educational for all of us. I hope you remember how to do a sterility workup.'

'I've been on the tapes for a month.'

'Good.'

'They got your message. There she is. Pretty little thing, isn't she? Not very frightened. What is that dazed look? She isn't that drunk.'

'I think it is called faith.'

'Well, she's in for a rude awakening. We'll have her on *Rorqual*'s rakes in about eighteen minutes.'

Iris repeated her prayers as the whale bore down on her with its mouth open. The roar of water against the rakes became deafening. She squeezed her eyes shut. The arched palate swept over her, swallowing her trembling raft into darkness. A resilient grate caught her. She opened her eyes to see a satyr – half-goat and half-man – standing over her. He was looking down at her with an oddly gentle expression. Assuming that the mythical beast was there to cure her barrenness, she prostrated herself at the hooves. The raft was now her bed of flowers. She closed her eyes, waiting.

'She seems badly frightened,' said a gentle male voice. 'Help me get her out of here.'

The giant that picked her up was coarse and brutish, with hard, calloused hands and a voice to match. Numbed by her elevated blood alcohol, she slept through the night on a heap of blankets in the laundry area. Dawn brought several of ARNOLD's wives, who offered salty clam and tomato juice. They showed her to her new quarters under the poopdeck.

Centaur Larry visited her on the second morning. She wore a soft, brightly coloured kilt.

'The wives told you who I am?' he said.

'Yes. You are the one who will cure my barrenness.'

'I'll do my best. Want me to show you around the ship?'

She nodded and took his arm; her knees were still a bit weak.

They circled the ship on the main and again on the freeboard. She saw ship organs; some did things to the catch, others did things to the crew. Her impression was one of intelligence and power – yet all of her contacts were with humans who seemed quite ordinary – gentle. It was hard to believe that *Rorqual* had had a successful career as a battleship.

'This is our White Room. We have a Medimeck and a Mediteck who will assist me.'

She eyed him, puzzled.

'They will help me cure your sterility problem – your inability to have children.'

'Oh.' She nodded.

'The first battery of tests will be done on blood and some cells from your vaginal pool. The White Meck can handle that.'

She winced at the needle. The results flashed upon the screen.

'Looks like you're a female – ovulating – no disease – and no tumours. Fine! Now, the next examination will involve some optic records and X-rays of the uterus. Climb up here.'

'Well . . .' said Larry. 'We're in luck! I think we found the cause of your problem – blocked cervix. Hang on, this might hurt.'

Iris sat on the cot with a tear on her cheek.

'Sorry,' said the centaur. 'But we found it and fixed it at one sitting. I'll give you two weeks to heal that dilated cervix and you'll be ready for your first pregnancy. Excited?'

She wiped away the tear silently.

'Well, I'll let you think it over. Come on, I'll walk you back to the wives' quarters.'

'Who will sire my child?' exclaimed Iris.

'Captain ARNOLD,' said Larry.

'But I thought that you—'

'I'm sorry, but as you must know – I'm part mechanical

horse.' He laughed. 'All of the King's embraces are fertile, as you can see from the poopdeck.'

'King?'

'That's what we call him sometimes. He picked up the nickname during the war with the Hive. I think he'd conquer the world if it would stand up and fight.'

She seemed disappointed. 'This is necessary?'

'Yes,' he said. 'Next year you must be a mother. The God-whale has spoken.'

ARNOLD stepped into her cabin on his way down to the evening meal. He left her blinking and bewildered. She wandered out into the corridor. Hooves galloped up behind her.

'Need a lift? Hop on,' said Centaur Larry.

She mounted slowly, wrapping her arms and legs a little tighter than usual. He didn't comment, just kept up his usual light-hearted banter. Her mood was deep blue through the meal. ARNOLD announced that they sailed to the Hive to trade a load of tuna for a moment of sharing. The giant warrior wandered among his wives, witty and playful, teasing before taking one off to his quarters.

Iris leaned on Larry, whispering: 'Why her?'

'She rubs herself with lemon.'

'Lemon?'

'Yes,' explained Larry. 'ARNOLD's wives have their own hierarchy. Those with the most male children have the most authority. They decide among themselves who will wear the citrus. The rest is up to ARNOLD and his nose. Lemon peel is easy to detect when the aromatic oils are rubbed into warm erogenous zones – pleasant.'

Iris relaxed and smiled. Lemon seeds would be on her list of things to take home.

'Want a ride home?' asked the centaur.

Iris climbed on his meck back. Again he noticed a distinct hug. 'Have you seen ARNOLD about your pregnancy? It's time,' he said.

'I did. At least . . . I think I did.'

Larry smiled. 'That's the way it is with the Captain. Consider yourself a mother.'

She rested her forehead against his back as he loped down to her cabin.

Four motorized barges waited at Two Mile Reef. Their yellow-suited Nebish crews fidgeted nervously as Benthic children frolicked in the waves.

Rorqual appeared on the western horizon. Centaur Larry scanned the barges with the long eye.

'Our Hive friends don't appear too happy about coming Outside.'

ARNOLD studied the sensor readings for a long time before answering. The back of his neck bristled. Everything read safe and green.

'I don't want the little bastards to be happy about anything,' grunted the giant. 'If I had my way, they'd starve. But *Rorqual* thinks she can learn something from that damned planet brain, so we're buying time.'

'Is it safe?' asked Larry. 'Isn't it possible that the CO might gain control of our ship if they link brains?'

'Trilobite doesn't think so. He says that he tried it once – piggy-back. The link was weak, too weak for control, but strong enough for good data transmission.'

The first barge brimmed with ice chips and tuna. Nebishes started weighing anchor. ARNOLD shouted a curt order. '*Rorqual*, put a grapple on the bare. No one goes anywhere until we get our sharing. Have you got the linkage set up?'

'Trilobite hasn't reached the top of the cliff yet.'

'OK. Start filling the second barge, but keep R-1 on the first one.'

The short, fat, thick-suited crew members of the Hive barge watched the powerful grapple nervously. Had they known how many of their number that grapple had killed, they couldn't have remained on their feet. As it was, two did faint.

'Linkage established,' said the ship.

*

264

The festivities at Har Island dragged on into the night. Iris felt a little insecure with ARNOLD's wives. Her contact with the giant had been brusque. His attitude towards her hadn't changed: it was casual, distant. He was performing a service. Now she carried his child.

'Have a guava?' offered Opal.

Iris accepted the greenish-yellow fruit. It was about the size of an apple and tasted excellent.

'Are you one of ARNOLD's new wives?'

Iris lowered her eyes. 'I am bride of the Godwhale for a year.'

'Oh,' said Opal in a matter-of-fact tone. 'They're taking a northern cruise this season. You'll see a lot of ice.'

'You've been there?'

'No. I chatted with Trilobite. He's down at the water-line now, sniffing around for bits of things left over by some ancient civilization. If you want to know the latest gossip, ask him. He's always sharing *Rorqual*'s shipmind. Between them they know a lot.'

'Why are we heading north?'

Opal shrugged. 'They traded a good cargo of tuna for a chance to share with the Hive's collective mind. I guess they found some clues to our deity, and they're going to check them. I think it is just a good excuse to explore another Ocean. They get restless.'

Iris glanced at the crowd near the fire. 'They?'

'Those three!' said Big Opal. 'That horse's half, Larry; ARNOLD; and my husband Har.'

'Har is going?'

'Yes, the silent gargoyle is always included whenever those other two go off on some harebrained adventure. Larry and Big Har were in the Hive together – Tweenwallers. Now that they watch for the deity, Har is quite excited. I think he is the only real believer.'

Iris studied Opal – still hard under the grey hair and wrinkles, a grandmother a dozen times over. The young girl took another guava from her hostess. 'You have a nice island here.'

'It's going to be too quiet after the men are gone,' said the older woman with a shrug. She stood up and circulated among her other guests.

Iris went to the beach for a lonely swim.

Several hours later Iron Trilobite approached the fire with a wet girl in tow – Iris, bride of Nine Fingers.

'I found a midnight swimmer,' said the meck, 'a sea nymph who was missing the party.'

Anonymous invitations came out of the darkness.

Iris let go of the ornate tail and clamped her hands on her wet hips, breasts moving, eyes glinting in the firelight. 'What party? There's no dancing!'

The beverages had put most of the men down on one elbow. They planned to sleep right where they were. Another violent dance – more of a mating ritual than anything else – was too much to ask.

Larry checked his mannequin's charge: ample.

'Centaur mode, please.'

Mannequin arched its pelvis back, separating its four legs. He was a bit shorter, but the goat-like satyr appearance was replaced by a horsey shape. Optics studied the woman's rhythm. Hooves beat a synchronous tattoo. She turned towards the mythical beast and smiled. 'Dance!' she shouted. They whirled and swayed to flutes and drums. The seawater on her skin was replaced by sweat. She climbed on his back. He reared and galloped off down the beach.

'What got into you? You seemed so sad before the swim,' said Centaur Larry.

'I had a long talk with Trilobite out there,' she said. 'I found out that ARNOLD is a genetic Carbon Copy of you.'

'So?'

'Then this child I carry is your child!'

Larry trotted out of his warm cabin on to a sunlit winter deck – thirty-four degrees; light, sticky snowflakes melted on his shoulders. Chunks of bright, white pack-ice glinted at him from a dull grey ocean. The long eye was spotting icebergs. The snow-removal crews sang their chantey in rhythm with the shovels.

'Would you chauffeur me around the deck?' asked Iris, standing olive-skinned in the door of a companionway.

Larry stopped, pawing the snow. She brushed off the saddle area, noticing the new chamois pad.

'No frost?' she asked.

'No frost. An adherent perineum can be uncomfortable. Mount up. I brought a two-holed poncho if the weather worsens.'

Her breasts and belly warmed his back as he reared up and pranced through a snowdrift. Her legs tightened their straddle. He loped and jumped a coil of hose. She became short of breath with her laughter. He slowed, gauging her endurance.

'Take it easy,' he said. 'I don't want anything happening to my descendant in there.' He reached back and patted her abdomen.

The wind picked up. They donned the poncho to watch an iceberg go by. ARNOLD came out on the deck wearing his angel wings and three layers of polymer foam.

'I don't think this is going to work in the Arctic Ocean,' he said. 'I've tried a quick dip in this icy brine and almost froze my lungs. We'll have to use the one-eyed Meck Tuna in the basin.' Then he noticed the two heads above the poncho. 'What is that wanton female doing? Making a pack animal out of you?'

Larry grinned. 'We're just sight-seeing in the northern latitudes – very educational.'

'You two don't look very scholarly,' said ARNOLD, tweaking Iris' toe.

'I like to ride,' giggled the gravid female.

'I imagine,' mumbled the giant angel, 'but don't get used to it. As far as I know, Larry here is the nearest thing we have to a horse on the whole planet, and you can't take him back to your husband.'

She tightened her hug under the warm folds.

'Where do we begin searching?' asked Larry.

The Hive gave us eighty-two degrees twenty-three minutes

north, nineteen degrees thirty-one minutes east. The bottom is about five thousand metres down.'

'It's a job for the Iron Tuna anyway,' said Larry, galloping off into the snowstorm. Iris pulled her bare feet up. The angel watched them go, wings freezing and drooping.

The child was strong and healthy – black hair, brownish skin, and dark eyes. Iris was pleased.

'I will be sorry to leave it when I return to my husband,' she said.

'There is no need. You will take the baby with you.'

'That is impossible. Nine Fingers is a king. He is very proud. His crown goes to his firstborn son. This child would not be welcome.'

ARNOLD nodded. 'I understand a king's feelings, but you are a bride of the Godwhale. Your child is more than a test of your fertility – it carries a king's genes. It belongs in a throne room, and it belongs with its mother.'

'But my husband will not be happy.'

ARNOLD grinned. 'He will accept the child if it too has only nine fingers.'

The little mother gasped. 'No. A crown isn't worth that much.'

'You want your son with you, don't you?'

She looked at the small, round face sadly. She didn't know. The dark, little eyes blinked up at her, trustingly.

'Is there any other way?' asked the mother.

'I see none,' said the giant.

Larry studied the child. 'It's a shame, really: the child has more of the brown than the olive. He actually looks like the King's child. Wait, there may be a way. *Rorqual*, can you dig up old optics of the King and Queen to compare their pigments more precisely?'

The ship matched the skins with mixtures of bright primaries through a sliding filter of brown and olive. The dermal colour index was printed out as a six-digit number: three digits for primary mix and three digits for the dull filter. When the child was compared, he came much closer to the light-skinned King.

'Good,' said Larry. 'Babies are usually lighter than their parents at birth. He might darken later, but right now he matches the King. Now, if we mix a pigment to match the mother – olive – and tattoo the tenth finger darker—'

'I see!' said ARNOLD. 'We tell the King that the mother's genes supplied the extra finger.'

Larry nodded. 'By the time genetic theory reaches the island, the child will have his rightful place beside his mother. They'll learn that acquired characteristics aren't hereditary: a lost finger doesn't show up in offspring. But the tattoo will be magic enough to win the child a home right now.'

The giant chided the centaur for showing so much interest in the child: 'You're too soft. Why, if I didn't know better, I'd think the infant was your child – not mine.'

'And we know that is impossible.' Larry smiled.

Larry studied the charts of the wreckage. 'There are miles and miles of it down there: fragments of fuselage and super-structure. And entire fleet of Harvesters must have gone down. We're just looking at an old graveyard – or some floating city was scuttled here during the Age of Karl.'

'Maybe,' said *Rorqual*, 'but the sedimentation pattern suggests that it has been there less than a hundred years, certainly much less than a thousand. The attached marine life is all recent. There is no trace of calcium or silicon buildup by organisms before the worldwide Ocean kill.'

'That recent?' mumbled Larry. 'But you and Trilobite had searched the Oceans thoroughly. There were no Hive vessels of this size and number – just an occasional hovercraft.'

The Iron Tuna found a long fragment and sent up the measurement. 'This is no hovercraft,' said ARNOLD. 'Here's an outline of something nearly a mile long!'

The scale printout gradually took on detail. Smaller frag-ments with similar characteristics lay nearby. These were hoisted to the deck and studied.

'Here's the letter P and there's an I. *Pi*? The pieces don't fit. Maybe it is *ip* ... "ship"?'

'Look at the scale model of that mile-long fragment. *Rorqual* is copying it because it's too big to bring up. Good girl! Give a model of all the bigger fragments. Maybe we can assemble it here on the worktable – like a jigsaw puzzle.'

The irregular fragments took shape – oblong segments of hull.

'Looks like a whale. Another Harvester?'

'It can't be! Look at the scale. It must be four or five miles long!' exclaimed Larry.

'A floating city. It must be a city. But where in the Hive could it come from? Twenty years isn't that far back. *Rorqual* had a good sharing with the CO and there was no record of it in the Hive. Odd.' ARNOLD scratched his chin – male stubble. 'Here are some more letters – *RO*. Isn't that a Greek letter?'

'*Rho*,' corrected *Rorqual*. 'This is just a word fragment – *RO*. The R piece fits behind the previous P piece. We have a *PRO*.'

'Well, *Rorqual*, you have enough data to tell us ... a five-mile-long hull with the name *PRO* and an *I*,' said Larry. 'Search your memory.'

'Nothing in the Hive. No surface ships of the pre-Hive era. No floating cities. Negative. Negative. Negative,' said *Rorqual*. 'But when I go back to the era of the Komputerised Aerospace Research Lab – KARL Era – I find a spaceship with the name of "Procyon Implant" that fits these characteristics. But that ship Implanted out successfully on a trip eleven point three light years long.'

'The Dever's Ark!' exclaimed Larry. 'It didn't make it? Could it have just circled the sun and fallen back to Earth after thousands of years?'

'Possible,' said *Rorqual*.

'That would explain how the biota returned to Earth. Implant starships are set up to seed a planet. We've been looking for a machine built by the Dever Clan – my descendants.'

Big Har, who had remained silent, picked up a crusted relic

270

from the wreck. 'This is all that remains of our deity? A dead machine?'

Larry was almost in tears. 'They failed? Ira, Jen-W[5], Dim Dever . . . failed?'

ARNOLD scoffed: 'I would expect the Hive to fail!'

'There was no Hive then,' said Larry. 'Just cyberdeity OLGA and KARL, her servant. The Golden Age! The land population was only one percent of what it is now. Look at the species that were on the Ark. None of these survived the harsh competition with the Nebish.'

'Then Man failed to reach the stars,' mumbled ARNOLD. 'What is so terrible about that? Maybe Man wasn't meant to succeed. After all, we are just animals – a higher animal, perhaps – but we eat, sleep, mate, and die like any other creature. Why get all emotional about an effort to see space? It happened a thousand years ago!'

Larry moved his mannequin over to the port and gazed out into the frozen, grey Arctic sea. 'I like to think that Man is the highest creature in the Universe – that Earth is the most important planet – and that I am . . . well . . . at least significant.'

ARNOLD apologized: 'I'm just a warrior. For me to go into battle with those daydreams would be very bad. I might hesitate. But you have always been a deep thinker. I'm sorry if I offended you. Let's eat.'

Har's appetite was poor. 'I still feel as if we have a deity looking over us. We prayed for food to return to the sea and it did – after thousands of years of sterility. It takes a deity to do that – perhaps a deity guiding a starship?'

Rorqual reassured Big Har: 'It is good to have a deity, and there is solid evidence that the entire Universe was built for intelligent life forms on this planet, if we accept the cosmologist's premise that a Creator would sign his work.'

Larry's eyes lit up: 'Of course! The anthropocentric-universe argument: $gy = c$! The most fundamental constant in the Universe is the speed of light. What is it – exactly?'

Rorqual printed out: $c = 2.997925010 \times 10^8$ metres per second

'Yes. Now if we multiply Earth's gravity acceleration in meters per second per second (m/sec²) by the Earth year in seconds, we'll have speed (m/sec). *Acceleration* times *time* equals *speed*. For planet Earth this speed is precisely light-speed; or at least it was when our first anthropoid ancestor set foot on the ground.'

ARNOLD frowned. 'You mean that this constant can be measured everywhere in the Universe – and our planet's gravity times its year equals it?? What is this math? In round numbers?'

The screen glowed reverently: OLGA's formula:

$$98 \text{ m/sec}^2 \times 3.0 \times 10^7 \text{ sec} = 3.0 \times 10^8 \text{ m/sec}$$

'Also used as index for hospitality when evaluating the planets of distant star systems.'

ARNOLD nodded. 'Close – only a two percent error.'

Larry smiled. 'That error vanishes if we get down to exact figures. Light-speed is a bit less than your figure – 2.9979×10^8. That never changes. The year is a bit longer each century – about two-thirds of a second. Now it is about 3.15577×110^7 seconds, but when Man's prosimian ancestors appeared, the Earth year was precisely 3.065×10^7. Gravity varies slightly from equator to pole, but the site of Man's oldest fossil ancestor has a g of 9.78 m/sec². Now the more exact formula is:

$$9.78 \text{ m/sec}^2 \text{ times } 3.065 \times 10^7 \text{ sec} = 2.9979 \times 10^8 \text{ m/sec}$$

'And that comes out right on the nose! The year was a bit shorter before prosimians, and longer after – so there was a time when the formula was accurate to an infinite number of decimal places.'

ARNOLD continued to question the math. 'I suppose it comes out the same no matter what units you use – feet per second? Miles per hour?'

'Of course. Just keep the units the same all the way through.'

'Does it come out like this for all the planets?'

Rorqual ran a quick check: 'The formula only gives ten

percent of light-speed for Mercury, sixty-six percent for Venus, and seventy-five percent for Mars. The outer planets are many decimal points off.'

'Interesting,' said ARNOLD. 'But if Venus or Mars were a bit larger or slower they'd be right in the formula too. Maybe all biologically rich planets fit the formula.'

'Maybe,' said Larry. 'But this in itself makes the cosmologist very happy. Such an orderly Universe!'

ARNOLD asked *Rorqual* for another printout. This time he wanted to study fossil mankind. 'Why go way back to the prosimian? What's wrong with the first hominid – that Miocene pongid, Proconsul? Why not use that year?'

Larry frowned. 'That year was 3.1416×10^7 seconds long. In the formula $g \times y = c$ the answer is light-speed plus an error of plus one and a half percent. Don't let the figure 3.1416 excite you: it is *pi*, the ratio of the circumference of a circle to its diameter. However, its appearance here, in the number of time divisions in a year, is just an artifact of our unit of time. Unlike light-speed, which is a universal constant in any units.'

ARNOLD continued to study *Rorqual*'s printout, which grew and became decorated with brilliant colours, elaborate designs, and miniature pictures. The ship enjoyed all the man-minutes and was actually doodling an illuminated manuscript of geological ages. 'I think I see now,' said the warrior giant. 'There seems to be an abrupt change around the time of your prosimian, *Palachthon*. The chalky Cretaceous ends with a bang – about a third of all animal families were wiped out: dinosaurs, marine reptiles, flying reptiles, ammonites, molluscs, and calcareous nanoplankton. It looks as if your formula does have some magic. I think that someone put this massive extinction in the fossil record, like a bookmark, so we would notice it.'

ARNOLD rolled up the elaborate printout and sat on it. He cleared the table and filled another bowl.

Har's appetite returned. He now felt that he was on the right planet – where cosmology argued for a deity with a penchant for numbers.

'There have been other extinctions,' mused Larry. 'About

two-thirds of the Trilobites were wiped out at the close of the Cambrian.' He smiled and glanced at the shovel-shaped meck at his side. 'And I suppose Iron Trilobite will find some satisfaction in knowing he was used for a "bookmark" too. But the most massive extinction was this recent spread of the Hive. Except for synthetic genes, our planet was essentially sterile!'

Rorqual continued to chart the starship wreckage. The scale model grew.

'Looks like a bunch of peas in a pod,' said ARNOLD.

'That's the idea,' said Larry. The pod is the outer superstructure. Each pea is self-contained and can act as a re-entry vehicle.'

'Why are so many peas missing?'

'Oh, we just haven't found them yet ... or ...' Larry's face lit up with ecstasy. 'Of course! The peas were dropped! It is possible that the ship made the round trip to Procyon, leaving biota on the new planet before coming back to reseed Earth.'

ARNOLD was fascinated. 'How can we know for sure? If Man Implanted to one planet, there must be other accessible stars he could have reached. I'd like to believe that our species could excel at something besides war.'

'Yes, warrior!' Larry smiled. 'We could find the answer to that if we located a piece of the starship's spine – the cephalic bulge, which might house a portion of the brain called the amygdale, or almond. Memories are solid-state in there. All her magnetic bubbles and ionic thoughts are probably gone. That was a rough landing. Implant starships are built in space to live out their existence in the nullgrav and vacuum between planets. Only their pods can live in an atmosphere. Re-entry must have been a harsh way for such a powerful cyber to die.'

The amygdale was located and dissected from a four-mile-long segment of ship spine. It floated in *Rorqual*'s wake, cradled in a foam cocoon. Neurotecks made hookups. The ship probed.

'It has no personality – just memory banks.'

Larry nodded. 'That's the almond. What do you see regarding the Implant?'

Rorqual was unusually slow in answering. 'The retrieval stem is Haganoid, but somewhat nonstandard. I haven't unscrambled the storage sequences yet. They are not linear. Allow me more time.'

'No rush,' said ARNOLD. 'We'll start back to Har Island. Maybe we can set up the almond in the jungles and probe it at our leisure. It will have an interesting story to tell.'

They attached the macramé to the lobulated white 160-×-120-×-120 foot mass of neurocircuitry and ploughed eastward through the pack-ice. All hands waited anxiously for news of the space colonists.

'Wiped out?' exclaimed Larry.

'One Implant apparently did so poorly that the starship wrote it off as a failure,' said *Rorqual*. 'I am still unscrambling the details, but there is evidence for two separate Implants: the first, about a century after launch, succeeded – doubling in population twice under observation. It was this second attempt, much later, that failed. Both planets were biologically hospitable (gy=c), but there was a competitive life form on the second planet.'

'Which star system?' asked Larry.

'The first may have been Procyon. The second is not identified, at least not yet.'

ARNOLD studied the memory logic of the almond. 'I can't understand it either. We'll have to get the starship's own retrieval system working to sort this out.'

'But we can guess,' said Larry. 'The Procyon Implant could account for several pods and several centuries. Earth could be the second planet (*gy=c*). We know we received an Implant about the time the starship re-entered and crashed in the Arctic. The Hive could be the competitive life form. Those poor colonists wouldn't have a chance to study the Nebish with those crazy bowmen flying around.'

'Impossible,' said *Rorqual*. 'No starship could make a round trip to a star and not know it had arrived back at its home sun. Earth's geography hasn't changed at all in a few dozen centuries. The Oceans were empty, true – and the Garden flora was sterile – but it wouldn't take the starship and its crew long to figure things out.'

Larry just waved his hands. 'But we know the ship spoke to Trilobite just before it crashed into the sea. It was acting mighty funny. Some of the pods seeded successfully, bringing back our extinct species. But these landed outside the Hive – in Oceans, small empty islands, tropical lagoons. I'm certain that the Hive would have wiped out any that landed on its Gardens. Judging from this jumbled almond, the starship was having cerebral difficulties. It may not have been able to help its colonists on Earth.'

ARNOLD stood and gazed at the horizon. 'Our ancestors returned to Earth and died at the hands of the Hive, and we couldn't help them!'

'Maybe,' said Larry. 'But you know how many little islands there are ... A few probably survived someplace. We'll come across them in our travels.'

The beach was practically empty as the Godwhale nosed into the sand. Only Opal and a few of the elders were on hand. It was an hour before sun-up, and most of the inhabitants of Har Island still slept. The decks were quiet, solemn. Opal twisted her flowered lei nervously. She relaxed when she saw the stoop-shouldered hulk of Big Har. He came out on the deck carrying a glistening white walrus tusk as long as his arm.

'Are you alright?' she asked as the crane set him on the sand. He nodded and turned to wave. The ship backed off quietly and was gone before the sun rose.

'Why are you so quiet? Couldn't you find your deity?'

Har started walking slowly towards his hut. 'We found her,' he said, 'only she was dead.'

Opal put her arm around her husband's shoulder. What could she say.

'But we think we found evidence of an even greater deity – just a clue – a hint. A deity so powerful that creation of whole planets is just a casual hobby – something to play at number games with.'

276

'What do you mean?'

He pointed down. 'This planet, so huge that I can't even understand the numbers, was put together and set in orbit around the sun to match some silly formula. The gravity times the year equals this universal constant called light-speed. The moon might have been a fine adjustment in the formula – to lower our gravity and provide drag to shorten our year so the numbers came out exactly. Exactly! Creation was just a game!'

Opal hugged him lightly. 'Now, now, even a deity needs a little recreation. Our home isn't really a bad place – even if it was made as a hobby.'

Har searched his hut for thongs and hung the tusk over the doorway. Opal noticed the scrimshaw: engraved letters and pictures.

'What's that?'

'A prayer.'

$$gy = c$$

'A prayer?'

'Yes OLGA's prayer – to let the Creator of planet Earth know that I got the message: a thank-you for our home.'

'Your deity isn't dead.' She smiled.

'I don't know how long *They* live. Earth was built a long time ago – billions of years. I just don't know ...'

Larry chatted with Wandee on the long ear. Both were wrinkled and grey.

'Are the lights still out?' asked the centaur.

'Yes, but the deathrate has dropped back to normal. I never realized how dependent we were on the Hive's circulatory system – air, water, sewage. Whole cities were wiped out when the energy organ blew. Fused our best machine shop too – killing our most skilled. I managed to survive by climbing up to the platform and foraging in the Gardens at night. Almost got killed by a Hunter this morning when I overstayed.'

Larry shook his head. 'Well, I guess it will be a long time before you are ready to trade with us—'

'Oh, we're ready now!' she said excitedly. 'If you have food – any kind. I'll see to it that we get some barges out to the reef. What kinds of things do you want? With a promise of calories, I can get most anything through the CO.'

'What about the new Chairman?'

'Oh, we don't have a Chairman right now. The CO is trying the headless-committee method. After Furlong's egregious mistake there'll be no carte blanche for a long time.'

Larry frowned. 'I hadn't realized the CO valued individual human life. Ode and Drum – was it their deaths that put the onus on the Chairman?'

'No. Failure did. Before Furlong, your Benthics were just a few naked savages. Now they are many – with a strong navy and the infusion of ARNOLD's warrior genes. Our Hive is clearly down a point. Furlong was blamed.'

'Conflict is unfortunate . . .'

'But necessary,' she said. 'In the eyes of the Hive, Oceans are just a food source. Citizens starve. Do you realize our population density?'

Larry tried to extrapolate from one of the island communities where 'crowded' meant fifty per square mile. In those cultures many calories came from the sea. He knew the Hive density was much higher. 'Five hundred per square mile?'

Wandee laughed bitterly. 'I wish it were true, but you are two decimals off: fifty thousand per square mile, for every mile of all the major land masses – totalling 3.5×10^{12} for the planet. That is why we literally eat each other and process our sewage and garbage – to shorten the energy cycle, close the loop in the nitrogen cycle. The CO feels the hunger of the dying Nebish. Ocean calories are needed.'

'Perhaps we can help each other – trade our catch for your manufactured products and tools. I'll work up a shopping list and get back to you.'

'Fine.'

*

'You did what!' exclaimed ARNOLD.

'But she is your mother-figure – such a nice old grey-haired lady—'

'Se's a member of the Hive and as such can't be trusted. If you give them a shopping list they'll know our weaknesses.'

'Look,' explained Larry. 'They built those Harvesters. What can they learn if we just order a few replacement parts? It will cut down on our own ship time. All they want is a few tons of extra plankton – calories. We can spare that. Besides, it gives us a chance to study their technology too. But I doubt they'll be much of a threat in the near future: they can't even get their lights back on – and they starve.'

AROLD glanced at the ship. 'What do you think, old girl? Is it safe to deal with the Hive?'

'Negative. The Hive will always be a threat to those who live Outside. However, the benefits of trade outweigh the hazard for the foreseeable future.'

'Why do you say that? Three trillion Nebishes with a planet-wide brain? Isn't that a threat?'

Rorqual sounded confident. 'When I shared with the CO I felt the burdens of the cities. They are so overwhelmed with basic bodily functions that they have no energy or time for philosophizing. They are so busy with today's technical problems that they forget the basic theories. They remember Einstein's equation, $E=mc^2$ but they forget OLGA's equation for a habitable planet, $gy=c$. When I tried to reach old fossil records I found abundant silly details about some of the more colourful creatures like the thirty-foot Devonian placoderm and the larger reptiles. But no thought was given to important details of the expanding universe, the age of elements, chemical evolution, or paleoclimates. Why there was no record of the Gum Nebula, the largest known nebula in our galaxy!'

ARNOLD shook his head. 'You and Trilobite think too much. I guess it was all those centuries of wandering around alone, ruminating. OK. If you think it is safe to trade, we'll trade. But keep your guard up!!'

'Yes, Captain. Shall I print out the items we need?'

'Fine – with copies to Larry, Tool Room, Electroteck Foreman, and Stokers.'

Copies of the shopping list were passed around at the evening meal. Larry was spooning up a sweet compote of fruit and syrup, getting some on his chin and the list.

'Why do we need these permalloy garnet wafers for the "bubble brain"? Aren't we growing our own?'

'Yes,' answered ARNOLD. 'But we're only getting two point five megabits per square inch. I guess *Rorqual* wants to compare quality.'

Larry nodded. A form of technical spying!

He read on: one thousand joules per nanosecond neodymium glass rod for lighting the ship's fire. Microwave gear in the one-to-ten gigahertz range. Sandwich-hetero-structured diodes of gallium arsenide substrate with doping using a variety of elements: tin, aluminium, silicon, zinc, and germanium. Super-conductors of tantalum disulfide and pyridine with an inter-calated crystal structure and periodicity of twelve angstroms. Deuterium. Tritium.

Larry folded up his list. 'I can't see anything wrong with the list – pretty basic junk for a teck to play with. I suppose it wouldn't hurt to increase our supplies.'

ARNOLD nodded. 'Send it to Wandee.'

Larry walked into the tool room to find Slot Machine stretched out on a work bench. Her 34-26-36 android frame had a bulky pelvis to house the primordial rusty box. Three square navels blinked out of soft syntheskin, reading: bar, cherry, lemon.

'Back again?'

'Fire in my skull this time,' she said.

He detached her scalp and apron, rolling her on to her side. Reaching overhead, he pulled down the power key and opened her service panels. Neck and shoulder circuits were bright and shiny, winking back at him with silvery beads and wires. The neural web inside the skull resembled a dusty cobweb – soot. He pulled down the viewer and attached it to his forehead. Blowing carefully with his nitrogen gun he checked each chip.

'Here it is! Another of those damned Hive chips exploded!' He pulled over his forehead brace and leaned into it as he made the microcuts. 'I don't know if it's worth it. I seem to spend more time putting these in and taking them out than you do using them.'

'What about those in my brain box?'

'I'll take a look at your Big Board when I finish here.'

'I wouldn't want to lose my mind. Isn't there some way to check them now – to predict which are going to fail so you can do preventative maintenance?'

'No,' he said. 'I've put some in my own mannequin. They check out perfectly every day, then go without warning – *poof!* Mine are the motor coordinating system. When they go I'll be ataxic or paralysed.'

He lifted out the charred chip and placed it in the diagnostic slot of the circuit analyzer. Tiny probes began a systematic checkout. Larry glanced at the results.

'Just the same as before: a hole in the centre, all the junctions melted and fused – useless. That crater must be a millimetre in diameter.'

'A bomb?' she said, recalling the Hive's propensity towards wiring explosive loyalty into things.

'I wonder . . . Let me put a spying optic over your Big Board. There are hundreds of Hive chips in there. If one goes, we'll have visual records, and can analyze the defective chip as it was immediately before the burnout.'

He finished inside her skull and closed. Moving down her back, he detached the posterior thigh and buttock plates. The big Board pulsed and glowed like a multicoloured honeycomb under a dew-spangled spider web.

'There is a lot to watch here,' he said, thoughtfully. 'I'd like to be able to get 500× resolution.' He reached for one of the better meck eyes, setting it for nine hundred frames per second. Using solid-state switching and focusing, he'd have an image of each chip twice a second. 'There! This won't prevent your next burn, but we might be able to find out what caused it.'

She started to leave – a 34-26-38.

'Sorry about that, but the spy takes up a lot of room. Hopefully, we'll find the cause of the trouble and have you back down to a thirty-six-inch pair of hips soon. Don't forget your apron.'

'After she left, he pulled the service plates on his own mannequin's forelegs. 'Might as well spy on these chips too,' he grumbled.

During the next few days he stayed away from the rail and wore a life jacket. He didn't want a sudden attack of tremors to throw him into the sea.

Larry was on his pre-dawn deck stroll when his chip went. There was an audible *pop*, followed my the acrid smell of burning insulation. His mannequin stumbled. He swayed against a stack of crates.

'Help!'

One of ARNOLD's wives helped Larry back to the tool room. He flushed the panel with inert gas and pulled it. His left leg locked; satyr mode.

'*Rorqual,* can I have the playback on my left leg optic? Give me 5× at first. Now, go back to the flash. There it is! Give me a 50x of that junction just before it flashed. Now a 500×.'

ARNOLD walked in. 'I heard you had a fire in your pelvis.' He grinned. 'Is that rusty box teasing you again?'

'Damn,' mumbled Larry. His eyes were glued to the scope. With his left hand he ran the optic sequences back and forth with time lapse. 'Damn the Hive. Look at this chip. They purposefully put in a timing device for self-destruct. See that whisper filament? Watch it grow. With each electron another ion is added. When the gap is closed . . . ZAP! The chip burns out.'

ARNOLD nodded.

'I'll take it down to the drawing room and have an Electroteck set up a processing bench for these. Well check them all as they come in. The Stokers say the heavy isotopes of hydrogen from the cities are not very pure, but provide a good raw material for extracting our own deuterium and tritium. I guess we'll have to treat all of the Hive's items as unfinished products.'

Larry handed the defective chips to the giant.

'It seems like such a waste of time,' said the centaur.

'At least it tells us something about the Hive quality control. And the price is right – a few dead fish.'

The giant left the chips in the E-lab and walked over to the garnet farm. 'How do the Hive wafers work out?'

'Fine, but I guess there isn't much they can do to ruin and expitaxial film, just as long as you keep it three milli-microns thick and use a single-crystal substrate.'

ARNOLD studied the blow-up prints. 'The pattern of Ys and bars looks sloppy.'

'I know, but we can get around that by using them in cyber units that have "learning" circuits.'

Wandee acted as the broker for the commodity exchange, trading perch and herring for joules, gigahertz, and megabits. While the cybers, CO and *Rorqual,* haggled over exchange rates, the little grey-haired lady tried to keep the human touch in the trading.

'And how is my son?' she asked.

'That is classified information,' said Larry. 'I can't even open up the optic channels. If you want to see him you'll have to suit up and spend a lot of time on the market barges. He sometimes goes there with the catch if his ship is handling it.'

'Is he well?' she pressed him.

Larry sighed. 'We have a standard answer for all such inquiries from the Hive: *couldn't be better!*'

Iris wrapped up her son and picked up the bundle of possessions she had accumulated. Larry stood in the doorway to help her with her burdens. She tied on her lavalava – added some leis to cover her large, lactating breast – and stuck a flower in her hair. She climbed on his back, took the infant from the aide, and rode him out of the doorway, up the ramp, and on to the foredeck beside ARNOLD. Ring Island was just ahead.

Larry pawed restlessly.

ARNOLD watched the natives chant and toss flowers at

their Godwhale. The string of green biscuits in the whale's wake was collected between canoes.

'We've given them a god,' said the giant, 'easy enough when their problems are small.'

'And when they're unsophisticated,' added the centaur. 'Look at their serene expressions. They've found their deity and know that they are loved by her. That should make them feel pretty secure.'

The mean of *Rorqual* remained aloof as the Queen's homecoming celebration picked up steam.

'Notice all the skin colours,' said Larry, 'olives, browns, yellows...'

'So...? Like any of the islanders.'

'I was just hoping I could recognize one of the Procyon Implant's rainbow mix. Remember the stills of that herb island I visited with White Belly? The fuselage in the swamp might have been a pod from the starship – to explain the radiating Gardens. If there had been humans in the Implant, they could have migrated south—'

'To these islands?' said ARNOLD. 'Possible, I suppose. We'd need genotype records from the Implant and "gene flow" maps of the islander's migrations to be sure.'

Larry nodded. 'The almond might tell us which of the rainbow mix were dropped on Earth. If some of the rare antigens were included we could search for them. It might take the rest of my life to complete the study, but it would be interesting to find out.'

ARNOLD just shrugged. 'You do what interests you. As for myself, I don't see the difference between a primitive gene surviving the Hive as a Benthic – or as a starship passenger. Either way you are dealing with a basic set of human traits leapfrogging into the future and losing their cultural heritage. You're the only one around with a personal knowledge of our history, and I can't see that it does you any good.'

'Insight?' said the centaur.

'You think too much as it is. Like your interest in $gy=c$. All it proves is that our planet might have been built at the whim of a superbeing. I was built at the whim of the Hive. I try to ignore it. We'd all be happier if we were accidents of Nature.'

'Maybe . . .' said Larry.'

Rorqual backed out of the cortege of ceremonial canoes. Larry stood on the foredeck sniffing his garlands and waving. Mannequin pawed restlessly. ARNOLD leaned out of the portal whispering.

'Did you see the look in Nine Fingers' eyes when he saw that tattoo? I never thought a dark finger could make that much difference.'

'Just another miracle in the psychology of fatherhood.' Larry smiled. 'He wanted a son. Now he has one. Until they study genetic theory, there is no doubt in their minds that the child is the true young prince of Ring Island. He has his father's colour except for the finger, which he got from his mother.'

'Obviously,' agreed the giant.

The aide interrupted them with a report of the island's annual catch and census.

'It looks like our opening the reef was just what they needed. The lagoon's fish population is way up. They even caught the white shark on one of the night throw-lines. Look at the size of the tribe! In a few years they should be up to a hundred again.'

'That's about right for the land – two square miles. They need that many to maintain the arts of boat and net.'

Larry frowned. 'But I don't want to give you the impression that people should cooperate and work together.'

'No, of course not,' laughed ARNOLD. 'We just visited this island so I'd have someone new to sleep with.'

Larry shrugged. 'Well, Nine Fingers wanted a prince and you were the only King around – a real Hive-certified King Rooster!'

Laughter across the waters.

The young King held his new son high so everyone could see. 'Our women are fat. Our babies many. The lagoon is rich. Gardens grow tall.'

Iris praised the young lad who had caught the white shark. She talked of her voyages in the Godwhale – meeting angels, centaurs, and dwarf Hive dwellers. Her gifts included a bucket of ice and a description of a land where such delicate white stuff extends from horizon to horizon. As she talked it melted away.

Truly, a wondrous adventure for a young Queen! Nine Fingers' crown sat more comfortably on his head as his olive-fingered son grew tall and strong.

Rorqual cruised another Ocean. On her screens she carried the prayer:

$$gy = c$$

Planet Earth was still hospitable towards Man!

T.J. Bass (Thomas Joseph Bassler) was an American science fiction writer and doctor, principally known for his 'Hive' stories. The first of these, published in *Galaxy Science Fiction* and *If*, were combined into the novel *Half Past Human*, which was nominated for the Nebula Award in 1972. Its loose sequel, *The Godwhale*, was also nominated three years later. His work explored the theme of overpopulation and was notable for its strong command of biological extrapolation. He died in 2011.